BODY O

Eleanor said, "I hope you
mistake."

"If it's about where N
no, it's not a mistake," I said.

She reached for her chair and lowered herself carefully into it, her eyes not leaving mine. "In your blood I found anti-bodies to viruses that have not existed for decades. Your lungs held traces of exhaust products of machines that haven't been used in a century."

"Could you date these phenomena?"

"I'd say about the time the Sleepers were from. Or even before. Your results overlapped with theirs."

"Pretty good. Would you accept 2023?"

She closed her eyes for a moment. "I don't want to. But the facts are there . . . "

PRAISE FOR *TIME FUTURE*

"Rich in detail . . . *Time Future* shows that Maxine McArthur has an astute mind, a ferocious sense of detail, and the capacity to become one of the world's most distinguished SF writers."　　**—*Nova Express* magazine**

"With considerable talent, McArthur blends a well-researched technological and cultural background with elements of mystery and crime drama, and characters that leap visually off the pages all into a gripping experience."

—fictionforest.com

"*Time Future* is fascinating and Ms. McArthur's aliens are truly not human."　　**—sciencefiction.com**

By Maxine McArthur

Time Future

ATTENTION: SCHOOLS AND CORPORATIONS
WARNER books are available at quantity discounts with bulk purchase for educational, business, or sales promotional use. For information, please write to: SPECIAL SALES DEPARTMENT, WARNER BOOKS, 1271 AVENUE OF THE AMERICAS, NEW YORK, N.Y. 10020

TIME PAST

MAXINE McARTHUR

ASPECT®

WARNER BOOKS

An AOL Time Warner Company

If you purchase this book without a cover you should be aware that this book may have been stolen property and reported as "unsold and destroyed" to the publisher. In such case neither the author nor the publisher has received any payment for this "stripped book."

WARNER BOOKS EDITION

Copyright © 2002 by Maxine McArthur
All rights reserved. No part of this book may be reproduced in any form or by any electronic or mechanical means, including information storage and retrieval systems, without permission in writing from the publisher, except by a reviewer who may quote brief passages in a review.

Published in arrangement with the author.

Cover design by Don Puckey
Cover illustration by Jim Burns

Aspect® name and logo are registered trademarks of Warner Books, Inc.

Warner Books, Inc.
1271 Avenue of the Americas
New York, NY 10020

Visit our Web site at www.twbookmark.com.

W An AOL Time Warner Company

Printed in the United States of America

First Aspect Printing: May 2002

10   9   8   7   6   5   4   3   2   1

Acknowledgments

Thank you to the following people: My agent, Garth Nix, and editors, Kim Swivel and Jaime Levine; readers Michael Barry (who remembered the implant), Jennifer Bleyerveen, and Viki Wright; relativistic adviser Antony Searle; the Canberra Speculative Fiction Guild—thanks everyone; Bruce Missingham, for the inspiration of his thesis on the real Assembly of the Poor; Marianne de Courtenay, always there; Brad, "Fixing it is only a way to show you understand how it works"; my family, who never complained; and all my other friends who helped in ways they probably don't want to know about. Most of all, thank you to Tomoko, for showing me what had to be written.

Life can only be understood backwards, but it must be lived forwards.

—Niels Bohr

Maureen was a comfort and an inspiration to me during the

TIME PAST

TIME PAST

The maze of paths stretched around me. I was lost. Tents and shacks crowded onto narrow dirt tracks. Piles of decomposing rubbish blocked some tracks. I tried to pick up my direction by the sun blazing across the river, but it was too late in the day.

In this month of April 2023 tent cities occupied river banks all over Sydney. The out-towns, as they called these barrios, also sprouted in the former parks and sports fields of the suburbs as the poor and homeless were forced out of the inner city by rings of police checkpoints that kept the rich and privileged safe.

If you walked from the out-town through the factories of Rhodes, across the murky Parramatta River, through the red-roofed, drug-sodden streets of Meadowbank, and up the slope; if there was enough wind to disperse the brown blanket of pollution, then above the hills and roofs of the suburbs you might see the city towers penciled against the sky. Over there lived the people who said in opinion polls, *illegal immigrants deserve to live like animals*.

Illegal immigrants like myself. I'd bet nobody had come as far as I had—in time, or in space.

As I retraced my steps, hoping I was heading east, people began to wander out of shacks to sit in front of them or stand chatting in the cooler evening air. A child struggled with a half-full bucket of water as she crossed the lane ahead of me. Three men standing beside an open doorway watched me all the way down that lane. I felt a prickle of fear between my shoulders until I left their gaze behind.

I didn't stand out physically—we all wore ragged T-shirts and either trousers or sarongs, and my space-pale skin had tanned in five months of exposure to the savage sun. What worried me was that I was carrying cash, with which I'd intended buying a black market laser, only the seller hadn't shown up at our rendezvous. I felt everybody could see the tattered plastic notes in my pocket.

I wasn't used to carrying money. In my century, food, water and shelter are basic rights, not something that must be bought.

This part of the out-town stank of petroleum. It was built on concrete slabs that used to house a refinery. The slabs were stained with dark grease and even the soil between them was hard with it.

Oh hell. My stomach rose as the smell of garbage and open drains mixed with oil. Have to be sick. I bent over a drain and threw up into it. Full of rubbish. Bones, shit, scraps of unrecyclable plastic. Stiff, bloated rat.

I wiped my mouth on the hem of my shirt. Didn't feel better. Mouth dry and foul, head pounding. I should have known the black market dealer wouldn't bother to turn up. Should have listened to Grace, who told me to stay in bed when I got sick. "Haven't got a clue, have you? How to look after yerself when you're crook," she'd said.

Of course I didn't have a clue. In my century we didn't get sick.

Grace Chenin helped me when I first arrived in the out-town, and I'd lived most of the time with her. As far as she knew, I was Maria Valdon, a political refugee who'd paid to be smuggled into the country then, like many residents of the out-town, been abandoned without ID or money and drifted into the out-town. It was such a common story here, nobody gave me a second thought.

Who would believe my real story? That I was Alvarez Maria Halley, space habitat systems engineer, flatspace drive mechanic, and head of a space station orbiting a planet thousands of light years away and nearly a hundred years in the future. That I arrived in the out-town because the ship I was testing malfunctioned and marooned me here on Earth.

I couldn't tell them I was stuck in this time and space unless I re-entered the jump point I came through. That would involve explaining the use of hyperspace to a species that couldn't even provide all of its members with clean drinking water, let alone devise a unified field theory.

To re-enter the jump point I needed a jump-capable ship. None existed on Earth in April 2023. But in three weeks this would change.

On May 1, the Invidi will arrive on Earth and identify themselves as peaceful aliens. They'll bring medical and agricultural technology that will allow humans to transform this world into a better place. In 2060 the four alien species of Invidi, K'Cher, Melot, and Bendarl will form the Confederacy of Allied Worlds. Twenty-five years later, Earth will join that Confederacy, which by my time, 2122, will have grown to thirteen members.

It must happen, because I'm here. The fact that a human traveled to the past in a ship using Invidi technology proves that the future will happen as it's supposed to.

Doesn't it?

I shook my head to clear it of useless speculation, and stubbed my toe on a piece of loose concrete. Leave the theory for later. Right now I needed to get back to my work place and put this money away safely.

The sun had dropped behind the uneven line of buildings. Hope I'm on the right track now.

I'd gone looking for a black market laser because I needed it to contact the Invidi once they arrived. I was planning to use a reflecting telescope's dish, inverted, to send a pulse along the short-range channel that the Invidi ships use. For tracking control, I used the computer in my work place, and an antique digital processor. The only component I hadn't been able to find was the laser.

I couldn't buy one openly because I didn't have a National Identity Card or a police registration certificate. The former would prove I was a permanent resident, and the latter would show my arrest record, if any.

Someone yelled something unintelligible at me. A small woman in a scrap of bright dress. She shooed me over to the other side of the path, then bent down and chucked a bucketful of dirty water where I'd been walking. All the voices in these lanes spoke a language unknown to me, although I'd been here long enough to recognize it as either Vietnamese or Laotian.

These people probably had the same problem as me—no official identity.

In the first decade of the twenty-first century millions of refugees and illegal immigrants tried to find a new home in Australia after unexpected climate change and a series of natural disasters damaged Western European economies, and the ascent of fundamentalist politics in the USA made that country less accessible. In Australia, the Residential Restriction Law of 2010 originally proposed settling the tens of thousands of illegal immigrants in restricted residency areas.

It was at this time, Grace told me, that the new ID card system was brought in.

"It wasn't the card so much as the zoning that pissed people off. They shouldn't have cut us off from the harbor," she'd said.

She resented it, but that was the extent of her resistance.

Her own fragile links to social services depended on her job and keeping out of trouble.

As soon as I arrived in the out-town I learned that, if caught, I would be sent to a holding center, where I could be detained for up to a year, then processed—my details, including DNA, would go into the official database as "illegal," and unless I could prove refugee status, I'd be sent either to a restricted area or to some far-off part of the country to work. Many people in this position simply ran away from their enforced work, but they had no ID card and dared not apply for one because a record of their DNA was already in the official database. Better to evade capture upon arrival and then make enough money to buy an ID made on the black market. In my case, all I wanted to do was evade capture, period.

It wasn't hard to remain free, providing I stayed in the out-town. Which left me without access to reasonable health care, money, and what passed in this era for advanced technology. Some tradeoff.

The hum of traffic was louder now, but I couldn't see from which direction. The out-town was so flat that you came upon things suddenly.

Judging by the way my feet hurt in the cracking rubber sandals, and how dry my throat was, I'd been walking long enough to get home twice over. I didn't care now if people stared. Maybe I'll ask someone and hope they don't take advantage of me.

I'd never get lost on the space station. If you walked for long enough, you came back to where you left. One of the advantages of living inside a torus.

I snorted at myself. Funny thing to get nostalgic about. The station, Jocasta, had problems of its own, many of them similar to the out-towns. We'd always had refugees there too.

Jocasta orbited an uninhabitable planet on the edge of

Confederacy space. Because we were an Earth-administered station, and because Earth was a minor member of the Confederacy and humans were not allowed to use the jump drive in their ships, we relied on the Confederacy for trade and defense. Which was fine when the Confederacy was feeling obliging. When they were not, we were thrown back upon our own resources. Jocasta had a large population of free labor, many of whom stayed when their contracts ran out because they couldn't afford the passage back to their home stations or planets.

We also had a significant population of refugees, who'd stowed away through the jump point at some stage on Confederacy-registered freighters. Many of the masters of these ships were as unscrupulous as the people smugglers who moved groups of people from country to country in this century. Some of the refugees were fleeing from persecution or war in their home systems. They made it to Central and then had to keep going to avoid being sent home again. Others just wanted a better life somewhere else.

So the out-town situation felt uncomfortably familiar. Overpopulation, intercultural (or, in our case, interspecies) conflict, lack of jobs, and crime. But everyone on the station did have equal access, at least in theory, to health and social services, including food, security, and education.

It was in the Confederacy as a whole that the real inequalities lay. The thirteen member species were divided into the Four founding worlds and the remaining Nine. The Four kept a stranglehold on the rest of us because they controlled the only way to travel the vast interstellar distances between the member worlds—the Invidi jump drive.

At last, a place I knew. This lane with three blue tents should lead to a footbridge across a smaller river. I was too far west, because on my right I could see the motorway barriers and hear the sporadic roar of vehicles. But I could then head east, past stained brick factory buildings now used as apartments, across the footbridge, and under the motorway, where the noise of the vehicles echoed like spaceship engines in an enclosed dock and the smell of urine and filthy water would have made me throw up again except that I didn't want to stop there.

Once over the river I headed northeast into my own part of the out-town. Shacks and tents were set on old factory grounds near the riverbank, but on the far side the trodden dirt tracks led into paved streets, which in turn led onto a larger road, down which vehicles drove north and south. Houses were brick and wood over here, and some of the original owners remained, refusing to flee from the real or imagined dangers of the out-town. Beyond that, you could see the tall Olympic hotels, secure behind their electric fences and serviced by private ferries.

Electricity could be tapped off established lines in this part of the out-town, and there was a sewerage system, although it had been designed for factory effluent, not human waste, one of the reasons for the foulness of the river water.

The problem with electricity was that the gangs wanted payment for illegal lines and many of the out-town residents, like myself, had no money to pay for it. No tribute, no electricity. The gangs were as ruthless as militias. They controlled the trade in illegal drugs and fake IDs, which made them all-powerful here. The only plus was that police seldom ventured into the out-town and therefore we were never asked to show identification we didn't have.

I found it difficult to comprehend a government that was content to ignore the out-towns, on the condition that their people didn't make a nuisance of themselves to the important parts of society, that is, those parts that could vote. A sordid bargain, in which the losers were the young, the sick, the elderly, and the very poor. I hated the way that the Four ignored much of the misery on non-Confederacy worlds, too.

Grace laughed at my dismay, when she'd drunk a few beers, which was often.

"They used to call it 'outsourcing,' darl. Means the gov'ment gets business to take all the stuff off their hands that's a hassle. You know, unemployment payments, pensions, telephones. It's the same with the gangs. Gov'ment doesn't have to worry."

I pointed out that governments usually didn't exact interest payments of up to fifty percent on late payment of their services, or terrorize those who couldn't pay.

"But the boys," she meant the gangs, "keep order a lot better than the cops did. Keep the muggers in line."

One of the few forces working to change the terms of the bargain was a tiny umbrella organization for community groups called the Assembly of the Poor. This was where I "worked," if you could call the few dollars I received from them pay. The Assembly was part of the Earth-South network, but we didn't receive much support from EarthSouth, which at this time was still a network of grass-roots organizations. In the social confusion following the Invidi arrival it would finally achieve mass support.

The Assembly office was in the upper story of a wooden house in Creek Road, which was a narrow dead-end street. Its asphalt was full of jagged holes, and the houses, which once stood in separate yards, merged into one another in clusters of additions and extensions. Some of the spaces between houses were filled with rusting parts of cars and machinery. Others held drums and plastic buckets of growing vegetables.

Today, the betting shop on the ground floor of the wooden house was open, and Indian music swirled out into the street. A hand-lettered sign next to the side door that led upstairs to our office read: CONSCIENCE IS NOT

ENOUGH. Blue letters on a yellow background. Under this rallying call of the EarthSouth movement, smaller letters declared: IF YOU'RE SICK OF LOSING, JOIN US. IF YOU WANT SOME POLITICAL POWER, JOIN US. LET'S MAKE THIS TOWN A FIT PLACE TO LIVE. Someone had crossed out an "e" in "losing." Below these exhortations sat a logo made up of four words in the shape of a face, the first word curved to make a fringe, the last, a frowning mouth: ASSEMBLY OF THE POOR.

On the side of the house local children had painted a red, green, and yellow mural of birds and trees. Some of it was still visible under black swathes of graffiti.

I dodged a heavy man who came out of the shop counting a handful of betting slips, waved a greeting at Mr. Deshindar who ran the shop, and fumbled inside my shirt for the keys, kept on a string around my neck. The lock on the barred iron door caught, then clicked open. I dragged it aside enough to slide in, then locked it behind me. Paranoid, yes. There isn't much of value here, except our old computer, and the solar panels and recycled car batteries that we used during electricity cuts. And my telescope.

I went up the dim stairs and into the top of the building. I still felt queasy and my legs ached from the long walk, but at least I'd made it here. Daylight was fading and I wanted to put the money into our strongbox before I went back to my tent. I'd kept my own cash at the Assembly ever since the tent was ransacked and money taken from it, soon after Grace moved out.

The office was a single room, illuminated only by a dirty skylight and windows that let in the afternoon sun if we forgot to lower the blinds. Papers covered most of the threadbare green carpet and three rickety tables that served as desks. The drawers of two huge filing cabinets stuck half open, contents bulging. Nelson Mandela smiled from a faded poster on one wall at an infonet portrait of Marlena Alvarez on the other. *Talk to your enemies,* said the text below Mandela, but Alvarez didn't smile back. Perhaps she didn't like being an internationally recognized symbol, shared between human rights, women's rights, and social justice movements. Like the Assembly of the Poor, which tried to service all of these as best it could.

We helped our member groups apply for funding, and the director, Abdul Haidar, lobbied local government. The Assembly itself was always in need of money. I was the "technical staff." Florence Woo, the other staff member, wrote submissions for funds, that is, begging letters.

When I came for the job at the Assembly, I'd said that I was involved in the EarthSouth movement in Vaupés and named the largest town near Las Mujeres, sure it existed in this time.

I'd been using stories of my great-grandmother's life to explain my presence in the out-town, masquerading as someone who knew Marlena Alvarez, the founder of the EarthSouth movement, the best known of the popular social justice movements in the early twenty-first century. At least, a century later it was the best known.

Alvarez was the mayor of the village of Las Mujeres from 2011 to 2017. My great-grandmother, Demora Haase, had been her chief of police. I grew up in that village hearing stories of Marlena. Her life, her sayings, her death by an assassin's bullet in 2017. It was easy to put myself in supporting roles in the events my great-grandmother used to talk about, events that to these people happened only a few years ago.

I poured myself a drink of water from the jug on Florence's table. Her papers were in neat piles.

Drinking water was the biggest expense for everybody in the out-town and in the surrounding suburbs. Since I arrived there'd been perhaps four days of rain, and none in the past three months. The tent cities had no piped water, and the water that came through the old pipes to these houses was often undrinkable. Water trucks came around regularly, but they charged just enough to make it difficult for a person on a subsistence wage to pay. Which meant most of the out-town struggled. We could boil piped water most of the time and get by. The last alternative was river water—nobody, seeing the rubbish and waste that ran through the drains, would willingly drink that.

One of the things the Assembly worked toward was getting water supplied free to everyone. Eventually we hoped to arrange sewerage as well as regular garbage collection. The enclosed environmental system of the space station recycled everything except a portion of heat waste, and I found it hard to believe this society still condoned the use of fossil fuel-burning engines and allowed production of nondegradable plastics. Still harder to believe was that some sections of the same city were left at below subsistence level, while others enjoyed the luxury of space and safety.

I knew how hard it was to persuade those with privileges to share with the less fortunate. On Jocasta we had enough space in the uppermost of its three rings to comfortably house most of the refugees and unregistered residents who stayed in the lower ring. But the upper ring residential area was owned and controlled by members of the Four—our "upper classes," and do you think they'd give up their extra space? No more than the power-holders of this city would let the out-town residents into the harbor area or downtown.

I felt too tired to work on the damn telescope, sweaty from the walk and the hot room . . . suddenly the claustrophobic heat became more than I could bear, and I pulled up the dusty blind and opened one of the windows. A hot, dry breeze entered, but at least the air was moving now.

I needed to explore other options to contact the Invidi.

What if I can't get a laser? Arrival is only three weeks away.

I groaned inwardly and switched on the small globe suspended from the roof girder in the middle of the room. Then, after first putting my cash in the strongbox and sliding it back behind one of the filing cabinets, I took out the telescope from its box under my desk and sat on the floor beside it.

My knees creaked as I sat, and it worried me that something else was going wrong. I thought I knew this, my body. I'd lived with it for thirty-seven years. Now it was behaving like an unreliable machine and the things that happened to it here were frightening. I couldn't control the incursions of viruses and bacteria, and what they did to me. My body was alien, a flimsy thing that didn't work as I expected it to.

I found myself heeding Grace's warnings about dangerous places, dangerous times of day, aware that physical damage here could be permanent; conscious of the frailty of my own flesh and bones, conscious that the medical treatments I used to take for granted would not be made until decades after the Invidi come. In this decade, a broken bone could take months to heal. Bruises remained for weeks.

Don't think of that. Think of getting back to your own time, where you won't have to worry—at least, not as much. Think about the telescope.

A fat tube with ungainly legs, it sat waiting for its computer connections to come alive. The lens was in place, and a hell of a job I'd had finding a workshop that would let me grind it. I was still accumulating pieces of hardware in order to motorize the tracking. For the time being, the scope had to sit static on its mount. I opened the toolbox, selected a screwdriver. The mount needed to be more stable.

I stood up again with a grunt, found the page I'd scribbled notes on, sat back down again. Most obliging of amateur astronomy groups to post telescope construction manuals on the infonet. After Grace had laughingly instructed me in basic computer usage, I found there were manuals for everything on the net, from bombs to kitchen renovations. Including the hacking manuals that allowed me to develop my computer skill further.

The floor shuddered slightly as someone rattled the door downstairs. The sound of male voices floated up through the open window.

I stood up, heart beating much faster than it had a few seconds ago. Maybe they want the betting shop, not the Assembly.

The door rattled again.

Maybe if I ignore them, they'll go away.

"Hey, Maria," called a familiar voice.

Two

It was Grace's older son, Vince. Some of the tension in my shoulders relaxed.

He'd probably either be trying to borrow money or looking for a place to hide something illegal. That's what he used to do when Grace lived with me. At least, I assumed the neatly wrapped packages he used to leave in Grace's tent were illegal. No reason to hide them otherwise. I lifted one once and it was heavy, the heaviness of metal. I asked Grace if Vince's group was connected with one of the larger gangs. "I don't want to know," was all she would say.

I turned on the weak yellow bulb on the stairs as I went down and looked through the bars. "Hello, Vince."

He stared at me with his usual sulky expression and jiggled his hands in his pockets as he spoke. In spite of the heat he wore a short blue jacket with the collar turned up, jeans, and a black T-shirt. It infuriated Grace that he always had cash to buy clothes.

"You seen Will?" he said. Will was Grace's younger son, ten years old.

"No, he hasn't come here. Is he out alone?" I heard my voice sharpen like Grace's.

"Just checking. So you can tell her I asked." He jerked his head back. "These blokes want to see you."

Four men stood behind Vince. I squinted into the

gloom—the local butcher and the bus driver I knew. His bus ran between the Clyde yards south of the motorway and the streets closest to the tent city. The other two men were strangers.

"You said she'd show us the tellyscope," said the driver. He poked his narrow nose up to the bars and stared up the stairs. The brim of his cap bumped the bar.

"Now?" I said. "And why? It's just a homemade telescope."

"That's what you say." One of the unknowns grunted from behind the butcher.

"Yeah. We don't like spies here," said the other.

I snorted. "Vince, have you been putting this stuff in their heads?"

"Not me." Vince shot me a look that said it was exactly what he'd done. He kicked the barred door. "I'm off then. If you see the kid, send him home. I'm sick of mucking around looking for him."

Left alone with the four men, I tried reason.

"Who would I spy for?"

"Migrant Affairs," the grunter said immediately.

"What would I tell them?"

"Names." He glanced at the others in triumph.

I felt both exasperated and concerned. "How would I contact them?"

The butcher nodded up at the office. "I seen all your radio stuff."

"That's not a signaling device," I said. At least, not to anyone on Earth. "Wait a minute."

I went upstairs, heaved the telescope into my arms. It kept slipping to one side, but I descended crablike down the stairs, placed it on the floor while I unlocked the barred door, picked it up again with a grunt, and shoved past them. Wish I'd gotten around to making wheels for the mount.

Outside the house, I crouched and eased the scope down

on the uneven concrete, hoping the dust-proofing on the casing and the screws would hold.

"Look through here," I panted.

The sky was quite dark now in the east, except for the glow of the city low down. Often I'd get better viewing in the south.

The butcher took first turn to squint through the eyepiece at what looked from here like a stretch of dull black sky.

"Well?" said the driver, leaning so close that I was afraid he'd push the scope over.

The butcher withdrew, rubbing his eye socket. "You wouldn't think you could see anything, would you?"

"Gimme a look." The driver pushed him out of the way to see for himself. "Huh, nothing special." But he sounded almost awed.

"Give me a go, then," said the grunter.

"Wait yer turn."

Most of them wouldn't have seen the stars properly for years. The skies of Sydney were as polluted as any other big city in 2023, and in my five months there, I'd never seen more than Venus just before sunrise or isolated dots that might have been constellations directly overhead, with the naked eye. Many of the out-town residents wouldn't even have seen the stars on their journey here, especially if they'd been jammed in the holds of boats sneaking past Customs patrols or drugged senseless in luggage compartments of aircraft.

On the rare moments I could see the stars, I loved the twinkling effect. I hadn't seen it since I was a child, having spent the past twenty-five years mostly in space habitats without surrounding atmosphere.

"My go," the grunter insisted. He squatted, looked, and became suddenly still.

They wouldn't see half the stars I saw from Earth as a

child, because in my time the Invidi had helped clear the pollution from the atmosphere, but even this view was more impressive through the telescope.

"I told you, it's just a hobby." I didn't try to keep the annoyance out of my voice and they all nodded and sidled back, except for the butcher.

"Yeah, well we had to check it out, y'know?" He looked hungrily at the eyepiece and wiped his hands on his apron, which smelled faintly of offal. "Reckon I could have another look sometime?"

"I don't mind," I said. "But not tonight, eh? I'm really tired."

"Right." He followed the others as they trailed away.

We needed the residents' goodwill because it wouldn't be hard to break into this old house. The people who lived in the tents and shacks along the riverbank knew the Assembly worked for them. They kept an eye on the office and we had to trust them, as we couldn't afford to pay for professional security.

I carried the telescope back inside and up the stairs. It felt a lot heavier now the adrenaline rush had worn off, and my knees wouldn't stop trembling as I made sure the computer was unplugged and checked the window catches were closed. Put the scope back—now I'm really too tired to do anything. I could push two of the chairs together and sleep on them. Or lie down on the hard green carpet— although the cockroaches made that an unsavory option. I could dump papers on the floor and use the table as a bed— it wouldn't be the first time. Or I could walk the three hundred meters back down the street and into the maze of paths to my tent.

Vince's words nagged at me. Had Will run off again? If he had, he'd be more likely to go first to my place. I sighed and locked the door behind me. Tent it is, then.

I'd shared the tent with Grace until recently. She picked

me up off the street when I first arrived in the out-town, lost and disoriented. She found me occasional mechanical jobs around the out-town and then the job at the Assembly. And she nursed me through virus-induced illnesses and bacterial infections, and negotiated with the local clinic to supply me with asthma medication on her health card. I owed my survival in this century to her.

When she lost her job packing pallets at a wholesale food distributor a month ago, she moved into her lover Levin's house, which was across the motorway near Parramatta Road. I chose to stay in the tent, despite Grace's invitation that I move with her; "Levin's got an extra room upstairs," she'd said. Levin's house backed onto his business and stood in an area with steady electricity and water supply, but Levin and I didn't get on at all. Grace said she moved in "for Will's sake." Levin resented my presence and the fact that I'd known Grace longer than he had. Will and I both resented Grace having anything to do with him at all.

I couldn't work out what his business involved—the shop front was a neat office, with a sofa for people to wait and a stack of magazines. I'd never seen anyone in there on the few occasions I went past in the bus or visited Grace. Grace said simply that he was a "local entrepreneur." She made it clear, in her blunt way, that she wasn't interested in talking about it. I wondered if he was connected with the gangs. Vince called him "Mr. Levin," and didn't talk much in his presence; that in itself was enough to make me wary of him. Levin occasionally hinted at some kind of paramilitary past, too, usually by mocking another person's less-than-expert opinion on firearms or military protocol.

Outside, the street was unlit except for irregular strips of light from windows and doorways. I tripped and stubbed my toe on raised pieces of concrete and potholes. As I left the paved area and moved between the out-town shacks, flickering lamps mostly replaced the electric lights. I could hear voices and see vague moving outlines in the darkness. Somewhere children giggled.

At the second corner down from Creek Road I passed through a yellow rectangle of light from the snack stall there. The woman inside waved her spatula.

"Nothing tonight, love?"

"No thanks," I said. My stomach at the moment couldn't tolerate a cup of tea, let alone slabs of potato fried in well-used grease.

"Night, then." She wiped the sweat off her mustache with a red and white checked cloth.

"Good night."

Her accent was unlike the accents of the majority of out-town residents—they used English as their lingua franca and to gain practice before paying off their fake ID cards and moving into suburban society, but it was not the mother tongue of most of them. Her accent was broad and local, and reminded me of Bill Murdoch.

Bill Murdoch was the chief of Security on Jocasta. He grew up on Earth in this very city, although at the end of this century, and his Earth Standard was as flat and idio-syncratic as the English in this time. Some days I could think about him and the station calmly—when the Invidi come I'll talk them into sending me back there and then Murdoch and I will pick up where we left off and every-thing will be fine. More than fine, perhaps, since he made it clear he was interested in more than friendship. He kissed me, after all. We hadn't done much about that more-than-friendship when I left; meals together when our schedules didn't clash and occasional off-duty walks in the station's gardens. Murdoch had been with me on the station for nearly five years, and when I didn't think about it too much, I could assume he'd be there when I got back.

It was when I did think about it, or in unguarded moments when I listened to local voices, that I was overwhelmed by longing to hear his voice. And consumed by longing to be on the station again. What if Murdoch's not there when I get back? He might have moved on, decided five months was long enough to wait. Why the hell didn't I tell him . . .

I spent many long out-town nights considering what I should have told Murdoch. Plenty of time to consider many things, while the sirens howled down the motorway and rats scrabbled along the roof and the couple next door screamed their nightly abuse at each other before rocking the line of tents with noisy sex.

I didn't even know which part of Sydney Murdoch came from. Comes from. Will come from. One day I thought I saw him, from the back. A tallish, heavy-chested man with a rolling walk. The unhurried persistence was so like Murdoch that I strode after him, pulse pounding in my throat. When he turned, I could see he was, of course, a stranger. No way Murdoch could get here. As a human he'd have no access to a ship that could bring him here.

As a human, one of the Nine, he couldn't use the jump drive. The Four—Invidi, K'Cher, Melot, and Bendarl—guarded their monopoly of the drive as zealously as the inhabitants of Sydney's inner city guarded their privileges. The Nine were limited to traveling on ships owned and operated by the Four. I wondered what happened back on Jocasta when the Four found out I had used a jump-capable ship to get here.

I hoped the three engineers who'd been involved in the research with me hadn't gotten into too much trouble. When we planned the test, I told them if anything happened and I didn't return, they were to blame the whole thing on me. Not that we expected anything to happen. Perhaps we should have put off the test until after the neutrality vote.

The station, and by extension the star system in which it was situated, was a candidate for the status of planned neutrality from the Confederacy. The Confederacy Council, which contained representatives of all thirteen Confederacy member worlds, would vote for or against this. We wanted neutrality because the station's residents were fed up with the Confederacy for a variety of reasons, including being left to endure an alien blockade for six months without assistance. The vote could have gone through already, it had been nearly half a year since we declared our intention to apply for neutrality. I'd been here on Earth for five months—what might have happened at home? Or rather, what will happen . . .

I nearly ran into someone on a particularly dark track.

"Watch it," a man's voice growled. A heavy body lurched past me, so close I could feel the heat of his breath and smell the alcohol fumes.

Stop daydreaming and concentrate on getting back to the tent safely.

A dog barked, hitting a corrugated iron fence with a thud that set my pulse racing again. I turned the last corner. In this lane there were no patches of uncurtained window light, only the glow from an open fire at the end of the lane. Laughter rose from the shadowed figures around it and tiny red dots from smokers winked on and off.

My tent sat halfway down the lane. It had canvas walls, pulled tight on a framework of hardwood poles driven deep into the dirt, and a thin sheet of corrugated iron for a roof. The wall that faced outward on the corner of the row also had a sheet of wood nailed to the framework outside. It kept out some of the noise, but on windless nights the tent was stifling.

The row of tents formed one side of a square that enclosed a courtyard paved with uneven brick fragments. The courtyard held a communal shower block and privy, a twisted lemon tree in a cracked plastic garbage bin, lines stretched between four sets of lopsided poles to hang washing on, and garden vegetables in rusting drums.

I pushed open the flimsy screen door. Inside, a wooden crate I used as a table-cum-cupboard was built around the central pole. I reached up and switched on the small electric lamp high on the pole. I charged the batteries once a week with the Assembly's solar generator.

The only other furniture was a chair of battered green plastic, a small pantry, and an old door propped on four bricks, covered with folded cloths. I couldn't sleep on a mattress like Grace. When she lived here she had flipped hers over one night, turned it on end, and sprayed pungent insecticide on all the insect life thus revealed. Shuddering, I told her a blanket was all I needed. She laughed at my squeamishness, but after that I slept on the door.

You should be grateful, I told myself drearily, sinking into the hard chair and staring at the ground. Six bricks marked the place on the other side of the tent where Grace's board and mattress used to lie. You should be grateful she picked you up and you're not stuck in a detention center. Grateful you can work.

And anyway, whose fault is it you're here? If you hadn't insisted on making the test run, if you hadn't insisted on beginning the project in the first place . . .

"Maria?" The small voice came from the doorway.

I blinked away tears that had somehow leaked out. Feeling sorry for myself again. "Will, what are you doing here?"

Grace's younger son, Will, wiry as a monkey and twice as much trouble, shuffled into the tent, slamming the screen door on its uneven frame.

"Wanted to see you."

I wiped my eyes hurriedly. "You saw me yesterday."

Yesterday he skipped out of school and the principal told Grace, who then came to the Assembly office in a foul mood. She yelled at Will, which scandalized Florence, and dragged him back to school.

Will sat on the chair and kicked his legs rhythmically. "When do the results come out?"

"I told you, middle of May."

"Can I come and look with you?"

"We'll see."

When he and Grace lived here, I'd helped him with his schoolwork. Sometimes we went along to the Assembly office and used the computer to do research on the infonet. While doing this, we'd entered a competition to design a spaceship engine. Why, I wasn't sure. We were both bored with his schoolwork. At the time, I'd had a vague idea that if the Invidi didn't come or, worse, refused to help me, I could start a career in aerospace. It was a challenge—how to use my knowledge without revealing future technology to this age.

"Did you tell them we moved to Levin's?" said Will, in time with his kicks on the chair. "So they know where to send my prize?"

"I told them. If we win, you mean."

If the company running the competition was genuine, they wouldn't be able to resist our entry. I had to use Will's name to get the necessary national ID number. Which meant putting Will's signature prints on the application. If we won, he got the prize, which was the whopping amount of twenty thousand dollars. I wanted to repay Grace somehow, but couldn't think of a way to do it that she'd accept. Aside from the problem of not having anything to repay her with. If Will won that money, I thought it would more than cancel the debt.

We hadn't told Grace about the entry, though. She didn't like me teaching Will anything except his regular schoolwork, despite his obvious ability. "I just want him to be normal, y'know?" went the litany. "Nothing fancy, nothing off the rails like Vince. Just get a decent job and lead a normal life. So don't fill his head with all that protest stuff, okay?" She approved of what the Assembly was doing in the out-town, but she didn't think it needed to preach.

"Does Grace know you're here?" I said, remembering Vince's visit to the Assembly office.

He kept swinging his legs, accompanied by little *boop-boop* sounds.

"Will?"

"She went out with Levin. I don't like it when they're mucking around. I told Mrs. Le I was coming here," he added defensively.

"What do you mean, 'mucking around?' "

"You know." He kicked the chair legs quite hard. "Kissing and stuff."

"Vince was looking for you earlier. Did you go home after that?"

"It's not home. It's Levin's place."

I couldn't dispute that logic. It was why I hadn't moved with them. "You can come too," Levin had said, with that mocking, dare-you-to-disagree look that would have been understandable on a teenage face, but sat strangely on a man who was at least thirty.

"I'm hungry." Will looked pointedly at the little pantry in the corner, raised on bricks like the bed. It was another converted wooden crate, lined with small-gauge chicken wire and fronted with the same material, to keep out rats.

"Nothing in there," I said. "Didn't you have dinner?"

"Don't like chook feet."

I sighed and wriggled my fingers around my trouser pockets. Maybe a stray coin . . .

"Mum gave me five dollars," he said. "We could get some potato cakes."

"We could get some fruit," I said firmly. The family who lived across the courtyard from our row of tents cultivated fruit and vegetables on a patch right down near the river's edge. They usually had some to sell. My stomach could handle something fresh, and it meant I wouldn't have to cook on the open grill in the courtyard, which was always filthy. And I wasn't a very good cook. In the twenty-second century I didn't need to be.

"I'll go," he said happily, and jumped off the chair as though he had springs on his backside.

Three

to cook on the open grill of the courtyard, which was at

Will and I had just sat down to a meal of mandarins and half a loaf of bread when Grace and Levin pushed open the door.

"Jeezus, you try my patience." Grace slapped Will's arm gently. He was sitting in the chair.

I stood up from where I'd been sitting on the bed. "Hello, Grace. Levin."

"G'day, Maria." Grace was about my own age, wary-eyed, round-faced, and running to fat around her breasts and stomach. She'd put on weight since she lost her job.

Levin, a long-bodied man with cropped dark hair and permanent stubble, ignored the greeting. He stepped around Will and sat down on the bed as though he owned the tent, legs spread wide in his tight black trousers. His eyes shifted continuously around the room and his big-boned hands grasped the edge of the bed with unnecessary strength. Levin's hands made me nervous. He balled them into fists even when his face was calm.

"He's supposed to be at home," said Grace to me. "Kid his age shouldn't be wandering around by himself at this hour."

"I didn't invite him," I protested. "He turned up here."

"Vince did," said Will. "Go out by himself. When he was eight, he told me."

"You're you and he's him, and you're different people. And I'm talking to Maria," said Grace.

"Grace, if you want me to baby-sit, say so," I said. "But don't attack me for nothing."

"I'm not a baby," protested Will, his mouth half full of bread.

"It's just an expression," I said. "You know that."

"You encourage him," said Grace.

"I do not."

"Send him back straightaway, then."

"I can't send him back in the middle of the night."

On the bed, Levin chuckled. "Studying history, Maria?" He waved a printed page at me. It was one of many in a pile hidden under the wad of towel I used as a pillow.

" 'On that fateful day in 2017,' " he read in an exaggerated tone, " 'who would have thought the portly figure of the unknown mayor would walk into history as a martyr of the fledgling EarthSouth movement. Would she have stayed away, had she known her fate?' " He picked up another page, then another. " 'Marlena Alvarez—the truth behind the legend' . . . 'Marlena Alvarez talks to *Le Monde*' . . . 'Did the EarthSouth movement begin here?' 'Mendoza on Alvarez . . .' "

"Leave them alone," I snapped, barely able to control the urge to snatch the pages out of his hand.

"You're wasting your time." He tired of teasing and let the pages drop. "Like you waste your time with that Assembly. EarthSouth is already finished. It will never amount to anything."

"I disagree," I said. "Look at the alliances they've helped forge among the environmental groups. And the restrictions they've got passed to protect labor."

"It doesn't make any difference," he said. "I grant you, Alvarez would have made a good leader. But without her, they're nothing."

I could feel my face flushing with annoyance. Alvarez didn't die so that some arrogant street thug could make fun of all that she and the other women fought for . . .

Grace tugged Will's hand and he slid off the chair, stuffing mandarins in both pockets as he went.

"If you two are going to talk politics, we'll be here all night," she said. "C'mon, Levin, let's go."

"Bye, Maria," said Will as Grace towed him out.

"Bye, Will," I called.

Levin shrugged and followed them. In his total self-centeredness he reminded me of a K'Cher and I tried not to let him get close to anything I valued. His touching the magazines seemed like a violation.

In the doorway he turned as though he'd forgotten something. "You went to the parts dealer today."

"How do you know?" Levin had connections everywhere.

"What is it that you want?"

"A kind of focused light beam device," I said cautiously.

"If you mean a laser, I can get you one."

"You can?" He couldn't have surprised me more if he'd suddenly begun to yodel. "I mean, that would be nice. But it needs to be a specific type, and they're out of production now."

"Why do you need it?"

I nearly said, *to send signals to aliens, okay?* but turned it into, "Part of the telescope assembly."

"Watching the skies. Can you see anything through the smog?"

"When it's finished I'll take it out of the city to look properly."

"Tell me the laser specifications and I will ask around."

"Around where?"

"I have friends."

"Why are you offering?"

He paused. "You are hardly in a position to be choosy." It seemed as if he'd been going to say something else, then changed his mind.

"I'll think about it." I was too tired to do anything more that night.

"Don't think too long," he said. "You get out of the habit of doing."

"Levin, you coming?" Grace called from outside.

He disappeared into the dark.

I latched the door behind them, although it wouldn't keep anyone out. Then I scraped the mandarin peel and bread crumbs off the table and into a bucket, over which I placed a piece of fibro and held it down with a brick to keep inquisitive rats from helping themselves.

Then I picked up the papers Levin had dropped, wiping each of them on the dirty blanket. Cleaner than Levin's touch. He was right. I was studying history. My own history, because Marlena Alvarez was my great-grandmother's best friend, and if not for her, I wouldn't have been born in Las Mujeres, because there would have been no village there. I was also studying the EarthSouth movement, which Alvarez had founded.

At least, my great-grandmother always spoke of Alvarez as if she single-handedly created the EarthSouth movement. I always thought that after her death in 2017 human rights and local autonomy groups across the world formed a chain of protest against oppression and poverty. The political upheavals following the Invidi arrival helped them bring their agenda into the mainstream of politics, while advances in medicine and agriculture allowed them to put many of their ideals into practice.

But Levin's comments about EarthSouth may have smarted all the more because I hadn't found much evidence of a united social justice movement in early 2023. From what I'd collected in written articles, downloaded from infonet archives, and heard from visitors to the Assembly, in these five years since Marlena's death EarthSouth was only an umbrella organization of loosely affiliated groups that met once a year in some countries, more often in others, and had only met twice internationally. The first meeting in 2018 attracted media attention, but during the second meeting in 2020 the Olympic sporting events received more coverage.

And Marlena Alvarez was only one of the "inspirations" claimed by the movement. Earlier icons such as Nelson Mandela and Naomi Klein also featured large in their pantheon. I wondered whether my great-grandmother might not have overemphasized Marlena's importance. Understandably, too, seeing that they worked and cheated death together in Las Mujeres for five years.

For five years after Alvarez became mayor, the women of Las Mujeres struggled to keep their village safe from government militias, private militias, guerrilla groups, starvation and disease. At least, that was what my great-grandmother's stories told.

She told how Marlena got the idea of moving everyone to a new camp, leaving the old village as a decoy, to be presumed abandoned. The guerrillas moved on to collect tribute from more lucrative sources.

How Marlena went alone and unarmed to talk to an army commander who wanted the women to inform on their vanished sons and husbands. He left, persuaded that the women had been alone for so long they could know nothing.

How Marlena's leadership united the heads of local governments enough to defeat the proposal to dam the nearby twin lakes and flood all the villages along the river.

Although I wouldn't have admitted it to Murdoch or any of my colleagues on Jocasta, these stories, this image of Alvarez, was a comfort and an inspiration to me during the long, hopeless months of the alien blockade. When yet another station system failed, or yet another squabble broke out between alien and alien, alien and human, human and human, in these moments I'd ask myself, "What would Marlena Alvarez do?" I trained as an engineer, and while I could direct the flow of a construction site or coordinate projects within a larger design, nothing prepared me to be solely responsible for thirty thousand people. Alvarez was an example of someone else who had made the best of a job she took on without training or preparation—she'd been a solicitor's clerk before becoming mayor.

I used to chide myself for relying on Alvarez's memory, but the parallels in our situations were obvious: we were both isolated, with limited resources, and surrounded by enemies who outgunned us. When the responsibility for Jocasta sat particularly heavily on my shoulders, it helped to think that Alvarez had found a way out. She had insisted Las Mujeres not align itself with any of the powers in the region, and the women stubbornly maintained their independence until the changes in local government laws of 2046.

Alvarez's insistence upon keeping neutral throughout the many wars and insurgencies that swept across the region influenced the EarthSouth movement's determined political neutrality. And her ideas influenced my decision to push for neutrality for Jocasta, although I didn't realize it at the time.

Since beginning work at the Assembly, I'd collected all the articles on Alvarez that I could find and downloaded as much information as I could from the infonet. And one memorable day, I watched her speak. It was a recording of a speech made shortly before she died.

It was early morning in the out-town about two months after I arrived. In the Assembly office Florence and I would work from seven to eleven, go home because it was too hot, then come back for a couple of hours in the evening.

On this particular morning, I found a reference to Alvarez in a file our computer could download, so I did, and fed it into "run video."

I cried out with surprise and slapped my hand over my mouth. Florence looked up from sealing envelopes.

"What's the matter?"

"Nothing," I mumbled, but she came and stood behind me.

"Alvarez? That's the San Diego speech, I think." Florence nodded to herself. "The only time she left her own country."

I wasn't interested in the details. The captions running at the bottom of the screen, the two smaller windows at the top that showed an edited history of the village and an explanation of the San Diego rally; all these were unimportant. Marlena was there, almost in person.

Beside the practiced movements of the suited man who introduced her, she looked small and awkward.

I thought she'd be taller. And I expected her to . . . glow, or something. Have an aura. But at first glance, she could have been one of the women who walked home from the bus stop each night from work in the factories, in her cheap dress and scuffed sandals. Graying hair pulled back from a large-featured face. Narrow dark eyes that glared from behind glasses.

Glasses. Nobody told me Marlena wore glasses. None of the photos showed glasses.

"You knew them, didn't you?" said Florence.

"Alvarez was well known in the district," I said distractedly. The glasses didn't fit what I knew about her.

The camera drew back to show Alvarez on the edge of a stage in a wide stadium, surrounded by a dark ocean of figures, almost engulfed in the spotlights.

Why am I here? Her voice echoed tinnily from the computer's inbuilt speaker. *You invited me to speak about the things that are happening in my country. But you know already. Why do you need me to tell you again? You are the ones who make the choice to go on as you have, or to act on behalf of others less fortunate who cannot act.*

"It's a real pity she's not around today," said Florence. She shook her head sadly and went back to sealing envelopes, dabbing them with a glue stick because they were cheap post office rejects on which the glue had long dried.

I said that conscience is not enough, but it is a good start. Don't let it stop there. You can go back to your comfortable homes after I finish talking, and you can forget what I say. Or you can think about it, but eventually you'll return to your job and your home and you'll forget. Or you can go home and do something. A small action is enough. But it must be an act.

She paused, removed the glasses, and smiled. It transformed her heavy features into beauty.

Then do it again tomorrow.

The speech was the same as I'd read in our history files, but it worried me that none of the contemporary reports mentioned my great-grandmother's stories, like Marlena talking to the army commander or the decoy village. There were other stories, less glamorous: how she stopped the dam work, yes, but mainly because she invited the media into her village, and the media told the world about the dam.

The media told the world about Alvarez, too. Now that I was here in the twenty-first century and saw the distortions in print and electronic media, I began to wonder how much we could trust of what they'd told the world about Alvarez.

In the tent after Will, Grace, and Levin left, I sifted through the flimsy pages that Levin had rearranged. Interviews, articles, news stories, later reviews of earlier articles. The big issue of a magazine called *Time* published on the first anniversary of Marlena's death, which I found by chance in a box at the dump when I was looking for wires. A lucky chance, because people usually sold old papers for recycling.

One of the interviews I'd printed from the infonet caught my eye. Alvarez had refused to cooperate with the new alliance government when it came to power in 2016, because it hunted down the militias who had terrorized the people of that region for decades and executed them without trial. "This is not the way to build a lasting peace," said Marlena. "You must stop the killing sometime."

I smoothed the paper below the grainy photograph—she wore no glasses—and read the last lines. "You have to be flexible," she said. "Things can change in ways you don't expect."

Like aliens coming to visit.

"I have never seen the wisdom," continued Marlena in the interview, "in resisting what you feel is right for today, in order to do something that may be right tomorrow."

I patted the edges of the papers into line and slid them inside the string bag in which I usually carried food or small pieces of potentially useful junk. I hadn't collected many new reports on Alvarez for weeks now. It seemed more important to complete the telescope and prepare to contact the Invidi when they arrived.

After five months here, I'd worked out that Alvarez might not be the hero I'd thought; she was a moderately successful politician who had a keen sense of justice, tempered by awareness of the need for compromise. Not quite the freedom fighter extraordinaire of EarthSouth legend and my great-grandmother's memories. Nor even the charismatic leader of my own imaginings.

Realistic or not, though, my image of Alvarez had helped

me through the ordeal of the Seouras blockade—cause enough for gratitude. And she would help generations of campaigners for planetary justice in the decades after the Invidi come.

I stepped out of the thin trousers and draped them over the back of the chair. Wash them tomorrow. Having to remind myself to do it was almost as arduous as the task itself. And hang them inside, I added silently. The day before yesterday somebody stole my other T-shirt and two pairs of underpants off the line in our courtyard. I couldn't afford to lose any more.

Four

In the dream I fall into the Earth. The blue and white ball rises, becomes a curved line, then a horizon, then finally fills my vision completely. It's different from the Earth of my century. The clouds are undisturbed by balloonlike weather controllers, there aren't enough comsats to make navigation difficult, and no big orbital stations. No wide, brown kelp farms in the oceans. Blue below, blue above. Nobody yells at me through a comm link for unauthorized entry, no Earth-Fleet fighters buzz my little pod in rude swoops.

Somewhere from beyond the dream come the niggling questions: Why wasn't I being shaken to the eyeballs or squeezed nearly senseless against the harness or hearing the whine and rattle of stressed systems and the sizzle of the pod's skin being fried? Shouldn't I be terrified and sweating and repeating the reentry protocols aloud to keep conscious?

What really happened was that the pod I took from the moon to Earth yawed and cracked across the structurals on one side and the paratube saved me with a jerk, holding me firm in midair as the pod fell away in pieces toward a black mass, then I landed with a clumsy thud onto soft dirt in the dark.

I know this, but in the dream the pod plummets toward the blue and I can't stop it.

Earth starts falling away from me again. Shrinks, falls

in upon itself as if someone has placed a black hole in the middle of the blue, and then it finally disappears. I drop into that point. You can't breathe in a black hole. Gravity crushes your lungs. Can't breathe . . .

Can't . . .

I pushed myself upright, hand fumbling automatically for the inhaler beside the bed. Not there . . . Horrible feeling, as though the air intake on an environmental suit had failed. Gasping for air that wouldn't come . . . Don't panic . . . my fingers found the inhaler and I shoved my face into it and sucked desperately. The chemicals took effect immediately. One breath in, one breath out. Easy.

I sat still, covered in sweat, and waited for the trembling to stop and my chest to lose that tight and trampled-on feeling. Prompted by the dream, my mind played through the scenes of my arrival, as if by revisiting them, I might find something I hadn't noticed before. Some clue as to what went wrong.

The ship I was testing, *Calypso II*, came through a jump point about three days' travel from Earth. With my twenty-second-century engines, that is. Using this century's pre-Invidi technology the same distance would have taken more than a year, which is about how long the original *Calypso* would have taken to reach this position.

The original *Calypso* left Earth on what its passengers thought was a journey to Alpha Centauri in 2026, and would have taken a year to get to the position in space where I'd emerged. So I thought I'd arrived in 2027. This was because the distance from Earth indicated that the jump I just completed had a "length" of ninety-five years, 2027 to 2122.

Calypso II seemed to hold together well, so after checking all systems I tried to go back through the jump point to my own time by repeating what I'd done when I piloted the ship toward the coordinates near Jocasta where *Calypso* had appeared.

It didn't work. I took a deep breath, let it out. I'd never used a jump drive before, this was only to be expected. Maybe I missed something. I checked the log, tried again. Didn't work. *Calypso II* continued in flatspace as though the jump point didn't exist.

I started to sweat. Ran a series of exhaustive diagnostics. Nothing mechanical at fault. Nothing in the navigational or control systems. But I couldn't get back through the jump point that should be there. *Calypso II* was on a short experimental flight, and my supplies weren't sufficient for more than a fortnight's emergency running. I also didn't have much fuel for flatspace thrusters. I could reach Earth—probably.

If I couldn't find the problem by the end of the fortnight I had two choices. First, I could do some fancy conversion work and divert energy from the flatspace engines to life-support systems, then sit around for months hoping someone from my own time would arrive with a rescue ship. Unfortunately, but necessarily, nobody knew that we'd been experimenting with a jump drive, and therefore just about everyone would think I had merely disappeared into normal space. And if the rescue mission didn't arrive, I'd have sacrificed my ability to move for no reason. In this century there was little space traffic near the solar system. The likelihood of my distress call being picked up by a passing trader was close to nil.

Second, I could recalibrate the flatspace thrusters and go to Earth. In 2027 the Invidi would have been here for four years. They'd have organized orbital stations, surely, so that they didn't have to live on Earth among humans. I wasn't entirely sure of the details of intra-system exploration in this age; I did know the first crewed expeditions to Mars didn't leave until the 2040s.

If I contacted the Invidi, they'd understand what had happened and hopefully help me to get back. They wouldn't know about the future ban on humans using jump technology. I wasn't sure whether my contacting them would give them information from the future, but hell, from what I understood of the timeline, all that had happened already.

So I headed for Earth with my twenty-second-century signal dispersal field operative, in the hope that I wouldn't show up on any human sensors. The Invidi hadn't given humans any engineering information or hardware at first, so human sensors should still be pretty primitive. I'd stretched the emergency running time to nearly three weeks by shutting off every inessential system and consuming as few resources as possible, so by then I was dirty, hungry, sleep-deprived, and thoroughly frustrated.

But the closer I got to Earth the worse I felt. There was no sign of Invidi presence. No ship signals, no residue from any kind of spaceship engine I was familiar with, no alien comm traffic. Only human signals, mostly on the same narrow band of frequencies and all of them on Earth, except for a robot probe gathering samples on Titan. When I reached the moon, being careful to keep on the dark side, I stopped and listened more carefully to the signals.

And it was there, huddled in my dark, foul-smelling, stale-aired cabin that had become a prison, exhausted, confused, and scared, that I learned I was in the wrong time. But this is impossible, I told myself, trying not to speak out loud to conserve oxygen, but by that time often it wasn't clear in my head if I spoke or not. News report after news report, entertainment program after program—what a lot of them—military communiqué after communiqué, all repeated the same unbelievable date.

This is your Moscow correspondent, bringing you the news on January 4, 2023.

Here's the weather, then, for Wednesday, fourth of January, 2023.

Kickin' in with the best quiz on the globe, this fine Tuesday evening, 3 January 2023.

I could understand the English, Spanish, and a little of the German—from my great-grandmother—and had to assume the other languages carried the same message. I was four years too early. The Invidi hadn't arrived yet.

Which is impossible.

I floated in the middle of the cabin and squeezed my eyes shut to keep out the sight of what might become my coffin. Don't panic, think.

Calypso left Earth in flatspace in 2026 and came out of a jump point at Jocasta in 2122. Six months later, I go back through that point and emerge at the coordinates *Calypso* must have left from. The distance from Earth to those coordinates indicated *Calypso* must have reached there and entered the jump point in 2027. Which means the jump should have been ninety-five years long. But I had emerged at the coordinates in 2023 . . . 2023, oh, gods . . . which makes a length of ninety-nine years between now and my time of 2122.

No jump we know changes length. They are always fixed in space—invisible until activated, but always in the same spot—and always have the same length, or "correspondence." Otherwise what would be the point of having a jump network? That's how the Confederacy maintains order, by keeping all member worlds on the same timeline.

Yet not only had *Calypso* used a jump point that was not connected to the Confederacy's Central jump network, but it seemed to have shifted back in time.

What the hell should I do?

In the end, I kept my original plan, prompted by the date. The only way I could find out if the jump point was still connected to my world of 2122 was to either repair my jump drive myself or ask the Invidi. As I couldn't do the former, I'd have to wait for the Invidi to arrive. And the Invidi arrived on Earth in May 2023. May 1, to be exact. All I had to do was survive five months on my own planet.

If I'd known what that involved, maybe I would have stayed in *Calypso II* and tried to stretch and convert my fuel for five months.

But I didn't, I left *Calypso II* tethered in a deep crater on the dark side of the moon and took one of the escape pods down to the planet.

The Single Escape Vehicle was popularly known as a "turd" because of their simple shape and the fact that if you needed to use one, you were deep in it. This one lived up to its reputation by malfunctioning, then disintegrating at about seven kilometers above the surface, and I floated down in a damaged paratube that eventually caught in short, thorny bushes on a hillside and dumped me. Sand and small, sharp rocks made a mess of the environment suit's insulation, so after I finished shaking with the release of tension, I buried it. All but the boots. The scattered remains of the pod I could do nothing about. I hoped it would be buried soon in drifting sand and dirt. I didn't really care, I just sat there for a moment and contemplated how nice it was not to be dead. Then the cold seeped up from the sand, which grew harder and harder, and merely not being dead wasn't enough. I had to find a town, somewhere to wait out the next five months until the Invidi came.

I knew when I was, but where? The stars said the Southern Hemisphere, but I didn't think it was my home continent. I didn't get as far as the Indian Ocean. Which left Australia. Murdoch's homeland.

Might as well walk as sit here.

The sun rose. I was in a landscape of straggly trees, sharp grasses, prickly-looking shrubs. Lots of unfamiliar birdsong, among it a peculiar gulping cry, and a liquid warble that made me glad just to hear it. A wire fence drooped to the ground unmended. This sign of human habitation heartened me and I followed the fence to a road. But there were no houses and no sources of water. I finished the pod's emergency water rations too quickly.

I kept walking along the side of the road. It didn't look well maintained. The edges of the bitumen mix were crumbling and there were holes every ten or fifteen meters, some big enough to cover a quarter of the black surface.

The heat reflected off the road became worse as the day dragged on. I kept my outer shirt over my head as radiation protection, but by midday my head was aching so much I had to stop and sit beside a bush. Mouth dry, eyes full of dust. Not one vehicle in about six hours. They'd had groundcars in this period, surely. If so, none of them traveled this road.

A little later a hum in the distance became a growl, then a roar, and a long groundcar stopped with a hissing of brakes at my frantic waving. The driver waited for me to rattle open the cabin door. He glanced at me sideways from pale blue eyes with lines radiating from the corners. Suspicious and distant.

"Long way from anywhere to be walking."

I nodded, unsure of twenty-first-century idioms. At least I understood his words. English.

"Car break down? Or somebody dump you?"

I nodded again. He gave me a drink of water, which I gulped down. The groundcar lurched into motion again. Unsettling at first, then soothing, the road rolled on endlessly, straight and gray, away from the sun. Eastern seaboard, I thought sleepily, population centers. From a photoimage above the window, a small dark woman hugging a young child smiled down at me. A dangling woven ball with a tassel rocked in front of them.

I must have fallen asleep, because the next thing I knew, the vehicle was stationary, the driver outside talking to another man. Dark outside, except for lights on poles beside the road and bright lights over a low building beside it. The driver said I'd better get out unless I wanted to go through a checkpoint.

"They sent them back." He pointed at the photoimage. "Guess helping you might even things out."

He liked the boots. I gave them to him in thanks for the lift, and found myself in the out-town.

Night, nowhere to stay. I didn't even remember going to sleep against a wall somewhere, but had a rude awakening just before dawn. Someone held my shoulders and covered my face while another grabbed the medkit and scanner I'd brought with me from the paratube. They disappeared into the warren of shabby buildings before I could stagger to my feet.

I'd thought that the moment I opened my mouth I'd be marked as an outsider, but nobody gave me more than a quick glance. Snatches of words in languages other than English drifted out of open doorways, people walked quickly along streets of small houses with red roofs. First I needed food, then shelter. Economic system should be money-based. I had no idea where to start.

I met Grace at the Help House near the church on Roma Street. I didn't understand that the House was a charitable organization, providing food and a few clothes for nothing to the destitute and temporarily destitute. They said they didn't need any work done, and Grace, who was there with a box of clothes to donate, laughed at me when I turned away in disappointment. If you want to work, she said, you can clean up my shower block. I went back to the out-town with her and cleaned the communal shower in the courtyard and fixed a couple of leaks in the pipe with a temporary patch.

"If you can fix things," Grace said, "that's a different story." She fed me, then introduced me to a friend who owned a repairs workshop and said, "She'll work for coupons and a rec-cert, won't you?" looking at me in a meaningful way I totally failed to comprehend. "You do baby-sitting?" she asked. The word conjured up bizarre images, and while I dithered, she continued. "'Coz you can stay here for a while, if you don't mind keeping an eye on my ten-year-old when I'm on night shift. I don't want no business done here," she added hastily. "It's not that I'm fussy, but you get some weird punters these days, and the kid" . . . I said I'd be very grateful to stay, having deciphered the "sitting" part, and only a little while later worked out what she meant about "punters." The option didn't appeal to me and I was glad I'd met Grace before being driven to consider it.

For the first few weeks I was too busy coping with attacks by local viruses on my unprepared immune system. At first I thought my twenty-second-century medical regulators had been disabled in some way by the jump to the past. Then I realized that they were probably still working, which was the only reason I was still alive.

When I finally experienced a few hours without feeling sick, I wanted information about the town, about the world, about my ancestors, and I needed to work out a way to contact the Invidi when they arrived. To do this I needed access to a computer, those ugly, primitive boxes that had to be physically connected to a source of electricity most of the time. Primitive maybe, but they were expensive by the standards of the out-town, and Grace certainly didn't have one in her tent.

The local store ran noninteractive broadcast programs, what older people called TV and younger ones called vidnet. It was the only place within a couple of streets that had a screen. Or I could access the local library's network, which connected only to other public libraries; or I could use the Net Café over the other side of Parramatta Road, but I'd have to borrow someone's account as you needed an NID to set up a new account. At the café I could surf the older internet, but most of the information I needed, for example about military communications satellites and higher level scientific information, was on Safenet, which was another system entirely and which had far stricter controls. So I tried to study ways to access different systems without authority—"hacking."

About a month after I arrived I found another temporary job with a mechanic. I picked up the essentials of the work quickly, but it was an hour's walk each way and there was no infonet access at the workshop.

One day, about a month and a half after finding that job, I was walking back to the tent by a different route and saw the words "EarthSouth Movement" on a poster outside an old house. I went inside to see what it was, and found myself in the Assembly office. A tiny, neat woman with a stern voice asked me if I'd come about the job. I said yes. She said Abdul's just stepped out, you can talk to me until he gets back.

She introduced herself as Florence Woo and asked me why I wanted the job. I said, having seen the posters and the slogans, that I'd been involved with the EarthSouth movement in South America. And that I needed a job closer to the out-town. We don't pay much, said Florence, naming a figure about half of the tiny amount I received from the mechanic. By now I knew that illegal immigrants couldn't hope to be paid fair wages for any job. But I saw the computer on the desk and calculated that the drop in pay would be tolerable if I didn't have to spend most of it at the café. And I could keep giving rent to Grace.

Florence said she'd "discuss" my application with Abdul. When I went back the next day, she said I'd got the job. Which was, I found out, a combination of mechanic, electrician, and computer repairperson.

None of which would come in handy when I got back and found myself ex-head of station, which would happen if Earth was annoyed at the way I'd borrowed funds to complete the *Calypso II* project, then thoughtlessly become lost in the past. If the jump point maintained its correspondence of ninety-nine years between 2023 and my own time of 2122.

I swung my legs over the side of the bed, being careful to first whack the ground with the short stick I kept handy for that purpose. Rats usually stayed around the outside garbage heaps where food was freely available, but I'd put my bare foot on a large cockroach once and the memory still made me shudder.

The dirt felt cool and gritty under my toes as I felt around for my sandals. Bluish white light snuck through cracks in one side, from the floodlights across the little river, where a clinical waste incinerator ran twenty-four hours, seven days a week. On the door side of the tent, yellow light would grow brighter, then fade again as somebody carried a lantern or torch along the track.

I reached for the jug and poured a glass of water. Sometimes it calmed the wheezing from the asthma attack. The water tasted stale and sour, although it was bought, filtered stuff. Even Jocasta's recycled water tasted better than this.

I finished sipping and leaned forward with my head resting on my folded arms on the crate table. A change of posture sometimes helped with the wheezing, too.

During the day I could think about telescopes and contacting the Invidi, and all the minutiae of daily life. I'd never imagined all the small, dreary tasks that had to be done to function at even this century's standard. All these *things,* out to get me. Like the viruses, lining up to get past my immune system. I wasn't used to taking care of anything but my job. On Jocasta, food preparation, cleaning, and waste disposal was done for us, silently and mostly efficiently.

But now, in the hours of darkness and silence here on Earth—unlike on the space station, where we have night-shift workers, and aliens who work their day shift at night, and the whole complex machinery of life support and recycling hums on in the background—in the hours when everything shuts down except the incinerator, my memories of the past creep up on me. My past, but this world's future.

I can see the chain of events that led to my being stuck here in the past quite clearly. A line of dominoes, set up in some pattern only the Invidi can understand. Every night in the out-town I sit wheezing in the dark and line them all up in my mind. Every night I give one of them a push, and watch as the line falls.

First—although, depending on which domino I push, it might not be first—there was the Abelar Treaty. Named after the star system within which Jocasta is situated, the Abelar Treaty was designed by me and my advisers on Jocasta and was signed by two alien races and myself, as governor of the Abelar system and therefore representative of the Confederacy. This was in early 2121. The treaty made the two alien races, the Seouras and the Danadan, co-monitors of each other's affairs within the Abelar system, which hopefully would stop their fighting with each other and destroying the neighborhood.

The Abelar Treaty was significant because when a different group of Seouras arrived several months later, we thought they also recognized the treaty. But these Seouras were different. Domino number two. Their heavily armed gray ships attacked the station and blockaded us from any contact with the Confederacy. The Seouras wouldn't say what they wanted, they just kept us prisoner in Jocasta.

For nearly six months we tried to find ways to circumvent the blockade or communicate with the Confederacy, and to keep the station's residents safe and fed. Six months of hell. Then domino number three arrived—a ship called *Calypso* appeared suddenly and activated a jump mine, which killed all but three of the crew. This was in January 2122. *Calypso*'s presence was a mystery at first. It couldn't have traveled from Earth to Jocasta in flatspace within fifty years, which was how long the cryogenic sleep system was set to preserve the crew. On the other hand, human ships were not equipped with jump drives, nor was there a recorded jump point in the place where *Calypso* appeared. It couldn't have jumped from Earth to Jocasta, because no jump points existed off the Central network. So we thought.

The *Calypso* crew's plan was to head for Alpha Centauri from Earth, and after fifty years of frozen sleep, to decelerate and look for habitable planets in that system. A mad idea, and if they'd arrived on schedule in 2076, they would have found a small but thriving Melot station there. But instead they arrived near Jocasta. And we couldn't tell how long they had been asleep.

Calypso's arrival signaled the end of the Seouras blockade. When we talked to the crew, they told us that an Invidi called An Serat helped them to leave Earth. We suspected then that *Calypso* might have jumped from a point somewhere along its course to Jocasta. I thought of An Serat's help as being domino number four, although a little out of time.

It certainly set things off on Jocasta. I wanted to take a look at *Calypso*'s engines, because I thought the Nine should be able to have jump technology. Our resident Invidi, An Barik, wanted *Calypso*'s engines so the Nine would not have a chance at learning about them. A terrorist group who'd infiltrated the station also wanted the engines so they could use the jump drive to help them fight the Confederacy. And, finally, it turned out that the Seouras ships we had been resisting for six months were in fact ships of a different alien race called the Tor, who had taken the Seouras prisoner and forced them to communicate with the station for the purpose of . . . getting hold of *Calypso.*

I tended to lose track of my dominoes at this point. Sometimes I put in extra ones for the gray Tor ships and the imprisoned Seouras. The Tor ships contained no live Tor, an aggressive alien species who'd fought a war with the Invidi for nearly a century. But after the Tor withdrew suddenly from Invidi space less than a decade ago, Earth time, we'd seen no sign of them. We never found out if the Tor ships had been traveling for millennia in flatspace, or if they appeared from their own jump point.

At any rate, the closest gray ship found out about *Calypso* and tried to take it.

Murdoch and I stopped them by damaging the gray ship using a bomb he planted inside *Calypso.*

The gray ship was damaged and retreated, leaving a field of debris behind.

Some of the debris contained pieces of *Calypso*'s engines. I salvaged those engines and started the *Calypso II* project.

In June 2122, I left Jocasta on a test flight and ended up in 2023. Which should be impossible. Dammit, where did I go wrong?

Someone knocked. Or rather, pulled the piece of string at the entry that rattled the pieces of pipe I'd hung in the center of the roof. A gentle *clackety-click* that roused me from my thoughts.

At first I thought it was the wind, grown strong enough to rattle the whole tent. But then it sounded again.

It had to be someone from the neighborhood. One of the gang that collected Grace's "rent" would have simply pushed open the door and demanded payment. Maybe something had happened to the Assembly office.

An uneasy lump in my throat, I wrapped a sarong around my waist and stood near the door.

"Who is it?" I called softly.

"Halley, is that you?" a man's voice called back.

In this century nobody knows my name is Halley. Nobody speaks a language called Earth Standard because it hasn't evolved yet.

No, it's not possible. Must be an hallucination. That flu's caught up with me.

"Hello?" I said cautiously. Then thought how ridiculous it was, standing there talking through a screen that provided no protection anyway. I opened it, hand shaking.

"It's me . . ." said the man on the other side. In the dark his face was indistinct, but his voice and his smell and his rhythm of breathing was Bill Murdoch's and I was backing up until my legs hit the bed.

He stepped into the room. "Halley, is it you?"

Then he lifted something up close to his eyes. Something small with two arrays of blinking lights in patterns. I recognized it as a directional indicator.

The sight of that small piece of twenty-second-century technology anchored my wits. I reached up the pole in the center of the tent and switched on the bulb.

In its weak yellow light Murdoch looked at me and breathed a sigh of relief. "It is you. For a second, I thought I'd got the wrong place."

He wore an old T-shirt and sarong, with thongs on his feet like any resident of the out-town. For a moment I saw him as a dark, heavy-chested stranger with lines on his face that could be either from worry or laughter. Then he was just himself.

He grinned. "Hey, don't go all wobbly on me."

I shook my head, beyond speech. An immense bubble of loneliness popped inside me.

"I'm really here." To demonstrate the point, he stepped forward and hugged me.

I let my face be squished against a warm, firm chest damp with sweat. Reached around with my arms and felt his solidity. Gods, he really *is* here, and I'm shaking and my face is wet. Am I laughing or crying?

"Bill, how did you get here?" I said, muffled. Stupid question—the same way I did, obviously.

His arms tightened for a moment, then relaxed. We separated awkwardly. Uncertain what to do, I reached for the water bottle and poured him a glassful.

"It's filtered," I said, unable to tell in the dim light whether his expression was distaste or anxiety.

He gulped it down and drank another. Put the glass on the crate and looked around the small space. "Is this it?"

"Is this what?"

"Where you've spent the past five months?"

Five months. The same length of time as I experienced. So he must have come through the same jump point that I used, and it had stayed stable at the same "distance" of about ninety-nine years—I left Jocasta in September 2122 and arrived here in December 2022. It was now April 2023.

"Halley? Is this where you live?" He was frowning in puzzlement, the expression familiar in the way it drew his brows together, making two deep lines between them.

"Yes. Yes, it is. When did you get here?"

"Just arrived," he said. "Yesterday."

Murdoch must have left in January 2123.

I ran my hand over my head, too many words competing to get out at the same time. I wanted to ask him how he got a ship to travel through the point, how he reached the surface undetected, what was happening back on the station, why he'd come alone, how he'd found me—although I had a good idea—and if he had a way to get back.

I took a breath to say the words, but it wouldn't come

into my lungs. Damn, damn. Furious and embarrassed at the same time, I dropped to my knees and scrabbled for the inhaler beside the bed. Where is the thing? I had it earlier . . .

Murdoch was kneeling down beside me looking worried, but I couldn't tell him what was wrong and didn't care because until I found the blasted inhaler . . . not under the bed . . . oh hell where . . . blanket, in . . . the . . . got it.

"M'sorry," I said as soon as I could speak, sitting on the floor. "Respiratory problem. Air passages close up." The hard edge of the bed board dug a trench across my spine and the packed earth was cool on my backside. One of Murdoch's hands rested on my knee, the other held my shoulder. He was shaking. I was shaking, with the teary relief that followed an attack.

"Are you all right?" he said helplessly. "Does this . . . how long has this been . . ." He peered closer at my face. "Jeezus, you look awful."

"Thanks." I wheezed the word with as much sarcasm as possible. He was so close. I could sense every centimeter of his body in a way I didn't remember having experienced before.

He didn't seem to notice anything, and leaned back against the bed beside me. "Don't be touchy. If you were on the station I'd hospitalize you on the spot." He waved his hand at the tent. "What is this place? I got halfway in here and thought I must have made a mistake."

My skin prickled where his arm and shoulder rested against mine. "It's where unofficial refugees, illegal immigrants, and asylum seekers end up. Also anyone else who wants to stay away from the legal system."

He grunted. "Lawbreakers, in other words."

"And drug users. Runaways. Homeless."

"Okay. I know what Earth was like in this decade, I read the history files."

"You'll find the details quite different." I felt clarity return. "First things first. Is your ship intact?"

He shook his head. "Sorry. Guess you want to get out of here." His voice was gentle.

Don't get nice on me, Bill, I'll break down. "Second, tell me how you got here."

Murdoch grabbed the hard plastic chair and straddled it in another familiar pose.

I sat cross-legged on the bed to listen.

Five

"An Serat sent me," said Murdoch. At my stare, "Make sense to you?"

"He must have met us here in the past. That's why he had to make sure you're here."

He frowned. "But that's . . . Anyway, you disappeared on your test flight. Big shock to everyone. But then Ensign Lee—you remember her? She mentioned to me that your signal cut out pretty close to where *Calypso* appeared. Aha, I say, and go to check on her navigational data, and she's right.

"So I go and have a little chat with the other three engineers on your team. They tell me you might have been caught in an anomaly of some kind. They weren't very upset, though. Gave me the impression they wanted me out of the lab so they could go back to work."

I grimaced, half embarrassed. The three engineers and myself had agreed to keep the real content of the research secret; if it leaked, I was pretty sure the Invidi would try to stop us. I hadn't intended to keep Murdoch out of the picture as well, even though that was how it turned out.

"After twenty-four hours we sent out search and rescue ships, as usual," he continued. "Must admit, when they didn't find anything over the next two days, I started to get worried too. I guessed you didn't have a lot of emergency life-support equipment installed. We had to cut down the search after that—you know how it is."

I nodded. If the missing person has no air left, there's no rush to find them.

He tilted the chair farther forward to look intently at me. "I didn't give up. But I had no evidence to give them that you were alive to be rescued."

I half smiled. "There was no evidence."

"Oh, yes there was." He let the chair fall back with a bump. "I took a look at your research notes . . ."

"How did you do that?" I sat up straighter.

"I'm chief of Security, remember?"

"And?"

"And it didn't make a lot of sense to me. Mostly equations and blueprints. But it was obvious even to me that you'd installed something other than a flatspace engine. Which wasn't in your project proposal, by the way."

"We thought it was safer not to say exactly what we were doing," I said.

"Like you didn't mention salvaging *Calypso*'s engines in the first place?" he said reproachfully. "I talked to Finke, too."

Hieronymous Finke, the salvage operator and independent contractor whom I'd asked to bring in the remains of *Calypso* after the gray ship spat it out, together with a lot of Seouras debris.

"Finke said he brought some space junk back for you and you stored it in one of the lower bays," said Murdoch.

"ConFleet was busy at the time," I protested. "I didn't want to bother them."

"Uh-huh. And you stored the junk as research material and paid Finke from the engineering budget. Nice bit of creative accounting, that. Veatch would be proud."

I suppose it had been naive of me to think that if we were successful, these minor transgressions would be overlooked. An unpleasant feeling, to have one's sins exposed one after the other. I remembered how I'd kept away from everyone, including Murdoch, over the next couple of months as I investigated what remained of *Calypso*'s engines. Maybe I was too angry at the Invidi, maybe over-reacting to the events of the blockade.

"I went back to your engineering colleagues," said Murdoch, "and told them I wanted answers. They were all a bit subdued by then—I think they needed to tell someone what had gone wrong. They told me you were probably at the other end of the jump point *Calypso* came through. Nothing we could do from our end."

He leaned forward again. "I thought, I can do something. I was going to go to ConFleet and request a rescue ship to go through the same jump point. At least, I wondered if I should do that, because if ConFleet caught you with Invidi jump technology you'd be under arrest in no time. But anyway, before I could do anything, transfers came through for all three of your engineering team."

"Whose orders?"

"EarthFleet for Josh Heron and ConFleet for the other two. Admiral's signatures on all transfers, no discussion. I barely had time to ask them what was going on; none of them knew. I went back to check whether I had enough evidence about the project and where you'd gone to take to ConFleet if necessary, and what do you know? Lee's navigational data was missing."

"What about the research results?" I said, not really wanting to hear the inevitable answer.

"Some of it had security seals on it. Above my level. Some of it had been 'transferred' and disappeared into a bureaucratic muddle."

"Sounds like An Barik's been busy."

I meant our "local" Invidi, An Barik, who had been the Confederacy Council observer on Jocasta for several years before the Seouras blockade. An Barik lived on Jocasta but didn't socialize in any way with other species, and only appeared at official functions when absolutely necessary. We suspected he'd been able to contact the Confederacy at any time during the blockade but chose not to. It was difficult to understand why, but as far as we could see, his reason was so that nothing would happen to prevent *Calypso* arriving.

He nodded. "Yeah, that's what I thought. So I went to see him. Tried to, that is, but I never got any response that made sense. I started to get really worried. It was over a month since you left and everyone was saying how sad, a tragic accident, let's get on with our lives."

"I'm sorry, Bill." I looked up from where I'd been tracing circles on the coarse brown weave of the blanket. "I meant to tell you."

"You mean, you didn't mean to get lost."

"Right." I don't know what bothered me more, that he knew me well enough to accept I'd put off telling him, or that I had, in the excitement surrounding the test flight, put it off too long. "So, um, what happened after that? Did you go to the Confederacy and tell them what you suspected?"

"No-o," he said slowly. "I waited another couple weeks. I mean,"—he flashed me a quick smile—"you've got out of some difficult situations before this. And . . . I dunno. I didn't want them to arrest you for possession."

"Thanks."

"And then the orders for my transfer came through."

"You?" Hell, I messed up Bill's life too. The three engineers were a different matter—they'd all accepted the risks and wanted to be part of the project. But Murdoch didn't even know what we were doing.

"Yeah. I didn't know what was going on for a while. Back to Earth, the orders said. By the time I contacted someone who knew something—an old mate of mine in

Finance—it was time for me to go. I took leave and stayed on the station and tried to get the transfer annulled, or changed, or something. No luck. So I started looking for An Serat. That was bloody difficult, too. I tracked him to a H'digh colony."

"You went yourself?" Travel quotas for private individuals of the Nine Worlds within the jump network were small and prohibitively expensive. I didn't want to hear that Murdoch had mortgaged his pension to try to find me. Or worse, put himself in the kind of danger that stowaways on Four ships faced.

"I pulled in a favor with Neeth—you remember, the K'Cher trader who tried to sell our planet?"

I did remember the incident, which had embroiled External Affairs, the Confederacy Bureau of Trade Investigation, the K'Cher League of Barons, and a network of small traders and pirates that covered the whole of Abelar system. Murdoch's Security team had prevented Neeth from being lynched.

"It gave you a berth to Rhuarl system?"

"Uh-huh. Serat seemed pretty much at home with the H'digh on Rhuarl."

"So what did he say?"

Murdoch narrowed his eyes as he remembered. "He didn't say much. Basically, that he'd been waiting for me. He told me he'd send me back to Jocasta and then to meet you. I waited around for a couple hours, then a H'digh gave me a pass back to Central in an unmarked transport."

"Who was the pilot?"

He shrugged. "I was in the passenger cabin, didn't see. But the fittings were humanoid-friendly, so probably a Melot. A Melot met me at Central, anyway, and put me on another transport. This one went from Central to Abelar. I tell you, by this time I was buggered from standing around waiting for Customs inspections and for the ships to leave. You know how they take hours from when the exit permit's approved to when the jump point actually opens. Not to mention the time getting to the points in flatspace. And then we rendezvous in Abelar flatspace with another ship, half a dozen Melot crew, no markings. I couldn't see the navigation details, but I reckon it was near where you disappeared."

That made sense. He'd have to finally go through the same jump point as I did; if he jumped from Central he couldn't have come to the past because those jumps on the Central network are all set at "present" time. Twelve o'clock in Central is twelve o'clock everywhere else.

"An Serat seems to have a lot of backup," I said.

"Yeah, but none of it official, you notice? No ConFleet or Confederacy Trader markings on anything. I reckon he's doing this without Barik and the other Invidi knowing. Anyway, they loaded me into a single-pilot fighter like a bloody droid. Not a word, not so much as a mind-your-step-don't-forget-the-emergency-exit. And the fighter went through the jump point on autopilot. Not a thing I could do about it.

"The fighter kept going once we left the jump point. I knew it was heading for Earth but I don't think anyone detected me coming in."

"Nor me," I said. "The only reason I can think of is that both your fighter and *Calypso II* contained an Invidi shielding device to avoid detection." My search of *Calypso II* failed to find one, but that didn't mean it wasn't there.

He nodded. "My ship was programmed already—it did nearly forty-eight hours' burn through the solar system after coming through the jump . . ."

"That's a day faster than I was."

". . . hit Earth's atmosphere and fried, and not a bloody thing I could do about it. I didn't enjoy that, I can tell you. Sitting there sucking my rations and doing my exercises, waiting for whatever An Serat—or whoever—had decided for me."

"I know the feeling."

"The life-pod worked fine and I ended up in the sea. Just off the coast, with a little raft to paddle in. Thoughtful, the Invidi. Bloke in a fishing boat picked me up. He was suspicious at first but I sounded enough like a local to pass. Said I'd got lost and spent the night drifting. Mist as thick as Jupiter. He wasn't going to make any trouble, the engines on that boat were too damn quiet for plain fishing. No lights or anything. He let me come inshore with him as a family member to get past the harbor checks. He didn't want anything to do with Customs.

"Then I tried to follow your signal . . . Good job that transponder is standard equipment now."

I twisted and felt under my shoulder blade. "That's what I wanted to say. It must be a different signal. I took the transponder out."

"Look for yourself." He passed me the locator, a flat square you could fit in your palm. The smooth syntal molded itself to my hand with heaviness out of proportion to its real weight. Its signal confirmation winked at full strength. I looked at the small thing, solid proof that there was a future and it wasn't all in my imagination. Then I looked up at Murdoch and smiled—he was even more solid proof.

He half-smiled back, mystified. "Are you sure you got the transponder out?"

I remembered a tiny, bloody splinter on Grace's finger. "Yes. Unless they put a backup in without telling me."

"Must be."

"That would explain why I still couldn't get past the alarms." I saw his expression of confusion. "When I tried to go into a shop in the city, something set off an alarm. That's why I asked Grace to take out the transponder."

He snorted. "How did you explain it?"

"I said it was a kind of microchip. They put them into

dangerous criminals in this country, but I said in my country political prisoners get tagged too."

"Jeez, what a century."

"But listen, even after that, I couldn't get through. I thought it was the Seouras implant, so I just kept away from wired places after that. Maybe it was a backup transponder."

"So if you want to go through any security barriers, we'll have to take out the backup too."

I wriggled my shoulders. "Ouch. I suppose so." It still might be the Seouras implant which was setting off the alarms, but if so we could do nothing. The implant was a neural connection originally installed in my neck by the Seouras at the time of the Abelar Treaty. I'd agreed to it, so that I could understand what the Seouras were saying and communicate this to the others.

Murdoch stretched, his shoulders making a faint popping sound. "Halley, why did An Serat send me after you?"

"I'm surprised he 'sent' you anywhere," I said.

I couldn't reconcile the idea of an Invidi and concrete action. Not that Invidi aren't good at getting people to do things, but they do it by maneuvering people into situations where we do what we want to do, only it ends up being what the Invidi want. Like An Barik exploited my friend Quartermaine's desire to know more about the Invidi and asked him to retrieve a device from *Calypso*. Like An Barik used my desire to protect the station from the Seouras to keep himself safe while he waited for *Calypso* to arrive. Or like An Serat used my desire to find out how *Calypso* worked to get me here in the past—although this one was guesswork on my part. Even like how the Invidi had used the Bendarl desire for expansion and the militaristic structure of their society to create ConFleet to keep order in the Confederacy.

There seemed no logical reason for An Serat to want

me or Murdoch in the past, yet he obviously did. Unless it was something on *Calypso II* that he wanted. Which didn't make sense either, because the only things of value on *Calypso II* were the engines, which had come from *Calypso* and An Serat in the first place.

"The only reason I could think of for him to send me after you," Murdoch continued, "was that he'd met me in the past and knew I had to get here. But why didn't he say that when he first met us on Jocasta?"

"He didn't want us to know. Because we'd know and maybe prepare against being sent here." I thought again. "No, it's already happened, hasn't it. Unless when we meet him in the past we tell him that he didn't tell us . . ."

"Bloody hell. You really understand this?"

I looked around at the tent. "I've had a lot of time to think about it. We need to separate the history of the history files from our personal histories. Our *desadas*."

He groaned. "No mystic terms, please."

Desada was one of the many Invidi words we knew but did not understand. The usual translation was "fate" or "pivotal life-moment." Quartermaine, my late friend who was also an Invidi expert, had thought it meant an experience that influenced the rest of one's life. I didn't agree.

"I'm redefining it. Think how pleased the linguists will be when we get back. I don't think *desada* is a single experience. It's the way the Invidi keep track of their own inner timescapes."

"Experience always runs the same way?"

"Sort of. If they're always jumping in and out of different places and times, it would be necessary to keep their own timelines."

Murdoch shook his head. "Hang on. Say I come back in time and start living my life here. I'm forty-four, right? Bill Murdoch in this history won't be born for another fifty or so years. What happens when that fifty years is reached? Will there be two of us? Which is the real one?"

"I guess you're both real."

"What happens when that child turns forty-four? Will he then travel into the past, and over and over?"

"I don't think so. You both have your own lives. Your *desada*."

He opened his mouth, shut it again. Rubbed his hand over his head and blinked tiredly.

"Unless it's a different universe," I added. It wasn't a theory I thought about often, for the simple reason that if it was true, we could do nothing but start over in this century.

"And the Invidi don't come, you mean?"

I nodded.

He snorted. "Then we're gonna find out the answer to the question that's been bugging everyone for a hundred years."

What would have happened if the Invidi hadn't come? Or, as far as we're concerned, what will happen if the Invidi don't come?

A wave of cold sickness made me shiver, and I drew my legs closer. If the Invidi didn't come, we'd be stuck here. Stuck in this place where the struggle to survive consumed the lives of those who had nothing, and the knowledge of their own futility diminished the lives of those who had everything.

No wonder they idolized people like Mandela and Alvarez. There was so little hope otherwise.

I shivered again and leaned back against the wall of the tent, feeling it give slightly, cool against my back through the thin shirt. Murdoch watched me, his face unreadable. His presence filled the tent. I could feel his warmth, reaching out across the bed, banishing the shiver. A strange feeling. Almost like the flush of H'digh pheromones . . . But that was ridiculous. Not here, not now.

"When did you find out it was this year?" said Murdoch. He turned the chair around and sat on it properly, stretching his legs out beside the bed with a grunt. "I didn't realize until I saw a newspaper on the fishing boat. A newspaper, would you believe it? Sort of brought it all home to me when the ink came off black on my fingers. Anything that messy had to be real."

"I tracked Earth communications when I was coming into the solar system," I said, ignoring the strange feeling of warmth. "That's why I had to come down to the surface and wait for the Invidi to come. I couldn't maintain life support in *Calypso II* by myself for five months."

I told him how I'd ended up on Earth, ending with where Grace took me in.

"We can't get back through that jump point without Invidi help," I went on, "either to repair *Calypso II* or lend us another ship. And unless we go back through that jump point, we can't get back to Jocasta in 2122. At least, I assume the point is stable now, since you came through it."

"Yeah, that's weird, isn't it? I'd assumed it took you to wherever the Sleepers in *Calypso* had jumped from."

"That's what I thought, too."

"So what happened? How did we come through the jump point in this year if that point hasn't been created yet?"

I rubbed my neck where the Seouras implant formed a roughly circular, raised area under the skin. "I don't know. That same question's been driving me mad. All I can think of is that the correspondence was somehow shortened when *Calypso* jumped. Or lengthened when we jumped. Another thing I can't work out is why it takes the Invidi so long to get here."

He thought about that one for a moment, then scratched his head tiredly. "Come again?"

"Think about it—neither of us came through the Central-Earth jump point, right?"

"The point we did come through is on a different jump network?"

"Exactly. But we've always been told that's impossible. There is no other jump network. So either the Invidi have been putting one over on all of us . . ."

"Or some of us. The rest of the Four might be in on this."

"Maybe. Or . . ." My voice trailed off.

"Or what?"

"Or, I don't know. Something else. Something to do with the jump being fixed now but not when *Calypso* went through it. My point is that an off-network jump point being opened ought to have brought the Invidi rushing here to investigate immediately, not five months later. Unless," I said, half to myself, "this was as close as they could calibrate it. After all, their time scale is presumably hundreds of thousands of years, so five months is incredibly accurate."

Murdoch stared at me. "Hang on. You're saying *we* brought the Invidi here?"

"Too big a coincidence otherwise. Jump point opens, they pick it up, come to investigate by opening a jump point on their own network between here and Central. Earth is then connected to the other worlds on the network."

"Whoa." He leaned back, nearly fell out of the chair, and righted himself. In the blue pale light of dawn his face looked pasty. "Doesn't that bother you? That we're responsible for the single most cataclysmic change in recent human history?"

I shrugged. "It did at first. Now I try to see it from An Serat's point of view."

"Which is?"

"He knows I build *Calypso II* using *Calypso*'s engines

and come back here. He sends you here from 2122 because he knows he met us here in the past and he needs us to be here so his past self knows to send *Calypso*."

"That's a circle."

I nodded. Whichever domino you tip, they'll all fall eventually.

"Halley, why'd you do it?"

I could see the line of dominoes clattering down. One, two, three, four . . . "Do what?"

"Take *Calypso II* through the jump."

I met his eyes. They were honestly puzzled, and a little hurt. I didn't want to hurt Murdoch.

"I had to know if it would work. If it really was a jump drive in *Calypso*."

He frowned and spread his hands helplessly. "What now? You've found out it is. What if the Invidi in this time help us get home—what are you going to do with the drive then?"

"Make sure everyone has it. That way the Four don't have their stranglehold over us. We might finally have some equality within the Confederacy."

He chewed his lip doubtfully. "Dunno how that's going to help the neutrality vote. Only thirty-nine days to go."

"Thirty-nine?" So little time. Ten days until the Invidi arrived here. If we couldn't contact them or they couldn't help us immediately, we might not get back in time for the vote. Not that we can do much to influence the outcome, but I wanted to be there.

"Getting the jump drive will help the Nine," I said. "If we win the neutrality vote, that will help the Nine as well because we'll be showing the Confederacy that they can't keep everyone as part of their system forever. It's a long-term investment."

He stood up suddenly, swung his arm around to indicate the tent. "Like long term, the Invidi helped us clean up this mess?"

I said nothing. I was thinking of Marlena Alvarez and her views on long- and short-term policies.

"Lots of nasty things can happen in the short term." He echoed my thoughts uncannily. "Like living here." He lowered himself onto the bed beside me. I saw it through his shocked, fastidious gaze—no more than an old door with stained and threadbare cloths folded on top. Like one of the dirty mounds people slept on at the entrance to the bus station.

"I don't have any money."

"But you're from the future," he protested. "You've got all this knowledge . . ."

"Most of which I can't use," I interrupted. "Because I don't want to do anything that didn't happen."

"You're not making sense. Whatever we do here is pre-ordained? Suppose we . . . I dunno. Kill An Serat or something else that we definitely know didn't happen? Are you saying something will happen to stop us?"

"Hell, I don't know," I snapped. "I'm an engineer, not a temporal philosopher. All I know is that when I got here I had no papers and no money to buy papers, and no papers means no job, which means you can't earn money. If I make an official refugee claim I get sent off to a reserve somewhere away from the city, from where I can't get out to meet the Invidi once they do arrive."

He looked at me. Enough beams of bright morning sunshine shone through the cracks in the tent material to illuminate the dusty lines on his face and the hollows beneath his cheekbones. He must have walked all day and most of the night. I remembered how I'd wanted a second chance to tell him . . . Now that he was here, I found it hard to think what it was I wanted to tell him.

"Thanks for coming," was all I could manage.

He leaned back on one elbow and smiled, a rare and delightful expression. "You . . . it was worth it."

I didn't have a reply. His presence meant I didn't have to face getting back alone. It meant I hadn't been dreaming about the future, and Jocasta and everything else. I caught my hand rubbing the implant and stopped.

Murdoch cleared his throat and rolled off the bed. He went to the door and stood looking out. I wondered at the way my eyes tracked his movement, lingering on things I never noticed before.

"Great opportunity to see the old town at its worst," he said.

I winced at the distaste in his voice. In a way, I was responsible for him feeling like this; I brought him here. "It is pretty bad."

"What happened to all the trees?"

"The trees you remember probably haven't been planted yet."

"What about the harbor?"

"You need a special pass to get into the inner city. I think they're rebuilding parts of the harbor area to cope with the rise in sea level."

"Special pass?" His distaste turned to disgust.

"For U.N. delegates, people in jobs associated with government, selected businesses. Supposed to be protection against terrorism."

The door pipes clacked and the door swung open. Before I could even stand up, Will burst in.

"Hey, Maria, can I have breakfast with . . ." His vivid face darkened with almost comic swiftness when he saw Murdoch.

"Will, this is my friend Bill . . ."

"McGrath," supplied Murdoch. "G'day, Will."

"Is your name William too?" said Will, recovering. He was in one of his sunny moods.

"Uh-huh. But I had an uncle with the same name, so everyone called me Bill. Right from when I was a baby."

As they chatted, I held my forehead in my hand and stared at the stains on the crate top. Murdoch's here—I'm still trying to cope with that, and now it's morning.

Six

Three days later Murdoch met Grace. She dropped in at the tent as I was about to leave for the Assembly.

"Hello, Bill McGrath," she said. She must have heard about him from Will. She settled into the chair.

"Bill, this is my old, um, tent-mate Grace." I'd told him about Grace losing her job and going to live with Levin.

"Hello, Grace." Murdoch smiled.

"You're not from Sydney?" Grace glanced at the pantry like Will did, but I wasn't going to invite her to stay for a cup of tea. I had to get to work.

"No, up the north coast. You from round here?"

"I moved here when I was a kid. From out west." Her eyes wandered over the mattress we'd borrowed from Florence's brother's best mate's sister-in-law, placed on a board on the bricks where she used to sleep. "You staying long?"

Murdoch nodded seriously. He was completely at ease with Grace. Then again, the only people with whom Murdoch didn't seem at ease were diplomats and Invidi.

"Been out of the country. Got back recently, thought I'd drop in and see Maria," he said.

"Bit out of yer way, though, wasn't it?"

"I didn't mind."

Grace raised her eyebrow at me in what she probably thought was a meaningful way. "Ah-huh."

I hefted my string bag, but Grace didn't take the hint.

"Is she easy to live with?" said Murdoch, with a sly glance at me. His mouth twitched.

"We had our ups'n downs," said Grace. "Didn't we?"

"Do you want to walk over to the Assembly with me?" I said finally, giving up on subtlety.

"I don't mind." She heaved herself to her feet. "Hey, Bill, is it true yer doing some work on those school grounds?"

"That's right." Murdoch had gone with me to take Will to school yesterday, after Will appeared yet again after breakfast, and ended up chatting with one of the teachers on duty in the playground. He'd been appalled at the rubbish, the graffiti, and the lack of repair of the buildings and fences. That's public education for you, said the teacher. I'm part of the public, said Murdoch. And he volunteered to do a couple of hours' work there.

"Good stuff," said Grace. "About time somebody cleaned the place up. Bone lazy, them teachers."

I resisted asking why she didn't volunteer herself. "Let's go. See you later, Bill."

"Ta-ta, Bill."

Murdoch waved solemnly from the sagging screen door of the tent as we walked up the lane.

"Nice bloke," said Grace. "Got the hots for you, too, I can tell."

"We're old friends," I said, picking my way around a line of broken plastic and filthy rags that spilled from a torn plastic bag. "We used to work together. I'm letting him stay until he finds a place of his own."

"Not your type, eh?"

All too easily, my imagination presented me with a situation in which I confirmed that Murdoch was "my type."

"I mean," went on Grace, heedless of my red face, "I

did notice the extra bed. If I had a hunk like that staying with me, I wouldn't make him sleep in another bed."

"How's Levin?"

"That's it, change the subject. He's okay." She glanced at me. "I don't expect it to last, y'know."

"With Levin, you mean?" It didn't surprise me, but Grace's acknowledgment was unexpected.

"Yeah. With his money and . . ." she started to say something but changed her mind. "He should be able to pick up younger women. But he reckons mature women know how to keep quiet." She flashed me a grin. "So I better, eh?"

We walked past the backyards of the houses on the street before Creek Road. One of them contained four, no, five now, rusting cars. And a modular storage shed, with a line of washing beside it.

"Why do you stay with him?" Stupid question, I thought immediately.

Grace looked at me as though she was thinking the same thing. Then she shrugged. "You not having kids, I guess you don't understand. I can't think only about meself."

We turned into Creek Road, the Assembly building last in the line of houses. The betting shop was just opening. The proprietor swept the dirt away from the entry and gave us a smile.

"Good morning, ladies."

Grace grinned. "G'morning, Mr. Deshindar. No ladies here."

They chatted happily. I stood and rattled my keys and stared at fresh graffiti that had blossomed on the side fence during the night.

During the night, when I lay awake, listening to Murdoch's heavy, even breathing. The day Murdoch arrived I realized how awkward the situation in the tent could become. Murdoch would be here for another ten days at least, more if we didn't contact the Invidi as soon as they came. An awkward situation not because I didn't want to sleep in the same bed as Murdoch. Quite the opposite—the more I thought about it, the more it appealed. If, that is, I wasn't mistaking the signals he sent to me.

But that was the problem—the more attractive I found Murdoch, the less I could consider sleeping with him. Henoit got in the way.

I was married to my H'digh husband, Henoit, for two years. Then I left, because I didn't agree with his extremist politics. He was involved with the anti-Confederacy group New Council of Allied Worlds, and their terrorism didn't seem to bother him. For seven Earth years we'd had no contact after I left him. Long enough to satisfy both Confederacy and Earth conditions of being legally estranged. I put him out of my mind.

Then he appeared on Jocasta in the middle of the crisis at the end of the Seouras blockade. He told me that, as far as he was concerned, nothing had changed. H'digh law and custom do not recognize estrangement, not even when one of the partners dies. I thought this was ridiculous and said so. He said that it was because the marriage vow continues beyond the death of either of its participants.

Then he was killed in the battle at the end of the blockade. It shocked me, but he chose to betray us for the New Council, so I didn't spend a lot of time mourning. Afterward, the situation on the station settled down and I began to work on *Calypso II*. Then I started to get "visits" from Henoit. It happened every time I had any sexual pleasure— even just release of tension alone at the end of a long day. All my physical reactions were the same as when he was there. Perhaps I had some of the infamous H'digh pheromones left in my system. But this time, unlike when he was there in the flesh, I didn't need to worry about compromising the safety of the station or the personal consequences of losing control or what he really wanted.

It was as though my pleasure sent a signal that was bounced back at greatly increased power and in a changed form—like when I made love with Henoit. His signature all over it. All over me.

I didn't know if it would happen when actually making love with anyone else, because I hadn't had a chance to find out until now. But since Murdoch arrived, every time my thoughts about him drifted in a vaguely lustful direction, I'd get that feeling of Henoit looking over my shoulder. If I allowed my relationship with Murdoch to become a full-blown passion, I was certain I'd feel as though I was also responding to Henoit.

Murdoch would not understand, especially as he'd met Henoit on Jocasta and knew what a bastard he was. I knew what a bastard he was too, but that didn't stop me getting off on his memory. Or whatever it is.

What could I say? *Sorry, but when we make love I'm doing it with someone else as well.*

No, it was better for both of us if Murdoch slept in a separate bed.

"Maria?" Grace's voice seemed out of place for a moment.

"Sorry, yes?"

"I'm off. You and Bill come over for dinner on Saturday, eh? Anzac Day special. See you later." She slouched up Creek Road toward the main street.

I smiled at Mr. Deshindar, who was now setting out his noticeboards, and unlocked the side door. It annoyed me how Grace disappeared as soon as work was due to begin. She could give me a hand sticking envelopes or something.

I hadn't shared living space with someone for a long time, and the next few days saw some more awkward moments, caused mainly by two adults trying to live in such a cramped space. Where to get changed? In the shower block when we could, but often the other people in the row wanted to use it. Who would get up first? There wasn't much room to maneuver around the tent.

In the end, Murdoch turned over while I got up and changed, then I went outside while he did the same. He was a tidy man, and my habits occasionally eroded his temper.

"Bloody good thing you don't have more than two changes of clothes," he grumbled, fishing these items from among blanket folds or off the back of the chair. "You put your tools away, why not these?"

We talked. About the Invidi coming. About Jocasta and the future. About his past, of which I knew embarrassingly little. As Security chief, he knew my background, but I felt I should have made more of an effort to know more about his than the basics of where he worked before coming to Jocasta.

"I was on Mars the job before Jocasta," he said from his side of the tent one night in the dark. "They resented me—an upstart from Earth coming in and ordering them around. Mind you, that was why they picked an outsider for the job—too much corruption, everyone in one another's pockets. I was fighting my own people more than the criminals." He was silent again.

"The girls didn't like it, either. That's my partner and my daughter," he added. "Irena."

"How long were you on Mars?"

"Standard three-year secondment. The girls went back after two, though. No fun for them. Irena was thirteen. The Martian colonists are too proud, sometimes. Their way of being independent, I guess. Anyway, when my three years finished, I left too."

"You went back on Earth?"

"For a while. Then I joined EarthFleet."

"Why did you join EarthFleet?" He'd been in the civilian police force long enough to have had a senior position.

He turned over, the board creaking under his weight. I couldn't see his face in the darkness and wondered if it had been the wrong question.

"She . . . my partner. She found someone else, been living with him the whole year I wasn't there." He paused.

I was going to say, *I'm sorry,* but that seemed ridiculous. I was glad he came to Jocasta. So I said nothing, and after a moment he spoke again.

"I was going to stick around because of Irena, but then I thought she'd never settle in if I did. And at the time I didn't know where I'd end up working. There were lots of problems with corruption in the force that year. Bloody mess it was. EarthFleet came round looking for high-level recruits and I thought it was time to get out."

He hadn't seen his daughter for five years, most of the time that he'd spent on Jocasta. I knew that, because his record said he hadn't taken Earth leave since joining Earth-Fleet. She'd be a young adult now. I felt obscurely guilty for keeping him away from her.

"Do you miss her—Irena?"

The board creaked again. His blanket flapped as if he was furiously rearranging it.

"I did at first, because she . . . wanted me to go. She took her mother's side, all the time. Then just before the blockade, she started sending me letters again. Said she was sorry and she wanted to see me when I came home again."

And now I'd dragged him a century further away from her. I felt definitely guilty about that.

"Something to look forward to when we get back, eh?" His voice wasn't as steady as usual, and I was glad of the darkness.

* * *

"Maybe the Invidi will call us," he said. We were walking along the paths from my tent to the Assembly. "Why bust yourself trying to contact them?"

"The lack of time, for a start," I said. "Assuming time passes there at the same rate it passes here, like with an ordinary jump point, in thirty-four days the neutrality vote goes through. Seeing that I sort of started it, I'd like to be there."

"And?"

"I don't know exactly what will happen once the Invidi arrive. Do you?"

He nodded slowly. "I see what you mean. We only know general history, not the details."

"Yes, and this time we *are* the details, and the history files don't tell us if we get home or not."

"You think the Invidi will help us get home?"

"An Serat sent us here, they're responsible for us." If the Invidi had a similar concept of responsibility, of which I wasn't at all sure.

"They might just tell us to stay. It's our planet, we should be able to fit in here."

I stopped and glared at him. "Are you just being devil's advocate or do you have a point?"

He stopped, too, and looked at me, not quite reproachfully, but in a way that made me turn my glare away. I shouldn't snap. Our situation wasn't his fault.

"Why Valdon?" he said.

"My father's name."

"Writer, wasn't he?"

"That's right. Why McGrath?"

Murdoch began walking again. "McGrath is my brother's name. He took my sister-in-law's family name when they got married."

"I see."

"He's a bit of a dead loss, my brother."

"Why?" I said, slightly shocked. As a child, I'd always wanted a brother or sister, and didn't like the idea of not appreciating the one you had.

"Sits around communing with the universe—that's what he calls it, the rest of us call it being a slob—and painting pictures."

"I didn't know you had an artist in the family."

"It's not as much fun as it sounds." He thought for a moment. "What about that ancestor of yours—Alvarez? Did you look up info on her?"

"She wasn't my ancestor. She was a friend of my ancestor. And she died five years ago."

"Yeah, I know. But she was famous, there must be a lot of stuff floating around about her."

The thought of Alvarez was almost painful—I'd been betrayed by my own expectations. "It's funny, but she isn't as well known now as she is in our time."

"You mean the Earth movement hasn't got going yet?"

"EarthSouth. That's part of it, yes." I'd come to the conclusion that the reason the EarthSouth movement took a long time to become a political force was because it was a genuine grassroots surge and the people at the grassroots were often, as Marlena said, *too busy staying alive to play politics and too wise to expect anything to come of it.* "It's almost as if our history files manufactured Alvarez."

"You mean she wasn't a real person?"

"Of course she was real."

We stopped again to let a small boy drag a line of empty drink cans on a string across the path. He stared at us with solemn, dirt-encrusted eyes before toddling away, the cans rattling behind him.

"But it's as though . . ." I paused, embarrassed now. There were bound to be discrepancies between actual events in the past and our historical records. It didn't matter to

Murdoch if Alvarez was a hero or not—I was the one who'd made an icon out of the woman.

"She's not what you expected," he said shrewdly.

I looked at him, surprised and comforted by his understanding. "That's right."

"This isn't what I expected either." He waved his hand at the potholed street and the ramshackle extensions that made a slum of once-neat bungalows. "But it doesn't mean I was wrong when I thought of Sydney . . ."

This time he paused, then caught my encouraging eye and continued. "On Mars I'd look up through the skylights and see those damn canyon walls and maybe a sliver of sky. And I'd think of this town, with the water and the bright sunlight and the trees. What I mean is, seeing Sydney like this doesn't make that any less right. Any more than you seeing more of the real Alvarez makes how she helped you wrong."

He glanced at me. "End of speech."

"How do you know what I thought about Alvarez?"

"I guessed." In response to my skeptical frown, he continued. "I thought it was a good idea at the time. God knows, you needed some help. You never told any of us much."

It was true. I hadn't talked much to anyone during the Seouras blockade. Murdoch didn't know until the end how they communicated with me through the implant. It had hurt like hell. The implant was the main reason I'd been avoiding doctors since I arrived in the out-town. Its nonhuman origin would be obvious to them.

I swallowed, feeling sick. "I don't want to think about it."

The greatest shock from that whole chaotic episode was, for me, the realization that An Barik had not helped us when he could. Presumably he had the support of the other Invidi. The idea of Invidi as humanity's benevolent benefactors lost much of its credibility for me after that.

So when An Serat had explained his action in sending *Calypso* forward in time as being to help the Nine, including humans, get the jump drive, I questioned his real motives.

An Serat's action meant we did get a version of the drive, in the sense that my engineering team on Jocasta managed to put together *Calypso II* out of an old freighter and what remained of *Calypso*'s engines. The core of those engines had been protected from the explosion. At the time, it had seemed an incredible stroke of luck. But I should have known better than to associate luck with a species that could see the future. At least, more of the future than we can.

We turned the corner into Creek Road.

"You know what was the worst part of it for me?" he said.

I shook my head.

"People dying. And watching you disappear inside yourself, not letting us help."

I stopped, shocked. "Bill, I . . . I didn't know. You never said. Not that I would have listened, I was so wound up with tension the whole time."

He patted my arm. "Don't do it to me this time, okay?" He smiled, and a woman in a blue cheongsam glanced at him as she passed and smiled, too.

"I won't," I said, the sick feeling gone.

We reached the Assembly and climbed the stairs to the office. Inside, I unlocked the cupboard beside the filing cabinet and pulled out a box from among the brooms and bits of string.

"Is that it?" Murdoch caught my eye and added hastily, "It doesn't look like I expected, that's all."

Certainly the archaism "telescope" conjured images of sleek and sophisticated instruments.

"Think of it as camouflage," I said. "If it looks like junk, nobody's going to steal it."

My telescope might look like a stubby bazooka on spider legs, but it worked.

"Basically, I've programmed a digital signal processor— or I will have, by next week, to a wavelet-based comm system, otherwise we'll have the rest of the planet listening in. I'll connect it to the laser—when I get one. The computer here can control the tracking. There's plenty of connecting line . . . they call it fiber optics. It'll connect the inverted reflector to the laser."

"So what's the plan?" Murdoch sat back on his heels, unimpressed with my clever design.

"It depends what the Invidi do when they get this message. If you remember, their ships appeared in at least ten places, over major city centers on all of the continents except Antarctica. I'm assuming one appears over Sydney, seeing that it's the seat of government and of the U.N."

Murdoch thought for a moment. "I think you're right. I remember learning something like that when I was in school."

"They'll know someone is here, because they'll detect my ship on the moon. I can set a beam-splitter to bounce their reply to us if they send one."

"They can locate the source of the signal if they want to."

"Of course."

"What if they don't notice it?"

"I told you, the signal won't be affected by radio wave disturbances . . ."

"No, I mean what if they don't realize what it is? You said the short-range comm system is used for service bots. Maybe the opsys will just filter your message before an Invidi sees it." He grimaced. "Or put it in their In file.

Knowing Confederacy bureaucracy, they'll get back to you in a century or so."

"There is no Confederacy yet," I snapped.

"Anyway, even if they do respond, how are we going to go and see them if we haven't got IDs?" He ran a finger along the barrel of the scope.

"I don't know. Not having an ID has been my main problem since I arrived here."

"Black market?"

"Too expensive. IDs and addictive drugs are the main revenue of the gangs. They keep the price of both high. It would take me two years at this rate to earn enough."

"This money thing's a bugger."

I nodded and tweaked a connecting cable absently.

"Right." He stood and stretched. "I'm off to the school. Might have a bit of a look around, too."

"What, out there?"

"I'm a native, remember?"

A thought struck me. "What if you meet your great-grandparents?"

He waved the possibility away. "They're still up on the coast, both sides of the family."

"Are you sure?"

"Yeah. It was my grandmother who moved. We've all been here ever since. Will be here," he corrected. "Jeez, plays hell with your tenses, doesn't it? Anyway, what does it matter how many of my family we meet? We can't change what's already happened."

He reached the door, but then turned back toward me.

"How about Griffis and the others?" he said curiously. "They must have electronic profiles somewhere on infonet." The three survivors of *Calypso*'s journey should have been well into their preparations by now. They had planned the journey for years; An Serat's help was merely a bonus.

"I thought about it." I had looked them up. Hannibal

Griffis, the leader of the *Calypso* crew, was listed under several organizations dealing with human rights and environmental issues, position "retired." Not true, of course. By now he'd be working with the secret space exploration group that coordinated the *Calypso* expedition. Rachel Dourif, the youngest member, was a student in Paris. And I'd found Ariel Kloos, one of their systems engineers, in a list of contributors to conference papers on AI systems.

"But the Sleepers never met us before," I reminded Murdoch. "They'd have remembered us when they arrived on Jocasta if they had."

"Shouldn't we try to warn them? Break this causal loop, or whatever you call it?"

"It's already happened."

He dragged his hand down his cheeks in frustration. "No, they won't leave for another three years . . ." He considered. "D'you reckon something would happen to stop you if you tried to meet them?"

"I don't want to tempt Fate, or whatever gods of time-space work the Invidi magic."

He grinned. "That's the scientific attitude, all right."

"It's a principle of engineering," I said coldly. "If it isn't broken, don't fix it."

"Anyway, can't you work your way around their computer systems? You're supposed to be the engineering genius. You could give yourself a huge bank account."

I wasn't sure if he was serious or not. "Other way around. Sophisticated equipment is expensive. To buy it you need cash or a bank account. To get a bank account you need an ID. But you can't make the ID without the equipment or pay someone else to do it without money."

"I get the point."

I stood up, knee joints stiff, and went over to one of the desks. "Hacking into their systems is not that difficult in itself, if you can adapt to how primitive the interface is." And, I reminded myself as my hand searched for the wall switch, if you remember to turn it on.

"But the tracking protocols in this time are efficient," I went on. "If they track me to this terminal it's a jail sentence. If I'm in jail, I can't contact the Invidi. And we can't get home." The computer on the desk made its usual preparatory clicking and whirring noises.

Primitive did not mean easy to use. I hated the inefficient, limited tools they called computers, hated the inorganic quality of them. Superficially, the interactive surfaces were similar to ours. No holoviewers or voice activation here in the out-town, but the screens weren't too hard on the eyes. Some miniature versions were like our handcoms, although clumsier. The keyboard input mode threw me at first—we tapped in commands to our interfaces on the station, but not on keys. Or we used audio or visual modes.

The user interfaces were confusing and getting inside them carried all the frustrations of being blindfold in a two-dimensional maze—every few paces I'd come up against another blocked path. In the Confederacy, interface use at anything more than an everyday level was more like a conversation. You'd discuss with the system what could be done and what couldn't.

"See you later, then," said Murdoch, and left.

Seven

Will was the only person who enjoyed dinner on Saturday night. Grace and Murdoch sat in Levin's backyard cooking sausages until the mosquitoes became too savage, then retreated to the house. A single-story brick veneer, it backed onto the shop front of Levin's "business" and boasted three rooms down a long hallway and a main room down the shop end, in which sat a televid, sofa, and dining table.

I arrived late, bad-tempered because a deal on a laser had fallen through. It was the wrong kind, hopeless for what I wanted. Who'd have thought it could be so difficult to get my hands on such a simple tool? And yet something like fiber-optic cable was practically lying around waiting to be taken away. Impossible to predict what would be easy in this century.

"Where's Levin?" I said. I might just have to take him up on his offer to find a laser for us.

"He'll be in soon," said Grace. "Have a sausage."

"They're good," put in Murdoch. His plate held nothing but greasy smears and some sauce. Both he and Grace were drinking beer. Having fun, while I wandered around getting hot and filthy looking for the essential component we needed to get home.

"Hi, Maria," yelled Will from in front of the televid.

"Hello, Will."

I poured myself a glass of water. If I did have to negotiate with Levin, I wanted a clear head.

"How many slices of bread?" said Grace.

"One." It was thin, tasteless stuff, smelling of its plastic packaging.

"You oughter eat more." She shook out a slice of bread,
placed two blackened sausages diagonally across it, and
smothered the lot in tomato sauce. "Blokes might pretend
they like skinny women, but really they want a bit of backside to grab on to."

"You . . ." *should know,* I started to say, then changed it
to, "you been busy today?"

"Oh, yeah, real busy. I haven't got a job and it's a hol-
iday." She smiled at Murdoch to show it was a joke, and
popped the top of another can of beer.

I folded my bread around the sausage and watched the
sauce dribble out. "I only asked because we could do with
a hand at the Assembly. Getting posters out before the
march, that sort of thing."

"Yeah, I'll give you a hand," she said expansively.

Levin came in.

He entered through the shop door. We could hear the
key turn in the lock, the door open, close, and the key click
again. Then footsteps down the hall. Heeled boots, not sandals.

He made a good entrance, standing for a moment in his
black jacket as though he were part of the darkness behind
him.

I stood up, mainly because I didn't want to finish the
sausage.

"Levin, this is an old friend, Bill McGrath. He's in town
for a while and he dropped by."

"Evening," said Murdoch. He stood too.

The two men were about the same height, although Levin

might have been taller if he didn't stoop. Murdoch weighed at least ten kilos more.

They faced each other with a sense of caution that nobody could have mistaken for politeness.

Grace padded in bare feet to the refrigerator and took out a beer, which she passed to Levin automatically. He took it without looking at her and sat down beside her, opposite Murdoch.

Murdoch and I sat down again. I glanced at the clock—only eight-thirty. Maybe if I pleaded a headache we could go.

"Where are you heading, Mr. McGrath?" Levin often spoke with strange formality.

"Nowhere special." Murdoch stared at Levin around a slow mouthful.

I hoped he wouldn't antagonize Levin before I had a chance to ask for help procuring a laser. I glanced at Grace to see if she'd noticed the tension, but she was half watching the televid over Levin's shoulder.

"I just thought I'd drop in and see Maria," said Murdoch. "Nice bread."

"It's from the corner shop," said Grace. "You gotta support your local businesses, I reckon."

And she didn't have to carry it all the way from the markets.

"How did you know Maria was here?" Levin asked Murdoch. "I thought she knew nobody in this country?"

"We met just after she arrived," said Murdoch smoothly. "She said she was going to Sydney. I asked around when I got here."

"What is your line of work?"

"This and that. I've done a bit of security work in my time." His eyes rested on the other, considering. "How about you, Mr. Levin?" He hesitated just enough to be noticeable on the name, long enough to hint a challenge.

Cut it out, Bill. I tried to signal him with my eyes.

"I trade," said Levin. "In hardware."

"I didn't notice a warehouse," said Murdoch.

"Middlemen are necessary in any industry," said Levin smoothly, and took a long draft of his beer.

I wiped sweaty hands on my trousers and wished for a small hyperspace tunnel to open between now and the end of the night. Then I wouldn't have to sit through this.

"You hungry?" Grace said to Levin.

He smiled at her, then dropped his gaze to the plate of sausages. A fly had sneaked in and was hovering over them, deterred only by occasional waves of Grace's hand.

"No," he said. "I'm not hungry."

Grace shrugged and picked up her beer again.

Will appeared at her elbow, after playfully punching Murdoch on the way and getting tickled. "C'n I have another sausage?"

"Yeah, go for it," said Grace. "Bread's there."

"Don't want any bread." He pulled a conspiratorial face of disgust to me, then bore off two sausages to his place in front of the vidscreen. Cartoon voices kept up a constant flow of inanity.

Levin had ignored Will completely. "Are you staying long, Mr. McGrath?"

"As long as I need to," said Murdoch. He was leaning back in his chair again, outwardly relaxed, but not tilting the chair like he'd done before Levin came in. His feet were now firmly on the ground, ready.

Ready for what, I wasn't sure. Could Murdoch see something in Levin I'd missed, or was this some kind of male rivalry thing?

"Hear the news about the airport closing?" Grace said.

"No," I said. "Which airport?"

"Are you planning a trip, then?" Levin's lip curled.

The sarcasm reached Grace. She flushed and put her can

down with a crunch. "Course not. Just making conversation. No need to get shitty."

"Which airport?" I said.

"It does not affect us directly," said Levin. "Who cares?"

"You sure?" Murdoch said slowly. "The newspaper said police suspected some of the guns came from inner-city gangs. Like around here."

"What news?" I raised my voice.

Grace leaned over, as though she was ducking the almost palpable waves of hostility that crossed the table between Levin and Murdoch.

"They found some guns at the airport, looks like the owners panicked and ran. It's shut down today while the cops sniff around."

All I knew about air travel was its hideous expense due to the cost of fuel and the security involved.

"When I was a kid," Grace continued, trying to catch both Levin's and Murdoch's eyes, "everyone caught planes here and there. Well, nearly everyone," she amended. "We only did it once, when Auntie Jen got married in Perth. That was a brilliant wedding. Everyone was pissed for three days. We kids sank Uncle Ray's ute in the river and nobody noticed till weeks later." She grinned. "What a year that was."

Levin leaned back in his chair and watched the cartoon. His attitude said he'd heard this story before.

"You ever do anything stupid when you were a kid, Maria?" said Grace. "Not that you think it's stupid at the time. Just fun."

I could remember several ridiculous escapades for which my grandmother made me pay dearly later, but I didn't feel like sharing them with Grace now.

"Maria looks like she's had a bad day," said Levin, abandoning the televid for more immediate entertainment. "Maybe she hasn't found what she's looking for."

"What do you mean?" Grace looked from me to Levin.

"Nothing." I scowled at the tabletop because I didn't want to ask Levin for help but knew I'd have to.

"Whatever." Grace scowled back and turned to Murdoch. "How's the work at the school going, Bill?"

"He's getting popular," put in Will.

"It's a lot of fun," said Murdoch. "I haven't played with kids for a long time."

"I'll wait for you outside," I said to Murdoch. Grace had begun to explain recent changes in the public school system to him at length, interspersed with an explanation of why Vince had never finished ninth grade.

Levin met my eyes, and followed me to the back door.

"You need my help," he said. It wasn't a question.

"Yes. I need a laser for my telescope."

"Which one?"

"I need something I can program to a repetition rate of between ten and a thousand Hertz, a main wavelength of five thirty-two and a pulse width of about thirty picoseconds." I slapped at mosquitoes that descended out of nowhere. His face was expressionless and I had no idea if he understood, or even if he was joking with me. "So, how much?"

"Probably about two hundred."

"You're kidding," I said flatly. "These things are nearly junk, I could get one for free."

"Not easily. And not soon."

"How much of that is your commission?"

He said nothing.

"I can't afford two hundred. I can barely afford fifty."

"That's regrettable."

"Come off it, Levin. You know how little they pay me."

He pretended to study his boot.

Murdoch came out, stubbing his toe on the brick step as I did every time I visited.

"Fifty, then," said Levin. "Are you in a hurry?"

Yes, I screamed inwardly. I need it by tomorrow.

"The sooner the better." I mentally ran through a list of people who might lend me money.

He turned back inside without further word.

Murdoch narrowed his eyes. "What's all that about?" he said as we started walking.

"He's going to try to get me the laser for my array. I couldn't get it again today. Haven't been able to find one as junk, either."

"I don't like him."

I shrugged. "Nor do I, but that doesn't mean he can't be useful to us."

"What does he do, run drugs?"

"I don't think so. But I'm sure he's got something to do with weapons and the gangs. Don't know what, though."

"Charming bloke to do business with."

I felt a rush of irritation with Murdoch. Here I was, doing my best to get us home, and all he could do was quibble about details that I had no control over.

"I'm not entering into a trade agreement here. He gets me a laser, I pay him, finished."

Murdoch's voice in the dark sounded abstracted. "Yeah, right. But I'd like to know more about him."

Eight

To pay Levin, I scraped the money together with a loan from Florence and the result of a hasty job done for the local electronics retailer. Murdoch didn't like the borrowing. "You won't pay it back if the Invidi send us home," he said.

I didn't like it either, but we didn't have a choice. If we wanted to try to contact the Invidi as quickly and as efficiently as possible, we needed the laser. I could almost feel time on both sides of the jump point sliding away beneath me. We would have only twenty-four days from when the Invidi arrived to get home for the neutrality vote, which would be 29 May 2023 here, and—hopefully—late February 2123 on Jocasta.

Levin produced the laser on Tuesday. I couldn't believe he'd been so quick. He woke me up early in the morning. The stubble on his chin was darker than usual, as though he'd been up all night and had not yet shaved. I stood in the doorway of the tent, Murdoch peering over my shoulder.

Levin took the money, stuffed it carelessly in his pocket, and handed me a small cylinder.

I checked it carefully, to his unconcealed amusement. The laser fitted all my specs.

"You don't trust me."

"Just sensible business, making sure of the goods. You're a businessman. You should understand."

"Indeed. My goods are always genuine."

"What other sorts of goods can you find?" I rolled the laser in my hand. "Goods that might be more dangerous than this?"

He raised his eyebrows. "A good businessman—or woman—does not question their source of supply."

"A good businesswoman doesn't deal with someone who could land her in jail," said Murdoch behind me.

"There is no danger of that." Levin scowled. For the first time since I'd known him he seemed to be tired and grumpy like a normal person. "What does it matter to you what else I deal in?"

"If you deal in weapons," I said, "it would make me nervous. Seeing how so many weapons get into the hands of children. Like Will and Vince."

"If I did, and if I said, *oh sorry I'll stop,*" Levin mimicked my tone, "it wouldn't matter. They'll get their weapons somewhere else. They want to die."

He caught our astonished gazes. "If they had some hope in life, they wouldn't need weapons, would they? Or drugs."

"So you just see yourself as the supplier?" said Murdoch.

Levin laughed. "Oh, no, Mr. Policeman. You don't get a confession from me."

"What do you mean, 'policeman'?" said Murdoch.

Levin shrugged. "You might not be now, but you have been at some time, McGrath. I've known a lot of coppers. I recognize the flat-footed walk and the way you can't keep your nose out of other people's business."

Murdoch kept his face bland. "I told you I did security work."

Levin's face was also expressionless. "I did think you might be useful to us. We can always use ex-coppers who know the ropes. Like we can use good hackers." He stared at me. "Interested, Maria?"

"Who's 'we'?" said Murdoch.

"Not interested," I said.

Levin turned away without saying anything further.

We stood outside the tent and watched him stalk away into the early morning, his black jacket a distinctive blot until he turned the corner.

"Bloody suspicious, if you ask me," said Murdoch. "He might not have a warehouse, but his garden shed's full of fertilizer."

"So?" I was thinking of the program alterations I'd have to make to the digital processor.

"Used for homemade bombs. And he's got a couple of drums of other stuff, too."

I stared at him. "You've been snooping around Levin's shed?"

He blinked back at me innocently. "No, I helped Grace clean out the spare bedroom. We took some stuff out to the shed, and I happened to have a squizz at what's in there."

I opened my mouth to protest, shut it again. Murdoch's proximity in the tent doorway was making me almost as hot and breathless as if Henoit had stood there. I cleared my throat and stepped away into the fresh air, shaking off the sensation.

"Only three ways he could have gotten this laser," I said when I was breathing normally. "He's got access to old stocks, or to people who have access to old stocks. And there aren't many. Or he's got black-market connections, which is what I thought anyway. Black-market electronics is a huge business. Or . . ." I wasn't sure of this last one.

"Or?"

"Or he's got contacts in the official defense industry,

because now it's the only place this type of laser is used. They need it for some of the older weapons."

"That might be how he supplies the gangs," said Murdoch with distaste. "He probably does know people in the industry. Does he really believe you need the laser for a telescope?"

I stretched. "What else might he think?"

"He could be worried you're working for a competitor, making weapons. Homemade stuff."

"He might be worried because you're snooping around."

"Good job I did, now we know what he's like."

"The deal with Levin's finished, stop worrying about it."

The pale apricot stillness magnified the sounds of a door banging, voices raised in the neighboring street, the mutter of people roused too early from sleep. In the background, the ever-present hum of the city, the irregular beat of the motorway. The out-town was peaceful at this hour. Tin roofs, wired window frames, crude verandas, all softened by the gentle light.

"But why is he helping you? Doesn't make sense." Murdoch persisted. "He could be setting you up."

"For what? The police aren't going to arrest me because I've got a homemade telescope."

"No, but they'll arrest you for being an illegal if Levin informs on you."

"I know that. But we've only got until Friday. Three more days, counting today. I didn't have time to look anywhere else."

"I suppose it's safe," he grumbled. "But I don't trust him."

"Forget Levin. Where did you go yesterday? More snooping?" He'd stayed out until nine or ten P.M. I'd struggled unsuccessfully against worry that he'd been mugged.

"Talking with Vince."

"Why?"

"He's not a bad kid. Him and his mates are pretty typical, I reckon. They're loyal to their small group and damn everyone else. But from another angle, they're just making themselves a safe place because nobody else will make it for them. Sensible, really."

"Most of Vince's behavior doesn't strike me as sensible."

"Doesn't mean there's no logic behind it. You just gotta figure out what it is."

"Like an alien species."

"Yeah. You might not sympathize, but at least you'll understand a bit better."

"Or like donkeys," I said absently.

"Wha-at?" Murdoch gaped at me.

"It's an old story." I wished I hadn't mentioned it. "My great-grandmother used to tell us this story about donkeys."

"Go on."

"She said that when a donkey stops in the middle of the road, you give it a whack with a stick, right? But the donkey doesn't learn not to stop on roads; it learns that by stopping it can make you angry."

Murdoch grinned. "A different logic."

"Yes. It used to remind me of K'Cher. You have to find out how that logic works or you end up expending a lot of energy for no purpose and both of you get frustrated."

It's strange, the things that remain in your memory from childhood conversations, from details and scenery you never realized you were noticing at the time. These things bridge time and space as successfully as Invidi jump drives.

I came back to the tent late that night after fitting the laser. I'd have liked to do a test run, but the glue on the fitting had to dry more and I needed to be there in the morning before Florence arrived, to pack it up out of her way and safely away from prying eyes. Now that I'd finally put it all together, we couldn't risk theft or damage.

Murdoch was already asleep, sprawled facedown on his mattress, the light on and a newspaper by his trailing hand as though he'd fallen asleep reading it. I'd sent him back to the tent when he came to pick me up at about ten o'clock. He didn't complain, but he looked tired—perhaps the twenty-first-century viruses were undermining his immune system too.

I turned off the light, undressed and got into bed, but couldn't sleep. My thoughts kept scurrying around in familiar circles. When I shut my eyes I could see the details of the telescope assembly. Every creak of the tent pole, every distant thud or clatter seemed magnified. I found myself listening to Murdoch's regular breathing. He sounded so comfortable, I was overcome by a callous urge to disturb him. I imagined sitting beside him on the bed, sliding my feet beneath the tattered blanket, putting one hand on the back that rose and fell so peacefully . . .

My breathing caught again, not from asthma, but from the feeling I used to get when Henoit, or any H'digh for that matter, walked into a room and the effect of their pheromones hit me. As though the slightest touch of anything upon my skin would be the signal for immeasurable pleasure.

Imitations of H'digh pheromones were exchanged galaxy-wide as aphrodisiacs, and it was said that humans who experienced sexual acts with them were forever "tainted"— they retained enough of the pheromone to send other humans mad with desire. It was also said that these tainted humans did not live long, as they became quickly insane. I had always dismissed this as space-talk, particularly as I had neither gone mad nor sent other humans crawling up walls.

Now, I wasn't so sure. Maybe I had enough pheromones left in me to activate the pleasure center of the brain. Not that it felt like the brain had much to do with it.

Images of Henoit kept popping into my mind; Henoit on Jocasta, appearing out of nowhere, arrogant and unrepentant at his terrorist activities. I hadn't seen that lean, muscled figure for seven years, but he'd looked as young as ever. Henoit when I first met him, an exotic unknown who couldn't quite explain why he'd chosen me to be his mate; Henoit saying we were destined to bond; Henoit's eyes meeting mine for the first time on our first night together . . . but here I stopped.

Any further and I'd embarrass myself by waking Murdoch, and embarrass myself further by not caring.

Humans have spent over a century trying to dispel the romantic notion that two people are suited to each other and each other only, drawn together by Fate. Then we find that the H'digh have built a whole society around that same notion. And it works nicely, thank you. For them. *Nor death shall us part,* ran part of that damn couplet Henoit used to quote at me from a marriage song.

Why did I marry him? I was flattered, I suppose, even though later he said that the attraction felt by two bond-partners was not the same as ordinary sexual attraction. I was curious, too, about H'digh sexuality and society. I wanted a stable relationship—eternity sounded pretty long term. And maybe I was also feeling what he felt.

Could it be true that Henoit was my soul mate and we were still bound together even after his death? Even as my rational engineer's mind laughed at the idea, Henoit's voice echoed in my head, the words just beyond hearing. The tone, regret. Or perhaps that is what I wished the tone to be.

I don't know how to get rid of him. Or if I want to. How can you get rid of someone who isn't there?

* * *

The day before the hoped-for Invidi arrival I was flat out at the Assembly, preparing for the May Day march. Nobody knew, of course, that it would be the last official May Day in human history, although the name remained in popular usage until nearly the turn of the century. I remember my grandmother calling it May Day, not First Contact Day, which she said reminded her of a tasteless joke about adolescent dating.

The Assembly had no funds to prepare information pages or elaborate placards for the march, but some of the neighborhood youths had been bribed with bottles of carbonated drink to letter a plank with the words "Assembly of the Poor" on one side and "EarthSouth Movement" on the other.

One of the youths was a graffiti virtuoso, and his lettering angled perfectly. The background to the letters was covered completely with a dense carpet of flowers. At least, they looked like flowers until you got close, when you realized that it was a stylized vulva. The placard was finished in time, though, and Florence didn't notice the "flowers" at all.

A wild dry wind blew all that week, and the placard's surface was gritty where sand had blown into the wet surface. That same dry wind scattered refuse and pieces of loose building material all over the tracks and made walking in the dark dangerous.

We spent that day coordinating the groups who would come on the march with us, and giving people instructions on how to behave, that is, how to stay away from police. The police, it seemed, took even local May Day marches quite seriously. The riots of 2010 and 2012, when thousands of police and demonstrators were killed worldwide, still smarted in their memory. For years, Florence said, they banned gatherings of more than twenty people, but recently they'd been more lenient.

Tomorrow the Invidi would arrive. They'd better. I'd waited so long for this, and now I wanted some answers to my questions. Why did *Calypso II* not arrive in the past in the same year that *Calypso* jumped, in spite of using the same jump point—does this mean the Invidi have been lying to us about the jump points and the jump network being fixed? Will we be able to return to Jocasta in our own time using the *Calypso* jump point? How did the jump point get there in the first place?

Not that "first place" has much meaning. The dominoes are stacked in a circle and touching any one brings them all down. All the events are interconnected. I wondered if that's how the Invidi see the universe—as endless interconnection. No wonder they sound obscure to us linear creatures who see time flowing neatly from past to future.

Flowing from today to tomorrow. And none too soon, as far as I was concerned. The future on Jocasta may have its problems, but it was nothing compared to life in the out-town.

By the time Murdoch came to pick me up at eight, I'd set up the telescope, ready to activate the signal as soon as we knew the Invidi were within range. I didn't want to risk starting sooner, there was too great a chance one of Earth's security forces would pick up the signal and trace it, especially after that airport incident. Once the Invidi arrived, confusion should make this worry unnecessary.

I was ready for a little advance celebration. We'd survived this far—it seemed cause enough to congratulate ourselves.

We sat beside each other on my bed in the tent and ate greasy chips, washed down with cold beer that rapidly warmed, leaving pools of condensation on the crate top. I looked sideways at Murdoch and let the reins on my imagination loose for a while. He was so close and warm. The muscles of his jaw tightened smoothly as he chewed. I let my eyes drift down his arms.

The never-forgotten feeling of H'digh arousal surrounded me. I could feel my heart beat faster, and somewhere a voice was saying, *Feel with me . . .*

"I'll be glad to get back. This place stinks." Murdoch carefully smoothed the cellulose wrapping that the chips had come in, put the wrapper beside the kettle, and sat on the edge of the bed. I was sitting farther in, with my back against the wall.

The warm, sexy feeling disappeared with his words, then crept back. His shoulder was close enough for me to reach out and touch. The T-shirt stretched taut over its roundness. Like a tune on the edges of hearing, I could feel Henoit's presence.

So what? What are you afraid of? That Murdoch will think you're possessed or something? For all you know, you could die tomorrow and not meet the Invidi. Then you'll regret never having slept with Murdoch . . .

I said the first thing that popped into my head. "Are you sorry you came?"

He didn't laugh. He looked steadily at me, and I felt heat rise up my neck and face.

"Why do you think I came?" He reached over and traced his forefinger up my arm.

I held down the shiver it provoked. "Because you needed to arrest me?"

"Because I couldn't bear not knowing what happened to you," he said. And climbed on the bed so he straddled my outstretched legs. "Because I couldn't bear maybe never being able to do this."

He leaned forward. I leaned forward. We kissed.

Pleasure ran into my gut like fire. Murdoch made a short sound that was between an exclamation and a moan.

Crash.

The door banged open and Will ran in.

Murdoch and I pushed each other aside clumsily.

Will stopped, seemed about to run out again, then said, "Hey, Maria. Can I stay with you?"

I was breathing too fast. "Does Grace . . ."

Will looked down. "She said it was okay. She and Levin were . . . um, busy. She said you can bring me to the march tomorrow. Vince brung me most of the way here. Oh, hi, Bill."

Surely not even a ten-year-old could be that ingenuous. He must have fled Levin and Grace "mucking around," only to find Murdoch and me doing the same. We could hardly turn him away.

"H'lo, Will," said Murdoch weakly. He let himself flop back on the board. "Oh, boy."

I rubbed my arms, where the hairs stood on end. Damn.

Murdoch and Will dropped off to sleep quickly. My breath began to catch and I sat up, sucking in air.

Tomorrow—no, later today—the Invidi would be here. Blue shafts of floodlight played on the walls of the tent like echoes of patterns in spacetime I could not begin to understand. A friend once said to me that the Invidi held the index to the book we were all living. Today we'd be given our first glimpse of the entry that was our own history.

No, thank you. I punched the blanket lightly. When the Invidi come, they won't be expecting humans from this era to be familiar with their systems. Their security will be geared toward other, more physical threats. Hannibal Griffis had mentioned an assassination attempt. This was as good an opportunity as ever to get our hands on information about the jump drive.

I wanted *Calypso II* back, and I was prepared to take

as much other information as I could. Much of my adult life I had used technology I did not understand, was not given the opportunity to understand. When I finally acquired what I thought was a jump drive, it turned out to be something different. I'd been literally taken for a ride.

I did not intend to return to our own time empty-handed.

Nine

In the dream I chase an elusive figure along a street in a place like the out-town. Overhead in the apricot sky hovers an Invidi ship. But the underside of the ship is the same color as the sky and nobody else notices. If I stop to tell someone about the Invidi, I'll never catch my target. And Henoit, blast him, keeps whispering in my ear, *Nor death shall us part, Nor death shall . . .*

I didn't know why I woke. The only sounds in the tent were Will's soft wheeze, Murdoch's rumbling snore from his mattress, and an intermittent *tap-thud* from the roof as the wind lifted a loose corner and set it down again.

Will's leg weighed on my stomach like a girder. I pushed at it and squirmed away. He twitched once, then flung his arms wide and took up more space. I slid out of bed. Murdoch's wrist timer, placed on the crate, showed two A.M. Too early for the Invidi, surely. May first had only just begun to crawl across the Pacific.

When I opened the door, the growl of the city sounded louder in the darkness, punctuated by sounds muted during the day—overhead roar of high-flying planes, the whine of vehicles from the motorway to the south.

The sky was its usual dull brown-gray, orange on the horizon. Not a star to be seen, not even straight overhead. Around me, the irregular shapes of shacks and tents. The smell of open drains, strong enough to have shape itself. And another smell I couldn't quite identify.

A dog barked a couple of lanes away. The skinny yellow creature that guarded the iron scrap gatherer's cart. Another dog, farther away. Then another, closer. In the next lane maybe. Too many dogs barking.

I looked up. Could the animals sense an alien presence?

A sleepy voice yelled shut up at the dogs. Then more voices yelled, several blocks away. I realized that the other smell was smoke. Coming on the wind, which gusted dust and heavier particles into my face. A hot, dry wind, blowing from the west.

I turned back to shake Murdoch awake, and far off somebody yelled the word.

Fire.

"Get up, Bill."

He sat up and automatically groped for his trousers. "Whatsup?"

"Fire. Don't know how bad."

"Shit." He rolled over and grabbed the two water bottles. "You got anything important here?"

"No." I grabbed my inhaler from beside the bed and shook Will. "It's all at the Assembly office . . . Will, come on. You have to get up."

More voices outside, slap of sandals on the earth. *Tap-thud* from the roof.

"Move it." Murdoch shoved the bottles at me and picked up the still-groggy Will.

I stepped outside and was nearly bowled over by a woman and two men running. The woman held a scrunched-up blanket and was sobbing.

"Which way's it coming from?" Murdoch said behind me.

I could hear more noise from the riverside. "We go this way." I pointed south and went ahead.

People milled about in the light from open doorways. Only a few moved purposefully like us. The comments we overheard were merely curious, and I wondered if we had been premature in fleeing.

What's going on?

Fire down the road.

Not that bloody bonfire again. I told 'em I'd report that . . .

What is burning?

I turned to Murdoch. He put Will down and held his hand.

"Where are we going?" said Will. "Is it a real fire?"

"I don't know how big it is," I said. "Maybe it's only a small one, but you can't be too careful." Twenty-five years of living in enclosed artificial environments had given me a healthy respect for fire and the way it sucks away oxygen.

"You'd better go to Levin's," I said to Murdoch. "Grace will be worried."

"What about you?" His voice was sharp.

"I'm going along to the Assembly. See if I can get the telescope out." I held out one of the water bottles and started to go back past them, but Murdoch got in my way.

"Hang on. We don't split up. Too much chance we never find each other again."

"Bill, the scope's our best hope of contacting . . ."

Will was staring confusedly from my face to Murdoch's. Down the way we'd come there was a loud crash. More people began to run. In the distance a siren sounded.

"It's today," I pressed. "I won't have time to make . . ."

"That's why we got to stay safe." Murdoch had to yell for me to hear him over the crashing, crackling sound and the babble of voices. When I looked back, smoke billowed upward, lighter gray against the dark brown-gray sky.

He picked up Will again and shoved me. "Go on."

I hesitated.

"I didn't come all this way to lose you now," growled Murdoch, and shoved me harder.

"Maria, let's go," whined Will.

We fled with the rest of the out-town. We started off in the direction of Silverwater Road, thinking we'd walk south along it to Levin's house where Grace would be waiting, but with thick smoke in our eyes we became confused in the maze of small lanes. People pushed us the other way, toward the river.

Will kept his eyes squeezed almost shut, whimpering. My feet were sore and battered from tripping on stones and rubbish. The water bottles dragged at my shoulders until we had to pass along a lane, where the heat and crackling loomed from both sides.

"On his hair." Murdoch directed me to soak Will and then we dribbled the rest on each other and ran through the lane.

We ran for what seemed like hours, but it was only a few minutes. The noise of the sirens grew behind us but the smoke had thinned. Those who'd run, like us, now mingled in the street with the residents of shacks and houses who came out to see what was happening.

"Where are we?" I croaked.

Murdoch shook his head. When he tried to speak, he doubled over coughing.

"I want to go home," said Will.

"Which way is it?" I said.

"I don't know." He began to cry.

"It's okay." Murdoch rubbed his back and held him close, in between coughs.

The smoke-filled dark whirled around us. I asked a man in yellow pajamas which way was south, and he pointed back the way we'd come. Surely that can't be right. I felt sick and put my head down, one hand on Murdoch's shoulder.

"Vince!" squealed Will.

Murdoch and I whirled around and there was Vince, puffing and coughing like us. He didn't look singed or hurt, but his face was shiny with sweat and at the sound of Will's voice his teeth flashed in a grin.

"Hey, you got out too."

He led us easily away from the edges of the out-town through streets gradually clearer of smoke, then under the motorway crossing to Levin's place, chattering with what must have been relief at finding someone he knew.

"I got stuck back there, was visiting Mikey over near the racecourse. You remember Mikey, Will? Used to dunk you in the water tank. Come and hold hands, mate. Yeah, and then all shit breaks out, they reckon it was somebody smoking and all that dry rubbish went up. Fire engines took their time. I reckon they couldn't care less. They prob'ly think, good way to get rid of the rubbish and all that crap."

I followed, too exhausted to query Vince, Murdoch holding my hand instead of Will's. Behind us a cacophony of sirens, voices, wind, and the breaking-up of flimsy dwellings. How could the Assembly office have survived this? Today the Invidi would arrive and I was back to square one.

Be grateful we're alive, said the voice of common sense. We seemed to walk for much longer than we'd run from the flames. Houses around us.

Grace's voice in the darkness.

"Will? Thank God." She grabbed him in a fierce hug. I looked back in the direction of the river flats and the sirens, but couldn't see anything except a faint glow in the sky above the ridge of the motorway. A shift in the wind brought a whiff of burning rubber, stronger than the smell that permeated our hair and clothes.

"You two okay?" she said. "Come inside."

"I'm okay too," said Vince pointedly.

"Thanks, darl." Grace bestowed a wet kiss on his cheek and Vince recoiled.

"Yech. I'm off." He started to slouch away, then turned back. "Levin around?"

"He went off about nine," said Grace distractedly, and shooed Will inside.

I grabbed Murdoch's arm as he went to follow her. "Bill, we need to go back and check the Assembly. Maybe the fire didn't go that way."

In the glow from the open doorway I could see the sympathy on his face. "Wait a little while. When the fire's out we'll go and see if it's safe."

"But the telescope . . ."

"Yeah. I know."

I didn't want sympathy. I wanted to smash something in rage at the unexpected contrariness of things.

Ten

Grace shut the door of the bedroom and sat with Will until he went to sleep. Murdoch and I washed off the worst of the grime and soot in Levin's bathroom.

I watched the brownish gray water swirl around the old porcelain of the hand basin and couldn't help thinking of hopes being washed away. Today the Invidi would come, and I had no way of contacting them. I would grow old—the pale, haggard face in the mirror seemed to confirm it—in this cursed century, while in my own world the neutrality vote finishes one way or another and Jocasta moves on, with the Four Worlds continuing to dominate the Confederacy, and there's not a damn thing I can do about it.

I couldn't get the smell of smoke out of my hair without having a shower, and using Levin's shower was not something I wanted to do. Not rational, but I preferred to leave the stink in there, a symbol of my defeat.

In Levin's living room reporters on televid told us what was going on two kilometers to the north. Sirens blared and we couldn't tell if they were outside or on the screen. Behind the reporter's circle of light, fire trucks siphoned water from the river onto what looked like a huge bonfire, and dark figures moved in front of the flickering light. It looked like the shanties of the main out-town over on the old oil company site. Made of old construction material, wood, and canvas, they must have fed the flames like tinder.

... for years, surrounding communities and charity groups have been telling local government about this fire hazard. Miraculously, there have been no reports of fatalities. Dozens of people have been taken to hospital with minor injuries and smoke inhalation ...

Only those too injured to run away first. Nobody from the out-town wanted the prying care of a big hospital, where they had to fill out forms with nonexistent ID and health-care numbers.

It's not known how the fire started, but the police have not ruled out the possibility of arson ...

Murdoch, who had showered with every evidence of enjoyment and who sat toweling his hair on Levin's sofa, laughed derisively. "They think people torched their own homes?"

"They don't think our tents are homes," I said.

He twisted around to look at me properly. "You okay?"

"I'm going to check on the Assembly. The main fire was over on the Rosehill side. And the fire trucks were coming as we walked this way, I heard them. Creek Road's probably all right."

He sighed, then stood up. "You're right, we should go and look. Even if the house wasn't damaged in the fire, there could be looting."

One more thing for me to worry about.

We went out the back door. It was still dark, but in the east the orange glow of the city was lightening further. I shivered. There was a chill in the air that I'd never felt before in Sydney. A cooler season on the way.

We could still hear sirens. People were clumped in groups along the road, talking. It seemed two theories were the favorites: that anti-immigrant groups had torched the shanties, or that it was part of a gang fight over territory.

Some part of the out-town had paid protection money to a different gang or something, I couldn't work it out from the snippets of conversation we heard, but Murdoch listened carefully.

We crossed Parramatta Road, deserted under broken streetlights, detoured around Will's primary school and over the footbridge that spanned the motorway.

The roads here, though closer to the fire, were nearly empty. We passed an elderly man walking two small dogs. Three boys on bicycles laden with newspapers passed us. Lighted windows glowed in a couple of houses, but most were still sleeping. Despite the haze and smell of smoke, it might have been the dawn of any day. But it's not any day. Today the world changes. Fatigue and thirst hit me suddenly and I wished I'd drunk more than a glass of water in Levin's bathroom. Never mind, it will be worth it when we contact the Invidi.

"Hang on." Murdoch grabbed my elbow and I staggered to a stop, dragging my attention back to the present. There seemed to be a commotion ahead of us. At the intersection of the next road, the telltale blue flashing light of a police car.

"Just stroll along and see." Murdoch linked his arm in mine and we sidled along the road, finally camouflaging ourselves behind a couple in matching dressing gowns who'd come out of their caravan to see what was happening.

A heavy feeling of apprehension dragged at my stomach. Just short of the corner we stopped to watch three policemen as they spoke to a dog walker coming from the direction of the fire. They allowed the dog walker to pass, but they might not let us.

"Do you think they'll bother with people going in?" I said quietly to Murdoch.

He shrugged. "They can take you in on the spot for being without an ID, can't they?"

We strolled casually away from the police, back down the street we'd come. If we turned up the next one, we could cut across to Silverwater Road.

I cursed under my breath. Nothing was easy in this damn century.

Murdoch squeezed my arm. "We'll get there."

But police lined the whole length of Silverwater Road and watched the bridge. We'd have to go back south, walk beside the motorway, then follow the river back up north.

"What's their problem?" I moaned. "Surely they can't suspect the whole suburb of arson?"

"I reckon it's the march," said Murdoch. He watched a bus trundle along, decked in bunting. "They're keeping an eye on possible trouble spots."

"Which won't be here. How can people whose homes have burnt down cause trouble?"

I looked down the road. The Assembly and my telescope were just over there, so close. The Invidi could be here any minute. History said their ships arrived simultaneously over big cities. But no matter how hard I tried, I couldn't remember exactly when and where the Invidi ships first appeared. "May first" covered a lot of hours in this age, when Earth had no single time. Every human child of my generation knew the Invidi's first message, it was part of our shared heritage. So why couldn't I remember exactly when they'd said it?

By the time we retraced our steps to the edge of the motorway the sun had risen and was warming our backs.

"No good." Murdoch's voice jerked me out of my daze.

The space along the edge of the river beside the unused railway track was cordoned off with police tape. One blue-uniformed man walked along the tape, then along the side of the battered brick building that backed onto the riverbank.

"Shit. What do we do now?" Heedless of the policeman, I squatted on the edge of the path. Across the river we could see smoke still rising from a dark mass of burned buildings. Yellow glimpses of a fire truck. A few figures moving near the wreckage. Cars parked close to the river path, unable to get in farther. Behind us, the muted roar of the motorway.

Murdoch squatted beside me. His shoulder felt warm and solid through my thin T-shirt.

"I guess we gotta wait." He sounded as tired as I felt. "They'll probably pack up by midday. Afternoon at the latest."

"What if somebody loots the Assembly while we wait? Or the Invidi arrive?"

"You can still signal them afterward, can't you?"

"Probably," I conceded. "But there's going to be a lot more interference then." His words reminded me I might have to make adjustments before the signal could be sent, and pushed my impatience further.

"We'll have to try to sneak through backyards." I stood up. "Work our way past the police and over to Creek Road."

"That's a good way to get arrested," said Murdoch, remaining seated. "Calm down and wait."

I contemplated going without him, but part of me knew he was right. I looked up at the blue and apricot sky above the smoke haze. No alien ships up there yet.

"I got it." Murdoch stood up with a grunt of stiffness. "We go on the march."

"Why?"

"Aren't you interested in the last May Day of human history?" He saw my expression. "Seriously, the police might put on a show, but I bet they won't actually stop the march. So long as some idiot doesn't attack them."

"So?"

"So if we go on the march, we can detour around the police checks. The big meeting's at Macquarie University, isn't it?"

"Wherever that is. Florence took care of those details."

"Well, we can start off with the march, then break off and cut back through West Ryde afterward. Or we can go part of the way, then come back along the far bank of the river. If Silverwater Bridge is still blocked, there's always the footbridge farther along."

"I suppose so," I said doubtfully.

"You want to go?" Murdoch raised an eyebrow at me. Better than sitting here waiting. "Let's go."

He nodded, relieved. If I didn't know him better, I'd say he only suggested it to give me something to do while we waited for the Invidi to come.

FIRST PASS 5 174

Eleven

"I shouldn't've come on this," grumbled Grace. "Me feet hurt like shit. May Day, Labor Day, what crap. I haven't even got a job . . ."

My feet hurt too. Dirt and dust chafed in the sensitive skin between first and second toes. I was tempted to take my sandals off altogether, but the footpath was too rough and hot. The edges had crumbled into the mess of holed asphalt at the side of the road itself, forcing us to walk in single file. A long line of bedraggled people, many in smoke-stained clothes. I'd spoken to Abdul earlier—he was up at the front of the line, carrying a banner he'd kept at his house on Campbell Street. He hadn't been to the Assembly and told me I should stay away until he could go and check if it was safe. I made no promises.

"When you're young," said Grace suddenly, "you think you're gonna be able to do it. Change the world. Look at the mess our parents made of last century. Not anymore, we thought. I remember sitting out there on the edge of the harbor, watching that word 'eternity' burn across the bridge on New Year's Eve and thinking this century's gonna be different." She sighed and limped on.

"What about now?" I said, half interested, half wanting to keep my attention on the sky.

"Now? You know, things happen. I couldn't find a job,

then I lost the ones I did get. Then I met Vince's dad and things were so bad and so good at the same time I never knew if I was coming or going. Then we left him. And he died.

"Now I'm nearly forty and this century isn't any better. It's getting worse. And I keep thinking of Will going off the rails like Vince. I get this sick, hollow feeling in me stomach, you know?"

"Will's not going off the rails. He's fine."

She sighed. "I hope so. You asked me why I went off with Levin." She looked around and dropped her voice. I had to strain to hear her when a truck went past.

"I lost my job, so no more proper healthcare, no more train pass, no more . . . you name it, when yer out of work, you don't have it. Levin was an extra chance, I took it."

It will get better, I wanted to say. Not immediately. But from today, things start to change.

"You know what they're saying about the fire last night?" Grace added after a moment. She'd dropped back behind me.

"No, what?" I looked up at the sky above the city, stubbing my toes again on uneven concrete. The sky remained empty.

"They reckon it was those Cabramatta gangs come up here, didn't get the action they wanted, and torched the place."

"Who reckons?" Personally, I thought the fire had probably been started by someone's careless use of a cooking fire, and been spread by the wind among flammable building materials.

"I dunno, everyone. But you know what they say." She put her hand on my shoulder to support herself while she pulled a stone out of her sandal.

"What?"

"No smoke without fire."

I turned, shocked, and saw her grinning at me.

"Joke." She chuckled, and swept on ahead. I couldn't help grinning back.

We'd gone through Rhodes and crossed Ryde Bridge about half an hour ago, and would soon join another group of marchers at Ryde Park where many of the groups were gathering before the long walk to Macquarie University. This would be a good chance for Murdoch and myself to slip away and head back southwest to get to the Assembly.

What if I was wrong about time and the jump points? There seemed no explanation for the way we'd jumped ninety-nine years instead of ninety-five. Murdoch and I might have simply wandered into another universe, one in which the Invidi never came to Earth, or in which the Bendarl got here first and enslaved the indigenous population like they did on Achel. I looked up at the sky, blue above and gray at the edges, and had to tell myself again, *It's today*. The fire, the march, all the events of this present were so close, the prospect of an alien first contact so far away.

We left the main road, to everyone's relief, as trucks kept trundling past too close to us, some of them swerving to avoid potholes. This must have been a lovely area once. Small brick bungalows and churches. One, two, three churches. Oak trees sheltered us from the sun as we passed, but their roots had made a broken mosaic of both footpath and road to trip over. Their lower branches were all gone and graffiti continued from the wall around the church onto their trunks. Barbed wire around one of the church walls, broken glass scattered over the footpath outside it.

Onto another large road, fewer potholes. Not only trucks, but a couple of passenger cars passed, their windows black and impenetrable. I looked for Murdoch, to ask him if we should split off from the others, but he wasn't in sight. Grace walked up ahead.

On either side of the road, three- and four-story buildings with smooth walls were set back from the footpath, alternating with smaller shops. Most of them had heavy bars on the windows. Behind the bars, colorful displays showed glimpses of a world I'd seen only on televid. Racks of coats in gradations of brown from fawn to chocolate, black sequined dresses on mannequins; men's suits hung like dead crows against a wall; silver, red, white, and yellow machines for kitchens and bathrooms; textured materials covering window after window of sofas, beds, chairs . . .

It was like the extra pages tucked into the newspaper. I hadn't taken seriously those pictures of hundreds of varieties of things, thinking it was an exaggeration. Nothing like that in the corner shops and markets of the out-town area. But here was a multitude of things, lined up for anyone with money to buy. I forgot to look at the sky and peered in the shop windows, feeling like I did the first time I saw the mercantile section of a Confederacy port. Amazed, bemused, and embarrassed at my own gaucherie.

Used to the species-based discrimination within the Confederacy, Earth's economic discrimination confused me. So senseless and extreme. Would the K'Cher, for example, exploit a world so much that the inhabitants had no food or shelter? They wouldn't care about much beyond whether the world could produce enough for their trading needs, but surely they'd try to induce the best conditions for productivity . . .

I sighed and checked the sky again. No sign of the Invidi.

Murdoch fell into step beside me.

"Where were you?"

"Checking the crowd. A lot more people in front of us."

"If *they* get here this morning we'll all see the show." I glanced up at the sky, which was now eggshell-blue. "What's the time?"

He tapped his empty wrist. "Must've left my timer in the tent." He peered in one of the shop windows. "Looks like about eleven."

"We need to get back to the Assembly," I said with renewed despair.

He nodded. "Let's get a drink at the park first, though. Didn't you say there'd be refreshments there?"

I had to agree. I wouldn't make it back to the out-town without a rest.

We passed a café with a televid screen, and I wondered for a moment if the Invidi had already arrived and official sources had suppressed the news. But that wasn't what the history files said happened.

Into the park. Tents around the edges, people living there. On a bowling green in the corner of the park, a group of elderly people stared as we walked thankfully off the hot street and sank down on the cleanest-looking patches of brown grass.

We could see more marchers gathered on the other side of the park. Some were dressed in bright costumes, some had painted their faces in red or green or yellow. They stood in groups of twenty or more, talking and chattering. Some of them picked up their placards and started moving out of the park. Two tall men wore black masks with a curious logo on the back of their heads—the symbol for nuclear power scored over with a red cross. By comparison the out-town crowd seemed dull and disorganized, everyone trailing along at their own pace in twos and threes, sometimes in a family group.

Then the music started. Six people in green clothes played a lively jig on pipes and horns that woke us all up.

A couple of the out-town marchers who had brought pipes joined in.

A group of women held their banner and performed some kind of mini-play involving much yelling and gesticulating for media reporters with cameras and recording equipment. A truck parked on one side of the park said YOUR CHANNEL on its side.

The ground around the pond in the middle of the park was crowded with people buying drinks and snacks from the stalls set up there. Many of them seemed to be local residents rather than marchers. Many sat under the trees or under beach umbrellas, ready to watch the show.

It's not merely disorganization, I thought, but a disparity of purpose. The out-town crowd wants justice on a local scale. The red and yellow and green people and the black-masked ones want progress on a global scale.

If Marlena Alvarez was alive, she'd mold this crowd. They'd follow her. I wish, sometimes, that I was more . . .

Like her. Like I thought she was.

I remembered the dowdy figure with the hesitant voice and glasses. Maybe she couldn't have united the crowd after all.

Murdoch tapped my arm and pointed. The Assembly of the Poor group was squeezed together beside one of the trees. Grace waved at me. We joined them and shared cups of tea from a chipped, foam-covered flask that one of the women had brought. I recognized her, she'd lived two lanes across from the Assembly, on the border between the tent city and the proper streets. I asked her if her family's shack was damaged in the fire. "We was okay," she said. Her English had a soft lilt. "But one of them fire trucks clipped a pole and half the loo came down. Good job no one was in it." She smiled to show the last bit was a joke. I smiled back. If her place was all right, the Assembly would be safe too.

The music set all our feet tapping. I looked at their tired, sweaty faces and felt glad I'd stayed here. Glad I'd seen this small, dusty corner of history. And how important it was.

Murdoch went and filled our water bottles at one of the stalls.

"We can go now, I reckon." He shaded his eyes against the glare and looked over to the main street beyond the park. "The police still have their checkpoint over on Victoria Road, but I saw a bloke in a van from that big furniture warehouse near Rydalmere, and he said they're gone from Silverwater Bridge."

I took a swig of water from the bottle and felt better. With any luck we'd get the telescope set up in time. When the history files said the Invidi arrived on May first, they might have meant the day of May first in Europe or North America, which would be early tomorrow morning, our time. It could be later tonight.

Rachel Dourif, one of the Sleepers from *Calypso,* said, *Everyone remembers what they were doing on that day* of the Invidi arrival. She also said, *I couldn't forgive them for taking over our future.*

What about children like Will and Vince, who may not have a future unless the Invidi come?

Murdoch and I eased away from the Assembly group and threaded our way back to the road, the sun hot on the backs of our necks. I turned to look once more at the sky over the city. Something flashed silver and I thought it was an airplane banking.

Only it wasn't banking, it was hovering. And it was far too large to be an aircraft. Far too large to be anything made by humans.

I reached out and grabbed Murdoch's arm.

"Ow. What are you . . ." He followed my trembling finger pointed east. "Shit. It's them."

Behind us in the park, somebody with a radio receiver stuck to their ear was yelling. The media reporters were running toward the edge of the park, cameras raised. The pipes faltered, then stopped.

Two media helicopters rattled overhead toward the city.

"What is it?" Grace came up behind us, shading her eyes and frowning over the tops of the heads in front of her.

Neither Murdoch nor I answered. I couldn't speak at all. They're here.

"It's a UFO," someone said.

"One of those hoverjets," suggested another.

"Must be big if we can see it from here."

"Hey, over here!" someone yelled. There was a rush out onto the road. Murdoch grabbed my hand and we were carried along with the crowd. I looked for Grace but she'd been whirled away.

We ended up in front of an electronics shop near the park. A whole window full of televid screens. All showing the same image.

Blank, fuzzy blue. The bottom half of the screen was full of lines and blocky angles. The blurring cleared, and we realized it was the city center seen from above, probably from a helicopter. Then that disappeared and we were looking at an Invidi ship.

It hung motionless in the sky. Must have been about a kilometer up. Faintly pulsing with a greenish light on the lower surfaces. Nobody could possibly mistake its bulbous diamond shape for a plane.

Thus it ends, I thought. Our anthropocentric universe, gone with the simple overlay of that shape on the sky.

Then the audio channels of radios, televids, public announcement systems all over the city crackled. A mechanical, unaccented voice.

We are the Invidi. We come in peace.

Exactly as the history files said. My knees went watery with relief. We didn't screw up. Everything is as it should be. The image on the screen blurred as my eyes filled with tears. Murdoch's arm, heavy and damp with sweat, squeezed my shoulders. His voice low in my ear.

"Right on time. Reliable bastards, aren't they?"

Twelve

If we didn't get our signal off soon, the rest of the world would begin trying. I imagined the number of amateur radio operators and astronomers who'd be even now reaching for their emitters.

"We have to go." I turned to wriggle out of the crowd but they were packed tight, three deep, all watching with faces still slack with shock. I found myself pressed chest to chest with Murdoch, slightly off balance. He couldn't back up or turn around, I couldn't step sideways.

He put his hand on my hip to steady me and I found I was breathing quickly. I could hear the beat of my own pulse in my ears, and feel the thudding of his heart through the muscle of his chest. Without thinking, I pressed closer. An impulse impossible to resist. I could smell human sweat and also a pinelike scent—H'digh sweat.

Murdoch drew a short, sharp breath and his hand tightened on my hip. Then it relaxed again as I pulled away, stumbling over the person next to me, forcing a way through the line.

"I'm sorry." I was furious at myself for confusing him, at Henoit for intruding, at the Invidi for coming before we could get our signal set up. Most of all, furious at not being able to enjoy the feeling of Bill's body against mine.

He ran his hand over his head and cleared his throat.

"Halley, I know it's not the time, but we gotta talk about this."

"We will," I said, and grabbed his hand. "Later."

We hurried down the middle of the main street. Every car had stopped. Some of them stood with doors wide open while their owners got the news.

"Damn." I stopped. "I should have made sure Grace was all right."

"She'll be fine," said Murdoch. He kept glancing at the sky in the east. Everyone in the street kept stopping what they were doing to look up.

We walked down Victoria Road, passing through groups of people huddled together in shock. The shining point of light over the city was hidden now, but we stopped to listen to the first, barely coherent announcement on public media on the televid in a café. On the screen, a white-faced official assured us everything was under control and exhorted us to remain calm and keep listening for more news. The white-faced café owner kept making cups of coffee. There were at least ten cups set neatly on the counter and he was twisting the espresso machine handle again.

We kept walking. I looked at Murdoch. "What do you think happens now?"

He frowned as a man ran out of a shop doorway in front of us carrying a carton. Another man followed, calling out for the first to stop, waving his fist.

"Hard to say. These bits don't get into the history files, do they?"

We knew that the official response would be cautious, that for a while governments thought it could be a hoax, despite what their scientific and military advisers told them. But we didn't know what ordinary people did on the day the Invidi arrived. Did they pick up their children from school and go home and cook their dinners as usual? When you come to think of it, what else could they do?

Many of the people in the street wore blank, shocked expressions. A woman in a white dress cried continuously as she walked, oblivious to stares or pats of comfort from strangers. I saw kindly people twice steer her out of the way of poles before we turned a corner.

In front of one house, a red-faced man in a gray business suit, out of his own territory, harangued an interested crowd on the theme of "it's all a hoax." It said much for the strangeness of the day that he hadn't been mugged yet.

"They don't believe it." Murdoch looked back as four children capered in a doorway and made "alien" faces at passersby.

"It's hard to take in at once. This is so far from . . ." I waved upward. "All that."

"That" being places that were not of this planet, words spoken by beings who were not us, a universe no longer empty. For a fleeting moment I shared their sense of wonder.

It was nearly four when we crossed the river and walked back into the world of the out-town. The air was still thick with smoke.

Two buildings in Creek Road were gutted from the fire, and the nearby shacks gone. Other houses had escaped with only smoke damage. The Assembly building itself still stood, although the outside walls were blackened and sodden black mush around it showed how close the fire had burned. The betting shop downstairs was waterlogged, but the fire must have been doused before it grew strong enough to do more than darken the walls. All the windows were smashed and the door swung open on its hinges.

"Don't like the look of that." Murdoch pointed at the windows. "Someone's been in here."

The side door was open too, the stairs slippery with

water and papers. Papers that had drifted out the open door of the Assembly office.

"Look out for glass," Murdoch said behind me.

I hardly heard him.

Someone had systematically stripped everything from the walls and bookcases and flung it all in the middle of the room, which was now a soggy mass of half-burned paper and plastic. They had set a fire here, too, but it hadn't had time to burn properly. The computer, battery, and strongbox were gone, although I'd taken all my money from the strongbox for the laser. The box containing my telescope was also gone. The bastards had even taken my box of primitive tools, which took me months to find in junk piles and then recondition.

I couldn't find an expletive strong enough. I drew breath, stopped, felt my chest grow tight with the pressure of un-expressed frustration. Then realized I truly couldn't breathe.

"Damn," I gasped, scrabbling in my pocket for the inhaler. Had I even brought it out of the tent last night . . . ?

"What's the matter?" Murdoch's voice sharp behind me.

I tapped my chest, unable to talk. Not in the other pocket, either. What the fuck does it matter anyway? If we can't contact the Invidi I'm going to die in this goddamn century . . .

Got it. Down the bottom of the pocket. Murdoch's large hand warm around mine as he steered the inhaler up to my face.

In, out. Not going to die today.

Murdoch shook glass and soggy papers off the upturned chair and set it to one side of the door, away from the worst of the mess.

"Sit there. Don't move. I'll go and check on the tent." His sandals flapped on the stairs.

I sat in the chair, not caring that the moisture on the

seat was soaking into my trousers. I was glad he'd gone
for a while, because at this moment we didn't need me
breaking down. Breathe, Halley. Don't think about anything just yet.

Light footsteps on the stairs. Florence poked her head
carefully around the door.

"Hello, Maria." She trod carefully inside and hung her
large black handbag on the remains of the door instead of
on the corner of her desk. "Were you here last night?"

I shook my head. "We just came."

"I came to see if we'd been looted." She looked carefully at each part of the mess.

"Was everyone all right at your place?" I said.

"Yes, thank you. I would have come sooner, but this
other business with the aliens took up most of the day."

I waited to see what else she had to say. Disbelief? Anxiety?

Florence merely took a pair of thick rubber gloves out
of her bag and pulled them on. She stepped carefully over
the fallen desk leg and, squatting on the other side, began
to sort rubbish into piles.

Murdoch looked around the door. "Tent's gone completely. G'day, Florence. Everyone okay at your place?"

"Yes, thank you, Mr. McGrath."

He looked back at me. "Tent's wiped out. At least there
was nothing much to steal there. Except my timer."

Except my collection of Alvarez material. My anger
drained away until I just felt sick.

Florence clicked her tongue. "I wonder what fun they
get out of this. And of course the police will be too busy
chasing aliens to do anything about it."

"I'll be back later," I said abruptly.

Florence nodded without looking up as I picked my way
over the debris and slid down the stairs.

Across the river, the tent city looked like the aftermath

of a battle with old-fashioned explosives: flattened, blackened rubble broken by dwellings or areas that had somehow escaped the flames.

"Why do you think they took all our stuff?" My voice wasn't as steady as I'd hoped.

"Probably took everything in all the empty houses," said Murdoch, who'd followed me outside. "Not just ours."

"What a waste of time it all was."

"Getting the telescope ready, you mean?"

I nodded, not trusting my voice.

"They might contact us, find you like I did."

"With the transponder? I don't think they will. They don't go out and look for things. Remember the Invidi on Jocasta? They stay put and let trouble come to them."

At the end of the street a wide mass of smoking debris blocked the way to the tent city. Two boys about Will's age looked up from poking the pile with iron bars.

"We'll have to find another way to contact them," I said.

"Can we use ordinary radio?" Murdoch said.

"We'll have to try. And as soon as they decide to land, we'll go and watch. See if there's a way to sneak in and get to see them."

He sighed tiredly. "You'd think we could just go and say hello."

"You, me, and the rest of the planet."

Will met us at the door of Levin's house. His face was solemn but his body twitched with excitement.

"Hey, the aliens are here! We finished school at lunchtime. They reckon there's no more school."

"Which aliens?" asked Murdoch.

"The ones in the ships. Are there other ones?"

"Could be all sorts of aliens out there."

Will didn't get the joke, which wasn't surprising. Nobody would get the joke for another sixty-two years, until Earth joined the Confederacy.

Another small boy waved at Will from the back entry. Will dashed out between us with a hurried "see you later."

Grace appeared and blocked the doorway while she yelled at Will, "Don't you go anywhere. Stay in this yard." Then she turned to us. "Glad yer okay, you two. What do you think, eh?" She gave me a quick hug and led the way into the house.

"I thought she'd be cranky we left her at Ryde," whispered Murdoch.

"Me too," I whispered back.

I headed for the bathroom. All I wanted at that moment was to get rid of my smelly, sticky coating of smoke, dust, and sweat. My hair felt almost solid with muck.

The pipes produced only a trickle, but Levin had buckets of tepid water in his bathroom. This time I had no problem with using his bathroom and couldn't remember why I'd minded this morning. This morning seemed a long time away. I scrubbed and then sluiced myself on the tiled floor, and watched runnels of brown water trickle out the hole in the floor, making slow, hypnotic patterns around the raised edges of the tiles. My clothes went into the last twenty centimeters of water in the bucket, to soak.

"Maria, you finished?" Murdoch's voice, full of guarded concern.

"Nearly, why?"

"Don't fall asleep in there."

"Huh. Can you ask Grace if I can borrow one of her sarongs?"

When I came out, feeling closer to human, Grace sat in front of the vidscreen in the living room with her two old neighbors, Phuong and Eric. It was a shock to see Phuong, usually trim and neat, looking grimy and exhausted too.

You didn't notice it as much with Eric, who was always dirty.

Murdoch sat on a chair and leaned his elbows on the table. He smiled at me and pointed at another chair.

"You reckon this is for real?" Grace waved her beer bottle at the screen.

We watched a wide-eyed commentator sputter his report while the same image of the Invidi ship I'd seen that morning floated in the upper part of the square.

"Looks real to me," I said shortly. For all Grace's offhandedness, two backpacks with emergency supplies and water containers stood at the back door, ready for her and Will should they need to run.

"I'm glad you're all right," Phuong said to me. "We looked for you last night but there were people everywhere."

Eric grunted and popped the top off a cold beer. As an afterthought, he reached down beside his chair, grabbed another one, and slid it across the table at Murdoch.

"Dangerous in the dark," Murdoch agreed, and popped the beer. "Anybody seen Levin?"

"Not since yesterday," said Phuong.

I poured myself a glass of filtered water. It wouldn't have surprised me if Levin had been part of any unrest leading to the fire. Or, at least, part of the looting afterward.

"Incredible," breathed Grace. Her eyes, fixed on the Invidi ship, had a glazed look.

"The government's working out what to do now." Phuong turned his head to speak to Murdoch. "They're trying to stop all private communications to the ship in case some crackpot says the wrong thing. Science groups are pissed off, but the gov'ment wants to keep it simple."

"Can the authorities jam the whole ionosphere?" said Murdoch, raising his eyebrow at me.

"They'll use satellites to jam the space around the ships."
Which is why, I thought gloomily, using shortwave bands
probably won't work. What am I going to do? Short of
physically approaching them. At the moment, I was too
tired to move anywhere at all. I leaned on the table beside
Murdoch.

A hurried meeting of the Security Council had agreed
no military aircraft were to fly within several kilometers
of the twelve alien ships hovering at various locations all
over the world.

"Who's talking to them?" said Phuong.

"The heads of governments, I s'pose," said Grace.

"Is there anything to eat?" said Murdoch.

Grace turned back to the screen. "How can you eat at
a time like this?"

Eric proffered a soggy bag of chips. Murdoch took a
couple, I refused with a grimace. The televid voices ham-
mered at us.

*In the United States, reports from Alabama, Georgia,
and New Mexico of mass cult suicides have been confirmed.
At least three thousand believers . . .*

"It's like the terror wars," said Phuong. "You think it's
never going to happen, then it's all over the news. Some
people can't take it."

"Didn't anyone see them arrive?" I said. "Surely NASA
has some probes out there?" If no one registered the
Invidi approach, it would support my theory that they had
some sort of field dissipation device, presumably in Murdoch's ship and probably built into *Calypso II*'s engines as
well.

"What does it matter?" Grace spread her arms, nearly
tipping beer into Phuong's lap. "They're here. Shit, they're
really here."

The screen changed to a collage of images accompanied by a voice-over. Different Invidi ships had appeared in evening, daytime, and morning skies over different cities.

. . . showed no hostile action. At present they seem to be waiting for our reply. A spokesman for the Eastern States said they are awaiting a go-ahead from the U.N. Security Council . . .

"Why can't I get Channel Five?" Grace asked me.

"It's broken. I told you weeks ago."

"Shit." She fiddled with the controls, but the channel stayed the same.

. . . and the Pentagon says their experts are still considering the evidence.

Eric burped. "They don't believe it either. I reckon it's some publicity stunt."

"They acted pretty quickly to jam communications, then," I said sourly.

"And what would they publicize?" said Phuong. "It's gone too far for that."

The screen cycled rapidly through reports in search of fresh news. I wanted to look at some of the aerospace and astronomy reports, but Grace kept flicking between the two channels we could receive.

"They want to take over completely," said Eric. He'd been giving the matter some thought. "I reckon they'll declare a state of emergency and crack down on the unions . . ."

Murdoch stared at me and I shrugged. Eric never knew quite who "they" might be, but he had definite and often conflicting views on what "they" would do in any situation.

"Tell you what." Phuong grinned. "They'll have to change the immigration laws now. 'Illegal alien' will take on a whole new meaning."

They all chuckled. I jiggled my feet and wondered where I'd get a shortwave radio at such a time. No money to buy one—I still owed people for the laser. A trip to the dump might produce one, but how to fix it? My tools had been taken from the Assembly office.

. . . amateur astronomers informed this site that . . .

"Hang on." I shot forward and stopped Grace's hand on the controls.

. . . at two twenty-five eastern standard time. This larger mass is in a geosynchronous orbit at twenty kilometers and appears to be of a different configuration to the smaller ships.

So they'd found the main vessel.

I'd have to keep watching to find out the coordinates of the ships' first appearance. Since I knew where the jump point from Earth to Central had always opened, this information would confirm whether or not the Invidi came from Central.

NASA believes information from their deep-space probes may have been blocked. It is now available.

They all looked at each other, the beginnings of real fear in their eyes.

"D'you think we should get out?" said Phuong softly.

Silence for a moment. Then Eric laughed. "Where to?"

"They said they came in peace," said Grace dubiously. "Besides"—she took a swig—"if they are a threat, there's fuck-all any of us can do about it. But I reckon Eric's got a point too. If we're not careful, the government'll use this as an excuse to crack down on us."

"Why?" said Murdoch, genuinely curious.

"I dunno." Grace looked embarrassed. "Keeping their act clean in front of the aliens, that kind of thing. Making sure we don't complain to them about what shits the government are."

"Maybe it'll force the government to give the out-towns better services, to prove to the aliens they are humane. Or they might be so busy with the aliens they'll leave us alone," said Murdoch.

The others guffawed good-naturedly. "Better services, sure," sniffed Grace.

Phuong wriggled into a more comfortable position. "All over the world people will be doing this. Watching and wondering what's going to happen."

I thought of my great-grandmother in her village. "You mean the fifteen percent of the world who can afford vidscreens."

I left them for the illusory peace of the street outside. Come to think of it, my great-grandmother had always seemed quite calm about the Invidi arrival—perhaps she didn't find out until later. Something to be said for living in the country.

"What's eating her . . ." Phuong's voice faded.

The house emptied and filled throughout the night with neighbors, Grace's ex-workmates, Will's friends, and finally some distant relatives of Grace's who had trekked from a different out-town. Some believed the aliens were real, some didn't, but they talked, ate, drank, slept in front of the vidscreen, woke, and talked again. Levin came back with a group of men and they spent hours talking in the inside room. Murdoch went to sleep on the floor next to four small children. I sat and nursed a headache through news reports and a thousand eager speculations about whether the aliens were real or a hoax, what they might look like, and what they wanted. A hundred years later we still haven't figured out that last one.

Some of the news reports grew increasingly hysterical. Army reserves were called out. The air force flew patrols beside no-fly zones around the Invidi ships. Presidents of at least four nation-states assured their populaces that their defense networks were intact. The head of state here appealed for calm and exhorted everyone to stay at home and not to stockpile goods. It hardly applied to the out-town. What goods? And where could we go?

Before dawn, I walked around the back of the house and out into the street. It was still full of people. Nobody wanted to go inside, to shut themselves off from the reassurance of other people, the reassurance that we, at least, had not changed.

In the small circle of light outside the house opposite, several dark figures pointed upward. A tiny point of coruscating color hovered in the murky glow above the city. It must be the Invidi ship, higher than it had been during the day and lit so as to be visible to human eyes. Obliging of them. The display should convert many of those who still thought it was a hoax.

A chorus of excited voices rose inside the house. A scrum of Grace's relatives burst out and left, waving.

"What now?" I asked Grace, who emerged last.

She yawned. "They're going to land."

"Here?" I looked up stupidly, half expecting to see the green glow of Invidi levitation fields above my head.

"Yeah, 'coz the U.N.'s here and all. I reckon it'll be the biggest party since the millennium."

"When?"

"Day after tomorrow, they said." She put her arm around my shoulders, and after a moment, I slipped mine around her waist. We stood and watched the one bright point in the starless sky.

"It's like someone dying," she said finally. "Pulls you out of yourself. Things you thought was important aren't anymore."

A bereavement—the death of humanity's loneliness. Of its independence, some would say.

"This morning seems a long time ago," I said.

"I'm glad we went on the march. It was sort of like farewell to everything up to today."

I nodded.

The sky far beyond the city was lightening, and my spirits lightened with it. The Invidi were here. We'd survived so far, and somehow, we'd be able to contact them.

"Or a new beginning," said Grace. "What's it going to be like for Will's generation now?"

I squeezed Grace's waist and turned to go back inside. "We'd better get some rest."

"Sleep?" She laughed. "S'pose we should. Seems weird."

"We'll probably find everything's pretty much the same tomorrow."

"Dunno if that's a good thing or not."

I couldn't afford for everything to stay the same. The Invidi were here, and I had to ask them how to get home. Tomorrow I would look for a shortwave radio, and when I found one, set it up to send a signal. Somehow I'd have to differentiate the signal from all the other noise the Invidi would be getting from Earth. The day after that, we'd go and watch them land. Even if we couldn't get near them at first, surely we'd get some clue as to how to go about it.

On Jocasta time was passing too. In twenty-nine days the neutrality vote would be passed and we'd see if the Confederacy trusted one of their "out-towns" to look after itself. I had to get back by then.

Thirteen

"We should've stayed at home and watched it on televid," said the man next to me. He wiped sweat off his upper lip with a disintegrating tissue and glanced at my feet as if debating whether to throw the tissue there. "You can see more."

"It's not some football game," said his companion. "This is history." He took the last cold beer from his cooler, replaced the lid, and folded his chair, ready.

Murdoch and I were part of a crowd that had come to see the Invidi land, spread for hundreds of meters along the beach that looked across Botany Bay to the airport. I was glad of the break, as I'd spent the previous day and night trying to modify a couple of old radios we found out back of the local electronics shop. With no success. I couldn't narrow the signal enough. The only reply I got was from a curious gentleman speaking what sounded like a Central Asian language. We were both frustrated to learn that the other wasn't the Invidi.

From the beach we could see, with the aid of binoculars, the huge expanse of the north-south runway and the cluster of airport buildings behind it. This was blocked off from the public with rolls of wire, troops, and vehicles, including a heavy armored vehicle with treads that Murdoch called a "tank."

The Invidi would land on the east-west runway, which stuck out into the bay like a long finger. From the point of view of the authorities, this runway was easy to cordon off and keep under surveillance. From our point of view, it was easy to see from the beach. The opposite bank of the bay would be even better, but it was closed off to the public, as were most of the roads leading into Mascot, Rosebery, and Sydenham, suburbs around the airport. We'd have needed a pass to go by bus or train into those areas anyway.

Instead, we'd taken a bus south to Hurstville, trekked through Rockdale, and walked all the way up the beach at Brighton-le-Sands until we couldn't go any farther due to the press of the crowd and also the police checkpoint on this side of Endeavor Bridge. The army held the other side of the bridge and the control tower.

Grace wouldn't come. She wouldn't let us bring Will, either, despite his pleading. Perhaps she still thought it was a hoax, or was worried that the aliens might come and scoop us all up.

She was not alone. Many people were panicking. Even in the out-towns, many shacks had been vacated in the past few days. The rich didn't need to run—they felt safe in their protected retreats in the north and on the coast. The poor couldn't run. Those in the middle wavered, not wanting to leave their hard-earned possessions but terrified of the unknown if they stayed. As this was a Sunday, many of them had decided to at least get away from Sydney for the day. Just in case. Roads and trains out of the city were packed.

The Invidi would land on the runway, where they'd be met by a select party of biologists, astronomers, and other specialists deemed suitably impressive but expendable in case anything went wrong. The major political leaders were keeping well back until their security services approved. Major religious leaders were being equally cautious.

"The welcomers will be from around here," said Murdoch.

I must have looked puzzled, because he explained. "You know, representatives of the original owners of the land. Have to say nice to meet you, welcome to the harbor, our place is yours. That sort of thing."

"Oh."

"The Invidi, if they've got any nous at all, will say thanks, pay their respects to the custodians of the land. You don't do this sort of thing at your place?"

"Not in Las Mujeres, no. We never had many guests."

There was no public access to the landing site itself. Despite well-advertised complaints, media reporters were confined to carefully escorted groups right back in the terminal buildings. Those who felt cramped by this drove up and down the foreshore roads, or rode in helicopters around the no-fly zone. They complained, too, because their satellites could not cut through the electronic interference. The authorities would allow only a few press representatives at the actual landing.

We were close to another large group that milled around the bridge on this side. It was hard to see where the ordinary crowd ended and they began, but they seemed to be a curious mixture of inner-city types dressed in sleek grays and outer-suburb workers of both sexes. They yelled at the soldiers on duty at the gate and waved placards at the press. The signs pleaded for their carriers to be allowed to meet the aliens. One sign said WE ARE THE CHOSEN. I wondered if they had any chance of being let in.

Murdoch saw me staring at them. "Nope." He kept his voice low. "You'd need a foolproof ID and a reason to go in there. Unless you can prove you're an expert in alien physiology . . . ?"

I could make an attempt at it—we knew more about actual alien physiology than anyone else on Earth at the moment. But I'd have to explain from where I arrived, why I didn't have an ID, and how I got the knowledge, or at least give a plausible reason for being unknown to the rest of the scientific community. I spent a few minutes imagining Murdoch masquerading as an eccentric biologist, then returned to craning over the heads of those in front of me. More waiting.

"They haven't absorbed it yet." Murdoch leaned back and lowered the lenses. "It takes a while to sink in. Then the trouble starts. People realize the implications. Remember the riots in Europe and North America? They had whole towns denying alien existence for decades."

"I know. Is it time yet?" The landing was due at noon and we'd arrived early to make sure of a place. Some people had camped here overnight. Murdoch and I had taken turns through the morning to sit on the sand and doze. I was sunburnt, even with a hat on, and red-eyed from staring at the bright waves.

The man on our other side yawned with an irritating yelp. He'd been doing it all morning. "I don't think they'll come," he said. "It's a hoax."

"It's only five to twelve," Murdoch said to me, after glancing at his neighbor's wrist timer.

The woman beside me bumped her broad bottom on my hip as she turned to speak to someone behind her. The brim of her sunhat scraped the top of my head yet again.

"Have a biscuit, luv?" She offered me a gingernut from the box passed along to her.

"No thanks." I leaned away from the hat.

She began to munch.

Somehow I'd expected the first historic meeting between human and Invidi to be more . . . momentous.

"Maybe they'll be late," said another voice. A couple of people laughed behind us.

I shook my head. Invidi were never late. Or early.

"I remember the Olympics," someone said. "Squeezed in like this."

"Yeah, the rich bastards got the best seats then, too."

We all laughed. Then silence. Murdoch's neighbor spoke again.

"We're gonna look pretty stupid if it is a hoax."

A media copter burred too close overhead and everybody covered their faces from blown sand. A couple of pithy comments whirled away in its slipstream and my neighbor waved.

"We'll be all over the world," she said, and waved again, but the copter had veered up and away to focus on the Invidi ship as it descended with little ceremony and less noise onto the runway.

The ship was a typical single-pilot barque, bigger than the little yacht our resident Invidi on Jocasta maintained, but smaller than the chemically powered shuttles humans used in this time. It hovered, reflecting green off the concrete, then settled with a sigh that actually came from the throats around us.

The glow around the vessel's base dimmed, and without further ado the hatch opened.

I leaned closer to Murdoch. "They haven't got much style, have they?"

"Nope," he said, also low enough for our neighbors not to hear. "K'Cher would've razed the landing zone and given us some fireworks."

"Mind you, K'Cher wouldn't care who was underneath the thrusters."

"True."

I looked around—all the faces showed such wonder.

Some recoiled in disgust or horror, but most were lost in contemplation of the incredible.

"It's true, it's really true." Tears streamed down the biscuit woman's face.

Behind us someone prayed. "Lord, thank you for letting me live to see this."

I felt so alone. Everything changes now, I wanted to scream at them. It will never be the same again.

But in that moment, when three Invidi rolled down onto the runway under a bright sky, nobody was thinking of the future. The present held enough wonder.

We threaded our way back among the groups of people who still lined the sand. Nothing had happened after the short welcome ceremony. Two Invidi trundled off to a large tent set up near the barrier that divided the east-west runway from the rest of the airport. According to the televid programs, that tent was where the initial talks would occur. We assumed the authorities were worried about disease or perhaps that the Invidi might do something drastic if let inside a real building. In any case, there didn't seem much more happening today, so Murdoch and I agreed to head home.

"So that's how it happened," said Murdoch. "I always wondered what it was really like."

I nodded. For a brief moment the Invidi had seemed unfamiliar, as if seen through my ancestors' eyes. Tall, thick, irregular shapes in silvery suits that draped, skirtlike, to the ground so that we couldn't see how they moved so smoothly in any direction. No distinct head, no features. Long, prehensile appendages in protective silver coils.

"We could go by boat." I noticed the sails far out in the bay for the first time. "It's not far across that channel."

Murdoch shook his head and pointed to the sleek shapes of Customs ships dotted around the bay. "Plus they've probably got the whole perimeter wired. And see those poles on the fence?"

"The thin ones?"

"Yeah. Those probably have visual pickups, with infrared for night vision. Pretty primitive, but good enough to keep us out."

"Bloody hell."

A young couple beside us drew back a little and eyed me worriedly.

Murdoch edged closer to me so there was no chance of us being overheard. "Let's think what we're going to say to them."

I didn't bother dropping my voice. It didn't matter if I was overheard—there were plenty of UFO-lovers around today. "We'll say to An Serat, you made sure we'd get here and now we want to go home. We'd like help with repairing our ship and getting it back through the jump point." I rubbed the Seouras implant in my neck impatiently. "Get me in there to talk to them, Bill. We've only got twenty-seven days until the neutrality vote goes through."

"I've been thinking. If we make it back to our time, what are you going to do?" he said.

"We will make it back. We don't belong here."

"Then we need to work out a way to keep you a free agent when we do," said Murdoch. He held my arm as I skidded down the side of the dry-grassed verge and onto the hard black of the road. "As soon as you enter Abelar space, EarthFleet Security is going to hold you for questioning about *Calypso II*. And I guess ConFleet will be waiting to find out where you've been without leave for five months."

A young woman looked at him curiously from under a wide-brimmed straw hat, and he waited until she shuffled forward out of earshot.

"Unless I've arrested you already," he said slowly.

"What?"

"I can say I got a tip-off about where you'd gone. Brought you back for questioning. If you're in my custody, they can't drag you off until we've processed the first . . ."

A series of strident whoops from behind made us both jump. The noise was projected from a slow-moving groundcar, its red, shiny surface visible through gaps in the crowd. We tried to climb the half meter onto the verge from the surfaced road but the verge was crowded too, so we were forced back into single file along the shallow runoff ditch. As the alarm grew closer and louder it was accompanied by the low hum of an electric engine and by cries of surprise and pain from the crowd. The sleek, bullet-nosed shape crept forward and people fell back on either side. Its windows were pearly and opaque—impossible to see who was inside.

Murdoch shoved open a space on the verge, then reached over to pull me up beside him. The groundcar was about a meter away. I felt a strange sensation as though a giant hand had swatted me to one side, followed by a sharp pain that disappeared as swiftly as it came.

"Shit." Murdoch shook his hand that had held mine. "What was that?" He looked down at me and I realized I was sitting on hard, dry grass. Around us, people cursed and picked themselves off the road. The back of the groundcar disappeared slowly into the crowd. As we watched, it rose slowly on its maglev boosters and soared away, as if in relief at leaving the crawling ground life behind.

I shook my head, throat constricted. My body tingled all over.

"Theft-prevention device," said a burly man next to us. He pulled the brim of his cap down firmly. "They're not allowed to use them in pedestrian areas, but shit, who's going to stop them?"

"They" must be people important or affluent enough to have watched the landing from one of the unoccupied buildings in the airports.

Murdoch pulled me upright and brushed off the dust with abrupt, angry movements. "You all right?"

"A bit numb. Must be a static charge. Wonder how they insulate . . ."

Farther back in the crowd, a woman's voice wailed high and desperate. Another voice shouted for an ambulance.

"Heart attack, probably," the man in the cap said, and walked on.

We hesitated. Murdoch turned and pushed back against the flow. I started to follow but was stopped by a wave of nausea. Bloody hell. The crowd was moving again and I didn't dare sit down for fear of being trampled. Nowhere to lean—the closest fence was over to the right beyond a wide ditch. I stood there, sick and indecisive, until Murdoch returned a few minutes later.

He shook his head in answer to my unspoken question and we walked in silence for a while. At last a copter with a red cross flew overhead and landed back at the scene of the tragedy.

Murdoch sighed and rubbed his eyes with his sleeve.

"Don't think they'll be any use. Bloke in his eighties or so. That's a good age for this century, isn't it?"

I nodded.

"Yeah, thought so." He said nothing more and I thought he'd finished, then he spoke quickly, without looking at me. "Every time something like this happens I get sick to the stomach. Shouldn't be this way."

"Something like this?"

"People with power not using it properly. Innocent people getting hurt." He risked a glance at me. "It pisses me off."

Back on the station he had always been scrupulously

fair in his dealings with both residents from the Four Worlds, those from the Nine, and the many species of refugees. I remembered now that he had originally been sent to Jocasta because he was unpopular at his previous post for accusing fellow officers of accepting bribes. The station manager, Veatch, himself one of the Four, had always found it impossible to persuade Murdoch that the K'Cher and Melot residents deserved special security privileges.

"We got it at home too," he said, echoing my thoughts. "But in this time it's worse."

We walked for nearly an hour before finding a bus with standing room, a bus that headed away from the harbor, away from the future and back to the out-town.

Fourteen

A week later, already 7 May, and we were still sleeping at Levin's house, no closer to talking to the Invidi than on the day they arrived.

U.N. troops and army squads kept the public at bay. There were more media people than before, if that was possible, and the whole area was still a shambles. The government made cautiously optimistic announcements, which included phrases such as "meaningful dialogue" and "considering the unprecedented nature of the situation." They were only human, after all, and must be as confused as everyone else.

As the days passed and the Invidi threatened nobody, the number of visitors to their "embassies" grew, until there was a constant twenty-four-hour stream. The heads of state of this region all had their turn, and now all of the U.N. organizations were forming delegations. Large multicorps were already sending researchers in with government scientists and academics. "They wanter see what they can sell the aliens," joked Eric one night. "Good thing it wasn't the K'Cher that got here first," muttered Murdoch. I agreed. Earth's future defined by an alliance between human capitalism and the K'Cher was an unpleasant thought.

The Invidi had spread their landing vessels impartially between rich and poor nations, north and south. In some places, the public had already been granted limited access. Not here, though. I seemed to remember from the history files that restriction of access to the Invidi and their technology had been one of the main reasons for the fall, in the 2030s, of many of the entrenched governments and the systems that supported them. People didn't see why everyone should not share the bounties that the Invidi offered so freely. Blockers of addictive drugs, for example, or virus neutralizers. When the huge drug companies that had always monopolized new medicines attempted to do the same with the Invidi gifts, there was widespread outrage.

Maybe restriction of jump-drive technology in the future would prove the downfall of restrictive Confederacy governments also. The longer they kept the Nine Worlds out of the secret, the greater the resentment and anger would grow. I could feel it growing in myself, every time I thought about time passing on Jocasta. Twenty two days from now, the Confederacy Council, representatives of all thirteen member species, would vote to pass or refuse our request for neutrality. I wanted to be there, considering I'd made the initial request.

Such a wondrous thing, the jump points—on Jocasta we could share time with places so far away that the human mind cannot comprehend the distance. We were lucky to be on the jump network. Nobody knew why the Invidi didn't increase the number of points. Some speculation had it that our contemporary Invidi cannot create new jump points anymore, and that the network is merely a technological legacy from past ages. But that didn't make sense, because the latest addition to the Confederacy was the Neronderon, who joined only five years ago. Which led to another question that had never been satisfactorily answered—how do the Invidi know at which point in a species' history to open a jump point? What if they'd made a mistake and appeared in Earth's Middle Ages? I didn't like the idea that the privilege of being part of the jump network might depend on an arbitrary Invidi decision. Playing God, that's what it was.

So where did that leave us? Seeing it was likely we'd brought the Invidi here when the jump point from Jocasta opened. And how did An Serat send *Calypso* to Jocasta? Through jump points not on the network, obviously, but this was the first time it had happened. Nobody suspected jump points could exist off the network. If the Invidi could create jump points at will, why hadn't they done it before? And why did the jump point have a ninety-five-year correspondence when *Calypso* traveled to Jocasta, but ninety-nine years when *Calypso II* and Murdoch's ship traveled to Earth?

Too many questions. Why do I get the feeling I'm never going to get any answers?

Four days after the landing proper we had gone to see the site again, hoping for inspiration. The expedition had involved leaving before dawn to catch the early bus, and much walking up and down the beach, from which we could see the east-west runway.

Those four days I had fiddled with scavenged and borrowed radios in attempts to send a message to the Invidi, with no result. I'd taken Murdoch's locator to pieces with inadequate tools and given myself severe eyestrain in the hope of being able to use its components to boost the signal somehow. And we'd brainstormed ways to quickly earn large quantities of money in order to buy at least one of us an ID. All of the methods were illegal, and all of them carried too much risk of arrest to be worth trying.

The Invidi "embassy" sat on the runway behind two fences drawn across the tarmac from north to south. The fences were separated by three or four meters and stood about three meters high. Electric current ran through both, and they had jagged wire on the top. Small boxes at intervals were probably visual surveillance pickups. A similar fence had been set around the perimeter of the east-west runway, although it was lower. Hastily erected guardhouses and offices stood on the terminal side of the fence.

Murdoch pointed out to me the snipers on the roofs of the main tarmac buildings, the missile launch trucks at points around the perimeter, and the long, low warships in the bay beyond the runway. His considered opinion was that we didn't have a hope in hell of getting in by any route but the gate. "They've tightened up security," he said. "That first day, nobody knew what was going on. Now they're sure who they want in there and who they don't."

I sat down on the sand with a thud. There were plenty of other watchers, some of them obviously locals; others had come with beach umbrellas and food to make a day of it. Four or five boys about Will's age rumbled up and down the footpath on skateboards.

"What do you suggest?"

He sat beside me, knee joints cracking. "Anything but trying to sneak past those perimeters. I'm too old to even think about it."

"We could think simple," I said. "Walk up to the gate. Say we have to see An Serat, that we've got a message from the future and we can prove it."

Murdoch looked at me pityingly. "You've seen some of those alien hunters on televid, haven't you? No security officer with half a mind is going to let you in."

I drew concentric circles in the sand with a twig until they all overlapped. "I never thought we'd get stuck at this point."

"Nor me."

His voice was tired, but sympathetic. He was staring out past the runway with eyes narrowed against the glare, arms gathered loosely around his knees. We hadn't spoken about either our interrupted kiss on the night of the fire or my unintended come-on in the street on the day of the Invidi arrival. Since then we'd hardly been alone together, anyway, and when we were, we talked about the Invidi. We were too absorbed in getting past this problem.

He'd responded, of that I was sure. And so had Henoit. I didn't want to feel Henoit instead of Murdoch. At the moment I didn't want to feel either of them.

I'd taken my ovulation suppressants regularly on the station, but always on a two-hundred-day course. I wasn't sure when my last dose was, things having been a little confused on the station before I left. The obvious result had occurred and I was feeling lousy. It was a sobering thought, that if we got stuck in this time I'd have to go through this once a month for another ten years or so. My female ancestors were tougher than I knew.

I started drawing lines with the twigs. This line for *Calypso*. This one for *Calypso II*. Linear thinking, that was our problem. We had to stop it.

Neither of us said much on the bus trip back to the outtown. Grace and Levin weren't home and we collapsed gratefully on the sofa. Soon Will would be home from school.

Scraps of wire, soldering irons, pieces of solder, and smears of flux lay on Grace's kitchen table. I'd borrowed the tools from Le's electronics shop for the purpose of fixing Eric's shortwave radio. The Invidi arrival had stimulated a revival of interest in this hobby and I could see why. Far more interesting to try to tune in to alien communications than be spoon-fed telnet reports of whatever the authorities wanted you to hear. The radio gave me a lot of trouble—one of those times I laughed at my assumption that because I could fine-tune twenty-second-century technology, I could do the same for that from the twentieth.

"You going to tidy that up?" Murdoch poured us both a drink of water. "Wasn't successful, eh?"

"I need a bit more time," I said shortly, sweeping the locator into a cardboard box with the radio tools.

Murdoch sighed. "Maybe you're right. We should just walk up and say we need to talk. We could use your implant as proof we're telling the truth."

I couldn't tell if he was serious or not. "It might still take weeks for them to test and process us. If they don't detain us first."

"And you say we don't even know if we can get back to our own time? That the jump point correspondence might have altered?" He blew out in the same frustration that twisted my stomach.

I dropped the box heavily on the floor beside the tele-vid and kicked it in beside the wall. "I want to talk to them *now*."

"I didn't know you were a VIP," said a mocking voice. I spun around.

Levin slouched in the doorway. "Why should the benevolent and all-powerful, wonderful aliens want to speak to you?"

"None of your business."

"It'll take you a lifetime. You know there's a waiting list of years even for scientists? How is your meeting the aliens going to benefit humanity?"

More than you can ever guess, I wanted to say.

"Grace and I will be going out tonight," Levin said. He padded across the room and peered into the refrigerator. Wrinkled his nose at its emptiness. "Buy some beer for when we get back, will you?" He pulled a handful of coins and small-denomination notes from his pocket and left the pile on the bench.

"Who do you think you are?" I said under my breath.

Murdoch watched, arms folded, from the other side of the room.

I wanted to ask Levin about the fire, as I'd wanted to ask him for days now. When he came back the day after the Invidi arrived, he'd said merely, "What a pity about the office." But I couldn't exactly say, *tell me if you helped the gangs riot and told them where to find the telescope.* Not when we were staying in his house.

"And a couple for yourself, if you like." He left, humming.

As the front door slammed I turned to Murdoch. "Bill, I think it's time we got rid of my backup transponder."

He stared at me. "Why can't you leave it in?"

"Because we might need to get into a place with security detectors in a hurry."

"Are you planning something?" he said suspiciously.

"No, but I think we should be prepared." I had nothing particular in mind. Only that I couldn't sit here thinking about the Invidi without doing something.

I pulled Grace's medkit from the top cupboard, dusted off cobwebs, and carried it over to the table.

"You mean, cut it out?" Murdoch stared askance at the small, flat blade I proffered. "I thought it was easy to remove."

"It would be if we were at home." Twenty-second-century medical technology could suck the transponder out through my skin or simply dissolve it in there. "The other one was below the right shoulder blade."

"I can't cut every bump on your skin," he protested.

I placed a bottle of disinfectant and a piece of clean rag next to the medkit, sat cross-legged, and drew my shirt up under my arms, trying to keep the front of it covering my breasts. My left hand found the fine, raised line of scar tissue where Grace had taken out the first transponder. My fingers felt cold. "That's where the first one was. Where do you think they'd put a backup?"

"On the other side?" Murdoch's warmer fingers traced around my shoulder blade.

I wriggled. "That tickles. You can press a bit harder, you know."

"That okay?"

"Mmm. Kind of like a massage."

"We could do that, too." His voice wasn't quite joking.

I wondered what his hands would feel like on the rest of my back.

"Is that it?" he said.

I shook myself mentally, then reached up with my right hand and found a tiny bump, no more than five millimeters long. "That's what the other one felt like."

Something moved in the corner of my vision and unease shivered my skin. I turned sharply.

"Hey, careful," protested Murdoch.

Levin stood in the doorway. When he knew I'd seen him, he stepped inside. "What are you two up to? I come back to get my keys and what do I find?"

I yanked down my shirt. "Nothing to do with you."

He swaggered past the table, pausing to run his finger over the medkit lid. "Well? You aren't the type for tattoos, Maria."

I glanced back at Murdoch. He shrugged, the blade ready.

"It's a . . . microchip under my skin. We're trying to take it out."

"A microchip?" Levin raised his eyebrows. "Never heard of them doing that to humans."

"I was in jail," I improvised wildly. "In South America. I told you I got away, didn't I? They do it to all their political prisoners."

"What did you do that made you a political prisoner?" said Levin.

"I formed an alliance with enemies of the state," I snapped, thinking of the Abelar Treaty.

Murdoch smiled. "Don't let us keep you."

Levin turned on his heel.

I faced the other way again. Murdoch pushed my shirt up and the tips of his fingers felt for the point under my shoulder blade.

Levin's footsteps had stopped. I glanced over my shoulder but Murdoch growled, "Keep still." He leaned forward and said in a lower voice, "He'll go if we ignore him."

But I didn't like the idea of Levin watching.

The disinfectant left a cold spot. A small, sharp pain overlaid the cold, followed by a warm trail that tickled down my back. A slight pressure.

"Got it," said Murdoch.

A floorboard creaked. Maybe Levin hadn't gone.

An opaque curtain seemed to fall over the room. I could see behind myself. A great dark shadow loomed there with something deadly in its grasp. For a fraction of a second I saw again the Q'Chn as it terrorized the throughways of Jocasta, a shimmering-winged killing machine. Blood spurting from a headless torso. Deck slippery underfoot in the dark. Screams. Henoit's voice in my ear. *Look out.*

I scrambled down and away from the table, stumbling in my panic to get away. Turned to face the thing behind me.

Levin stood beside Murdoch, craning over his shoulder at something on Murdoch's bloody finger.

They both stared at me.

"What's wrong?" said Murdoch.

"N . . . nothing." I was breathing hard.

"Turn around, then." He lifted the swab in his other hand.

I half turned, so I could keep an eye on Levin. Something cold wiped the tickle away with the sting of disin-

have weapons more powerful than the government will admit.

But, Professor, these aliens have traveled faster than light to get here. What could we possibly use against them?

Bond leaned forward farther, eyes shining. *The essence of the universe itself. Nothing can withstand the annihilation of matter.*

Aren't you worried the aliens might overhear us? The interviewer was definitely tongue-in-cheek by now.

They don't think we can be a threat. He nodded confidently. *That's their weakness.*

Murdoch folded his arms in the doorway. "This bloke's a few crumbs short of a full biscuit, isn't he? What's he talking about, nuclear fission?"

Grace placed a bowl of refried veg-and-egg in front of Levin. "Put your knees down, Will."

"Why?"

I shrugged at Murdoch. "Maybe something more exotic. Fusion."

"He'll have to tell us."

Antimatter. Bond sat back in his chair, having delivered his bombshell, so to speak. The interviewer made admiring noises and a background voice explained the concept of energy freed by the collision of matter and antimatter, assisted by a simplistic screen representation.

"If you're eating, Bill McGrath, you can make yer own," said Grace, sitting beside Levin and heaping egg on her toast. "Will, knees."

"Knees what, Mum?"

"I'll have Maria's." Murdoch squeezed next to me and broke my piece of overcooked toast in half.

Levin curled his lip at the screen. "That is ridiculous. No army could ever use antimatter weapons."

"There isn't enough antimatter accessible anyway," I said.

"What do you mean by 'accessible'?" said Murdoch through a mouthful of toast.

"Containment. I mean, it's been done, but none of their methods are portable."

"It would be a perfect terrorist's weapon," said Levin almost dreamily. "You would need only an atom, I suppose. And poof! annihilate oneself and one's enemy with perfect finality."

Grace, driven to distraction, snatched Will's bowl away and snapped at him to get ready for school. Levin disappeared behind his paper again.

"G'day." Vince poked his head cautiously around the back door. A young mustache clung to his upper lip, making him look scruffier than ever.

"What do you want?" said Grace, not taking her eyes off the vidscreen.

"G'day," said Murdoch.

Will jumped up and went to punch and whisper with Vince in the corner.

Peep-peep. Levin's phone.

"You get it," he said from behind the paper.

Grace put down her bowl and spoon and stood up slowly. "Wonder who that is."

She tapped in the vidscreen connection. The news broadcast faded, to be replaced by a plump man in a white suit. Vertical lines of worry between his eyes eased as his screen gave him a view of Grace.

"Good evening," he said. "May I speak to Mr. William Chenin?"

We all looked at Will. What had he done now?

"I'm his mother," Grace said.

"Ah. You are Ms. Maria Valdon?"

"No." Grace frowned over her shoulder at me, then back at the screen. "Who are you and what do you want?"

"I beg your pardon." He inclined his head. "I have to make sure I am speaking to the right person."

"I'm Valdon," I said, and pushed back my chair to stand too. "Will is here."

"Me." Will came closer and waved.

"My name is Matthews," said the man. "I am an employee of the aerospace development company, Suntel. It is my very great pleasure to inform you that the design submitted by Mr. Chenin and Ms. Valdon has won our spacecraft design competition."

We all jumped as Will let out a shriek of delight and knocked half the things off the table onto the floor.

"We won! Hey, Maria, we won!"

"I know this is a little sudden," continued Matthews, "but we'd like you to come and talk to us about your design."

"And the prize?" I said, watching Grace from the corner of my eye.

"The twenty thousand dollars will be forwarded to the financial institution you specify. Mr. Chenin is a minor, so there will of course be limitations in his case."

"Limitations?" said Will.

"Twenty thousand?" said Vince at the same time.

"Shush," said Grace. "Mr. um . . . "

"Matthews."

"Matthews. This is a bit of a shock. I'd like to discuss it with my son." *And you,* her glance at me said. "Can you call again in an hour or so?"

Matthews beamed, but the lines were back between his eyes. "No problem, Ms., um, Chenin. I'd like to add that as a special, additional prize, we have managed to secure a place for our winner to join in the first UNESCO delegation to visit the aliens."

My hands balled into fists of triumph and I wanted to

yell like Will. When I glanced at Murdoch he was grinning and shaking his head in disbelief.

"I don't know about that," said Grace. "We'll talk again soon." She reached out to cut the connection and Matthews's smiling face faded. "Okay, you two. What's going on?"

Grace didn't like it and I couldn't understand why. Will had participated as much as I in the actual design work. More, in fact, because once he understood the basic principles involved, I let him have a free hand, and the resulting design had all a child's extraordinary flair while at the same time being aerodynamically sound. It would have caught *my* eye. In the engine I'd hinted at a way of achieving many times the payload with only a few modifications to a propulsion system I knew they were already developing, thus promising immediate economies.

But Grace demanded to know why we hadn't told her, why we wasted time playing with graphics when Will should have been studying, had we ever intended telling her?

"I knew we'd win," gloated Will.

"The thing that upsets me was you didn't tell me," Grace repeated.

Vince muttered something about volunteering to use the money, and she rounded on him.

"I know you'd use it. You take anything that's not bolted down. Will's not like you. He's going to amount to something."

Vince glowered. "Fuck you, too. It's your fault I'm like this."

Grace grabbed a glass and drew back her hand but Murdoch caught her wrist in time.

"Get out, then," she yelled.

"I'm going, I'm going," Vince yelled back. "Not as if there's any reason for me to come here, is there?" He swept the remaining items off the table on his way out.

Levin merely pushed his chair back against the wall and watched.

Will burst into tears. "I thought you'd be happy . . ." The rest was drowned in his usual piercing cries.

"Ah, shit," said Grace. "Don't bloody scream, Will." She jerked her wrist away from Murdoch. He started to say something but she interrupted.

"You should understand." She had to yell at him over Will's crying.

Frustration dragged at me. "Understand what?" And then, because I couldn't help it, "Shut *up*, Will."

He stopped, astonished that I'd snapped at him, then began afresh, with a new note of desperation. I groaned.

"He's gotta study and work hard," she said. "Not sit around living off money we didn't earn. You must have worked hard to learn all that stuff," said Grace. We had to stand nose to nose to hear each other. Murdoch tried to calm Will.

"Vince never learned that," she said. "That's his problem." She paused for breath and looked at Will, who was snuffling in the loose circle of Murdoch's arms.

"Will, I'm proud of you. This is pretty smart."

"You take his money," said Will, pointing at Levin. "How's that different?"

Grace flushed dark red. "That's more like a loan. Till I get another job."

"What about me?" said Will thickly. "You never think what I want."

"That's not true."

"What's wrong with accepting the prize?" said Murdoch. "It's what you do with money that counts."

"Grace, listen." I put my hand on her arm cautiously. "I'm sorry for offending you. I didn't mean to. Whether you accept the money and whatever else they offer is up to you and Will. But at least let him go with the delegation. It's the chance of a lifetime."

It was probably the only chance we'd get for a while, too. I felt my face redden and avoided Murdoch's eye. Will wanted to go, right?

"I'm not going." Grace folded her arms and I had to drop my hand.

I risked a glance at Murdoch. "We'll go, then."

"I thought you two didn't have IDs," said Levin. "They won't let you in."

I cursed inwardly and Will's face fell.

Levin strolled around the table and cuddled Grace in a proprietary way. She twitched, but didn't move away.

"I'll talk to a mate of mine. He can get them IDs," said Levin.

Murdoch's face reflected the astonishment I felt. It was swiftly followed by suspicion. "Why?"

"Special occasion, that's why." Levin raised his eyebrows at Murdoch. "Don't you want to go and see the aliens?"

"Yes," I said, before Murdoch could protest. "Thank you."

"Thanks, Levin," snuffled Will. Grace held out her arms and he rushed into them. Levin stepped back in distaste and kept going down the hall.

I turned to follow him but Murdoch grasped my arm first. "We need to check you're not still setting off security alarms," he said in a low voice. "If it's the Seouras implant, no point in even trying to get through those gates."

"We'll do it first," I agreed, then hurried after Levin, who was standing inside the door on the shop side. The front shutters were down and the room dark.

"Why did you offer?" I said.

"Don't you trust me?" His voice was mocking.

I thought of Henoit's voice warning of a dark threat behind me. "Not really."

He waited.

"If you can get us IDs," I said, "why didn't you offer before?"

He tensed, then relaxed again. "Because you're up to something and I don't know what it is."

"We're not up to anything."

"We work on many levels, Maria. You will find that you can fit into one of them."

"You want me to join you?"

"There is nothing to join, no organization. We work for the same ends but we are not one."

"If I don't, will you still get us the IDs?"

He smiled with his mouth only. "If I say no, will you agree?"

"No."

"Someday you'll be glad to work for us."

I shivered, like when Henoit's voice warned me. Then I thought of a less sinister motive—if she accepted that prize money, Grace would soon be much richer. By helping Will, Levin was keeping in Grace's good humor. We were coincidental. It should have made me feel better, but it didn't.

Murdoch went out later and came home after ten. Grace and I had gone over the details of the prize—she was considering putting it in a trust for Will. We talked about going to see the Invidi with the delegation. It was to be in a week's time, at the landing site. Grace still didn't want to go. She looked tired, and went to bed a bit before Murdoch returned.

"Where have you been?" I let him in the back door.

Murdoch kicked off his sandals and slumped on the sofa

beside me. "Looking for Vince. Couldn't find him. He's not with his usual mates."

"Why are you so worried about him?"

"Dunno. He reminds me of me at that age."

"I can't imagine you were anything like that."

He stretched his legs and braced his shoulders against the sofa. "In some ways. I was slow, and it took me a while to find what I wanted to do."

A short silence, broken by the sound of Will's feet running down the hall and into Grace's room. Music drummed faintly from next door.

"Bill? Let's give Levin a chance. Maybe he can really help us."

"I don't trust the bastard. Why's he being so nice all of a sudden?"

"He probably wants Grace to accept the money so he can sponge off her for the rest of his life. Or maybe he really wants to help her and Will. She knows him better than we do, you know."

Murdoch grunted something like, "Wanna bet?"

I sighed. "So he's not trustworthy. But hopefully we'll be gone before he can prove it."

Fifteen

The morning we went to meet the Invidi was bright and dry.

We left Grace and Levin at the station where the hovercar came to meet us. Grace was less censorious than I expected. She cooked a special breakfast, made sure Will's hair was brushed and his clothes neat, and told us to behave. She even suggested a question for the Invidi—we'd all been told we could ask something. Grace's question was, "What do your people gain by coming here?"

Good question.

Levin was almost bearable. He bought Murdoch a pair of secondhand trousers, cracked a lame joke about not pushing any buttons on alien machinery, and gave Will a cap. The badge on it was an old army one, he said, and would bring Will luck.

"Have fun," he said to me.

I nodded in a friendly way, but only because he'd gotten the IDs for us. The night after he offered we'd gone with him to a photographer's studio about half an hour's drive west. There, a small, scared man called Wes had taken our photographs, scanned our fingerprints, and taken blood samples. Murdoch had been dismayed by the whole exercise. We got a bonus out of it; the studio had an advanced sensor array such as official buildings used, and as I didn't set off any alarms, we proved that my Seouras implant was not going to stop us getting through the checkpoint into the airport.

Vince arrived at Levin's just before we left and asked Will to get an Invidi autograph for him. He offered Will forty percent of the selling price in return. When Grace cuffed him, he merely growled back.

The whole street turned out to see us go, or so it seemed. People I'd never spoken to waved and called me by name, and a contingent of Will's friends trailed us to the station, chattering and cavorting.

"Nothing like keeping a low profile." Murdoch grinned.

Sunlight bounced off the harbor like applause as we flew over the airport road Murdoch and I had traveled a long week ago. The hovercar touched down closer to the runway than we'd stood then. At the bump and faint lurch of landing Will looked at me and laughed aloud. I grinned back, infected with his excitement. In the seat behind us Murdoch craned his neck in an attempt to see ahead.

The car purred toward the first set of gates. Will bounced up and down until we got out.

"Hello, I'm George DeLucca." The U.N. official at the gate was a tall, light-haired young man who shook our hands in a distracted way.

The three of us were subjected to a polite security question-and-answer; do you have any weapons on your person, any drugs, have you been in a different country in the past few days, do you carry any gifts, did you pack your own bag, and so on. A handheld sensor was passed over us, IDs and all. Nothing registered, and I breathed again.

Then we were directed to a line of ten, no, twelve ground vehicles, each containing room for four passengers. Some of the vehicles carried only children, others had an adult with them. Brown heads, black heads, blond heads—UNESCO had gathered children from all over the globe, their corporate sponsors having agreed to anything for the chance to be part of this.

We clambered into our vehicle. Faces peered at us from the others.

DeLucca smiled broadly, seemingly as much relieved to get going as we were.

"Welcome to the tour." He indicated two men in gray suits who stood waiting, one middle-aged, the other young, with long hair pulled back.

"These gentlemen will interpret for you if you need to talk to each other. You'll find we don't need interpreters to talk to the aliens. First we'll go to the Welcome Hall and meet two of our new friends. Then we'll have a short tour of the Invidi embassy on the east-west runway."

A small voice piped something from another vehicle. It was not in a language I understood, but the word "Invidi" was recognizable.

"Can we see the ships?" translated the younger man.

"You certainly may see the ships," replied DeLucca, and this was duly relayed by the interpreter to the child who'd asked the original question.

I shifted my feet impatiently. Thank goodness we had voiceboxes and efficient translators on the station—imagine negotiating with aliens like this.

The whole cavalcade trundled toward the buildings at the edge of the water. These groundcars were older than the hovercar and slower, fossil fuel burners from a more profligate age. Jeeps, Murdoch called them. But easy to repair and maintain and, he whispered, not subject to electronic interference, intentional or otherwise. The air tingled on our cheeks. The hot spell had broken at last and autumn was here.

"There they are!" called one of the children.

Two silver oblongs towered over the human figures beside them. My heart thudded in ridiculous anticipation as we drove closer. How many times have you spoken to an Invidi? I chided myself. You're one of only two people on the planet who know what they look like under those suits. Relax.

We got out of the jeep and walked the last twenty meters or so. Once again I mentally bemoaned the Invidi's lack of diplomatic skills. They could at least roll a few meters forward to greet us.

One of them surprised me by finally doing that. He crept in our direction with an almost imperceptible motion, silvery folds of the suit swaying. Will grabbed my hand and held on tightly. I squeezed back and smiled reassuringly. Another child whimpered. Murdoch reached out to pat a shoulder.

The Invidi spoke from its concealed voicebox.

"We greet you. Please join us. We will talk."

For a second I didn't understand the words. They seemed to be a jumble of Spanish, English, Earth Standard, childhood German. Then they became clear, but there was still a strange echo in my ears.

"What language did you hear?" I whispered to Murdoch.

He blinked. "English. Eventually."

The translation matrices for these Invidi voiceboxes were not as complete as the ones we were used to. No wonder, they'd only been listening to human languages for a few days.

One of the younger children stepped forward. She carried a spray of white flowers. Flimsy things, but big enough for her small hands. The man with her started to lift her up, but one of the human attendants waved him away. They didn't know where the Invidi kept their faces.

The child held out the flowers and recited her message in a clear, singsong voice.

"The children of Earth welcome you. Please be our friends."

The newsnet commentators will love this.

In a slow, slow response, the first Invidi lowered a small upper tentacle like a silver cord and touched the flowers, then the girl's hand. She stared at it, fascinated and unafraid. I remembered seeing a naked Invidi tentacle in a room on Jocasta once. Soft, it had been, and covered with tiny hairlike cilia.

The silver cord hovered.

The child looked over her shoulder at the adults, uncertain. She raised her eyes up the vast bulk, then back down to the flowers, considering. Then she reached up and pressed the stems firmly against the cord.

"You can have these. It's a present."

We waited.

The tentacle closed around the stems. "Thank you," said the Invidi.

The child smiled in delight and one of the media people clapped. A collective sigh of relief rose from the other adults.

The courage of these ancestors of mine amazed me. That they should be able to stand before the unknown and not falter. That they could accept the existence of vastly superior beings with dignity. Did the Invidi realize what it meant for humans to allow their children to come here? As far as we know, each Invidi individual is created by genetic manipulation, with the consensus of their whole society. I wondered if they could comprehend that presenting our children was the greatest gesture of trust the human world could make.

Maybe the parents of these children all believed what they were told by the authorities about the Invidi being safe; maybe some of them had been paid well. But whoever had pulled the little girl's hair tight in tiny plaits this morning must surely have wondered, even if for a moment, whether they were doing the right thing. It took courage to send a child here today.

I looked at Murdoch. He was scanning the area with his eyes, looking away from the group and back again, alert and absorbed.

"Let's go inside," suggested one of the attendants. The Invidi changed direction by simply rolling backward.

"It's An Serat," I whispered to Murdoch as we all followed the two silver figures. Four or five media people skipped around the outside of the group.

"Are you sure?" He tried to see over the heads between us. "They all look the same to me."

"The voice is the same."

He still looked doubtful.

The building was a hangar, with aircraft maintenance equipment secured on the walls and high ceiling. Rows of chairs were arranged in a half circle around a wooden dais flat on the ground. We all maneuvered for the best positions in the front seats. To Will's disgust, we ended up in the second row.

The media people arranged themselves around the walls. The meeting was to be broadcast live by satellite all over the world, although the tour afterward was restricted.

One of the senior attendants, a thin, stooped man in his fifties, stood on the dais with the two Invidi.

He smiled brightly and spoke slowly, his voice echoing in the space. "The Invidi ambassador will give us a short talk, and then you can all ask your questions."

Murdoch shifted beside me and rolled his eyes. "You'd think they could get someone who at least looks like he enjoys the job."

"Shh." Will prodded me.

The attendant stepped back off the dais, and one of the

Invidi followed him. It rolled back out the door, leaving its companion to field all questions.

"We come from far star systems," began the Invidi I thought was An Serat. "We use a travel technology which is beyond the present capability of your science to understand. We do not come to your planet with any intention other than to become your peaceful allies."

He wasn't good at this. The words were spoken flatly, with no pause to indicate he knew an audience was listening. Had the Invidi ever contacted a noninterstellar-spaceflight-capable species before? All of the other Nine Worlds species entered the Confederacy after they'd achieved a high standard of spaceflight within their home systems. Maybe the Invidi experience with humans showed them it was too much trouble to coddle a species into maturity. But there would be no Confederacy until 2065. Come to think of it, nobody seemed to know or care how the Four decided whom to contact and admit to the Confederacy after they'd formed their core group.

"Does anybody have a question for our friends?" said the senior attendant with an insincere smile. The interpreters translated. A forest of small arms shot up.

"What do you eat?"

The Invidi answered immediately. "We absorb a prepared combination of the appropriate amino acids and trace elements that our metabolisms require."

"How do you move?"

He demonstrated by rolling back, then sideways and forward. "We manipulate a tractive device on the bottom of these suits with a neural interface."

"Do you have children?"

"We do not breed using sexual reproduction." A few sniggers followed that one, mainly from boys about Will's age.

"How can you talk to us?" This question I could only follow through the interpreter.

"We build a device which deciphers the principles and structures of your languages and adapts our input to make it comprehensible to you. Therefore you will hear our reply in the language most familiar to you."

"What's your name?"

"Serat," was the eventual answer. I winked at Murdoch.

"Do you have music?"

"We have structures which fulfill some functions of your music."

"Do you sleep?"

"We experience periods of altered consciousness, but not as regularly as you do."

That was news to me. Maybe it explained why, on Jocasta, An Barik had sometimes been unavailable for weeks at a time.

"Why do you wear those suits?"

"We cannot survive without them in your atmosphere." Serat began to rock slightly as he neared the end of the questions. Impatient?

Will had thought hard about his question, refusing offers and suggestions from the rest of us. He had kept it a secret until now. It was his turn.

He stood up, face tense, one hand picking nervously at his trouser leg.

"Are you going to help all of us, not just the rich people?"

The question echoed out of proportion to his thready voice. Every whisper, every scrape of feet and sniff in the hall, ceased. I put my hand on Will's back.

"We help all of you," said An Serat, and the hangar erupted in applause.

They did help all of us. From my own time of 2122 I could look back upon nearly a century of post-Contact history and say with conviction that they kept their promise. Their medical and agricultural technology was given freely to whoever asked for it. They stood back then and allowed us to work out how to structure a world where nearly every child born could live to old age. Whatever quarrel I might have with the Invidi over the way they abandoned Jocasta, whatever doubts I might have about equality for humans within the Confederacy, I could not deny that we couldn't have repaired the Earth so quickly without them. We might not have done it at all.

"Now we will drive over to the landing area and take a brief look at the ships and the Invidi embassy." The senior attendant wiped his forehead with a folded handkerchief and eased his collar.

The children began to file out, flanked and headed by the media people, who were rearranging their cameras to get a good view of the children as they went off to see the ships.

I stood up and shoved chairs aside to get to the front beside An Serat. He towered over me.

"I have a question," I said.

DeLucca turned from where he was shepherding children out the door. "Question time's over," he said.

"It's only a short one," I said. "An Serat, can the Invidi make jumps off the Central network?"

DeLucca looked expectantly at the Invidi, and when no reply came, he touched his ear and nodded. "I think that's a little outside the scope of this meeting, Ms. . . . Valdon. Shall we go on with the tour?"

I ignored him and continued to speak to An Serat. "I think you want to talk to me about this as much as I want to talk to you. You know who we are."

DeLucca nodded to one of the attendants, who reached for my arm, but Murdoch stepped between us.

"She's not dangerous," he said quietly.

Still no reaction from the Invidi.

"Don't you want to know how we got here?" I said.

Will pulled my arm. Most of the others had left. He looked curiously at the Invidi, but obviously wanted to go and see the ships more. "Come on, Maria. We'll miss the best part."

The Invidi swayed and the surface of his suit rippled as the tentacles beneath it moved.

"We talk," he said.

I turned to DeLucca. "Alone. Please."

He glared. "Impossible. We don't know . . ."

"This is correct. This ones only. We talk," An Serat interrupted. DeLucca went into a huddle with his earpiece, then nodded to the other attendants, who backed slowly away from me.

"Maria . . ." Will was nearly crying with frustration.

"You can ride with me." DeLucca patted his shoulder. "In the front jeep."

Murdoch smiled at Will. "Go on, mate, we'll catch up with you later."

Will shot me a look of puzzled anger, or pleading, I couldn't tell which. Then they left, followed by the second Invidi and the attendants. Only An Serat, Murdoch, and myself remained.

Sixteen

"**D**o you know who we are?" I said

"I . . . we find your ship," the Invidi replied. "I recognize you. I do not recognize you." An Serat somehow looked at me, then Murdoch, without making any movement.

"I came later," said Murdoch dryly. "Your future self sent me."

Murdoch's details weren't in *Calypso II,* so this Serat didn't know him.

"Then you know we are stuck here, out of our own time," I said. "Because our ship's jump drive is disabled. We'd like to ask for your help to repair it and get back to our own time."

An Serat shifted a little. "Your ship carries elements familiar to me. Tell me more about *Calypso.*"

For a moment I was astonished, then realized he must have seen the specs of *Calypso II,* which included where we got the engine.

"We used the engine from *Calypso.* You sent . . . will send it to Jocasta."

"That's . . ." began Murdoch helpfully, but Serat interrupted.

"I know. Who are the Sleepers?"

Murdoch sidled closer to me. "Is it okay to tell him all this?" he muttered.

"He's seen the record," I said out of the corner of my mouth. I raised my voice again to talk to Serat. "The Sleepers are the people you help to get away from Earth in three years' time. You use their ship *Calypso* to get a jump drive to us in the future."

"I know about ship." Serat's voicebox carried an impatient tone I didn't remember. "I cannot see far. Paths are much clouded."

"What if all your people here tried to see?" I said. "Maybe you can see that we have to get back."

His tentacles curled and uncurled, a sign of agitation. "Unnecessary. Alone I am enough."

I felt impatient, myself. "Will you help us get back? I don't have the tools to fix my engines, you do. We must get back. There are things we need to do."

"I understand the means but not . . ." Serat's words made no sense. I had the feeling he was talking to himself.

Murdoch caught my eye and made a helpless gesture.

"Tell me of the Serat in your path," said An Serat normally. "Am I always the keeper of the travel paths?"

"I don't understand," I said.

"What your records call the network."

Murdoch frowned. "But you're not . . ."

I cleared my throat to interrupt him. "An Serat, is it possible to make jumps off the network?"

"It is not Invidi way."

"But we got here, so you must have created a jump somehow."

"The action is yet un-pathed. I cannot say."

This was no good. We didn't know what he wanted, how much we should tell him. Why, for example, did he seem to want to keep the other Invidi out?

"We would greatly appreciate some help in getting back

to where we came from," I said. "Seeing that you—I mean, your future self—is responsible for our getting here in the first place."

"I wish to know more," said An Serat.

I looked at Murdoch. We hadn't expected this. The Invidi normally did not pry or demand things. I wasn't sure of my temporal physics, but common sense suggested the less we told An Serat about the future, the better.

"I don't think that would be a good idea," I said.

"Do all of you feel that way?" said Murdoch. "Can we talk to the others?"

"I lead this group," said Serat. "Alone I talk."

That was clear, at any rate.

"Others should not know," he added, as if trying to make it clear.

We'd seen conflict between An Serat and other Invidi back on the station. An Serat was regarded as something of a maverick in the future. Perhaps he had always been a problem for them. I wished I knew more of the background to the conflict between Serat and An Barik, who seemed to represent the rest of the Invidi.

"Know what?" said Murdoch. "You are going to tell the others about us, aren't you?"

"You go now."

"What?" My voice rose. "You can't just send us away like that. We don't belong here."

"You're kidding," said Murdoch. His eyes on Serat were cold. "You send me back a century and then leave me here? No way."

The door burst open. An officer in a blue U.N. hat stood in the entry, flanked by two soldiers holding guns. For a moment, I thought An Serat had sent them a signal and they were responding.

The armed men immediately checked all angles of the

room. Satisfied we were the only occupants, they stood still, the weapons covering us.

Another soldier walked in behind them, carrying a box with sensor equipment on top.

"Excuse us," said the officer with no hint of apology. He bowed fractionally to An Serat. "Someone is sending an unauthorized electronic signal from within this building."

I chafed at the interruption. "There's nobody here but us."

"Won't take a minute, ma'am."

The soldier with the sensor advanced farther, until he stood in front of me. A quiet, tanned face. He nodded at the officer, who said, "I'm going to have to ask you to step outside, ma'am."

"Why?" I looked at him, at the projectile weapons on either side of us, cold tubes of menace.

"Our equipment indicates you are the source of the signal. You understand we have to be cautious. If there is some mistake, we apologize, but for the moment you'll have to come with us."

I met Murdoch's eye and he shook his head slightly.

We left An Serat standing there. One of the soldiers stepped in ahead of me and one followed behind Murdoch. What "signal" could it be? The transponder was gone, the Seouras implant was safe—had Levin's ID set off another, unknown security system?

The sky had clouded over while we were talking to An Serat, and it was cooler. The other Invidi stood outside with a third soldier. I could see small figures grouped around vehicles at the checkpoint onto the far runway. The children's tour was about to begin.

"What kind of signal is it?" I asked the sensor operator. He glanced at the officer and didn't reply.

"Empty your pockets," was the next order.

We did the same thing we'd done at the gate. Wrist timer, ID, comb, bus passes. The officer passed each item to be checked by a different set of sensors.

"This one, sir." The soldier held up my ID. "Don't know how it got past the main detectors. Might be a time-delay trigger."

"What's the signal for?" The officer asked me politely enough, but his eyes were hard, his young face tight.

"I don't know anything about a signal. As far as I know, that's an ordinary ID."

"She's telling the truth," said Murdoch. "We only came here to meet the aliens."

"What kind of signal is it?" I asked again.

The officer finally nodded approval for the soldier to answer. "Some kind of activation sequence."

The officer spoke into his head mike. "Go to alert. We have a possible situation Tiger." His fingers dug into my arm. "Activation sequence for what? A bomb? An attack?"

"I tell you, I don't know. Bill?"

He shook his head. "No idea."

Levin must have done something to the IDs so we'd be caught. The lousy bastard.

"Did you lend your ID to anyone recently? Did it leave your sight?" He rushed through the words, obviously not believing our innocence. He spoke into his collar again. "Did anyone else come with them?"

"We . . ." I began to tell him about Levin, when something clicked in my skull. Something about gifts and packing your own luggage.

I stared at Murdoch. "Activation. Presents. Bill, Levin gave Will a cap."

"Yes, but . . ." The initial skepticism faded swiftly from Murdoch's face.

"They have to get rid of it."

Murdoch turned to the officer and he was no longer a

casual visitor—like spoke to like. "Listen to me. We didn't plan this, but we think there may be a bomb or similar device with the child who came with us. Tell them to isolate his cap and take cover."

"His cap?"

"It's got a metal badge. We think the device is in there."

The officer glanced at the sensor operator, who nodded. "It's possible."

"Block the signal. Jam it," I said.

The officer spoke to his HQ and we waited for an endless moment before the signal operator frowned.

"Still going. It's a . . ."

I grabbed the ID from the officer's grasp and flung it on the ground. "Shoot the damn thing."

He stared at me, then drew out his pistol, aimed, and fired. The card shattered at the second shot. The operator shook his head. "It's stopped, but there's some reaction at the other end."

I couldn't see the figures beyond the checkpoint, a good hundred meters away along the runway.

"Full alert," said the officer into his collar. Sirens wailed across the water. "Situation Tiger confirmed. All mobile liaison units return to base. Unit Random Two, report."

Murdoch turned to the Invidi. "I advise your people to take precautions."

The alien spoke, with a different timbre to An Serat. "Your advice understood."

"You can see what's going to happen." I rounded on the Invidi. "Whatever it is, stop it."

The silver suit twitched all over.

"They can't contact Random Two—that's the jeep your child is in," said the operator. "We're sending a ground unit . . ."

His words faded, because in the next moment I was running through the gate and up the runway, without conscious thought. Behind me, Murdoch's shout whipped away in the wind.

"She's not armed!"

Hard asphalt, burning lungs. Gray sky wheeling overhead. I was never a sprinter, but I swear it took less than ten seconds to the next gate.

"Can't go through here." A firm voice, arm barring my way. I kicked out without thinking, somebody cursed. Squeezed through a narrow opening, the tarmac spread before me. Four jeeps reached a low building. A fifth, still in the middle of the runway, turned and started to follow the others. Another, carrying crash-suited soldiers, drove toward the lone jeep from a different building.

I ran on, waving frantically. Can't they hear the siren? Throw it away, Will. Throw it . . .

The bomb exploded.

One moment the jeep was there. The next, a small flash of unbearable light. The approaching jeep leaped into the air and something smacked me hard.

A single high note, far away. It distracted me from trying to get somewhere, do something.

Bumping sensation—someone's hands on my shoulders, shaking. Pain burned across my cheek as it scraped on the ground. Eyes, open your eyes.

I was sitting on the tarmac. Murdoch's face came into focus in front of me. His mouth moved but I couldn't hear any words. My fingers tingled and the shadows at the corners of my vision were edged with strange colors. The same high note over it all.

I pointed at my ears and shook my head. "Can't hear."

Murdoch mouthed, "You okay?"

I nodded. He sat down wearily beside me and put his head in his hands.

A round, glassy scar smoked where the tarmac had been seconds before. A sunken area in the center, leaking seawater, was echoed by another sunken ring around the edge of the blast zone. It seemed impossibly small for such a powerful explosion, until I realized that the Invidi must have detected and contained the blast, or perhaps deflected it upward. I'd been close to the edge of the containment and must have felt the beginning of the shock wave. The airport and everyone on it had been saved.

Except for the two closest jeeps.

Murdoch's shoulder jolted against mine. He wept with his face buried between his raised knees. I wanted to hold him but my arms wouldn't move. We sat there in numb silence until the soldiers came.

Seventeen

They put us in a small, bare room one floor above the ground, in one of the buildings overlooking the tarmac. We tried to explain, but nobody had the time to listen.

Murdoch sat on the floor against the wall and closed his eyes.

I looked out the window and tried to gather my thoughts, which dashed around in meaningless circles. Like the people and vehicles below, busy around the edges of the blast site, but not yet venturing onto it because it was still too hot.

Grace must know by now.

At that thought, everything else caved in. We'd brought Will here and now he was dead. Nothing else mattered.

I felt myself begin to shake. Murdoch looked up as I stumbled around. He said something I couldn't hear properly. I needed to be sick but there was no privy in the room, not even a basin.

I held both hands over my mouth and leaned against the cool glass of the window, which wouldn't open.

The sky had darkened further and soldiers were setting up lights around the blast site. On the far side of the burn mark, the other terminal building sat undamaged. Beyond the building moved the gray sea, and beyond that, lights and thronging vehicles and people on the shore. Copters flew over them, a swarm of black gnats clustering on the edge of the no-fly zone. The undamaged tarmac stretched back to where the Invidi ships waited.

I tried to concentrate on the shape of the ships, the size, which ranged from baby runabouts through shuttle-sized yachts to one larger vehicle I'd never seen before. Perhaps they'd stopped using them in the intervening hundred years, or maybe we were too far out at Jocasta for that kind of ship to . . .

It doesn't matter. Nothing matters.

I turned around. Murdoch was staring at the ceiling.

"They think we did it." I must have shouted, because he winced.

"What do you expect?" His voice sounded muffled, but audible.

"How could they think we'd involve the children?" My throat closed and I had to turn back to the window.

"It didn't worry Levin." Even half heard, Murdoch's voice was harsh. He rose stiffly and came over to the window, leaned his arms against the sill. His eyes, bleak and stunned, roved over the scene below.

"I thought I'd seen a bit of the galaxy but . . ." He coughed and rested his forehead on the glass. "We're not a nice species, are we? I never realized how . . ."

"Do you think he planned it all along?"

He shrugged. "Dunno. They might have had the stuff but couldn't work out a way to get it in."

"How . . ." My voice gave out.

"I dunno, okay? Some nanobug to eat through a covering. Doesn't matter now."

I looked out at the Invidi ships. "It's time to go home, Bill."

He followed my gaze. "Don't be stupid."

"It's the only chance we'll get. By now, Levin will be gone. We're the only suspects they have. An Serat won't help us. We can spend the rest of our lives rotting in a twenty-first-century jail or we can grab one of those yachts and run."

Murdoch look at me in consternation. "Jeezus, you're serious. For a start, you can't use an Invidi ship."

"How do you know? No human's ever been allowed to try."

"What about Grace? You're going to leave her, just like that, without trying to explain, without trying to help them catch Levin?" He dropped his voice again, with a glance at the door. I had to strain to hear over the ringing.

"What can I do for Grace now? It's my fault Will is dead. Do you think she'll want to hear what I have to say?"

"It's not . . . I hate the idea of running away. It's like we're abandoning her." Misery lowered his voice.

"It's either that or abandon our own time. Abandon everyone on the station. Because they'll keep us locked up for life over this."

"Not if we give them enough evidence to get Levin," he said.

"Do you really think we can do that? Do you think Levin will hang around waiting?"

He leaned his forehead against the window and ran his hand over his head. The glass fogged with his breath. "If we don't tell them about Levin, he'll get off scot-free."

"You don't know that. There might be a way to trace him from the blast residue. Or something." It sounded lame, even to me. I swallowed the sickness in my throat enough to get words past. "We have to go or stay. And I can't spend the rest of my life in jail here."

He stepped back from the window and looked at me. A gaze that seemed to go right through me. Then nodded once, decisively. "Let's do it, then. Nowhere to go but forward. What's your plan?"

"I, er." My mind remained blank. "If I distract the guard

by going to the toilet, you can get out and . . . sneak up behind him."

The muscles of his face relaxed a little. "You need a refresher course in anti-terrorist contingencies."

"Have you got a better idea?"

He thought for a moment. "Can't you short the power to the lock from in here?"

I examined the walls and ceiling. The single light source was set into the ceiling behind a glass cover, and too high for me to reach by myself. The switch must be outside the room. No surveillance camera, unless it was hidden in the light. We had no tools to either unscrew the cover or rip up wall panels to find wiring. I could stand on Murdoch's shoulders and try to smash it or pick at it with my fingertips . . .

"No time, even if I had the tools. They're going to come back for us pretty soon."

He nodded. "Only reason we're still here is probably because they want to keep us away from the media. You go to the toilet, and when you come back, I'll jump him."

"How is that different from my plan?"

"Okay, okay. I'm not in a creative mood." He retreated to the window and sat down on the floor. "I'm here, in an unthreatening position."

"That doesn't mean you'll stay there."

"It's a combat psychology thing. Trust me."

"Hey!" I raised my voice. "Hey, open up! Hello?" I banged on the door a couple of times then retreated a few steps.

The door opened and the young soldier stood at the ready. He didn't look much older than Vince, with the same lonely, underfed look.

"I need to use the toilet."

He looked at me doubtfully, eyes flickering to Murdoch and back again.

"To pee," I added. "You know."

"They'll be coming to get you soon," he said. "Wait until then."

"I'm busting. I can do it on the floor, but you'll have to explain."

He sighed. "Okay. You can't go at the same time," he said to Murdoch.

"I'll wait."

The soldier motioned me out the door with the muzzle of his gun, taking care to leave an open line of fire to Murdoch as well. The boy knew his job—it might be harder to get out of here than I'd thought. But infinitely easier from here than from wherever they intended to take us next.

The toilet was down a flight of concrete stairs and halfway down a ground floor corridor that seemed to run the length of the building. Green exit signs glowed at each end of the corridor. The soldier let me half shut the cubicle door.

"What's your name?" I asked from inside.

"Can't tell you that."

"No personal communication with prisoners, eh?"

He said no more and we ascended the stairs in silence. The stair lights activated automatically as we passed. I couldn't see any obvious surveillance cameras, but they might be built into the walls. Unreasonable to think there wouldn't be any in an airport building.

The rush of adrenaline as we approached the door made my heart jump painfully. My breathing faltered suddenly like blocked pipes and I forgot everything else.

"Shit." I dived for the door. My spare inhaler, the only thing they'd left us, was still in Murdoch's pocket.

"Hey!" The guard was as surprised as I was.

"Asthma," I wheezed, fingers scrabbling at the handle. "Medicine's inside."

It was a bad attack. As I slumped against the door frame and sucked for air that wouldn't come I was conscious of the soldier unlocking it as fast as he could. Then it opened and I stumbled into the room. Something knocked violently against me and I fell.

Through a fuzzy roaring I could hear curses and sounds of a scuffle, but couldn't do anything but fight for tiny gasps of air.

The inhaler attached itself to my nose and mouth, thrust down in Murdoch's hand. One, two. Slowly, small breaths. One, two.

One, two figures on the floor. One still, one moving. I uncurled and sat up. The moving one was Murdoch. He groaned and rolled over, then began to search the soldier's pockets. His nose dripped blood on the green and brown fatigues of the young man.

"Sorry. I wasn't much help," I said.

"You weren't any help." He sniffed and wiped his nose on the back of his sleeve. He began to unlace the soldier's boots. "Hope I haven't broken his jaw."

I peered at the soldier's face. His eyes were closed peacefully but his lips were bloody and a red, swelling weal across his lower face matched the shape of the gun butt. Sorry, sorry. I wish this didn't have to happen.

Murdoch tied the boy's hands with the laces, removed the boots, utility belt, and slid a two-way radio out of his chest pocket. He wiped most of the blood off his own face and pulled me to my feet.

"Come on. Better go before they realize he's out of it." He left the boots and belt inside the door. The U.N. cap went on his head and the gun loosely under his arm. It might fool the cameras for a second or two.

We wanted to get out of the building and go toward the ocean end of the tarmac where the Invidi ships stood. Hopefully they'd expect us to head the other way, to the barrier gates. We reached the exit at the end of the building without incident.

"Keep going," said Murdoch through gritted teeth behind me. We slipped outside.

Evening had closed in early and a thin rain fell from the dark gray sky. On our right, tendrils of steam stirred at the heat of the explosion site. Ahead, the tall, rounded shapes of the Invidi ships lay in shadow. Lights flooded the main area to the left and behind us, but fortunately this made our area darker. Beyond the faint hiss of rain rose the sound of voices and the rumble of engines. A sentry on the far corner of the building looked out at the lights. As we watched he talked into his collar, shook his head, and paced a little. The air had a wet, metallic smell.

Our shoes became soaked immediately and squelched on the wet asphalt. I looked back. The sentry had turned and was walking to the door. How long before the alarm sounded?

Five Invidi ships in all. Three lozenge-shaped shuttles, any of which we could probably manage, and two single-pilot yachts. The shuttles might not carry a jump drive, so the yachts were a better bet. The closest one towered at least twenty meters over us on the longer axis of its elongated, bulbous diamond shape.

We crouched in the shadow of one of the shuttles beside the yacht. Hope they don't have proximity alarms.

"What are you going to do if they're inside?" Murdoch murmured in my ear.

His body radiated warmth against my shoulder and hip, welcome after the cold rain.

"I think one or the other yacht will be empty. We know An Serat was the leader of the expedition. He should have his own ship. And he's probably still over at the main building."

"And if he's not?"

"We can ask him to come out and talk to us, then run past him. We can threaten him with the gun . . ."

"This,"—he shook the weapon—"is not going to frighten him."

"All right, so we ask him to come out and talk. But I still think they're empty."

Murdoch's voice hardened. "Let's get on with it. Which one?"

I pointed to the closer one.

He shrugged and took up a position farther down the shuttle's side, from which he would be able to see anybody coming from the buildings.

No lights glowed on the ship, either outside or inside. I stubbed my toe without injury on spongy material that spread in a doughnut shape around the base. I would have to clamber onto it to get close to the ship. Where was the entry hatch? Which part presented to an airlock?

Cold rain spattered against my face. The outer hull of the ship felt cool to the touch, but not as cold as a metal surface would have been, nor was it smooth. It was scored with myriad tiny trails.

I edged quickly all the way around the ship, running my hands up and down as I went. No levers, switches, handles, or even joins, other than the strange pattern. I was soaked and shivering and my hands were so numb I probably couldn't have opened a hatch anyway.

"What's wrong?" Murdoch loomed out of the dark.

"W . . . won't open," I said, teeth chattering. "Nothing on the surface."

"Bloody hell." His voice sounded as if he was looking the other way.

I looked back too, and saw more light than before streaming around and under the Invidi shuttles. Floodlights around the building now, not just on the tarmac. The sound of engines and shouting. They'd found out we were gone.

I ran to the other yacht, tripping over the spongy base and nearly falling flat. Murdoch followed more carefully.

Again I felt the surface of this next yacht, the tiny trails in a material that felt more like stone than metal. But this one had a different texture, harder. Or perhaps it was my numb fingers.

Not far away, a shrill whistle blew and dogs barked. I pounded on the ship's hull, not caring now if there was an Invidi inside or not. The men who set the bomb that killed Will and the men pursuing us with guns seemed far more alien.

"Let us in! Please."

The hull shuddered under my palms. Surely I didn't have the strength to shift it? Its surface crawled—all the patterns moved, as though a trillion threadlike worms wriggled against my hands. I jerked back.

"What is it?" Murdoch's voice by my ear.

"It moved. Like . . ."

My voice trailed away. Above us yawned a round, dark break in the hull surface. I reached up and felt the lower rim, level with the top of my head. The edge was smooth. I couldn't feel anything in the space beyond, although the air seemed warmer.

"Give me a leg up." I stuck one heel back at Murdoch.

Nothing for a moment, then his warm, firm grip closed on my ankle. He put his shoulder under my knee and heaved. Behind us the growl of engines grew louder. Jeeps.

I levered myself into the Invidi ship and rolled over onto a hard surface that sloped slightly downward. It was warm inside, and dry. The surface was faintly warm under my hand. Then a dim golden light grew, seeming to come from within the walls, floor, and ceiling of a small cabin. It gave me a curious feeling of being exposed.

The Invidi owner couldn't have been comfortable in here, there was barely five meters breadth or height.

Murdoch's head appeared suddenly as he jumped, then hung with his elbows over the rim inside. "You okay?"

"There's nobody here. Get in."

His head disappeared, his knuckles on the rim whitened with strain, then he shot upward and his upper body wriggled into the cabin. I heaved the back of his trousers and he swung his legs inside.

The only thing that looked faintly familiar was a chest-high band of indentations and lines on one wall. Otherwise, all the surfaces were the same rubbery, slightly porous material as the base outside, but warm to the touch. A welcome warmth, after the cold and wet.

"There's nothing here," panted Murdoch. He looked around the narrow space.

There was a shout outside, too close.

"Halley, they're nearly here."

I turned quickly to the band of indentations. I laid my palm on one after the other, searching for initialization confirmation. At the third try, the lighted surfaces pulsed slowly. Brighter patches and flecks flickered over the walls and ledges. At the edges of hearing, a hum began. The place where my hand had just been glowed in the shape of my palm. I touched it again and snatched my hand away with a cry.

The surface had prickled like an electric shock, but that was not what surprised me; with the physical contact came another kind of touch. I'd felt something travel up my arm, dissipate, then stroke the inside of my head. Not an invasive voice like the Seouras or the dreamlike state of Henoit's presence. It was more a question:

Hello? Are you ready?

"What the . . ." Murdoch swore as the floor bucked upward and deposited us in a huddle against the wall where the control panel pulsed.

"I think it's activated." My voice was muffled against

his shoulder. I pushed him off me and found that the floor was now a wall and the hatch had disappeared. The band of indentations had flattened down and out from the wall to form an obvious consolelike surface at a little less than waist height.

We couldn't hear anything from outside; the hum settled into an uneven murmur that reminded me of a cat's purring. The surface beneath us vibrated finely.

Murdoch stood up gingerly and patted the wall. "Where's the hatch?"

We both sprawled headlong as the cabin lurched again.

"What the hell is this thing?" He held my elbow as I got to my knees in front of the "console."

My handprint now glowed by my face. "Put your hand here."

"Here?" The glow disappeared under his wide palm.

"Do you feel anything?"

"Sort of a buzz. Look, we don't have time to play...Oh." He'd realized the incongruity of a human handprint on an Invidi ship.

"It appeared when I touched the console a second ago." Now that I looked properly, the pattern of indentations on the console seemed familiar. The rhythm of lights was regular, small blue ones intermingled with larger orange flashes. I'd seen flashes like that on a console somewhere, but not recently. It wasn't a good sign, I seemed to remember.

"Stabilize internal inertial compensation," I said loudly. Nothing changed.

"No audio," said Murdoch. "Aren't these ships supposed to be customized to the pilots?"

"They are in our time, but these are a century older. We wouldn't get inside an Invidi ship in our time, because they only open to the owner. Maybe Invidi cloning techniques aren't so advanced at this stage."

"Is that what they do?" Murdoch looked faintly ill. "I thought they just put character markers in the ship's interface."

I shook my head. "As far as I know, they start with the same basic genetic material as themselves. You know, like we're closer genetically to an Earth tree than we are to any alien humanoid."

I put my hand on the palm print and shut my eyes, resisting the urge to jerk it away from the initial shock and tingle. Think nice thoughts. Hello, I'm here and I want to go home.

Nothing happened, and I wondered if the first time had been a mistake.

"When you said let's steal an Invidi ship and go home, I did assume you'd been inside one before," said Murdoch. "You must have found out something in all those years of tinkering. Didn't *Calypso* give you a hint?"

The indentations on the panel re-formed themselves in my mind and I saw that the raised parts between them were what mattered. A seemingly random scattering of triangles. I traced them with my fingers. The orange flashes grew stronger and came closer together. Thruster control, I thought. We want to go up now.

"They're probably surrounding us," said Murdoch.

A door opened in my mind and an avalanche of sensations and information in unfamiliar forms swept over me irresistibly and I felt myself drowning but couldn't do anything to stop it . . .

Then I was gasping and coughing on the floor of the cabin. Murdoch sat back on his heels, chest heaving. He grabbed my wrist and held his thumb over the pulse.

"This might be . . . more difficult than . . . I thought," I panted, still dazed from an overload of the incredible. For a moment I'd felt . . . I didn't know what I'd felt. "What's wrong with you?"

He stared. "I just gave you mouth to mouth. You choked and stopped breathing for Chrissakes."

"Oh." My lips did feel numb. "Thank you."

I tried to gather my thoughts, but normal associations wouldn't come. Everything that was me, Halley, floated somewhere just out of reach, and the only thing grounding me was my attachment to the ship. "It's . . . some kind of mental link. Helps us use it." I retrieved my wrist from his grip and got shakily to my knees.

"Bloody hell." Murdoch leaned back and rubbed his face in despair. "We haven't got time for this. The army'll be swarming all over the place out there."

"I don't know . . ." I stood up carefully—for a moment I thought we'd begun to lose gravity, but then realized I was tilting sideways as I stood. The triangular pattern and the lights, where had I seen them before? I'd asked the ship for thruster control.

"We might have left the ground. Maybe the atmosphere, too."

"What?" He scrambled to his feet and stared at the panel with me. "How do you know?"

"A feeling. When I was, er, connected. And I also have the feeling this is Serat's ship."

"Shit." He stared at nothing for a moment, then began to prowl around the space, touching the walls and snatching his hands away as if worried by what he might set off. "I wish we had a viewscreen."

"Invidi mightn't use viewscreens. Plenty of species aren't as visual as we are." I stroked the edges of the more obvious triangles. It seemed to be the right thing to do, but I couldn't think why. *Edges give you the basic controls,* said a voice inside me, *don't you remember?*

Part of the panel glowed in a new pattern. It was like looking at the bones and veins in your own hand held up to a strong light. Little azure pulses of synaptic energy zipped past.

Viewscreen, viewscreen . . . *Up there, on the right-hand side. Leave your hand on the raised section, it will sense you're there.* The voice was that of Jon Heggit, my second in command when I'd been head of the Jocasta reconstruction project. I could hear his husky, spooky voice as he leaned over my shoulder and told me what he'd found in one of the completed center rooms. A Tor control panel. One that worked.

We've worked out a couple hundred basic interface commands. Amazing stuff. It learns so quickly what we want. His enthusiasm led him to ignore one of the precautions we'd evolved for dealing with Tor systems—always assume there was a booby trap. And he died.

"Did you do that?" Murdoch stared at an oblong window filled with stars. "You were right, we did leave the atmosphere. Looks like we've left orbit, too." He stomped on the deck. "Gravity field is on." When I didn't reply, "Something wrong?"

"Bill, this isn't an Invidi ship."

"Whaddaya mean, it's not an Invidi ship? You said it's Serat's ship . . . No sign of them following us, is there?"

I touched another couple of triangles, cautiously now. "I don't think so."

"What kind of ship is it, then?"

"It looks like a Tor console."

"Must be a mistake," he said flatly. "The Invidi were at war with the Tor for years. That's how Earth got Jocasta, when the Tor lost."

"I know that. But I worked on the early stages of Jocasta, remember? I know what Tor interfaces looked like. And they looked pretty much like this. This,"—I waved my hand over the console in front of us—"responds like a Tor interface would. That's how I got your viewscreen."

"What about this mental link thing, then?" He frowned. "Nobody ever mentioned that about Tor systems."

"No. But sometimes we wondered. Sometimes when we tried to outsmart a trap, it would seem like the system knew what we were thinking. We lost so many people in those first months."

He stared at me for a moment, then ran his hand over his head helplessly. "Last time we were in a Tor ship, it was holding the Seouras hostage and tried to kill us both."

"That was different."

"You hope."

"It's An Serat's ship, Bill, I can feel it. So maybe he's modified Tor technology for some reason. Maybe this is a special model."

"Then he's really going to be pissed off to have to wait for a century to get it back. That is where you're heading, isn't it?" he added. "To the jump point?"

"Yes, but I can't give such specific directions through this console. And I don't know how to activate the jump drive. Flatspace engines are no problem—I think. But to find the drive connection is another matter. I have to try the link again."

He swallowed. "Why don't I give it a try?"

"You did, nothing happened . . ." The panel tingled under my fingers. Something touched the edges of my mind. Inquisitive, interested.

Murdoch closed his hand over mine, lifting it above the panel.

"Wait. What am I supposed to do if you . . ." His fingers traced a circle on the inside of my wrist. "Dying's not good for you."

He had a point. A sore band was still tight around my chest and tiny bright dots danced around the cabin when I moved my head too fast.

"Watch me, then. See if we can talk while I'm doing it. If it looks like it's too much, break the link."

He frowned with frustration but we had no other choice; we had to know how to tell the ship where to go. And quickly, too, before the Invidi either followed us or asked their mothership to intercept us.

Besides, I'd been waiting to get inside an Invidi ship since my first days in the Engineering Corps, more than half my life. And this was as far inside an Invidi ship as anyone could possibly get. At least, a semi-Invidi ship.

I readied my hand over the panel.

Murdoch nodded.

This time no flood of information overwhelmed me, merely a slow trickle of images and concepts. I was conscious of Murdoch's presence through a thick haze. He was speaking and his hand shook my shoulder. I felt the movement, but not his touch.

" . . . hear me?"

My mouth felt clumsy and far away. "I can hear you."

"Where are we?"

The moment I heard his words I knew the answer.

"We're waiting. Between where we were and where we want to go." Nothing as flat as coordinates; I "knew" our exact position in the solar system right down to the chemical composition of the dust outside the ship and the tingle of radiation against its skin.

Murdoch's voice an insistent buzz. "Can we get home?"

Home. Home was Jocasta. The time—after Murdoch left.

The ship understood immediately. It was as easy as thinking where we wanted to go.

Eighteen

Maybe not that easy.

It hurt. What began as an ache behind my eyes grew and grew until I had to talk to keep concentrating. Half the time talking to myself, or the ship, the rest of the time to Murdoch. The ship didn't mind, but Murdoch got edgier and edgier.

"It feels like we've been in here about an hour." He fiddled nervously with the viewscreen controls and brought up a succession of images from outside the ship. Four views showed only dark space broken by a few points of light. Another was filled with bright gases. "I hope this thing has decent radiation shielding."

"It must. The Invidi have been in space long enough to think of something as elementary as that." I rubbed my neck where the Seouras implant felt tight. It felt like the pain was centered there.

"I meant, shouldn't we be at the jump point soon? Judging from what I can see of our position."

I nodded and pointed at the navigational display on the surface of the console where it curved up to meet the wall. At least, I hoped it was a navigational display.

"We're nearly there." My head throbbed as I leaned over to check on one of the lights.

"At the jump point?" He peered into the display, too. "That's the jump point? The yellow curly thing?"

"I think so. Not quite 3-D, is it?"

He blinked. "3-D for differently structured eyes. If the Invidi have eyes. Do they?"

"Depends on which expert you ask . . ." I rubbed the implant again. "Ow."

"What?"

"The blasted thing's giving me a headache."

"It's probably not used to humans."

"I bet it isn't."

"You're probably giving it a bigger headache."

"Thanks a lot."

He rubbed the viewscreen controls but the views didn't change. "Can't we see the point on the viewscreen?"

"It won't show unless we're right on top of it," I said.

"But in EarthFleet ships they show you this kind of glowing ball as the ship approaches a point." He curled his fingertips together.

"They do?" I would have been more interested if my head didn't hurt so much. "I was never on an EarthFleet ship when we jumped." EarthFleet ships went through jumps docked to ConFleet ships. I'd always been in engine rooms of ConFleet ships. "They must show you a holo or something. All we really see is . . ."

I checked our position, then leaned up to point at one of the screens. "You won't see anything until the drive kicks in. But it'll be about here."

Change now, I said mentally to the ship. The enabling connection—the "gate"—should open to the jump drive engines, if I'd understood the ship. Normally, jump-capable ships had flatspace thrusters of a particular configuration that contained this connection. In our time, the gate could be installed only by Central-registered stations and activated only by registered individuals, who were members of the Four. I just hoped this had not been the case in the time An Serat built this ship.

Something's wrong. We should be seeing a dot like a star rush toward us.

"Aren't we nearly at the coordinates?" said Murdoch, staring at the navigational display.

"Nearly," I said. We're there and nothing's happening. I pushed my hand down onto the console. The edges of the controls dug into my fingers as I tried to find order in the endless jumble of images and commands that overflowed my mind.

Jump drive. We need it now if we're to go back to Jocasta. Jocasta in 2122, at the other "end" of the jump point. Please activate the jump drive now.

Without looking at the display I knew we'd gone too far. I felt myself slump in disappointment, at the same time as Murdoch's exclamation jerked me back.

"There it is!" He grinned at me, his finger pointing at a yellow dot that grew brighter, glowing and growing until it took up half the screen. The ship must have enabled the drive at the last second.

The brightness flared. Murdoch looked away and flung his arm across his face.

The deck shifted under our feet, seemed to drop away. It's working. The jump drive takes over in a measureless second of stomach-dropping nothingness . . .

"We're home." Murdoch was shouting. He hugged me tight and shook me away from the console. For a moment his touch felt as if it were on someone else, or my whole body was numb. Then the warmth of his arms around my shoulders and of his chest against mine thawed the numbness. I squeezed him weakly in return. Lost a few minutes or hours there.

In the viewscreen we could see Jocasta.

The station's three interlocking habitat rings spun around the center cylinder and its associated docks, processing platforms, and recycling units. Six solid spokes connected the rings to the center. Viewed side-on, the line of the rings was broken by the center poking out top and bottom. From above or below, not that there's either in space, it looked like a white wheel whirling around a hub, in turn rotating around the unnamed planet the Tor laid waste decades ago.

We could see the Bubble, the raised bump of the command center on the upper ring. Light glinted off the banks of mirrors around the sunside of the rings.

"When did we come through the jump?" I tried to activate a communications signal, but none of the likely commands worked.

"A couple of minutes ago," said Murdoch. "You said something about drives but I didn't think you looked awake."

"I don't remember the time passing." I rubbed my head but it wouldn't clear. The flatspace thrusters must have kicked in without having to be recalibrated. This ship really was a special model.

He pointed at the screen. "Aren't we a bit far off to see all that detail?"

Never mind the screen, there was the shadow of something behind me. I kept turning around to check, but there was nothing in the cabin with us.

"What's the matter?" said Murdoch.

"Something's there."

"Where?"

"Behind me." I half shut my eyes and put my hand flat on the console again, holding my breath against the pain. Now I could see the shadow.

A long cylinder, covered with garish colors. A ConFleet cruiser, Bendarl markings, enough destructive power to pulverize a planet.

"Shit," said Murdoch. "Where did that come from?"

I opened my eyes properly and realized the cruiser was now visible on the screen, too.

A different series of lines lit the display, bouncing in waves.

"I think that ship is hailing us, but I can't get the comm system to work." I tried a random tapping, to no effect.

"Don't worry, we know what they're saying," said Murdoch sourly. "Identify yourself and prepare to be boarded."

"That's what worries me. I'm going to dock us at Jocasta."

"They're following, but they're too far out to catch us."

"Still can't contact the station." I ran my fingers down what I thought were the ridges allowing directional control, but for all we knew, the ship could have been reading my mind.

Murdoch leaned on the console beside me, his eyes moving from viewscreen to console. "Don't worry, they'll welcome an Invidi ship. Put us in one of the upper docks, easy to get in."

The ship aligned itself in response to my directions. The patched white skin of Jocasta's center section grew more detailed in the viewscreen as we approached. The airlock grew larger, a round mouth pouting outward from the skin, surrounded by clusters of clamps like crab legs and conduits ready to uncoil. A couple of flat oval maintenance droids known as "bugs" skittered several meters away before holding position.

We nudged the airlock cuff and felt the faint *snick-thud* of the clamps.

"We should put it into an inside dock later." I couldn't help yawning as I spoke.

Murdoch gestured helplessly at the cabin, then ran his hand over his head. "When you get your breath back, you can explain what the hell just happened. We made it through the point, obviously."

I shook my head, then stopped, as it made everything else shake. "For a minute it seemed like we wouldn't make it. I could have sworn we'd gone past the coordinates ..."

He flexed his shoulders. "We're home now." He squeezed my arm again. "Well done."

I yawned. My thoughts were losing focus as well as my eyes.

Below us a round hole slowly widened to a bit less than a meter. Murdoch approached cautiously, then his shoulders relaxed. "Looks safe."

We slid through the hole feetfirst and found ourselves in the airlock. The bare conduits, unevenly textured panels, and white light were familiar; the familiarity of a recurring dream. We were definitely home. The air had that distinct recycled whiff, like breathing into one's own shirt. Gravity set at slightly less than Earth normal.

Jocasta's center normally possessed close to zero gravity, but the Invidi had installed a field that could be activated to produce the conditions of gravity comfortable to each particular species. I hated the gravity field, mainly because after all these years I still hadn't a clue how it worked.

In front of me Murdoch tapped the airlock controls to open. The doors hissed apart.

Dimmer light, faces. The smell magnified. A human voice speaking Earth Standard.

"Human? But it's an Invidi ship ..."

Other voices in the background, excited.

"It's them!"

"Quick, tell ..."

"Did you get a reading for ..."

Murdoch tugged at my elbow and I stumbled with him out of the airlock.

A Melot face. For a second I stared in shock at the difference—the eyes and mouth were in the same position as a human's and the face shape was basically oval, but it was covered with fine golden scales. The ears were invisible under a caplike covering, and out of the side of the head protruded flexible antennae stiff with shock.

It was the suit that affected me most. An exquisitely tailored piece of sartorial engineering in translucent gray. The Melot wore it with restrained aplomb that was further removed from the out-town than Jocasta is from Earth.

"Veatch!" The strength of my pleasure at seeing him again made my voice crack.

"Commander Halley?" Jocasta's station manager remained still, his hands clasped behind his back, but his antennae twitched. Beside us, Murdoch's hand was being pumped by Helen Sasaki, the second in command of Security. Several other Security personnel waited to do the same.

I managed to smile. "You're looking well."

Veatch opened his mouth twice before words emerged. "My condition is satisfactory." He unclasped his hands, then dipped his antennae toward a human who stood a little apart. "This is Mr. Rupert Stone, of Earth's Ministry of External Affairs."

Stone stepped closer. Not as tall as Veatch, wearing his close-fitting mauve suit like a uniform. Short, pale hair. Cold, pale eyes.

"So you're Halley," he said in a smooth baritone. His eyes ran over me. "You're smaller than I expected." He sniffed fastidiously, as if to say dirtier, too.

I opened my mouth to retort, shut it again. Our twenty-first-century grime was more obvious under station lights and the smell in the lobby may not have been entirely due to recycling. Even so, I didn't expect to be insulted on my own station.

"Mr. Stone has been acting head of station for twenty-four station days now," continued Veatch. "Since you were officially pronounced missing."

So, External Affairs, the ministry responsible for Earth's role in the Confederacy, had taken the opportunity to put someone in charge here whom they could control. An obvious move. No reason for me to feel a surge of resentment toward Stone. External Affairs had always been pro-Invidi, and were lobbying actively against our neutrality petition.

"What's the meaning of this?" Stone waved at the airlock and the Invidi ship. "Are you the only passengers? Where have you been all this time? ConFleet and Earth-Fleet have both wasted time and resources looking for you."

I smoothed my shirt ineffectually and pulled my shoulders straighter. Wish my thoughts were straighter. "I was out of comm range."

"If you're alone, you're in trouble." Stone half turned to Veatch as if in confirmation. "The Confederacy could charge you with possessing Invidi jump-drive technology, I believe? And there are penalties for those who assist you."

Veatch inclined his antennae. "That is correct."

Sasaki and Murdoch turned to watch us.

"Veatch, how long is it since Mr. Murdoch left?" I said.

"Thirty-six days," Sasaki answered for him. "And every one too long." She elbowed past Veatch, grasped my hand in both of hers, and wrung it painfully. She was a tall young woman with a powerful grip. "Welcome back, Commander." Her round, solemn face blossomed in a smile.

"I'm waiting for an explanation," said Stone.

I half expected him to tap his toe.

Thirty-six days. Murdoch had been with me for twenty-four, and he had spent some time looking for An Serat. So the same amount of time passed here as on Earth. Which confirmed that the jump point between 2023 and 2122 was stable, just like those on the Central network. That is, it kept the same correspondence. So why did it not have the same correspondence when *Calypso* went through it?

A wall comm unit buzzed. *Mr. Stone. Message from the cruiser.* The voice was familiar. Ensign Lee, from the command section in the Bubble.

"Put it through," said Stone.

Cruiser. With a jolt I remembered the bright ovoid against the stars.

"What's that cruiser doing there?" Murdoch demanded of Veatch.

"It seems to be patrolling the system boundaries," he said.

"They can't interfere in station business at the moment, because of the neutrality," added Sasaki. "So they like to prowl around and try to catch ships either going in toward the jump point or coming out, and inspect them. There are rumors the New Council has sneaked a ship into this system. People are anxious because of the New Council's connection with the Q'Chn."

"This is the kind of situation," Stone began, "that reveals how foolish neutrality is. How can station administration possibly protect . . ."

A Bendarl snarl interrupted him from the comm unit. Everyone jumped. Bendarl always turn the volume right up.

Attention! Station Jocasta! We demand you return the Invidi ship and its pilots to us. They are in violation of . . . three Confederacy statutes and four Sector navigation regulations.

I shared a glance with Murdoch. They knew who was piloting the ship. Our ex-observer, An Barik, was probably behind ConFleet's orders, as he had been at the end of the Seouras blockade. Barik had presumably been trying to deal with An Serat for years. He must have known about our leaving Earth in Serat's ship and therefore of Serat's experiments with Tor technology. Barik had waited for *Calypso* to appear near Jocasta. He could probably "see" Murdoch and me coming back from the past as well.

My stomach clenched—what the hell could we do? I didn't want to give up the ship before I could figure out how it worked. I tried to think of a strategy but my head hurt and the implant itched and facts didn't seem to connect properly.

Stone drew breath sharply. "Commander, we must comply. I'm sure you'll sort it out."

He reached for the comm unit controls. Sasaki stepped forward.

"Sir, we don't have to . . ."

Attention! Station Jocasta! Respond! The Bendarl voice rose in near-hysterical impatience.

Murdoch glanced at me, eyebrows raised, then stepped forward too. "Hang on a minute, Mr. Stone."

"Why?" Stone looked at him suspiciously.

"We can't hand Halley over to them right at the moment because she's in my custody. And I'm not going to hand myself over until I've completed my duties. Have to go through due process," said Murdoch, deadpan.

"In your custody?" I said.

"What do you mean?" said Stone at the same time.

Stone and I eyed each other, neither certain enough to be openly hostile.

Murdoch nodded at Veatch. "Mr. Veatch knows what I mean. Until neutrality is approved or disapproved at the Confederacy Council, Jocasta operates under Earth law, like we always did."

"I see," Stone said slowly. "But what do you intend telling the cruiser?"

Station Jocasta! This is your last chance to respond to our hail!

"Wait a minute, I don't see," I said. "What does being under Earth law have to do with it?"

Stone tapped the comm link. "Ahem. Earthstation Jocasta to Confederacy of Allied Worlds cruiser *Vengeful*. Your previous message was not clear. Please repeat."

"Means once we've arrested you for something they can't arrest you for the same thing," said Murdoch, stepping back to give Stone room and taking my arm. "Did I tell you your rights?" He smiled as he said it and I relaxed a little. He had mentioned this on Earth. He was going to arrest me so ConFleet couldn't. Or something.

Our instruments show you received our message! sputtered the Bendarl.

"Really?" said Stone. "Possibly they need to be recalibrated."

We demand you return the Invidi ship and its pilots to us! They are in violation of . . . three Confederacy statutes and four Sector navigation regulations.

Stone glared at Murdoch.

"Which Invidi ship?" I prompted in a whisper.

"Which Invidi ship do you mean?" Stone's version was a study in well-meaning incomprehension. He put his hand over the pickup and whispered, "Really, Commander, I protest. We risk annoying them."

"Bendarl are always annoyed," I said.

Don't try to stall! the Bendarl officer growled low. *We want the Invidi ship that just docked at that station and we want the pilots.*

"Ask for the captain," I mouthed.

"I feel there has been an unfortunate misunderstanding," said Stone soothingly, with a glare at me. "I wonder if I might speak to your captain?"

The captain does not speak to such as you.

Stone tapped the link shut. "Why do we have to talk to the captain?"

"The exec will only put us on hold while she checks with the captain anyway," I said. "Might as well save the trouble."

Stone folded his arms. "Commander, unless you give me a proper reason, I have to at least hand over the ship. We can't risk offending ConFleet!"

Sasaki muttered something like "Why not?"

I tried to think, only it was such an effort. It seemed important that I didn't tell everyone that the ship we arrived in was some kind of experiment using Tor and Invidi technology. But I didn't know what to say otherwise.

"It might help us understand the jump drive," I said desperately. "All I need is a bit of time to investigate. Can't you say it's evidence in Murdoch's case or something?"

"Sounds okay," said Murdoch.

Stone opened the link again, his elegant brows curving down in a frown.

... you have ten of your minutes to surrender that ship and pilots!

"Really, if it's not too much trouble, I'd like you to connect me to your captain."

Silence again.

"What if they attack us?" whispered Stone, his hand over the pickup again.

Wait. The sullen voice disappeared but the connection was maintained.

"And what do you mean, help us to understand the jump drive?" continued Stone in a whisper. "We already know what the jump drive does."

"We don't know how," I said, keeping my voice low as well.

"Think of the publicity," Stone moaned, almost to himself. "Harboring criminals. That's not going to be good for business."

"She's not been proved a criminal yet," said Murdoch,

not bothering with the whisper. "Let them appeal in the proper way. We go through due process."

"I'm glad to hear that," said Veatch. "Perhaps we could do the filework now, then. Including your leave forms, Chief Murdoch. You failed to fill out the correct ones before you left."

Murdoch groaned. "Later, please. And what is the time?"

"2308 hours."

A different Bendarl voice interrupted. *Cruiser* Vengeful *to Earthstation Jocasta.*

I coughed to get Stone's attention and pointed to myself, then the comm link. Stone hesitated, nodded.

I stepped over beside the link. "This is Jocasta."

Who are you?

"Commander Halley, former head of station. You are?"

Captain, she said with heavy finality. *My second level told you to surrender a vessel and its occupants. Why have you not complied?*

"There are no Invidi-owned vessels docked at this station," I said. "That ship belongs to me."

It is stolen property.

"Who made the complaint? When and where was it stolen? I deny it categorically."

We will take it.

"If you try, we will complain to the highest level of the Confederacy Council. You have no docking permit for this station."

"Commander," Sasaki whispered excitedly. "Dan Florida's just brought a group of Confederacy Council delegates to the station. They'll be in danger if the cruiser attacks us."

I nodded thanks. "Captain, were you aware that members of the Confederacy Council itself are on the station at this time? Perhaps you should reconsider your options."

There are no options. You give, we leave. You don't give, we take.

"Sorry. No deal." I cut the link, prickles of sweat under my arms and down my back.

"Quite the prodigal, aren't we?" said Stone. "Arrive out of nowhere in a stolen ship, endanger the station, and expect us to be delighted? We should give them the Invidi ship, at least."

"No," I said.

"That ship is material evidence in a case not yet tried before an Earth court," said Veatch thoughtfully. "In my opinion we should not tamper with it in any way for fear of affecting the verdict."

Stone shot him a look of annoyance.

"Why didn't you tell the Bendarl I had you in custody?" said Murdoch.

"I didn't want to give away too much information too early," I said. "Knowing An Barik's political clout, he might be able to come up with some sort of waiver for the agreement."

Lee called Stone again from the Bubble. *Vengeful* was still idling near the system boundary closest to Jocasta, but it had sent a scout back through the jump point to Central.

"Calling up reinforcements?" Murdoch met my eye.

"Getting a second opinion, more likely." Would An Barik or any of the other Invidi advise them to break our neutrality agreement to take the ship? Was a Tor-Invidi experiment that important to them? And why wasn't An Serat here to meet us? He'd been waiting nearly a hundred years, I was sure.

"Well, Chief?" said Stone. "Aren't you going to take your prisoner to the brig?"

Murdoch flexed his shoulders. "Yeah, guess I should do that."

Sasaki frowned. "With respect, Mr. Stone," she said. "They look like they should go to the hospital first."

Dried blood still crusted Murdoch's shirt, and one eye was puffy from his fight with the guard. I must look even dirtier after being on the ground after the explosion.

For a second I was back there. The artificial lighting and low ceiling became a cloudy sky stretching all around, sea and seagulls, wind burning into my lungs as I tried to reach Will. Will, riding all the time too far away, riding away from me and I didn't even say good-bye . . .

I gulped back a huge lump of tears and then Jocasta solidified around me again. Sasaki was looking at me strangely but nobody else seemed to have noticed. Stop it, I told myself. Five hours but nearly a century ago. Forget it.

"I concur with Lieutenant Sasaki," said Veatch. "This matter can be resolved in the morning. In the meantime, I will consult with the Magistrate's Department regarding the legality of Commander Halley's position and that of the station itself."

"Bill, we need to put the ship away somewhere." I didn't trust the Bendarl not to take it from under our noses.

"Yeah."

We nodded at each other. I couldn't think of anywhere. I couldn't even remember the layout of the station.

"How about in one of the old fighter bays?" suggested Sasaki. She eyed us anxiously. "I'll put a tug on it now. Why don't you two go see the doctor?"

As we moved off, Murdoch looked back at her. "Nice of you to get a welcome party together."

Sasaki laughed in an embarrassed way. "We came up here to look at Mr. Stone's observation lounge," she said. "And I wanted to make sure everyone up here knew about the extinguisher test tomorrow. Then when the Bubble called us to say an unidentified Invidi ship was coming into this dock, we came up to see who it was."

"Just good timing, then," said Murdoch.

"Yes, sir. And I can't take credit for that." Her laugh sounded more comfortable this time.

Dr. Eleanor Jago, head of the Medical Department on Jocasta and also of the hospital, welcomed us back with perfunctory kisses "in case you're infectious—you smell infectious," requested that next time we returned unexpectedly could we do so during the day shift, and made us lie down to be tickled with diagnostic tools until she was satisfied we could be let loose on the station in safety.

She finished examining Murdoch first, so he could go and arrange for secure quarters for me, then took me off to her consulting office, a small room with one low bed, a row of panels, and a desk. She ran her instruments over me, then waited for the data to process. I sat on the bed and waited for the questions.

Jago was a little older than myself, and we'd been friends for three and a half years, four if you counted the missing five months. We didn't always agree on matters of station policy—she thought the administration should put more effort into securing medical supplies and expertise. For a while during the Seouras occupation I thought she blamed me for the death of her partner, who was killed when one of the gray ships shot at a team repairing one of the outer reflectors. We'd cleared that up, but something remained between us, and I wasn't sure if it was only my guilt.

"What have you been doing to your lungs?" she said, her eyes on a monitor.

"Breathing nonrecycled air."

"Well, go on," she said after a moment. "Where? You've been gone for five months. Give me an idea what happened."

"Well, yes."

"Where was this?"

"I'd rather not say." There was no reason to keep our journey to Earth's past secret from Eleanor, other than in the interests of objectivity, as she'd find out soon enough when she checked the results of our tests. But, as we walked down from the center, Murdoch and I had agreed we would keep information on the Invidi ship confined to as small a group as possible. "The thing I want to know is whether this technology could interact with my Seouras implant."

She sighed through her nose and brushed past me to tap up another monitor on her desk, a smaller one. She was a big-boned woman, but her economical elegance always made me feel . . . overdone. Uncouth. She stared at the monitor, her eyes moving rapidly as she used the visual interface. "I'm looking at those records now. But why should the Seouras implant have anything to do with Tor things?"

"Because the gray ship—the Tor ship—also used it to communicate with me, remember? And the Seouras were in the gray ship. Anything they used to communicate with my implant must have been Tor. You know how Tor programs corrupt anything else."

"Hmm." She blinked in silence for a while.

I fidgeted and adjusted the light range on one of the diagnostic panels. Already rumors would be flying about the arrival of the former head of station and chief of Security in an Invidi ship. An Invidi-looking ship, to be exact. It was outwardly Invidi, but inside, the Tor elements were obvious. Whichever of the Invidi built it, and I was willing to bet it was Serat, he had wanted to keep it secret from the others and also had no fear of anyone entering it accidentally.

"The trouble with that implant," said Eleanor finally, "was that we couldn't find any direct, measurable effects. There were plenty of indirect, long-term effects, including,"—she read from the screen—"decreased olfactory sensitivity, headaches, nausea, weight loss, mild paranoia . . ."

"I don't remember the paranoia," I interrupted. "You're saying you can't tell if the implant's been activated?"

"Yes. Unless you want to take me wherever you found this Tor technology and we can monitor your reactions to it in a controlled way."

"Which will take days, right?"

"At least."

"I haven't got days. I might not have hours," I said gloomily.

"What's all this about an Invidi ship?" Eleanor tapped the screen shut and looked at me again. "It's not the same ship you left in?"

"No, and before you ask, we merely borrowed it."

"And you're going to give it back?" She raised her eyebrows at me quizzically.

"After I've had a look at it."

She clicked her tongue. "ConFleet won't be keen on that. What's your status? Bill Murdoch said something about you being wanted for questioning."

"He's going to hold me here. It's temporarily neutral ground, and if the vote goes through, it will stay that way."

She scraped her chair back roughly. "I don't understand why you think neutrality will be any better than being in the Confederacy."

I stared at her. "But you supported us in the application."

"Personally, I think it's a good idea. Not so sure in my professional capacity."

"But we'll be free to choose policies that are better for the station."

"What does that mean, exactly?" She tisked at my puzzlement. "In concrete terms, how is it going to be better?" She ticked off items on her fingers at me. "We've established a steady supply of medications and treatments. New personnel are settling in. For the first time since I arrived here four years ago we've actually got a medical record for everyone on the station. All this is possible because ConFleet is offering protection. If the neutrality vote goes through and Central withdraws technical support as well as withdrawing ConFleet's protection—worse, if Earth admin withdraws too, what's going to happen to the infrastructure here?"

"ConFleet let us down when the Seouras came. How do we know they won't let us down again?"

She shrugged. "We don't, I suppose. But we're looking at an immediate interruption in trade as well—what happens to the contract workers, the businesses dependent on Confederacy materials and supplies?"

Pride prevented me admitting I didn't have answers to details. And if I didn't fix up my personal problems, I wouldn't be around when the neutrality vote went through. But there was one thing I did know.

"Eleanor, we need to be able to decide these things for ourselves. That's all. We might decide to continue with ConFleet protection. We might decide to provide businesses with bridging loans. We might decide to ask all traders to bring medical supplies as a condition of station use, I don't know. The important thing is that we decide these things for ourselves."

She sighed, unconvinced. "You could be right. And sorry to hit you with it when you've just come back."

"Believe it or not, it's something I thought a lot about when I was away."

"You'd better go and find Murdoch. He's not really going to arrest you, is he?"

"I don't think he's got much choice," I said gloomily. "If he doesn't, we can't support his claim to have brought me back, and he may be charged with possession of jump-drive technology as well."

"Was he in the same place you were?" She emphasized "the same place," obviously annoyed at my secrecy.

"For a couple of weeks."

"Thought so. Physically, he's not as affected as you." She raised her eyebrow speculatively at me, obviously wanting a report on our personal relationship, too, but I was tired and my mind was full of other, less pleasant things. Like the ConFleet cruiser waiting at our front door.

"Good night, Eleanor."

"Good night, Halley." She watched me go, one finger tapping the monitor frame.

I wish she wouldn't do that. It confuses the input sensors.

Nineteen

I left the hospital by its Alpha ring exit. Jocasta's corridors seemed very enclosed after the skies of the out-town. The wide throughway glowed blue in the night light. We kept diurnal rhythm on the station by tilting the side mirrors on Gamma and Delta rings, and by tilting the main reflecting mirrors above Alpha ring. Most species needed the illusion of some kind of day and night, and on Jocasta we kept a rhythm of twelve hours daylight, one each of dawn and evening half-light, and ten hours of darkness.

The Security constable who had waited outside Jago's office told me Murdoch had prepared one of the guest officer's quarters on Alpha. Better than the brig, I quipped, but he simply said yes, ma'am, and looked straight ahead. He had a large nose that he kept wiping with a cleanchif and his collar was done up crooked below an unfamiliar face. Perhaps he'd come to the station while I was away. It increased my out-of-place feeling, and I didn't say anything more as he escorted me back through Alpha ring. We passed through the neat streetscape of the sleeping business quarter, far removed from the bustle of lower-ring commerce, then along the Bubble's main corridor with its maze of offices to either side. Our destination was the ConFleet and EarthFleet officer and guest quarters on the other side of the Bubble.

It was warm after Sydney's winter, and the humidity up here in Alpha was comfortable, unlike down in Delta ring. The gravity was less, too, one of the benefits of living in the upper ring. Another benefit seemed to be satisfaction in being able to afford living where most of the station could not. Most of those who could afford it were from the Four. This caused much resentment despite the revenue that Alpha rent brought to the station.

It seemed so familiar. From the out-town, we could see the spires of the city and the highways curling across the skyline to the eastern coast, where those who could afford it lived a life that hadn't changed significantly for fifty years. We'd never be able to do anything about similar divisions here until we got out of the Confederacy. Neutrality wasn't an option, it was a necessity.

Small things caught my eye; a loose conduit that rattled, alien writing, the scents of food plus alien body odors, whiffs of cold machinery from maintenance panels, the rich, repellent smell of a recycling vent. In the Bubble, what seemed like kilometers of EarthFleet-blue walls, section headings, door signs, noticeboards. All familiar, but somehow removed from myself.

I kept remembering things from the out-town that I'd forgotten to do—a letter I forgot to give Florence, the milk bill that I was supposed to remind Grace to pay, Will's science project that we'd only half finished . . . a band of grief tightened around my chest and made me stumble on nothing, because my vision was blurred with tears . . . surely this would pass?

My grandmother said grief doesn't go away, it just gets older with you.

Murdoch had put my photoimage from Las Mujeres out on the desk of the guest quarters. The small rectangle stood alone on the polished surface; the interface monitor was built into the wall beside the desk and the controls into its top. The rest of the room was as impersonal as the desk. A small living area, a single sleeping room with narrow bed, a door off the sleeping room that contained a hygiene cubicle.

I peered in the doorway of the sleeping quarters and was surprised to see my other possessions: a red, gold, and orange scrap quilt, folded on the bed beside a small pile of nonregulation clothing, including a pair of battered running shoes. Someone had also laid out my paper books, a couple of small ornaments, and a red lacquer box inside a clear case. The lacquer box contained medal ribbons, a couple of old coins, a magnetic stud from my first construction job, and an old locker key.

Nice of Murdoch to try to make me feel more at home. But like the unfamiliar faces in the corridors, it merely heightened my feeling of being out of place. Part of me wanted to linger in the past. It had only been a couple of hours, for goodness' sake. Less than a day since Will died. Less than a day since I'd been a hundred years away. Less than a day since I'd been so desperate to get back here, where I'd imagined I belonged.

I paced from desk to wall, around the comfortable chairs and the convenient low table. On twenty-first century Earth they called the disturbance in people's diurnal rhythm when they traveled from one time zone to another "jet lag." So what was I experiencing now? "Time lag"?

The photoimage on the desk caught my eye and I stopped to look at it properly. Speaking of the past . . .

It was a monotone, 2-D photograph; the only thing my great-grandmother left me. The paper inside the clear casing was in its original form, faded and tattered around the edges.

Five women stood together on dusty ground beside a great fig tree, in front of a rough concrete wall. My great-grandmother, tall and scowling at the camera. Marlena Alvarez, plump and calm. Three others who had risked everything to say to the militia and the police and the gangs, enough is enough.

Five women beside a tree. In a town that had nothing. During the last decade of Earth's purely human history. In seven years the Invidi would arrive and everything would change.

The photoimage was as familiar as the reflection of my own face. I'd looked at those figures all through the blockade and drawn comfort from them. But then I went to their century and saw the world behind the image. Instead of a window into another world, the photoimage was now a facade covering a world not so very different from our own.

Alvarez seemed to look directly at me, a frown creasing her heavy brows. *If our world is like yours,* she seemed to say, *what are you going to do about it?*

It's all right for you, I thought. You never had any problem with the difficult choices. You never did anything and wondered later if you've screwed up completely.

In the out-town, Jocasta's neutrality problems had seemed a long way away. Now they loomed immediate and complex. So what? a voice inside me scoffed. Like Stone said, you're not head of station anymore. You should have known they'd find out about *Calypso II,* the voice persisted, and relieve you of duty, but you went ahead with it anyway.

I went ahead with it because getting the jump drive to the Nine is important. In the long run. I wondered if Alvarez would have seen the logic behind trying to keep hold of the Invidi ship. I didn't want to look at her photoimage. She wasn't the person I'd imagined, and even then I couldn't live up to her.

I turned to the bed and picked up each item of clothing, the books, the box. My hand shook as I held it and the things inside rattled. Things that were memoirs of a time when it was all right for me to be just an engineer.

Maybe it's not Alvarez who isn't the person I thought she was.

We couldn't have stayed in 2023 and explained to Grace, could we? It wouldn't have worked. An Serat knew what I'd do because I'd already done it. The whole thing, the whole stupid loop was a setup. That's what Invidi do— they let you act, and it turns out to be for them. No use thinking if I hadn't entered the competition, if I hadn't trusted Levin, if I hadn't salvaged *Calypso,* if we'd stayed . . .

A brief vision of what it might have been like flashed through my mind. What if we could have helped the police catch Levin? We could have helped Grace cope. The many-colored kaleidoscope of possibilities opened, then shut, leaving the gray present shutting tighter around me.

With a spasm of anger I hefted the box, ready to throw. Anger at An Serat, at the Confederacy, at myself . . . I didn't know what, but dammit, I wanted to smash something.

We had to choose—go or stay. We had to choose—clean up that mess or deal with the mess in our own time. And how I was going to do that, I didn't know.

My eyes met those of Alvarez and I let the box drop back on the bed.

"Well, what do you think I should do?" I said idiotically, and began to cry.

Twenty

From where I sat on the bed, the time indicator on the interface panel in the other room was a green blur. I wiped my eyes on the back of my ConFleet blue sleeve—dark navy, not EarthFleet sky blue. For years I'd resisted changing my Engineering corps maroon for this color, now I was stuck with it, for a while anyway.

When I focused, the green numerals said 0800. That couldn't be right. I'd only sat sniveling here for a few minutes.

The door buzzed.

"Door open," I said, then hurriedly wiped the rest of my face.

Murdoch peered inside, then came in. He carried a handcom and wore a nonregulation soft shirt over fatigues trousers, which made him look more like Bill McGrath of the out-town than Chief Murdoch of EarthFleet Security. I wasn't sure if that was a good idea. Right now I needed Chief Murdoch's advice rather than Bill's.

He stood in the doorway of the sleeping room. "You still up? It's 0300 here."

I peered at the timer again. The eight was indeed a three. "That would mean something if we knew how much time passed while we were in the Invidi ship."

"A hundred years or so, wasn't it?"

"You know what I mean."

He looked at my red eyes, then dropped his own sympathetically. "Yeah. Felt like a couple of hours."

The pain in his voice was too close to how I'd been feeling. I looked away so I could blink back the tears without Murdoch seeing. A sharp-edged lump blocked my throat when I tried to swallow. Talk. Talk so the lump will have to go away.

"Bill, why did Levin do it?"

His mouth was tight, holding in emotion. "I told you, I don't know. Could've been trying to see how strong the Invidi were. An attack on U.N. authority. A way to get rid of us . . ."

Levin had used us and there was no way we could get back at him. We'd been made fools of by a dead man.

"Is there anything in the files on him?" I said.

"Nope, I already checked. Doesn't mean he never did anything worse, though. Just that he never got found out. Or that the records were lost in the crashes of the thirties and forties, like a lot of that official stuff."

"But they didn't catch him for the bomb?"

"Like I said, we don't know. The records aren't good enough. We knew there'd been some kind of assassination attempt. But no details." His voice roughened suddenly and he cleared his throat. "What are we going to do about this ship?" He put the handcom on the desk. "That's an update on our situation with ConFleet, by the way."

He turned his back on the monitor and sank into one of the low chairs with a groan of tiredness. "Basically, if they come and get us, all we can do is file a complaint with the nearest EarthFleet rep from inside our Confederacy cells."

I left the sleeping room and sat in the chair opposite him. "What about you? Weren't you transferred?"

He grimaced. "Officially I'm still on leave. I'm hoping

they'll accept me bringing you back as proof that I'm a good lad and listen to my request for the transfer to be rescinded."

But if I have to be tried under Earth law back on Earth, I want you there, I nearly said.

"You know, Halley." He leaned forward, his elbows resting on his knees and his hands clasped loosely between them. "You might be able to wriggle out of the *Calypso II* charges with only a fine. After all, there's no proof now that it was a jump drive. And as for appearing on that ship, I can say an Invidi lent it to us after setting it to arrive here. But if we hang on to it now, we've got no excuse."

"I know," was all I could come out with. All my reasons and excuses had disappeared.

"I reckon we've got twenty-four hours at most," he said. "That's how long it took them to respond when we had the Danadan warship here, and after you told them about the treaty."

"Bill, you know how important it is that the Nine gain access to the jump drive," I finally managed. I glanced at the photoimage of Las Mujeres, but it was at an angle where I couldn't see the front.

"Yeah, I can see that. And I'm no fan of the Four." He reached out and grasped my wrist. "But how important is it to the station? Stone was right in one way—how is this going to help the neutrality vote?"

I wished he hadn't done that. The warmth of his touch triggered feelings that were inextricably linked with Henoit's presence.

"Stone is worried about the reputation of the station if we don't do what the Confederacy wants us to," I said. "But the Confederacy is the one that should be worried if they force their way in here."

"You mean, if they break the neutrality provision? It hasn't been confirmed or ratified yet."

"I know. But if the Four, represented by ConFleet, were seen to be interfering before the whole Confederacy Council has considered the case, maybe it would get us sympathy votes."

He let go of my wrist and rubbed his face. "Not from Earth, it won't." His voice was muffled. "External Affairs is disgusted with having to leave us to even temporary neutrality. They see it as losing a colony."

"They should see it as gaining an ally." The current Earth admin's attitude had always been two-faced. They expected us to follow their directions but never pushed our interests with the Confederacy. They abandoned Jocasta to the Seouras blockade, then moaned about us losing faith in them.

"So how does keeping the Invidi ship help the neutrality vote?" said Murdoch.

"The Nine also vote. Maybe some of them will support us."

"I just don't see . . ." He stopped, looked at me, then continued determinedly. "I understand why we need neutrality. We can't risk the Confederacy leaving us to the wolves like last time and we can't go back to being an Earth colony. Fine. But I don't see how getting the jump drive to the Nine is going to help any of us here and now."

I thought of Alvarez, and was glad the photoimage was hidden from where I sat. I rubbed my eyes, and wished I hadn't, because they were raw and stung.

"I'm not sure I know either." I've been chasing it so long, though, it's hard to think I might be wrong.

He said nothing, for which I was grateful.

"I think it's important we understand why An Serat was experimenting with Tor technology," I said finally. "If it is possible to create jump points off the network, surely we don't want the Invidi to have a monopoly on that information, too?"

"I dunno." Murdoch ran both hands over his head. "Is it any better for us or the H'digh or the Bendarl to have it?"

"The Bendarl will get it anyway, if the Invidi have it," I said sourly.

"If it is Tor technology, how did Serat get it?"

I'd thought about that. When Earth was connected to the jump network and we started learning about the rest of the galaxy, we found that the Tor-Invidi war had been going on for decades. That war must have continued from before the Invidi came to Earth, I now realized, if An Serat had used Tor technology in 2023, Earth time. The war never directly concerned humans and had always been part of the background of the Confederacy. When Jocasta was given to Earth, of course, it became a more personal matter, because we had to deactivate the Tor elements of the station, and they did not cooperate.

The little we knew of the Tor was from their savagely active technology. What kind of species, we'd wondered, would create artificial intelligences whose prime directive seemed to be to take over any other kind of mechanism? The Invidi told us nothing. Any query about the Tor met with a dead end. In popular mythology they were variously represented as monsters, half machine half life form, and as gods. It was frustrating to have information kept from us, and, in the case of rebuilding Jocasta, it had proved fatal for many members of the engineering crews.

"Maybe Serat salvaged something from the conflict, like I did with *Calypso II*," I said. "It could have been an official experiment to merge Tor and Invidi technology, but then why would Serat go to such trouble to make it an obviously Invidi ship on the outside?"

Murdoch nodded. "There's some secrecy there. Otherwise why has Serat been up against the rest of the Invidi for years?"

"We've only Barik's word for that." At the end of the Seouras blockade, Barik had implied Serat's helping *Calypso* had been without the knowledge of the other Invidi.

"But the Sleepers said the same thing," said Murdoch. "And Serat was definitely connected to the New Council. No respectable Invidi would work with those terrorists."

The New Council of Allied Worlds had tried to take the jump drive from *Calypso* because An Serat had told them about its existence.

"Anyway," I said, suddenly tired of speculation, "I think we should know as much as we can about the ship and what Serat's been doing. The more we know, the more bargaining power we have."

"Break their monopoly on information?" Murdoch shook his head. "We can try, I suppose. But you'll have to work fast. Because when ConFleet comes to get it, we're going to have to give it to them pretty damn quick."

I nodded.

He smiled, and reached out to touch my hair lightly. "You . . ." His voice trailed off.

It felt good. Henoit's presence touched the back of my mind as Murdoch's fingers had touched my hair. I knew this was not the time or place, but it was hard to look away.

We sat staring at each other across the little table with its EarthFleet logo: a rounded arrow shape against one large star, symbolizing Earth, and three smaller ones, symbolizing Mars and the colonies of Europa and Titan.

This is ridiculous. We haven't even kissed since that night in the out-town before the Invidi arrived. Keep your mind on business, Halley.

"Bill, how can I investigate that ship if I'm under arrest?"

He smiled wryly. "You haven't technically been charged with possession of jump technology because there's no solid proof. I mean, *Calypso II* isn't here. After all those records disappeared, I reckon they'll have trouble proving you did anything wrong at all."

"Maybe they'll 'find' those records if they need them."

"It wouldn't surprise me. But my report says you're assisting us to answer questions regarding EarthFleet resources used in your research activities. The charge will probably be misappropriation of funds. We'll refer the suspicion of possession—that's for appearing here in an Invidi ship—to the Confederacy when we've finished here, like we do with any Confederacy offense."

"Possession has always been fully prosecuted. And ConFleet will court-martial me."

"I think you should talk to deVries about that." He meant Lorna deVries, the chief magistrate.

"Veatch said he'd talk to her. I'll give him a bit longer, then call her." I yawned hugely. "Sorry."

"I'm sorry about the quarters." Murdoch waved his hand at the room.

"It's fine. Thanks for getting my things out. My old room is being used, I suppose."

"We had a big staff quarters rearrangement a few months ago," he said. "I signed for your stuff, being executor and all, but Helen Sasaki took care of putting it in storage. Getting it out tonight was her idea." He seemed about to say more, but stopped. There was a silence full of something.

"I'm sorry you got dragged into this." As I said it, it struck me that it should have been said sooner.

He snorted. "If I'd been worried about that, I wouldn't have gone looking for you in the first place."

More silence. I looked at his hands again, then at the dark curve of his forearm. His closeness filled all my senses except for the sixth, within which Henoit's presence stirred up and down my skin in a shivering wave.

I stood up abruptly. "We'd better get some rest. I need to be fresh to look at that ship."

Murdoch stood up, too, and shoved the table to one side with his knee. "Are you really sleepy?"

His arm slid up mine. I forgot Henoit and stepped into Murdoch's embrace, my body pressed against his, our faces close in the first tentative nuzzles of a kiss. His tongue licked the edge of my jaw and I reached up impatiently to turn his mouth to mine.

Déjà vu. We'd kissed like this in the out-town. The night before the Invidi arrived, the night of the fire. Will interrupted us. The pang of loss cut through pleasure. Murdoch felt the change and drew back.

"What's wrong?"

As if in answer, the door buzzed.

"Bloody hell," said Murdoch and took his hands away from my waist.

"Door open," I said hoarsely.

This time it was Veatch. He came in and stood, antennae drooping apologetically, just far enough inside the door for it to shut again.

"Commander Halley, please excuse this intrusion. Chief Murdoch, I was hoping to confirm your availability at 1000 hours to discuss and process the filework for your investigation."

"Veatch, why didn't you use your comm link?" I said.

"I did not wish to disturb you if you had retired."

He could have asked the interface if my room was on rest cycle. He must have something on his mind that he couldn't ask or say outright. The telltale signs of discomfort were there: antennae curled tighter than usual, shuffling four or five handcoms in front of him.

"Chief Murdoch, you also need to fill out your leave forms correctly," he continued, bringing the bottom handcom to the top of the pile. "Plus the groundwork for your charges against Commander Halley."

"I'm no sooner home than you're trying to get rid of

me," I said with deliberate humor, wondering if Veatch would get the joke. If he was relaxed, he could usually follow human humor.

"On the contrary, Commander, I am attempting to make it illegal for you to be arrested twice."

"Can't it wait . . ." Murdoch began, then caught my raised eyebrow and stopped.

"Do you think it likely ConFleet will break the neutrality provision to come and get the ship?" I said.

"I do not have sufficient information to estimate either way," said Veatch. "However, I believe they may make some kind of move later today. Mr. Stone's message should have reached An Barik or an alternative Invidi by then and . . ."

"Hang on," said Murdoch. "What do you mean, Stone's message?"

"Mr. Stone has continued private communication with An Barik since the Invidi left Jocasta," Veatch said, with an air of "didn't you know?"

"When was that?" I said. When I left, An Barik was living on Jocasta as the Confederacy Council "representative" rather than in his previous role as "observer." He'd still remained a virtual recluse in the Smoke, the non-oxygen breathers' section of the station.

"Approximately twenty days ago," said Veatch.

"Seven days after I left," said Murdoch, considering.

"Why is Stone sending him messages?" I said.

Veatch managed to convey the essence of a shrug without moving his elegant shoulders. "Perhaps it is an arrangement by your ministry," he said. "Perhaps An Barik asked Mr. Stone and he could not refuse."

"I don't see that this changes anything," said Murdoch. "*Vengeful* sent a courier with the news to Central anyway. An Barik will still hear about it."

I wondered why An Barik had stayed on Jocasta after

the neutrality provision came into effect. Opinion on the station was clearly against the Four's continued domination of the Confederacy Council and against the Confederacy owning Jocasta. It can't have been comfortable for him.

Unless he was waiting for us to return from the past. Our return must be a big enough "node" or disturbance in their fabric of time for him to "see." And he knew about *Calypso*'s arrival, my departure with *Calypso II,* and An Serat's involvement with the causal loop. Perhaps if he was here, An Serat couldn't or wouldn't come.

What had kept Barik away from Jocasta at the critical time of our return? Something more critical out there in the Confederacy, perhaps countering An Serat's influence. Or, conversely, our return with Serat's ship was not as critical as I thought.

"Does Stone know you know he's sending messages to An Barik?" said Murdoch to Veatch.

"I assume so." Veatch's eyes were pools of liquid innocence.

Humans are pre-programmed to rely on eyes for subtle clues to intention. Unfortunately, Melot signal their subliminal clues through other means, antennae or body position, and it takes a while to learn these. I was out of practice and couldn't place Veatch's intent in telling us about Stone. When I first arrived on Earth in the past, the endless array of human faces, unbroken by alien colors or features, seemed monotonous and oppressive. Now I was having trouble remembering which alien expression meant what.

Veatch certainly seemed more relaxed now that he'd told us about Stone. And he hadn't yet implied we owed him something in return.

"You mean you haven't told him," said Murdoch, resigned. "Like you didn't tell Halley when you were reading her mail."

It was unfair of Murdoch to bring up that incident, part of the events surrounding the Q'Chn we had on the station at the end of the Seouras occupation and therefore over and done with.

Veatch remained relaxed. "I have not discussed the matter in detail with Mr. Stone. However, I assumed that as he is generally an efficient and thorough administrator, he is cognizant of my arrangements."

I wasn't sure if that was a backhanded comment against my nontalents as an administrator or not. "Do you enjoy working with him?" I said.

"Mr. Stone shows some understanding of complex concepts of organization. I am impressed that your species is capable of this," said Veatch.

"That must make your job easier," I said, stung.

"It removes much of the necessity to recheck procedures. And perhaps smooths the interactive aspect of my job."

"It's late," Murdoch said. He reached out and put his arm around my waist. The open gesture of affection shocked me as much as it seemed to surprise Veatch, judging from the way his antennae stiffened.

"Let's continue this after we've had a couple hours' sleep, okay?" said Murdoch.

Veatch gathered his handcoms to his chest. "Yes, that would seem to be the best approach. Good night, Commander, Chief."

"Good night, Veatch," we chorused.

The door swished shut behind him.

Murdoch's arm was warm around my waist. I should go up to the dock now and study the ship. ConFleet or An Barik could arrive sooner than we expected and I'd lose the chance. But I was so tired . . . I shook my head angrily. What happened to all that energy I had during the blockade? Maybe age is catching up with me.

"What's wrong?" Murdoch squeezed gently.

"I was thinking I'm getting older."

"It's all that time travel, takes it out of you."

"I should go up and look at the ship."

"You're not going to find out anything if you're half asleep." He tugged on my arm. "Sit down, huh?"

"Bill, I haven't got time. We don't know when Con-Fleet . . ."

He tugged again. I sat, mainly to avoid overbalancing. Once seated, it seemed very comfortable. I leaned against him, as I'd done a couple of times in the out-town. We'd watched televid in Levin's house like this. But in Levin's house Grace or Will had always been present. Now it was just Bill and me.

Bill, whom I'd been kissing when Veatch interrupted.

This is not a good time to begin a liaison. Neither of us knows where we'll be tomorrow, let alone in the months to come. Henoit's presence is getting stronger every time I touch Bill, and we've got so many other things to worry about.

"Activate privacy lock," I said to the air. The interface beeped acknowledgment.

I half turned to see Murdoch's expression moving from astonishment to careful interest.

"Bill, do you think . . ." *this is a good idea*, was what I'd been going to say, but then he reached up to the back of my neck and stroked gently. An invitation. His other hand was cupped around my outer thigh. It moved slowly inward.

I couldn't finish what I was going to say because my breath was gone. When I gasped to get it back, my arms were around Murdoch's chest and my lips were on his.

*   *   *

Later, I curled with my back against Murdoch's warm bulk and watched the unchanging night light of the station stain the room blue.

We knew each other so well, except in this. I hadn't expected him to be a gentle, inventive lover and he had obviously not expected ... my responses. Which were partly a response to Henoit. Not that Murdoch knew that. He saw only the effect, as if I were responding to him alone.

Do you feel as I feel? Henoit had whispered in the ear of my mind. His touch brought something out of me to the surface of my skin to meet him. For the space of a heartbeat or the length of an orgasm I did feel how Henoit felt, see the same way he saw. In that space I was part of a consciousness not mine, not human. I could never describe it; we have no frame of reference for getting into another's skin.

It wasn't fair to Murdoch, because when I held him tight and pitched into pleasure I was holding Henoit's hot, dry skin and feeling his breath in mine. And for that second I wanted it to be Henoit.

Why couldn't Henoit leave me alone? But, oh dear, it is hard to resist such ... I wriggled in the bed, still smelling Henoit's scent, still half immersed in his voice.

It wasn't that he had possessed some exotic alien appendage that could be used to drive humans to extremes of arousal, as popular entertainment depicted. The mechanics of H'digh reproduction are fairly androgynous, like their appearance, and practical rather than exciting—a species in which most females conceive only once in their lives has to have evolved methods of making sure that conception occurs.

When I lay with Henoit, the quality of arousal for me had come firstly from the pheromones, which turned my whole body into a kind of tuning fork for pleasure, and secondly from the accuracy of his touch. Perhaps because, as bonded partners, he was inside me mentally and could feel what I felt, and adjust his touch accordingly.

But I never thought it would happen when I was with someone else. Murdoch's every caress, every shiver of our arousal, every touch of hot skin in the here and now, had an extra dimension. As though I was feeling with two sets of senses.

I rolled over and stretched myself full length along his side. Reached over and anchored my hand across his chest, laid my head beside it. When I shut my eyes to keep out the blue, I could feel his chest rise and fall under my cheek. His heartbeat thudded regularly in my ear, loud enough to drown out other memories.

Twenty-one

The door buzzed. My eyes stuck together and I tried to force them open, surprised that I'd eventually fallen asleep.

Murdoch half fell out of bed beside me and staggered into the main room. I heard him groan, "It's 0700. Don't you ever sleep?"

Murdoch in bed beside me. I rolled over onto the warm space he'd vacated and wriggled my toes there, savoring the strangeness of the feeling, wanting to etch it in memory before it faded to familiarity.

"I work to a Central day," said Veatch's voice.

That is, twice as long as we work. Better get up, Halley.

I rolled right over and out of the bed. Fished for the uniform trousers I'd left on the floor the night before. Earlier this morning, rather. At the third try I got them. My depth perception was out, focus too.

"May I come in?" Veatch's voice went on. "I have some information I think you should know."

The door swished shut. I pulled on the trousers and did up my shirt, realized it was uneven, refastened it.

When I looked into the main room, Veatch was standing near the door, where he'd stood last night. Murdoch rubbed the sleep out of his eyes beside him.

Veatch's antennae perked up. "Commander Halley. Considering the urgency of our situation, I felt it best that I should come early."

"Urgency. Yes." The strange Tor-Invidi ship, Rupert Stone, and An Barik. A Bendarl voice growling—ConFleet waiting to pounce. Murdoch's hands on me, reaching . . .

"Have we got a coffee dispenser in here?" I said.

Murdoch yawned hugely and pointed to an alcove on the wall beside one of the chairs.

"Allow me," said Veatch. He stepped over to the alcove and tapped at the dispenser controls.

I went back into the bedroom and shoved my face in the cubicle's airwash. The mirror in the cubicle was voice-activated and I was careful to say nothing. If I looked half as sleepy as I felt, I didn't want to see it.

Awake on the outside at least, I reemerged into the main room. It smelled of coffee. Murdoch was hunched over a cup in one chair and Veatch sat on the edge of the chair opposite. Another cup sat on the low table in front of the other chair, beside Murdoch.

The room was artificially lit, as it had been last night, but something in the quality of the light said morning. I sipped at the coffee and things began to slip into place. I must go up to the dock and investigate the ship. We had to know how it worked, and whether it was important enough for An Barik and the other Invidi to risk political embarrassment by breaking Jocasta's provisional neutrality to take it back.

Veatch straightened his collar. A small gesture, but unusual enough to ring a faint alarm bell. He'd wanted to talk about something last night, but Murdoch and I had been in no condition to listen.

"What do you want to talk about?" I said, too tense for subtlety.

"I, er, wish to know the details of your disappearance and arrival," said Veatch. "It is impossible for me to complete my report without knowing your previous where-abouts."

Murdoch shook his head. "Imagine that, not being able to finish a report for five months. And all I was worried about was whether you were alive."

I frowned at him. "Veatch, I can't tell you where I went. Not yet. It involves the Invidi."

"In what sense . . ." he began, but Murdoch interrupted.

"You mean finish your report about the *Calypso II* experiment, don't you?" he said, voice rising slightly. "You must have implemented those orders to transfer the three engineers. When I asked you what happened to the Engineering accounts for June, you didn't know about it. You didn't even know who was treasurer at that time. As for the information on Finke's freighter . . ." He leaned forward and tapped the table for emphasis. "How about my transfer? You passed that through without query, too, I suppose?"

Veatch drew back slightly. "I have no input into personnel movement orders."

Murdoch snorted. "You're station manager, aren't you? At that stage we didn't even have an acting head of station, so if you didn't object, nobody would."

"Chief Murdoch, you must understand that I am obliged under all circumstances, however personally disconcerting, to observe the protocols of the service."

I drained my coffee and put the cup down with a clatter louder than I'd intended. Not that I'd ever expected Veatch's loyalty. Or even his understanding. "So who was it?"

Veatch twitched in my direction. He'd started shuffling his handcoms again. "Who was what?"

"Who gave the orders to hush it all up?"

He hesitated, then laid the handcoms one by one on the table, like someone playing patience with 2-D cards.

"The orders came through Sector Five Division Three," he said. Sector Five was the branch of the Confederacy bureaucracy that handled affairs of the Nine Worlds. Division Three was Security.

"The orders were . . ." he paused, then continued delicately, "emphasized by An Barik. His advice was to follow them precisely. I did so."

Murdoch and I shared a glance. An Barik wanted my experiment with *Calypso II* kept secret. The immediate explanation was if news leaked out that a member of the Nine had used a jump drive, the Four would have to explain how that was possible and why everyone couldn't do it. The other explanation was that An Barik knew the *Calypso* jump point was off the network and wanted to keep that possibility quiet as well. Why hadn't Barik simply prevented me from taking *Calypso II?* I supposed, because he needed me to go back to 2023 and set off the chain of events that resulted in the Invidi coming to Earth.

"I'm sure you both agree I could not have done otherwise. Even had I wished it," he added unexpectedly.

"Why should you 'wish otherwise'?" said Murdoch suspiciously. "What's in it for you?"

Veatch seemed unembarrassed by the question. "If use of the jump drive becomes more freely available, the status quo in the Confederacy Council may be disturbed. In this scenario, there is some probability that nonaligned worlds such as ourselves may gain economically."

"And the other probability?" said Murdoch.

"The political upheaval may induce lawless elements, which were previously restrained by the presence of ConFleet, to attempt acts of violence."

Murdoch met my eyes and I remembered his comments the night before. *How's it going to help any of us right now?*

"However," Veatch continued thoughtfully, "I have considered this matter at length and feel it is highly unlikely that either outcome would prove particularly detrimental for this station and the Abelar system."

He waited for Murdoch's impatient "Well?" before continuing, his antennae perked with gratification. "This station is not on the periphery of the Confederacy in any sense other than that of physical distance which, as we all know and appreciate, is of little import in the present transport system which relies on the jump network. In fact, Jocasta's position close to a point on the jump network places it in as important a position as any other place close to a jump point, whether that be Earth, Chene . . ." which was one of the main Melot systems, "or Rhuarl, to give random examples."

"You're saying if we improve our insystem facilities, we could become a big center in this sector?" said Murdoch unbelievingly.

"But not if we lose the neutrality vote, right?" I said, understanding Veatch's reasoning. "If the Confederacy keeps control of who goes in and out of the jump point, we're never going to get the people here who could help set us up as a major sector player."

"An oversimplification, but I believe that is the gist of the matter," said Veatch, with nicely calculated condescension. "I do not think the Four Worlds will lose the monopoly over travel within the Confederacy. My experience tells me ConFleet will come and retrieve the ship you brought here, to prevent you from passing on the information. But this in itself will be a destabilizing influence, as it will demonstrate to the Nine Worlds and unaligned worlds that the Four are willing to break their own laws to protect their interests. The likelihood that we will earn enough votes for neutrality is greatly increased."

"Will any of the Nine support us, do you think?" Murdoch said.

"My casual opinion"—Veatch paused to make sure we realized this didn't commit him to anything—"is that we may count on support from the Dir, who reject K'Cher monopolies, and the Tell, although it is not clear why. The Neronderon may turn our way—they are unpredictable as yet. Achel possibly, because their new leaders are demonstrating a desire to take leadership among the Nine."

"None of the Four will vote yes, obviously," said Murdoch.

"The Bendarl do not like to lose territory. The K'Cher do not like to lose arenas for business. My people are divided on most issues, but generally we support keeping the jump drive confined to use by the Four. And the Invidi . . ." He paused.

"The Invidi?" I prompted.

"This is difficult to express." His antennae curled lightly once, then extended again. "The Invidi are like a child who insists on having a potentially dangerous animal for a toy. In my opinion, they are genuinely curious about other species and wish to engage with them on a variety of levels. But when those species begin to act in ways that the Invidi perceive as dangerous or disturbing, the Invidi lose initiative. It is a most curious phenomenon."

"If you can't stand the heat, stay out of the reactor," grunted Murdoch.

"Yes, but if it wasn't for them, we wouldn't have a reactor," I reminded him.

"All this talk of Four and Nine," said Murdoch. "You're one of them, not us. Why are you betraying your own kind?"

Veatch's antennae curled momentarily in outrage. His unblinking eyes narrowed. "I am doing nothing of the kind. I merely desire to continue a satisfactory occupation."

Murdoch and I had speculated after the Seouras occupation ended whether Veatch's masters in the Confederacy bureaucracy would want him back at Central. It looked like the answer was no.

"You'll try to run for a top position if we get neutrality, won't you?" said Murdoch.

"My present position is sufficient and I would like to keep it." Veatch shifted even farther onto the edge of his chair. "As part of that position, I have business here with you this morning."

Murdoch yawned, but his eyes were wary. "We're listening."

"You are familiar with the trader, Kuvai Trillith?" said Veatch. Murdoch and I both nodded and he continued. "Twenty-five days ago it came to me and asked me if I could assist in a problem of storage. A cargo of high-quality booster fuel, I believe, that exceeded the capacity of Trillith's own warehouses. Perhaps mistakenly, I agreed to lend it an unused storage bay in Level Eight of the center."

He paused to check we were following.

"Veatch, at the moment that's not a priority," I said.

"Perhaps you will think differently when I am finished." He inclined his head in gentle reprimand and I remembered the irritation with which I'd often sat through his convoluted explanations of protocol.

"Get to the point, then." Murdoch stretched back in the chair.

"If I state the point without providing the necessary background, how will you understand whether the point is reached or not?" said Veatch.

I jiggled my bare feet on the carpet.

Veatch glanced down and took the hint. "Unfortunately, the storage bay is designated an official area. And in consideration of services rendered previously to the administration by Trillith, I waived the surcharge."

"You let it use an official area without permission or payment," said Murdoch. "So what? We're worried about being arrested by ConFleet at the moment, not how you fiddle the files."

"I am not familiar with that particular human archaism," said Veatch. "However, I assure you this has some bearing on your position."

"You don't want Stone to find out," I said, suddenly understanding. "Or he already has, and you want to stop him acting on it."

Veatch inclined his head graciously. "Perhaps you could explain to Mr. Stone how difficult it is to balance the demands of the various interest groups on the station?"

Murdoch guffawed without humor. "This is a waste of time."

"Actually, I can think of a couple of issues Mr. Veatch may be able to help us with," I said, trying to signal him with my eyebrows. "Surely you can tell Stone that approval for emergency private use of the storage bay is waiting on a security check or something?"

"Trillith is too damn greedy for its own good," he grumbled. "But I'll see what I can do."

I smiled at him. "For example, Veatch might be able to enlighten me on how the Invidi treat those who break the rules of their society. Do they have punishment, as we do? Atonement?" I wanted to know if Serat not being here to meet us meant the other Invidi were preventing him from coming for his ship.

Veatch settled back in his chair and tugged at his suit to keep it smooth. "The Invidi, Commander? I am no expert in the Invidi."

"But you just told us about them," Murdoch said.

"In my capacity as station manager"—he glanced reproachfully at Murdoch—"I have acquired a degree of knowledge about the species of the Confederacy. I must say that the Invidi are particularly guarded in their presentation of their society to non-Invidi. However, based on the case of Tiepolo v. An Dorol of 2119—"

"Never mind the details," interrupted Murdoch.

"In summary, the Invidi do not have a system of physical restraint or mental reconditioning. They do not feel they have the right—and I may be mistaken in this, Commander—to restrict another's movement. I may add that my observation of An Barik on this station supports this interpretation."

I had to agree with him. An Barik had been almost a recluse and refused to have much contact with even other Four residents. When *Calypso* arrived and he tried to access its jump drive before anyone else, he'd used my friend Quartermaine to do the hard work.

"Why did Barik leave?" I said.

"I do not know."

I dragged my thoughts back to the neutrality vote. "What about the H'digh?" I asked, thinking of Henoit. A residual shiver from last night prickled the back of my neck. "How do you think they'll vote?"

Veatch considered. "H'digh domestic politics are extremely volatile. However, a conservative faction now holds the Confederacy Council representative posts, so it is likely they will vote no, in an attempt to restrain the New Council group and the radical groups within H'digh society who support the New Council."

Like Henoit. "Does the New Council still have the Q'Chn?"

Murdoch started to say something, stopped.

Veatch picked an invisible piece of fluff from his knee. "A good question, Commander. I fear the answer is in the affirmative."

Q'Chn were the genetically engineered warrior caste of the now defunct K'Cher empire. At the end of the K'Cher-Invidi war, four Earth years before the formation of the

Confederacy in 2065, the K'Cher agreed not to make any more Q'Chn and the galaxy breathed a collective sigh of relief; Q'Chn were formidable killers and the old K'Cher empire employed them frequently to enforce order in its colonies. Until the Invidi stopped them.

"Have the Invidi said how they defeated the Q'Chn in the war?" I said. "Surely they have a duty to the rest of the Confederacy to protect us this time."

Murdoch shifted in his chair and leaned back. "If they have, nobody's telling Security forces on the ground. Why should the Invidi bother? They're not the ones getting killed yet."

When one of these aliens appeared on Jocasta at the end of the Seouras occupation, we expected the worst. Five humans and one K'Cher were killed by it. But the Q'Chn we saw was different to the old Slashers—it thought ahead, it had the ability to wait and hide. It was more than just a biological killing machine.

The New Council had obtained Q'Chn genetic material and "made" their own Q'Chn, modifying along the way. But genetic engineering is an inexact science at best. They wanted a Q'Chn that was amenable to orders yet also an efficient terrorist; instead,. they had produced a cunning killer with nobody knew what desires and goals.

"The New Council won't be interested in Jocasta unless we're neutral," Murdoch said.

I nodded. Henoit had come to Jocasta to bargain for use of the station as a base. "Which is why some of the delegates will vote against us. They think if ConFleet is here, it will keep the Q'Chn out of a system that has a position on the jump network."

"And potentially into Central." Veatch sounded satisfied at our conclusions. "I estimate we will lose both Earth and the H'digh votes because of this issue. I should go," he added. "It has been enjoyable to talk with you again, Commander. Chief Murdoch, despite the fact that you are still officially on leave, Lieutenant Sasaki wished me to inform you that the civil unrest in Delta Section Three has calmed during the night . . ."

"Civil unrest?" I looked at Murdoch.

He shrugged. "Apparently there was a protest against the increase in time it takes to access the docks because of a new safety measure."

". . . and the fire extinguisher system test will be at 1400 hours, not 0900," finished Veatch.

"Thanks," grunted Murdoch without the slightest indication of gratitude.

Veatch inclined his head and left.

Murdoch rose abruptly. "He's always manipulating. Always got something on the boil, and you're lucky if you guess what it is before you get scalded."

"Maybe this time he's genuine." I sounded as unconvinced as I felt. "Bill, do you think he's right about the Q'Chn? That there are still some out there?"

"We've heard rumors."

"Is it likely?"

He shrugged. "You tell me, it was your ex who was so chummy with the New Council."

I picked up my empty cup, put it down again in confusion. Had Murdoch suspected something last night? Why bring up Henoit now?

"Anyway," he went on, "if you're worried about defense against the Q'Chn, don't waste your time. We can't defend ourselves against something like that. And if the New Council come asking for dock space, we'll be allies and won't need to worry about the Q'Chn."

"I don't want to be allies with the Q'Chn. Bill, defense is a problem with neutrality, isn't it?"

He nodded. "I guess the only thing to do is either build up a standing fleet of our own, or make it more profitable for people like the New Council to use the station, not attack it. After all, what would we have that the Q'Chn could possibly want?"

I didn't think the Q'Chn thought about things so logically, but it didn't seem worth debating. I went into the bedroom and pulled on my boots.

"Bill," I called, "are you going to keep that constable with me all day? It's a waste of your people's time."

"Regulations." He came to the doorway, fastening his jacket. "If we're going to use my custody of you as a reason to resist Confederacy charges, we're going to have to do it properly."

He patted his equipment belt, frowned, reached across to the desk for one of the handcoms there, and stuck it to the belt. "We could put you on bond for a while," he said. "Means you put up a payment and promise not to leave the station or communicate with anyone outside the station. We let you walk around."

"Like bail," I said. "Grace lent Vince money once to get one of his mates out."

"That's right."

"I overdrew already to pay Finke."

He grinned. "You can put that ship up, I suppose."

"But aren't you treating it as stolen property?" It sounded unorthodox to me. Stone wouldn't like it.

"That's a Confederacy problem," said Murdoch, almost happily. He was in a strange mood this morning.

"If you say so."

He sat behind the desk and tapped at the comm panel for a moment. "Come look in here."

I peered over his shoulder. He was in a restricted area of Security input.

"Okay," he said, "I've put in the details." He pointed at the retina plate. "Have a squint in there, so it can check with your records."

I stared at the plate until my eyes began to water. The acknowledgment light blinked on. I stretched my neck and stepped back. "Bill, tell me about Stone. Where was he before he came here?"

"Does it matter?"

"I need to know how he might react if ConFleet gets pushy."

He signed himself out of the secure area before replying. "I think he'll get out of their way. He was head of Audits—this is in External Affairs—for three years before he came here, and assistant secretary of Finance and Admin in the same ministry before that."

"He's never been off-planet before?"

"Only to Mars."

I snorted. "I know I wasn't Earth's favorite head of station, but who decided Stone would be better?"

"I reckon Earth wants to get us economically viable before the neutrality application. Then they can say, why bother with neutrality, you've got it all now." He looked at me sideways. "But then, if you'd been here, Stone wouldn't have got chosen at all."

I said nothing. The weight of mistaken choices sat heavy in my stomach, and the Seouras implant twinged as if it sensed the irony of how close I was to answering the question that drove me to make those choices. How did the jump drive work? That ship in our dock could tell me.

Murdoch seemed to be waiting for something. Then he shrugged, stood up, and we were face-to-face behind the desk. "You'll be with the ship."

"Yes."

"Have you thought of letting everyone know?" he said. "Sending the ship's specs to everyone you can possibly think of and hoping the information will go right across the Confederacy?"

"I have, but that will take time, and this isn't any old

jump drive. It's got Tor elements. Unless I look at it while I can, we may never get a second chance." A thought struck me. "My general access codes won't work anymore, will they?"

"No, they won't. I'll get Helen to put you back in the system. But I can't get you more than basic level stuff. Because you're officially missing and until I change that status, it won't recognize you for higher-level commands."

"I remember." I wish I hadn't helped Engineering develop those security measures. We'd had a problem with official supplies being rerouted by thieves who masqueraded as dead or missing officers, so we'd tightened up the system.

Murdoch stayed in front of me when I attempted to move past him. Put out an arm to block my way, but the arm ended up around me. "Halley, is it safe? You quit breathing last time."

"It should be all right. Nothing too bad happened after that first contact. And I won't be going anywhere in it. Just seeing what I can find out with diagnostic tools." I would have liked to stay and enjoy the sensation of his arm, but the ship was pulling at me with an almost palpable tug, and I didn't want Henoit whispering in my ear again.

"See you later, then." Murdoch let his arm drop.

"Right."

Awkward moment when neither could decide whether to kiss or not. Awkward moment solved when Murdoch brushed his lips on mine. His chin bristled me with two days' worth of stubble.

Twenty-two

It was about 0800 hours when I walked back through the Bubble to the nearest spoke. The uplift there would take me straight to the part of the center that housed the enclosed areas in which ships from our EarthFleet squadrons used to dock for maintenance, before they were decimated by the Seouras. Sasaki said she'd put the ship in there, probably for several reasons: it would be well protected against curious stares and isolated enough to be easily guarded; if ConFleet tried to locate the ship, the proximity of many other ships and the opsys core might confuse their sensors, and the docks offered easy maintenance access.

She'd also said the cruiser had done nothing unusual after sending the scout through the jump point, merely continued on its normal patrol pattern. I would gain a little time, too, because at this time of year, the orbit of Jocasta's planet took us farther away from the Central jump point's flatspace coordinates. It wouldn't take long for a ConFleet ship to cover the distance, but I'd be glad of even one extra hour in which to examine the ship.

This part of Jocasta was a pleasant open area between the Alpha ring section containing central admin and the hospital. Around me, low vegetation lined the double walkways. People in uniform or civilian suits sat on benches or walked between offices. The huge pillar of the uplift spoke blocked the path ahead, otherwise it would have continued curving up. The mirrors that lined the top of Alpha ring brightened the "sky" to pale gold above, almost too strong to look straight up. If you could look straight up, you would see the cylindrical center of the station, the hub connected by the lines of the spokes, and beyond it the curve of the rings on the far side.

Veatch's words echoed in my head. We were used to thinking of Jocasta as being on the periphery, as being unimportant. Hard to consider it wasn't necessarily so. The jump point was close to the station's orbit because, during the Tor-Invidi war, this had been a place of conflict and the Invidi ships, or Bendarl, perhaps, had to have had a way to get here. And how did the Tor get here? Through their own jump system, presumably. All we knew about the Tor was that they had possessed jump technology. When the gray ships arrived we first thought they'd come through an unknown Tor jump point.

I wondered if we'd find a Tor jump point somewhere out there, close to where the gray ships first appeared. Would it open for an Invidi ship? Would it open for a hybrid Tor-Invidi ship?

I stopped dead, trying to grasp all the implications of that idea. Had An Serat's ship been a project to infiltrate the Tor jump network? But if that was the case, why did An Serat attempt to keep it, and his subsequent assistance to *Calypso*, a secret from the other Invidi?

Voices and other footsteps echoed ahead. A mixed group of humans and aliens moved toward me, heading for the Bubble. Leading them was a lanky young man in civilian clothes. Even before I heard his voice, I recognized Dan Florida's slouch and the way he threw his hands about when he talked. Dan Florida, founder of Jocasta's only unofficial news media organization and presently the single member of the lobby delegation from Jocasta to the Confederacy Council.

I still felt guilty at how I'd persuaded the Residents Committee to vote for Florida as our lobbyist to the Confederacy Council. He'd been entirely too curious about the *Calypso II* project, and I felt that talking to Council members about Jocasta would keep him busy. As well as Jocasta receiving the benefit of his obvious talents as a lobbyist—persistence and persuasiveness.

"You should remember that this part of the station was one of the earliest built," Florida was saying as he approached. "This hall was the original command center."

The others stared up at the building he was pointing at, an unimpressive single-story community hall, now used as a temporary storage facility. I didn't remember it being the command center, but then, I didn't take over as head of station until the station's third year, after the first head had quit, two committed suicide, and the one in between was poisoned.

The people with Florida must be the Confederacy Council representatives that Sasaki had mentioned; a human woman in colorful caftan and two men in drab suits, five Dir, all wearing robes of a single guild with their hoods open, two fur-covered Achelians, and a high-caste Leowin attended by its retinue of smaller slaves.

Leowin are a species thought by everyone else to be distantly related to the K'Cher but they deny it vehemently themselves. They are bipedal by choice but can move just as fast on four limbs. Their upper manipulators are jointed, unlike K'Cher feelers, and their chests and abdomens flow into each other. This one wore a robe similar to that of the Dir, but in a more subdued weave and color.

"Hello, Dan," I said. The scene took me back half a year or more to the day Florida and I had escorted *Ca-*

lypso's Sleeper passengers on their first tour of the station. Their first tour of the twenty-second century.

Florida stared. "I heard the rumor, but I didn't believe it." He bounded forward and wrapped his arms around me in a bear hug.

I felt as though I'd been wrung out. He was as big and bouncy as ever.

"Good to see you back," his voice boomed in my ear.

I squeezed his torso briefly in gratitude at this welcome and hoped he wouldn't notice my eyes were watering.

"These are some of my delegates." Florida indicated the group with a flourish. "Consul Reo of Achel and his aide. Amartidjar of the Leowin. Count Quertianus, and his captains. Councilor Sarkady of Earth. Councilors, this is Commander Halley, Head of . . . former head of station."

I bowed to the Achelians and nodded to the count, a high-status Dir whose quick glance evaluated everything about me from uniform to body parts. The Leowin ignored me, as its protocols demanded.

Sarkady grasped my hand without turning a gracious gray hair and looked me over with eyes that might have been wise, or merely the result of a career spent trying to look wise. She wore a loose gown of bright-colored cloth that glowed in the humid air.

"Commander. Weren't you reported missing?"

"A slight misunderstanding."

"Presumably you'll be able to clear it up."

"I'm sure we will."

Sarkady nodded in turn at the two humans with her. "My aides." One, a human with pale mottled skin and reddish hair, shook my hand North American style. The other, seeing me flex my squeezed hand with a grimace, merely inclined her head. A trim, correct woman, she was like an older version of Ensign Lee.

"We're on our way to the garden," said Florida, ushering his charges ahead of us. "Come along now, we'll miss the best part of the morning," he chided gently. After minor jostling between the five Dir and the Leowin slaves, they walked on ahead of him.

"Where have you been?" he whispered to me.

"Nowhere interesting," I whispered back, then felt ridiculous. "Dan, I need to talk to you about Central," I said in a normal voice.

I wanted to hear his views on the likelihood of the neutrality vote being passed, and compare it to what Veatch had said. Florida might be brash and obnoxious, but he had a knack of making useful contacts and his verbosity could be an asset.

"Come to dinner tonight. A few of us, in the observation lounge in the center." He pointed upward. "Level Three."

"There is no observation lounge on Level Three." Then I remembered Sasaki's comment when we arrived last night.

He grinned. "Thought I'd catch you on that one. Will you come?"

"If I can." If I'm still here. And if I've figured out how that ship works.

"The new head of station . . ." he began.

"Acting head of station."

He raised an eyebrow. "Acting head of station decided it'd be impressive to sit and watch the stars spin around while we ate dinner. Don't want to miss that, do you?"

"You could have used one of the construction platforms," I grumbled, thinking of the complex logistics of redecorating a section of Level Three.

"Ah, but he wants the gravity field on. Can't have important guests chasing pieces of their meal in free fall."

And we'd get complaints from travelers who didn't want to step out of their airlock into Earth gravity . . . "Wait a minute. This is an official dinner?"

"You got it. Dress uniforms, antique cutlery, speeches, the lot."

"You sneaky bastard. You know I hate that sort of thing."

He grinned. "It'll be a great chance for you to reemerge, so to speak. Give you a taste of what happens at Central."

"I don't want to go to Central. That's why I sent you."

"I thought it was to get rid of me." He grinned as he said it, but his eyes were shrewd.

"You make a better lobbyist than I do, Dan."

"Maybe I believe in neutrality more." This time his face was serious, but I still had the impression he was laughing at me.

"What's that supposed to mean?" I glared at him but we'd reached the spoke and the agricultural section, and Florida was tapping open the entry with one hand.

He patted my shoulder with the other in odious sympathy. "Don't worry, Commander. I'll make sure you don't embarrass yourself too much."

The EarthFleet blue panels opened and warm, heavily oxygenated air rolled out to meet us with the unmistakable smell of growing things. Beds of vegetables, fruit, fungi and gillus rose in terraces to meet the reflected gold of the "sky." A diffuse, pale light covered everything. The fields were originally an eighth of this size and designed to merely augment the station's food supply. Under Confederacy neglect and alien blockade, however, we expanded them in order to survive.

"Lovely, just beautiful," Sarkady enthused.

"Charming," agreed the Achelian.

One of the Dir tapped something into his handcom and showed the result to the others.

"Dan, I have to go."

"Ah, to the mysterious Invidi ship that brought you home, no doubt? We haven't seen an Invidi, though."

I'd forgotten how fast rumor spreads on this station.

Florida looked down at me with a speculative gaze. "Did you know some of the officers have a betting pool? Guessing where you went."

I groaned. They should have better things to do.

"Until you came back with Bill Murdoch, do you know what the favorite was?" he persisted.

"That I blew up?"

"No. Odds on that you took *Calypso*'s engines and whatever they could do, and gave them to the New Council."

"What?"

Sarkady's female aide turned in surprise at my yelp of disbelief. I smiled feebly at her and lowered my voice. "Why would they think that?"

"Why do you think? Because you nearly did it last time."

I could have hit him. "That was a completely different situation. If our survival had depended on us allying with the New Council, then I might have agreed. But it didn't. And I certainly wouldn't join a group that allies itself with something like the Q'Chn."

Florida seemed unconvinced. "Methinks you protest too much. I think it's highly likely you took the prototype to the New Council. And now you've got your hands somehow on a proper Invidi ship and you're trying to get it past ConFleet and away."

Should I meet this drivel with the silence it deserves, or cut it off early?

"Dan, you can't spread unsubstantiated rumors like this. It's neither professional nor ethical."

The skin around his eyes flushed. "That's a laugh. What do you expect when you never give out information?"

"I'm not free to do that, and you're going to have to live with it."

"Don't blame me if people fill in the gaps, then."

We glared at each other. It made my neck ache, as he was a lot taller than me.

"You really don't give up, do you? Don't you have enough work to do at Central without manufacturing ridiculous rumors?"

"Plenty, thank you. I'm concerned about Jocasta." He spread one large hand. "It may surprise you, Commander, but I want neutrality as much as you do. I've worked with the ordinary residents here—hell, you know I came here illegally myself. I've seen what it was like here under the Confederacy, and it can't be any worse if we're independent."

"How is spreading rumors about the New Council going to help get the neutrality vote?"

"It's not. I'm not spreading anything." He shook his head, resigned. "I said that because I want you to know that a lot of us have a big investment—not economic, either—in an independent Jocasta. And it seems to me that your . . . research might get in the way."

"I won't let that happen," I said, uneasy at his perspicacity. "And I promise you'll be the first to know if we decide the information can be released," I said. "But it's a bigger story than me defecting to the New Council. Just wait awhile."

He hesitated, then nodded reluctantly. "It better be good."

"It's sensational."

The old fighter bays were in the sunside of the center, between where the slim cylinder emerged from the protective cocoon of the rings and its far end, which sprouted into a forest of unlikely looking wings and sails to harvest sunlight, emit heat waste, and other mundane functions that kept the station alive.

The uplift took me to Level Six. Normally it was full of floating figures and luggage, but today the gravity field was activated and a clamor of voices in different languages mostly voiced complaints at the heaviness of bodies and the awkwardness of containers. The gravity field certainly increased the time spent waiting for people to get out of one's way.

Most of the people were heading for Levels Four to One, at which ships were docked or from where they could access the outer docks or orbital shuttles. I took a corridor crawler—a lift that moved within the center—down from Level Six and I was the only passenger when it reached Level Eight, where Serat's ship had been placed.

Outside the airlock to Bay 12, a security guard waited. He nodded at me and let me pass without question.

Inside the airlock, the bay was like an ovoid cave, nothing obvious to show that the wall on one side could become a round exit. Gantries and grappling arms clustered around the edges of that wall, in readiness to fling ships without internal-use thrusters out into space. Lines in various colors showed the "floor" for when the gravity field was not in use, and indicated where maintenance and service machinery should be positioned. Despite the overall gray, these lines gave the bay a festive air.

The ship sat safely nose-up on the launch base, the center-side wall of the bay when the gravity field was off. Its smooth hull looked out of place against the reinforced surfaces of the bay, which were studded with maintenance stations and access points. Like a child's toy in a gun turret.

Three people stood beside it. Murdoch, another security guard, and, unexpectedly, Rupert Stone. I was taken aback, to say the least. I'd been looking forward to a quiet investigation of my . . . An Serat's ship, not more debate on whether to keep it or not.

Murdoch faced Stone and was pointing at the ship. The lanky security guard—Thoms, that's right—loomed beside them.

They must have got word that ConFleet's on the way,

I thought with a stab of despair. I'd have only an hour or less to look at the ship.

"What's going on?" My voice echoed impressively in the maintenance alcoves in the sides of the bay.

Murdoch looked up. "Thought you'd never get here. Didn't want to use your comm link in case someone heard."

"Is it ConFleet?" I said.

"Not as such." He waited until I was three paces away, then tossed me something small and hard. "Thoms gave me a call, like he was ordered to do if anyone came in here. I scooted up and found him"—he nodded at Stone— "putting that on the ship."

Stone watched us. His light eyes narrowed with hostility, his whole personality seemed more focused than last night.

"What's she doing up here?" he said. "She's supposed to be under arrest. Dammit, Murdoch, I'll arrest you as well if I have to."

"She's on bond and assisting us with our inquiries," said Murdoch, "part of which involves assessing possible threats to this station. Which includes this ship and"—he nodded at the thing he'd tossed me—"that device."

The small oval nestled on my palm in a familiar way. It had no distinguishing features, no cracks or bumps. The material felt warm and slightly velvety. Not cold and hard like ordinary metal. It felt like the Invidi device that An Barik had given my friend Brin Quartermaine to break into our security when the original *Calypso* arrived. The device that led Quartermaine to his death.

"What does it do?" I said to Stone.

He sniffed superciliously and said nothing.

"The last person to use this kind of Invidi device on this station died," I said. "Do you want to end up the same?"

He drew himself up straight, his gaze flickering anxiously at the guard. As if he'd just realized security could be used against him. "Are you threatening me?"

"Don't be an idiot," growled Murdoch. "She's telling the truth. You can't trust them."

"Where was it?" I said to Murdoch.

"He was trying to stick it on the hull. In an inconspicuous corner. It doesn't match anything in our files, including what little we got on that thing Quartermaine used." Murdoch glared at Stone.

"We couldn't analyze Quartermaine's thing," I reminded him.

Murdoch adopted what he seemed to think was a jovial tone. "Come on, Rupert. We're all in this together. An Barik's not here. We are. Tell us what's going on."

"I'm acting under orders from my superior," said Stone. He shifted uneasily and pulled his suit coat closer across his chest. "You people seem to forget that we need the Invidi. We need their protection. Think how much they've given us. We owe them."

"Did An Barik send a message buoy directly back to you?" I said. "Or did this order come through the Bendarl cruiser?"

Murdoch met my eyes and rubbed his head in frustration. Whichever the case, Stone had got the message past Security's communications monitoring. It was galling, the way the Invidi could skip around inside our systems.

Stone said nothing.

"What if it's a bomb?" said Murdoch.

I handed the small oval back to him quickly.

"You could endanger everyone," he continued. "For what? A chance to play spy."

I thought of Dan Florida's suspicions of my own spy activities. He'd got the wrong person.

"Not a bomb," said Stone, "he said it was a disabling device. Nothing violent."

"So we can't fly the ship away until he gets here. You believed him?" I said.

Stone glared at me.

Murdoch glared at him. "We can expect An Barik back soon then, can we?"

"I don't know," said Stone sullenly.

It made sense. The Invidi don't do their own dirty work. When they need to fight, they have the Bendarl and Con-Fleet do it for them. When they need someone on the ground, people like Quartermaine and Stone are keen to oblige. And, until recently, myself. In pre-blockade days, if An Barik had asked me to help him, I would have agreed without question. As Stone said, the Invidi helped us, we should help them. My memories of pre-Contact Earth nagged at me—Stone was partly right. The Invidi saved us from destroying ourselves, we owed them something.

"Bill, why don't we forget this whole thing," I said.

Murdoch frowned. His expression shifted rapidly from *are you mad?* to *what the hell are you up to?*

"I mean," I said slowly, "Mr. Stone believes he's doing the right thing . . ."

"I *am* doing the right thing," Stone almost shouted. "It's you two who are endangering the station."

". . . however much it may look like sabotage," I finished.

Stone blinked and was silent. Let him work out we're at a stalemate. If he didn't push about Murdoch's involvement in our being on the Invidi ship, Murdoch wouldn't push about Stone's private communications with An Barik.

Murdoch had worked it out, too. And hopefully he'd keep a closer watch on Stone from now on. "Yeah, well, I reckon we can be generous this once." He jerked his head at the door. "Come on, Rupert. You and I have got work to do. Residents Committee meeting, fire drill, concern about the cruiser . . ."

"You're going to leave Halley here?" Stone resisted Murdoch's hand on his arm.

"She's got her job to do," said Murdoch.

"But she's in custody." He sounded so frustrated, I almost sympathized.

"Yeah, and I've got her formally on bond, if it makes you feel any better."

"It doesn't," said Stone. But he allowed Murdoch to usher him out of the bay.

Twenty-three

They left me alone with the ship. A relief, in a way. I've spent most of my life alone, and much of that time in pursuit of some technical problem. Longer in the company of ships than with people. Sometimes I think I'm more comfortable with the former.

Could that be why your personal life is such a mess? asked an annoying internal voice.

It's not a mess, I told it crossly. My marital problems with Henoit came from his activities as a terrorist with the New Council. Nothing to do with my job.

I shook my head to clear it of that thread of thought, and walked around the ship, reconfirming my memory of its outer configuration. A bulbous diamond shape, no distinguishing features on the outside, no protrusions from the smooth hull.

I wished Heron and the others who'd worked on *Calypso II* were still here to see this. If they were, I'd ask them to help me go over it. As soon as we'd worked out this present mess, I promised myself to look up where they'd been transferred and tell them what happened. And I couldn't ask any of the present engineering staff for help—they'd either be arrested with me or end up transferred like the others.

I reached out a hand to the ship, palm up. It seemed

expectant, somehow. Perhaps I was more attuned to it now, but I could feel tension humming in the air. The name popped into my head immediately. *"Farseer,"* I said aloud. And the ship listened. Like a dog with its ears pricked, waiting. What a ridiculous simile. Ships don't have ears.

Farseer it is, then.

I considered asking Murdoch for the tool An Barik had given Stone, in order to try gaining quicker access to *Farseer,* but the risk was too great that the ship would be completely immobilized. Better to stick with my own methods. I checked the control panel just inside the dock's airlock entry. Outer space door, inner space door locks activated. Atmospheric controls green.

From the maintenance locker beneath the control panel I took a Level One toolkit then brightened the lights around *Farseer* before returning to its side. Setting my handcom to voice record, I began.

"The hull looks smooth, but tactile examination reveals indentations that feel approximately one millimeter in depth and width. These indentations follow no easily discernible pattern and seem to continue across the entire surface."

I paused and took out a gauge from the toolkit. It should pick up any information the handcom's more limited sensors missed.

"The first time I used this vessel, it opened without direct command when I traced one of these trails with my bare hand and thought of entry hatches. I'm trying the same thing now . . ."

And it worked again. Part of the hull moved, and suddenly an opening existed.

"It's not a sliding door. The opening part seems to actually dissolve back into its surroundings, rapidly. It leaves an entry of"—I glanced down at the gauge—"one hundred twenty by eighty centimeters. I'm going in now."

It looked the same as last time. Small cabin, floor-to-ceiling consoles or control surfaces. A definite floor, which showed its Invidi genealogy—they always used the gravity field. Dim to moderate lighting, orange-tinted.

"I'm trying access with the sensor gauge first." This was totally unsuccessful. The ship refused to recognize any of the gauge's universal access codes. In fact, it refused to recognize the gauge itself. All console and wall surfaces remained stubbornly unlit. This could be because the universal codes hadn't been developed when *Farseer* was built. But as the codes were based on Invidi access methods, I'd assumed *Farseer* would find something familiar in them.

"Next I'm trying the same method of access as last time. That is, direct physical contact with one of the control panels."

This was more successful. Successful in the sense that the panel lit up and began to show me information, but less so in that the jolt of whatever it was up my arm sent continuous needles of pain through neck, head, and shoulders.

On any ship with an Invidi jump drive, whether K'Cher, Melot, or Bendarl—I'd never been on an Invidi ship—the jump drive itself is inaccessible. On most of them, the drive is in a separate, sealed section. Only the master can activate it.

When I worked as a ship's engineer my job had always been to maintain the flatspace engines. Using the jump drive destabilized fuel ratios and the entire engine system required recalibrating after each jump. As even a minute antimatter leakage would finish the ship's journey very quickly, this was an important task. And always rushed, as ships' masters pressured engineers to get quicker and quicker after jumps. The only time I'd ever been able to take my time was when I piloted *Calypso II* from the jump point to Earth in 2023, and then I'd been worried about my supplies running out.

Jump-capable ships have thrusters of a particular configuration. That is, the flatspace engine has a drive-enabling connection—the gate. It seems to draw energy from the thrusters, hence the slight imbalance after each jump that we have to recalibrate. In all my previous attempts to understand the jump drive, because I couldn't actually get into the drive system itself, I'd been forced to concentrate on why the gate causes this imbalance. The gate was the closest I'd get to the drive itself.

Even with *Calypso II,* all we'd done was buy an old freighter that had had its jump drive chamber removed. Into that we put what seemed like a similar chamber from the wreckage of *Calypso,* and linked what we hoped was its gate connection with the freighter's thrusters. We hadn't actually opened the drive chamber. I had to recalibrate *Calypso II*'s thrusters after I arrived in 2023 in the usual way, which seemed to indicate *Calypso* didn't have a special drive of any sort. That is, it behaved the same as did ships traveling on the Central network. And yet it jumped to a point off that network. Whatever the secret of the off-network jumping, I didn't think it had been in *Calypso* itself.

Farseer's drive might be accessible. I wanted to see into that system. I wanted to take it apart and see how it worked.

First I had to map out what was in the system so I knew I was taking the right things apart, and so that if there were any Tor surprises in there, I'd know. I had to do it properly, through an interface, because I didn't trust the mental link to give me all the information. And I had to set up safeguards both for myself and for the station. Especially given *Farseer*'s Tor elements.

I didn't trust those Tor elements. We'd had so much trouble with Tor hardware in the early days of the station when I was still only site manager, before Jocasta was even named.

We'd used the Tor structure of the core and Alpha ring because the alternative was to build a station from scratch and the Confederacy didn't have the resources or the desire to do that. So we tiptoed around the booby traps and explored the mazes and tried to make it work to our directions. It did work, but even now, seven years later, the core was never trustworthy—you could go into it and find meter-wide sections encrusted with new connections, impassable. Not with live Tor technology, of course, more like our Invidi-designed connections were trying to prevent a revival of Tor activity.

This didn't seem to disrupt our systems, perhaps because everything was backed up in the rings and we ran regular observation teams to the core. But some systems, water circulation and atmospheric monitoring, for example, had to be coordinated from the center. Viewed as a whole, the Tor elements in the opsys were no more than one variable, but they could interfere significantly in an emergency by diverting power and information from important functions. As had happened during the Seouras blockade. Some of the other variables—the "extra" adjustments that half the population illegally made, for example, had been reduced since the end of the blockade.

But the Tor bits were still there. I didn't like it, this building a station on top of hostile hardware, however much we'd irradiated and restructured and overlaid the Tor systems with Invidi identity. In the early days of construction I'd often dreamed of being lost in a maze, booby traps on all sides, endlessly rewriting commands to overlay Tor systems, but the commands would unravel as I watched and the maze would close in.

of those old vids Grace used to watch. At the end of the secret passage the characters would find hidden treasure.

My hidden treasure was the jump drive in *Farseer*. My only break in twenty years spent working with and studying the jump drive. A chance to finally understand.

Understanding the jump drive will do so many things for humans and the rest of the Nine. It will open up the rest of the Confederacy worlds to us. Imagine being able to go anywhere on the jump network we liked. Before the Seouras blockade I'd been a Four Worlds supporter, in particular an Invidi supporter. Now, while I still believed they wouldn't deliberately harm us, I also knew they put their own interests ahead of ours, as An Barik did when he let Jocasta be blockaded simply because he didn't want to disturb *Calypso*'s arrival. Definitely, humans and the rest of the Nine need access to the jump drive.

It can't bring Will back.

The thought popped into my mind and stuck with all the adhesiveness of Seouras slime.

I found I was sobbing into my knees, rocking against the console-covered wall. The physical pain of contact with *Farseer* was nothing compared to this.

How long am I going to be haunted by the thought of Will's death? The memory keeps sneaking back, hitting me when I don't expect it, dropping me without warning into the abyss of loss. If only . . . here we go again. If only I hadn't entered that damn competition. But I knew we'd win—a century's head start is fairly conclusive. If only I hadn't taken Will along. Why didn't Grace put her foot down and forbid it? Usually she was so protective.

Because she trusted you.

I felt sick. *Farseer*'s golden light seemed too warm, the walls of the cabin too close. Damn An Serat for sending us back there. Damn myself for deciding my present on

Jocasta was more important than my present in the out-town.

How did he do it? I clutched at the thought because it wasn't part of that guilt. How had An Serat sent *Calypso* to Jocasta? How did we get to Earth from Jocasta and back again? How could a jump point exist off the network?

The handcoms made minute whirring sounds as they processed *Farseer*'s information. Surely the answer was in there.

Leaving aside the question of why *Calypso*'s jump had a shorter correspondence than *Calypso II* or Murdoch's ship, we could assume that An Serat was involved in possibly creating new jump points off the network. When I used *Calypso*'s jump drive in *Calypso II,* the flatspace engines reacted in exactly the same way as they did with a normal jump drive. So I felt safe in assuming that whatever Serat did, it wasn't with *Calypso.*

All of this supported the theory that the Invidi are able to create or open jump points at will, and not necessarily from Central—An Serat was on Earth at the time.

Opinion among the Nine is divided into two main camps on the nature of the jump drive. The first holds that the jump points are engineered wormhole mouths and that there is no such thing as a "drive"—what we call jump drive engines couldn't possibly process the energy needed to manipulate the mouths. The "drive" is just a way for the Invidi to track all registered ships that approach a jump point. At a signal from the drive, the Invidi open the jump points from Central.

This doesn't explain how the Invidi have less than perfect control of the Central network—the K'Cher and their subsidiaries use the jumps for shady business all the time. And where does the energy to open the points come from?

The second opinion says that the jump points are like bubbles in spacetime that are inflated to allow passage "through." The jump drive is necessary to propel the ship in a certain way (nobody can explain exactly how) to pop through the bubble. This explanation seems to give the Invidi godlike powers and doesn't really explain how they keep the network together.

I'd never bothered too much about which theory was more likely, because I thought that when I knew how it works, I'd know why. But the off-network jump points between Earth and Jocasta supported the latter theory. The "bubbles" are supposed to be there, waiting to be activated. Maybe the Invidi have always had this ability, but don't use it by mutual consent. You'd run into a lot of causality problems without the fixed jump network.

I sat up straight, let my knees go, and wiped my eyes with the back of my sleeve. That fits. If Serat went against the consensus of the other Invidi by opening a jump point off the network, they'd be mad at him. If he'd also been experimenting with Tor technology . . . I ran my hand along the warm, almost organic surface of *Farseer*'s deck.

Maybe it was the same thing. Tor technology—new jump point—*Farseer*. Maybe An Serat had used it to open new jump points off the network.

No, wait. I held my head in frustration. An Serat didn't use *Farseer*, we did. The off-network jump point was there in December 2022 because that's when I arrived from Jocasta. How could it be there before Serat had a chance to open it? Unless he opened it from the other end . . . no, that's the jump point where *Calypso* appeared.

My head throbbed. I'd go and talk to Murdoch, get an update on the Bendarl situation. See Lorna, ask her what my legal status is. And talk to Eleanor about getting rid of this headache. By then it might be possible to look inside *Farseer* and find some answers.

Twenty-four

Murdoch listened calmly to my excited talk of bubbles and Tor technology. The banks of monitors behind his chair cast a bluish glow on the top of his head and turned the shoulders of his olive-green uniform turquoise.

"So what you're saying is that we can't rely on that link you've got with the ship to provide accurate information." He poured a cup of tea from the bottle beside his desk and passed it over the mess to me.

"Yes, and getting enough information on the ship to begin investigating it is taking time." I looked for a place to put the cup among the handcoms, data crystals, and stacks of plastocopy.

"Drink it," he suggested. "It's been five hours since breakfast."

I stared at him. Five hours? I'd spent so long with *Farseer.* "ConFleet?"

"Holding position. Nothing's come back through the jump."

The tea was hot and sweet and did a lot to relieve my headache.

"How long will you need to get an idea of how it works?" he said.

I nearly laughed. For nearly a century we'd been trying

to get an idea of how the jump drive works. "I'll take as much time as I can get. A lifetime mightn't be enough."

"Don't think we can manage that long." He had that worried line between his brows again. He rummaged below the desk and pushed a wrapped ration bar across the desk at me as well. "Eat that. You look like you need it."

I unwrapped the bar and chewed its sweet crumbs. "What have you been doing?"

He shifted in his chair. "Getting back up to speed on what's been going on here while I was on leave."

I didn't think that was the whole story. He was looking at me as if trying to decide something. When I came into the office he'd jumped and placed the handcom he'd been reading obviously out of reach on the far side of the desk.

"And?"

He sighed and passed that particular handcom to me.

The screen scrolled slowly down what looked like a diary entry. The initial date said 12 March 2076, Mars City. The first human colony on Mars. The screen's first paragraphs concerned impressions of an official function to celebrate the colony's foundation in 2050. It was obviously a personal record of somebody involved with colony administration. Then it continued:

Father went home right after the ceremony, like he always does. He says it's because he prefers to watch the balloons from our place with the girls, but I remember he told me he doesn't like ceremonies. I said, thinking it was modesty, that someone who'd been involved with the colony since the beginning deserved to be honored. He replied, "It never mattered to her what I achieved." Until then, I never realized how strongly my grandmother's presence still haunted him. I knew Father was still young when she took her own life and the colony hadn't yet begun. Father

said she never got over my uncle's death. I can't for-
give her for leaving him, and us. It makes me all the
more determined to treat my daughters with equal
love and affection.

Below the entry, the database code and brief description: William Russ Chenin, Assistant, Dome Technical Division.

The name was familiar. In the years before the Confederacy was founded, William Chenin helped design the
improved habitat containment that replaced the first un-
wieldy Mars domes. The team's work was required reading for engineering students.

"That's Vince's son," said Murdoch. "Vince managed to
work himself through apprenticeships, then tech school. He
ended up on Mars." He paused. "Grace killed herself twelve
years after Will died."

I stared at the hard brown carpet. A wave of guilt and
grief choked me into silence. Nothing to say. How could
there be anything to say? Will and Grace had both been
dead for nearly a century.

I knew that. I knew Vince was dead, too. And Levin,
curse him. But it was as much of a shock as if a policeman had come to the tent in the out-town and told me
they'd died that morning.

If the Invidi were able to open jump points anywhere
off the network, it meant that in a sense Will alive existed
right there in front of me beside Will dead. Not before or
after, but beside each other, equally accessible. All our moments, superimposed upon each other but separate. How
did the Invidi bear this? No wonder they needed order.

"I'm going to see Jago." I stood up after a long pause.

"Have you considered," Murdoch said, "that maybe this
is one you can't win?" He stood up too, hitched one hip

onto the desk. Tucked his hands under his elbows as if he'd rather be doing something else with them.

I turned in the doorway. "What's that supposed to mean? I'm always trying to win?"

He laughed, although without humor. "Aren't you? Isn't that part of this whole preoccupation with the jump drive? Sure, you want to know how it works. But there are other fascinating bits of hardware in the universe. You can't stand them having it and not us."

I opened my mouth, shut it again. I've never denied that.

"I don't like it either," he kept on. "But I know I can't fight them in that particular arena. Last time you were lucky and you got us into another arena—that's the neutrality. Let's keep the fight there, eh? Then we might all have a chance of coming out of this ahead."

"You're saying let them take *Farseer,* forget about the jump drive and how An Serat used us to bring the Invidi to Earth and whatever other games he's playing that we don't understand? Go back as if it never happened?" My voice rose in disbelief.

"Yes." He leaned forward, quite serious. "Because it's not getting us anywhere. It's becoming a liability. And if you don't see that, that's a bigger liability."

I felt as if he'd switched off the gravity beneath me.

"Not only that, for Chrissakes. Don't you see that it's a bloody deal safer *not* to know anything about that ship? If we say, hell, sorry about pinching it but we don't know how it works, then they might let us go back to our old lives. Or not, I dunno. But personally, I'd rather not have ConFleet decide we need help forgetting."

"You think they'd wipe our memories?"

He shook his head doubtfully. "I hope not."

I can't let that stand in the way of finding out the truth, I wanted to say, but then, it wasn't just me, was it? Murdoch was involved. He'd sacrificed his job and risked his life to come and get me in the past, whether it was all part of an Invidi plan or not. ConFleet Security might even conclude Sasaki knew, too. And Eleanor Jago.

Maybe we can't win, at that.

I took the uplift to Alpha without noticing anything around me. Murdoch's words had stung. Partly because we'd slept together last night, and somewhere at the back of my mind was the unreasonable expectation that we'd cease to disagree from now on. Mostly because he'd never said anything like it before. During the occupation he'd disagreed with some of my decisions, but went along with them nevertheless. Even when calling me "obsessive." But now we had no protocols, no procedure to follow or rank to hide behind.

Of course I'm obsessive. All good engineers are obsessive. It's how we get the patience to keep trying different solutions when the first few hundred tries fail.

The jump drive is the key to the power of the Four in the Confederacy. Henoit and his New Council saw that. In trying to change the balance of power, they came looking for *Calypso*'s jump drive.

Will changing the balance of power in the Confederacy help Jocasta's neutrality?

No, put it another way; will changing the balance of power help the residents of Jocasta?

The potted plant by the door of Eleanor's admin office, up one floor from her consulting room where she'd examined me the night before, had grown larger and been joined by feather-leafed companions. On the wall, the same orange and yellow-toned weaving hung sideways. Eleanor said walls should help soothe the mind, and she kept her one interface monitor on the desk.

"That's new." A small holo-crystal on the front of the desk. The face of Eleanor's late partner grinned at me from under his wild thatch of hair.

Having Leo's holo close by must be a good sign—for a while she couldn't talk about him at all.

Eleanor sat down at the desk. She wouldn't look at me and her hands kept rearranging handcoms, data crystals, saucers, on the desk. She glanced at the holo and smiled. The sight of Leo seemed to give her the impetus to continue.

"When you disappeared I was so angry with you." She looked at me properly. "Thought I'd have to go through all that again." She pointed at the holo. "I was packed up ready to leave, but Bill Murdoch came to see me. He said he didn't think you were dead."

"Are you still angry?"

She smiled then. "Sort of. You could have told me what you were doing."

"I know. I'm sorry. I should have told Bill, too."

She pushed her chair back and paced once or twice across to the wall hanging and back. "I don't know why I'm nervous." She ran a hand over her smooth bun. "I hope you'll tell me I'm making a ridiculous mistake."

"If it's about where Murdoch and I have been recently, no, it's not a mistake."

She reached for her chair and lowered herself carefully into it, her eyes on mine. "Wait. Just in case we're talking at cross-purposes. In your blood I found antibodies to viruses that have not existed for decades. Traces of antibiotics, of all things. In your lungs I found traces of the exhaust products of machines that haven't been used for a century. Your respiratory system was irritated to a clinical degree."

"Can you date these phenomena?"

"I'd say about the time the Sleepers were from. Or even

before. Most of your results overlapped theirs to some extent."

"Pretty good. Would you accept 2023?"

She closed her eyes for a moment. "I don't want to. But the facts are there."

I leaned both elbows on the desk. "Could I fake those results?"

"Highly unlikely."

"We were there and we did come back. That's as clear in my memory as your facts."

"Did you get there in that Invidi ship in dock?"

"No, in the one we worked on here. Eleanor, that information, the results of your tests . . ."

"Is in a secure file," she said. "I know sensitive material when I see it."

"Send a copy to Murdoch, will you? He's got even more secure files."

"All right. But you can't keep this a secret for long. The technology . . ."

"Has existed since the Invidi came to Earth," I interrupted. "We knew nothing of it then and if it wasn't for my 'accident,' we'd know nothing of it now. What makes you think things will change?"

"Because you're involved."

I winced at that.

"You're going to fiddle around with it and work bits of it out and maybe change things." She sounded resigned.

"I don't think I'll have time for that. ConFleet will probably come to take back the ship soon. And if I'm not careful they'll take me too."

"Have you seen deVries? She'll know where you stand legally."

"I'm going to see her next."

She leaned forward, her face more animated. "Tell me—what was it like back then?"

"Inconvenient."

"I'm talking about how you feel, Halley. How it affected you."

I picked up Leo's holo-crystal, looked it over, and put it down. "That doesn't matter. We need to work out what to do now."

"How you felt then will influence what you do now."

It took a while to find the words. "I was afraid. That I'd die, of some stupid disease, all by myself in the past and never see you all again. Oh, damn."

She passed a cleanchif over the desk and waited while I wiped my eyes and blew my nose. "Why a disease?"

"Or an accident or something. People died so easily then. Ordinary people, on Earth. Died of cell mutations . . ."

"Cancer."

"Yes. Or because their organs failed. Children with faulty nervous systems from parents who'd used powerful drugs for fun. Or because they were standing on the wrong side of the street when some drunken driver came down it . . ."

I paused, noticed I was scraping the skin around the nails of one hand with the other, and stopped. "I'm no fan of the Invidi lately but, Eleanor, if the only thing they did was teach us to spend our resources on preserving life, then it was worth them coming."

"Did you know anyone who died?" She kept her voice flat.

"Yes," I said shortly. "By the way, did you find any signs my Seouras implant was active again?"

"Nothing pathological, no. But as I said this morning, we didn't find much before, either. Have you had any subjective symptoms recur?"

"Only when I'm in that ship."

"Don't use the ship, then." She put up a hand. "I know, I know. You have to use it."

"While I can."

"Is it worth all the trouble?"

I blinked at her, shocked. "Is what worth the trouble?"

"Working for neutrality and independence and all that."

"I know you have your doubts, but we'll make new contracts."

"I know. It's just that . . ." She tapped the desk in frustration. "Every time we settle down, someone turns the gravity off from underneath us again. Well, you know what I mean."

"I know. What we need, metaphorically speaking, is our own gravity field generator."

I called the head magistrate, Lorna deVries, from a public comm link in the hospital lobby, and told her I'd be right down.

Lorna deVries was chief magistrate on Jocasta before I became head of station. We used to play squash, in those days. She had a wickedly accurate backhand and an unerring sense of when her opponent was tiring.

She was at her desk in the far corner when I entered the huge, open-plan office. Her dark hair frizzed above her head and her black magistrate's gown had slipped half off one shoulder, showing bright cloth beneath.

"Halley, nice to see you back." She hugged me lightly and stood back to look at me. Lorna was one of the few people who made me feel tall.

"You look exactly the same," she said, and steered me over to her desk.

Not very encouraging, when you consider what a wreck I'd always looked like here.

She activated two privacy panels and enclosed us in a tiny alcove. "And it's nice to have you back," she went on, seating herself behind the desk.

"It's nice to be back, but . . ."

"But the problem is how long we can keep you here,

right?" She didn't seem worried. But then, she never seemed worried. "I talked to Jago. She says she found evidence of you and Bill Murdoch having been in the past." She paused, as if to give me time to deny the words. They did sound unlikely, delivered in her quick, clipped voice.

I nodded confirmation.

She leaned her elbows on the desk and steepled her fingers. "Do you have any idea what this information could do?"

"Not just information. The ship we came back in is part of some Invidi experiment."

Lorna let her breath out in a slow whoosh. "You can't keep out of trouble, can you?"

"What's my legal position?"

"Bill's got it right so far. He's put in a custody report. That makes you the responsibility of EarthFleet Security, which is acting on the charges they brought against you after you left so suddenly."

"That's unauthorized use of resources?"

"And facilities, yes. Misappropriation of funds. They'll need to process those charges before they can hand you over to ConFleet. ConFleet Security will probably charge you with absence without leave and possibly desertion of duty."

I rubbed at the implant in my neck. I swear it was getting itchier. A sense of being slowly suffocated. "What about the possession charges? They can't prove there was a jump drive on *Calypso II,* can they? So there's only *Farseer.*"

Lorna frowned. "What's *Farseer?* Halley, you know you're not supposed to withhold information from me."

"Sorry. That's the name of the ship Murdoch and I came back on."

"Oh. I'll have to do some research, but I'd say the Invidi aren't going to charge you with possession if you give the ship back. They won't want this whole can of worms opened up for the rest of the galaxy to sniff. You could give it back in return for ConFleet dropping the charges." She raised her eyebrows in query.

"Imagine what my life in ConFleet will be like if I do that." Short and nasty.

"Are you going to take up ConFleet's offer and stay on here, then?" If neutrality went through, ConFleet would give its human staff on Jocasta a choice of leaving and remaining in ConFleet, or staying and either becoming civilians or joining EarthFleet.

"I haven't thought much about the future at all, Lorna. I've got enough trouble coping with the present." And the past, I nearly added.

She pursed her lips and gave me her serious, handing-down-sentence look. "If you don't give the ship back, I'd say ConFleet will charge you and apply for extradition even before the EarthFleet charges are heard. External Affairs might just be annoyed enough with you for starting this whole neutrality thing to agree."

I opened my mouth to ask her how soon they could apply for extradition and get it passed, but she looked down and exclaimed loudly enough to make me jump.

"Aha! That's an idea." Looking up again. "Halley, you need to first ask for asylum under the MIA."

The Mars-Invidi Agreement on Species Rights basically states that all members of the Confederacy have the right to be understood and treated according to the standards of their own species. It was designed to prevent more technologically complex species from having too much power over others. In law, it means that a suspect charged with a Confederacy crime may appeal to a court of their own species or planet.

"You know," mused Lorna, "the MIA has the potential to change the legal structure of the Confederacy, if people would take it seriously. At the moment it's used only as a glorified extradition treaty."

"Asylum to Earth?"

"From ConFleet, yes."

"If ConFleet asks me where I've been, I'll tell them. Won't the Invidi want to avoid letting everyone know about this new jump point? I don't think they'll charge me."

She leaned forward. "If you give the ship back. If not, well, do you want to risk your freedom on how much control the Invidi have over ConFleet? And what about Murdoch? If they charge you with possession, he's likely to be included. And are you going to keep quiet about this jump point to Earth?"

"I don't want Murdoch involved." As for keeping quiet about the jump point, if An Barik and the other Invidi came to get *Farseer,* I supposed they would make sure we couldn't find or use the jump point again. Then the only proof of its existence would be the word of two humans, Murdoch and myself.

"Did they let you take the ship?" Lorna was making notes on a stylus pad.

"Not exactly."

"Theft as well," she groaned, and underscored a phrase. The interface beeped apologetically as it read the lines as an erasure.

"It was our only chance to get away. What if the ship is registered as evidence in an asylum case? They'd have to put it aside then, wouldn't they? Until the case is held."

She ran a hand through her boisterous curls. "I don't know, Halley. I'll have to check the relevant sources. I doubt we've got many precedents, which means anything could happen. And if we get orders to rush your hearing through . . ." She added, "Don't forget I won't be on the bench. Carr Val, the new associate, will be the judge."

"But . . ."

"I can advise you or I can try you, not both."

"Thanks, Lorna."

"Thank me when I've got you off." She stood up, an unconscious gesture of dismissal. "See you at Florida's dinner. I'll know more then."

"If ConFleet haven't arrived by then," I said gloomily.

"If they haven't arrived," she agreed. "I said that to Florida and he seemed surprised. I don't think he realized quite how dicey the situation is."

"He doesn't know about the ship."

"He was cocky that he'd got you to come to the dinner, you know."

"I think I'd rather be in the brig."

She grinned and waved as I wound my way through the desks. Her words made me feel a little more secure. In my fears about An Barik and the Invidi coming to take *Farseer,* I'd forgotten that the Confederacy had laws, and that we were still part of those laws, even with neutrality pending. ConFleet couldn't just sail in and take me away from here. At least, not until Barik got them permission. If they did, they'd be in the wrong and the rest of the galaxy would see that.

The most pressing problem was saving information from *Farseer.* I could record as much as possible by our normal data retention methods, but as the disappearance of our *Calypso II* records showed, recorded information could be unrecorded.

I needed another way to store information, and the only way seemed to be in my head, not the most reliable method, or hidden in a place someone like Veatch or Stone would not think to look. I could try to connect *Farseer* directly to Jocasta's core and speed up the process, but I wasn't sure how *Farseer*'s Tor elements would affect our opsys. It might react as though *Farseer*'s Tor elements were a disease and "cleanse" them, as we'd taught it to do with the original Tor elements of the station.

The worst scenario was if *Farseer*'s Tor elements were stimulated by contact with Jocasta and began to attack our opsys. I couldn't risk that. I'd have to be content with using normal methods and make multiple copies.

I rubbed at the implant helplessly and swore under my breath. A curly-haired EarthFleet ensign coming the other way along the corridor raised her eyebrows in disapproval and turned her eyes away as she passed me. I didn't recognize her face. Probably came with Stone. Things were changing on Jocasta and I wasn't changing with them.

Twenty-five

Outside on the throughway, I felt equally uncomfortable. The Boulevard, Gamma's main throughway that ran straight through Sections One to Four, had always been crowded, but previously it had been noisy with the bustle of stall-keepers calling to customers, customers talking about purchases, and a new type of music every ten meters or so. There must have been new regulations set about the music, because all I could hear was a thin background jangle.

The crowd looked more prosperous, too, and I heard more Confederacy Standard than Earth Standard. Gamma's residents had always been the most cosmopolitan on the station, but I noticed a lot more nonhuman Nine Worlds loiterers. Achelian, Dir, even a few H'digh and several groups of what appeared to be young artisan-caste Melot, dressed in bright, tight-fitting clothes. These latter were having fun—as I watched, one of them plucked a round fruit from a stall and carried it on his or her head for several paces, to the applause of the others.

Tourists? I must ask Veatch. The K'Cher trader Trillith had had a plan to begin a tourist run through the jump point from Central to Abelar. When I left in *Calypso II* the plans hadn't been approved by Central. Everything was pending until the neutrality vote was heard.

I let the crowd carry me toward the spoke in the middle distance. The spoke's bulk was less obvious here than in Alpha, because it was obscured more by the buildings that rose in closely staggered rows up the curve of the ring. The crowd meandered past stalls and stores offering every conceivable exchange, past the Middle Systems Trade Hall, past the small Security cabin in the middle of the section.

The mass of bodies trailed to a standstill to let past a group of Dir who were maglevving a huge trunk. In rowdy pre-blockade days this activity would have been greeted with yells of annoyance, catcalls, and a gathering of idlers, but today everyone in the crowd watched and waited politely.

I turned off the Boulevard and onto one of the throughways parallel to it. Shabbier stalls, less fashionable restaurants, the whole space narrower. Pedestrians here were either trying to avoid the traffic of the Boulevard, like myself, or wanted to enjoy a slower pace.

The side throughway reminded me of the out-town. Not the tent city, but the older streets behind; where red brick buildings that had once been factories and newer concrete blocks of three-story units squeezed the road between them. In the same way, the backs of low buildings that fronted onto the Boulevard rose straight on one side of the walkway and on the other residential units rose in staggered terraces to the upper limit of building permits.

If I wanted to be reminded of the tent city, I should go down to the Hill, I thought grimly. It had always been the darkest, most tiring—because of the higher gravity—and most crowded part of the station. I wonder if Stone continued the reforms we put in place after the blockade? Plans to repair the reflectors, reinforce weak structures, clear the throughways of unregistered buildings and add extra residences in Alpha to house illegal residents from Delta—the refugees and unregistered workers who'd stayed through the Seouras blockade and who were now official residents.

Being an illegal migrant myself in the out-town had changed my perspective somewhat. We'd always accepted refugees on Jocasta, in spite of the pressure they placed on our environmental systems, mainly because they had nowhere else to go in the Abelar system and couldn't afford the trip to Central. And also, because Marlena Alvarez had always accepted refugees into Las Mujeres. But I'd never realized before what it must be like, to be adrift in a context-less existence, not knowing everything that others take for granted; having nobody to rely on; to be always on the alert.

Ah, but you don't have time to go and look at the Hill, do you? You're too busy with matters of galactic importance.

I can't do everything.

No, you can't.

Something flickered at the side of the walkway. In the entrance to a side alley that was little more than airspace between buildings, a knee-high duct alcove had been lined with metal. Round knobs of holo-emitters lined the edges and there was a small plaque at the base of the alcove. The emitters glowed red, then went dull again. The show must have just finished.

I knelt down to look closer. The plaque said:

NOVEMBER 4, 2121, REMEMBRANCE DISPLAY. SPONSORED BY THE GAMMA SMALL TRADERS ASSOCIATION.

The fourth of November, the date of the fire. Two months before the Seouras blockade ended, we had a major fire on the station. For three days it burned, and it took another week before the state of emergency was lifted. Most of the fire was in Delta ring, in the Hill, but flames spread through one of the uplift shafts and started a smaller blaze here in Gamma. Two EarthFleet officers, four volunteer firefighters and a family in their home were killed in this ring alone. Half the sections on both sides of the spoke were damaged.

INSERT APPENDAGE TO VIEW, said smaller letters under the plaque. With a mixture of curiosity and sadness, I passed my hand inside the alcove to activate its sensors.

The holoimage flickered into life. I was looking at a view of Gamma ring—an overhead view of the Boulevard. But it wasn't as light as now. This image must have been taken during the blockade, after auxiliary and reflecting mirrors had been damaged in the initial Seouras attack, giving the scene a curious twilight feel.

This is Underway Terrace in Gamma Two...began a recorded commentary in Earth Standard, but it was in need of repair; it kept cutting out and I caught only isolated phrases, interrupted further by the voices and equipment noises around me.

People walked up and down the gloomy Boulevard in the holoimage. They looked shabbier than now, and there were more humans. In one corner of the screen a Security constable gestured at two Garokians who were trying to set up a stall in front of an Achelian merchant's store to clear away.

The scene changed abruptly. Broken images of the same stretch of throughway, but this time dark with smoke and filled with running figures. This was what Security pick-ups must have recorded before they went offline.

... terror as residents ran for their lives. The flames ...

Spread out from the spoke, yes, I know. My palms were sweating and I wiped them on my trouser legs. My heart was beating faster. God, it's as if it happened yesterday. Images of the out-town fire mixed up in my mind with the Hill. Screams in the darkness.

... equipment better maintained than in the lower ring. The firefighters were able to contain the fire here in Gamma, thus saving the rest of the station.

Not exactly, but what did it matter now? The pickup had changed to a handcom recorder and was now moving past a desolate row of blackened buildings. Smoke had stained the upper part of the ring vault in this section and the "sky," usually filled with reflected light and seemingly far away, loomed gray and close. It was like being in a dingy fishbowl. Humans with dirty faces stood, shocked and helpless, looking at the rubble. Two Achelians linked arms and rocked in distress.

If we'd had decent equipment and sufficient resources, we could have contained that fire immediately in the Hill. Nobody needed to die in Gamma. Familiar anger and frustration formed a tight ball in my stomach.

The holoimage was now cycling through the faces and names of the victims.

My stomach rose and I stood up quickly, ignoring the pins and needles in my knees and the brief dizziness. I don't want to see this. It's as bad as watching people in the out-town run from the fire.

You talk about the out-town as if it were terrible, I told myself, but the Hill is almost as bad. If you can't help these people in your own time, don't criticize people in that other time.

It shouldn't be that bad. Here, I can do something about it. I can try to make sure we're never in that situation again. I can't help Will, but I can do something for all of us here and now.

At that moment the extinguisher system test began.

From what Sasaki had said to Murdoch, it was supposed to be a simple alarm test. We had distinct extinguisher systems for each section and again for each ring. Fire, as we'd found out to our cost, was too great an enemy to give it even the smallest chance of spreading. But the alarm could also be controlled station-wide, and Security wanted to make sure they could alert any- and everyone if need be.

The alarm activated as planned. First stage—the alert. The audio rose and fell in a three-beat whine, at least, to human ears. Lights flashed from the edges of the reflectors on the top of the ring, so nobody could block one with illegal construction.

Then the second-stage alarm sounded, a louder, higher tone. I couldn't hear anything else.

But somebody hadn't done their work of separating the alarm from the actual extinguishers for this exercise. There was a loud clicking sound above my head. A heavy mass of white retardant powder whooshed out of wall and ceiling outlets and covered everything.

Even in the alley. Most of it came from an outlet in the side of one wall of the alley, but hit the other wall and blew over me and the Remembrance Display. The holoimage, basically a series of light beams, disappeared immediately, disrupted by the particles.

"Ah, shit." I tried to cover my face.

The trouble with retardant powder is that as soon as it settles, it changes into a slippery film that retards movement as well as flame. A bit like the slime I used to get covered in when I went to the Seouras ship during the blockade. Though the fire retardant is supposed to be easily shaken off when it dries, we'd always had hell's own trouble getting it off modular building surfaces and recycled uniforms.

The retardant burst ceased, as did the alarm. Voices shouted and cursed from the throughway, loud in the silence. I scraped slime off my face. Why do I get the feeling the station is trying to tell me something?

Twenty-six

I stopped off at one of the library stations in the Bubble after washing the crusts of dried retardant off my face and hands. Murdoch's excerpt from the history files had reminded me of something I needed to look up. I didn't know if the information had survived, but astronomical records might tell me something about *Calypso*'s departure. If they'd had instrumentation accurate enough to record the radiation from a jump point and if they'd been looking in that direction at the time.

The library station was a room lined with booths, with a storeroom on one side that held the limited amount of hardcopy records we had on the station—mainly books, scrolls, or data crystals abandoned when people left the station. I settled gratefully into a cushioned booth, laid my head back into the supporting headrest to look at the monitor on the opposite wall of the booth, and hoped I wouldn't drop off to sleep.

"History, Earth, year 2023, date 14 May. Show edited visual record, ocular manipulation." Short pause while the interface hummed softly. I stretched my toes uncomfortably in my new boots, which had given me blisters.

The monitor brightened and I blinked my way through subject headings. Normally using visual cues made me squint and I avoided the method, but it was certainly fast.

The history files for 14 May, the day we met the Invidi and left Earth, said nothing about a stolen Invidi ship. The file listed newspaper and visual media references to an explosion that most of the reports called an "accident," some an attempt by an "unknown, deranged individual" to damage human-Invidi relations. After that, security had been further tightened around Invidi "embassies" all over the world.

Then again, the history files were incomplete. The facts on the screen had been collated and edited to read smoothly, but the original sources, ranging from media reports to private diaries, were scattered and limited. There may have been news reports that didn't survive the century. Some of the security forces at the airport in Sydney must have seen two humans enter an Invidi ship, and more people would have seen that ship take off. Unless the Invidi asked the government of the day to suppress the information in the media. Or perhaps the history files had been tampered with during the century, not impossible seeing that the Invidi controlled most sources of information and barely understood Invidi technology was used to disseminate it. Like they'd kept all information about the Tor to themselves.

It was hardly surprising that the Invidi would want to keep it quiet that Murdoch and I had been able to use one of their ships. Our taking *Farseer* had probably, I reflected gloomily, been one of the reasons they decided to lock the Nine out of using jump technology in the first place.

I blinked my way to astronomical records. These were better preserved, and where there were gaps, it was obvious. Unfortunately, the year after *Calypso*'s departure from Earth, 2027, which was when the ship would have entered the jump point, was full of gaps. A bad year for infonet failures and data losses due to computer viruses. There was no reference anywhere in the last fifty years, either, to a jump point or even gravimetric disturbances at those coordinates. Until I went right back. I started searching in the relatively recent past because before the space program picked up in the 2050s, instrumentation on Earth wouldn't have been precise enough to pinpoint such a disturbance. But then, as I scrolled back over reports of the Invidi arrival I noticed an astronomical report from 16 May 2023. It detailed a major gravitational radiation source that suddenly appeared close to the solar system. The astronomers became excited about this, but the radiation peaked immediately, then dispersed, and they could find no explanation. A follow-up probe found nothing a decade later. The position of the source seemed to fit the coordinates where Murdoch and I had appeared from Jocasta.

Normally, jump points weren't detectable unless they were in use. When a ship entered, for a second only they sent out one sharp burst of radiation, which then ended as smoothly as a closing door cuts off the light. So why this uncharacteristic surge from the jump point two days after we left?

Think, think. I seemed to have exhausted all my mental energy working with *Farseer*. The semi-reclining chair was too comfortable. I stood up, tapped off the monitor, and paced up and down the line of booths. There were no other users on this side of the room, nobody to poke their head out of a booth and glare at me.

A stable jump point never leaked radiation after the point closed. Which indicated that the jump point Murdoch and I came through might have destabilized for some reason two days after we left. The type of radiation mentioned in the report seemed right. Had An Serat or one of the other Invidi in 2023 tried to follow us and for some reason the point destabilized? Or had they deliberately made it impossible for anyone to follow us? That would be my guess, unless . . . another big "if," *Farseer*'s Tor components helped to destabilize the point.

If that ninety-nine-year jump point was destroyed or made unusable, and if the correspondence was consistent, in another day the same thing would happen to that point at this end. We could expect a major burst of radiation from the place where we appeared in *Farseer*.

So how, then, did *Calypso* use a jump point in 2027 that didn't exist anymore because it destabilized in 2023? Maybe it still existed and the radiation surge was due to a different reason. We were still left with the contradiction in the correspondences between *Calypso*'s ninety-five year jump and our ninety-nine-year jump.

Was it not more likely . . . I stopped pacing and groped for the thought, my hand literally groping in air. More likely that there were two sets of jump points? One with a ninety-five-year correspondence from 2027 to early 2122, and one with a ninety-nine-year correspondence from late 2122 to 2023. The first one *Calypso* used. The second, *Calypso II*, Murdoch's ship, and *Farseer* used. The latter would destablize somehow and the former would be opened by An Serat when he sent *Calypso* in 2027.

I remembered how *Farseer* had seemed to pass the co-ordinates where I'd appeared. Maybe it entered a different point.

I groaned in frustration and left the library to get a Con-Fleet dress uniform from the Uniform Recycling Center at the edge of the Bubble. The uniform Eleanor had given me when we arrived back on Jocasta must have been old and much-recycled, because the retardant stuck stubbornly to the material in a whitish film. I might as well wear the correct clothing to Florida's dinner—don't want to insult the Council delegates. Hopefully I'd get a chance to talk to Florida about the neutrality vote. I could slip away and go up to Level Three to continue with *Farseer* halfway through the dinner.

"Don't know if we've got any in your size." The clerk,

a delicately boned Achelian, looked me over and narrowed her huge pupils. Her long claws clicked on the touch pads of the interface panel.

"Make one," I suggested.

She twitched her ears and the claws moved slower.

"We're busy today. When do you want it?"

"Now."

This time her eyes opened so wide they took up half her face.

"Now?" she squeaked. "You can't have it *now.* Regulations clearly stipulate you must apply for a day uniform three shifts in advance, dress uniform, six."

"I wasn't here the day before yesterday and I need the uniform tonight, so find one."

"You'll have to file a special request form from your supervisor."

I took a deep breath. "I do not have a supervisor. I am the ranking ConFleet officer on this station and I want a dress uniform *now.*"

She laid back her ears in doubt.

I reached across the counter to slap my palm on the recognition pad. The screen obediently displayed my name, rank, position—which was "pending"—and a head and shoulders image that dated from three or four years back, judging from the lack of gray hair.

"Oh, sorry," she whined. "I didn't know, did I?"

"Just give me the uniform. Make sure you put Engineering Corps insignia on it."

She rolled her eyes in a deliberate mimicry of human gesture.

The dress uniform was a dark red material, softer than the normal stiff, navy-blue ConFleet suit, but with a higher collar. Now that the Engineering Corps no longer used the maroon color, they'd taken it for the dress uniform.

I changed in the bathroom of the senior officers lounge in the Bubble and shoved my retardant-soaked uniform down the recycling shaft. Strange that the official-looking figure in the mirror should have been only yesterday living in a tent in a slum one hundred years ago. Yet when I shut my eyes, I could see the crumbling edges of the outtown's runoff ditches and smell the refuse. Which was the dream?

The collar showed ConFleet rank bars on one side and the star-and-bridge of the old Engineering Corps on the other. Both insignia stood out from the fabric like silver brocade. I ran my fingers through my hair, noted vaguely that it was getting too long and much grayer, and went off to the dinner.

First I checked, via a handcom connection, the progress of my mapping of *Farseer*'s systems. Slow, far too slow. At least another hour before I could make even an educated guess where the gate connections were. And I didn't have time to waste looking in the wrong place.

In the new observation lounge on Level Three, the corridor for a whole section on one side of the spoke had been converted into an observation lounge, the section next to it into a dining room. The gravity field was active, so we would stand with our feet toward the core and gaze at the stars and the rest of the station through the ceiling. Two security guards stood at either end to divert passersby around the long way or through the dock access on the space side. Down in Alpha ring two more guards stood at the uplift entry to make sure we didn't get any uninvited guests, and to direct the uplift straight to the center without stopping at any of the spokes. And Murdoch had said he'd keep a couple of his people at the entries to the observation lounge during the dinner.

All in all, a well-considered entertainment effort and

one, I conceded reluctantly, I'd never have thought of myself.

When I arrived the observation lounge was empty.
Through the wide doorway into the next section, waiters
and serving droids readied the food. I sat in a low chair
and leaned my head back. Above, the pale arms of the
rings encircled me, reflectors glinting in the unseen sun so
their long expanses seemed gilded. On my left the spoke
loomed and then diminished rapidly to a slim line inter-
secting the gold. The whole scene crawled with the movement of tiny shapes—ESVs, shuttles, scooters,
communication pods. Beyond the rings further shapes
moved, some no more than points of light trailing against
the unmoving stars.

Leaving aside any foolish jealousy about Stone taking
over, I still felt out of place. As though a part of me—
some large, sharp-cornered part—could no longer fit with
things here. They didn't need me here anymore. My hands,
spread on my knees, seemed out of place on the rich red
material; bony, flat-tipped fingers with bitten nails, square
palms, the backs flecked with tiny scars I hadn't bothered
to get erased over the years, newer scars from the twenty-
first century.

The doors swished open.

"Here we are." Dan Florida strode into the room, cir-
cling his arm in a flourish to the dignitaries behind him.
"And here's Commander Halley, enjoying the view without us."

There seemed to be more of them than I'd met in Alpha
ring. The five Dir had multiplied to more than a dozen, including invitees from Jocasta's Dir community, dressed in
a variety of guild colors. Several more Leowin, also, and
the two Achelians I met had each acquired a couple of es-
corts.

The Earth representative, Sarkady, was talking to Stone

as she came in. He was resplendent in a high-collared, long-skirted jacket in pale gray and she had changed her bright dress for another embroidered with threads of gold and silver.

I remembered Veatch's prediction—we'd get votes from Achel and Dir, but not Earth. And he didn't mention the Leowin. If they hated the K'Cher, they might even vote yes.

I shook Sarkady's plump, moist hand again. "Good evening, Councilor."

When she smiled, her eyes disappeared into her cheeks. "Good evening, Commander. I didn't recognize you."

Stone nodded shortly. Probably still mad about us taking his Invidi toy. I made a mental note to ask Murdoch where he put it.

Lorna deVries appeared in the doorway as we tried to find the right places at the round dinner table. She waved excitedly at me until I joined her.

"A courier just came from Central," she said in a low voice. "I received orders and I bet Stone did, too."

"From Earth?"

"Yes. I'm to make sure you're given no exit permit. And the Adjudicate's Office wants an opinion drafted on Murdoch's charges." She tugged one of my sleeves down absentmindedly. "Halley, they're serious about this."

"I know. I'm feeling more trapped every minute. Can I make my asylum application now?"

"If that's what you want. But it's a big step. ConFleet won't want you back afterward."

"They'll court-martial me if I stay. Make the application."

"All right. You'll have to come and voice-print it."

"That's okay. I'm not staying here long."

She grinned. "And you so fond of social gatherings. What a waste of a nice dress uniform."

"Oh, be quiet. Look, here's your place. And I'm over there near the door. How considerate of them."

We sat down and waited for the speeches.

Stone bowed neatly as all eyes turned to him. "Welcome to Jocasta," he said smoothly. "We are honored to welcome such a distinguished group of guests, both from the Confederacy Council and from our residents here, to Earth's only extra-system station."

Lorna caught my eye again but I looked away. If she wasn't going to mention the neutrality issue, neither would I.

"As you can see," continued Stone, "Jocasta is a valuable asset for the people of Earth, and our government has invested in it a great amount of resources, time, and personnel. I hope you will enjoy your time here, and please do not hesitate to bring any questions to me or my staff."

Florida fielded the ball neatly. "Thank you, Mr. Stone. I'm honored that the councilors accepted my invitation to visit the station. The residents of Jocasta certainly owe a great debt to Earth's government and EarthFleet in particular. Who among us could forget their valiant efforts to defend the station when the Seouras ships invaded this space?"

"Hear, hear," said deVries.

Florida inclined his head in her direction. "The time has come to revise this relationship to meet the changing needs of our population. This population, as the honored delegates saw today, now consists of mainly nonhumans. The station's decision-making processes must be rebalanced to reflect this. We do not feel that Earth can take responsibility for our fate—we must do this ourselves."

The reaction from the listeners was lukewarm, by any standards. Only deVries nodded and smiled. Veatch looked faintly disapproving, as always. Quertianus the Dir shook his head and the Achelian, Reo, muttered to himself and counted something on long, spidery fingers. Sarkady had kept the same interested expression on her face and I wondered if she'd gone to sleep with her eyes open. Trillith, the K'Cher trader, ignored Florida and persisted in talking to the Leowin, Amartidjar. They both sat, or leaned, at places set closest to the door.

Florida must have sensed he was losing his audience. "I would like to ask you to join me in an old human tradition, the toast." He lifted his glass. "To the future. May it be fair and prosperous."

"To the future," echoed Lorna.

Most of the diners raised their glasses, having either lived with humans or knowing of the custom.

I sipped a mouthful of champagne. The future—may it always be unseen.

The civilian waiters and an EarthFleet corporal served the delicacies appropriate to each species, moving between the round table and two laden benches by the other door. The light was soft, like candlelight without flickers. The level of conversation rose.

On one side of me Trillith leaned on a K'Cher stool far out from the table. On the other side, one of the Achelian diplomats waited while his escort sorted his food.

I fiddled with a fork. Lorna caught my eye from across the table. She raised her eyebrow in query and I glanced half over my shoulder at the door. I could go now. Lorna rolled her eyes. *Already?* the look said.

I wanted to go. The mixed aromas of the food and alien scents, the complex buzz of conversation, and tiredness all conspired to addle my thoughts. I'd be much happier in the dock with *Farseer,* waiting for results from the system mapping.

Trillith shifted its entire body beside me. I glanced sideways and saw with shock that its torso was mottled pale gray. Across the table Veatch also stared at Trillith, antennae stiff with worry. His hands slid off the table onto his lap.

The door whooshed open. Guttural voices echoed in the corridor.

When the Bendarl captain stepped through the door, I knew we'd lost.

pushed by an armed Bendarl. Sasaki looked at me, face hard and eyes confused, but all I could do was give her a quick look, trying to project *don't do anything, it'll be over soon.*

"You will inform your subordinates in the rings that they are to stand aside. This is an authorized inspection," said the captain.

"Authorized by whom?" Stone was the only person ignorant enough to question her.

"Let it go," said Lorna tightly to him.

Stone ignored her. "This is Earth territory and you are trespassing without a docking permit."

The captain turned in his direction and I activated my wrist comm hurriedly. "I'll tell them."

"No." The captain's huge six-digit paw snared my arm in a swift movement. I felt the link crush and the pain of her grip sucked the air into my throat in an involuntary cry.

"Shit," said Florida faintly.

"Use this." She released me and tossed a standard Con-Fleet-issue fieldcom onto the table. The flat box was bigger than our links—it was also stronger, and easier to repair. This kind of equipment would be obsolete, if not for the Bendarl preference for simple toys. They were supposed to use the station's comm system, as the usual docking permit states. But like Stone said, they didn't get a docking permit.

Trillith edged away from me as I activated the fieldcom clumsily with one hand. The K'Cher's color was now a pasty gray all over, similar to the pallor of Stone's face. Mine, too, probably. I flexed the fingers on my left hand and was relieved to find they all worked, however excruciating they felt.

"Halley to Murdoch."

The reply was immediate. "Murdoch. What the hell's going on? I'm getting reports of ConFleet . . ."

"Offer no resistance," I said sharply. "Is that clear?"

He only hesitated for a millisecond. "Understood. We'll stand back. What do they want?"

I looked at the Bendarl captain over my shoulder. "It's an inspection. Halley out."

The captain observed the room. "Let's clear this." To An Barik. "You wish these out of the way?"

"Safe," the Invidi said. The word echoed in the frozen silence.

The captain and two more Bendarl marines herded all the civilians into the far corner of the room. She was marginally more deferential to Trillith and Veatch, but they kept quiet, nevertheless. I hoped this behavior from the normally bumptious Trillith would encourage everyone to do the same.

We waited.

Sasaki and the guard, a young man with freckles standing out like a mosaic on his pale face, stood next to me. I wanted to pace, but when I tried, the captain growled and our personal ConFleet guard leveled his weapon suggestively. The Bendarl like projectile weapons, the larger and messier the better. Fortunately, regulations required that they use either standard stun charges in enclosed environments or hand lasers.

"Aren't they breaking the law?" whispered Sasaki. "We're supposed to be neutral ground."

"Who can stop them?" I said, then put my finger on my lips for silence.

The Bendarl captain prowled around the table. She sat in Florida's seat and sampled mouthfuls of as many dishes as she could reach. We all watched with horrified fascination as she ate.

"This's good," she said to An Barik around a mouthful. "Try some."

"Results slow," was the answer. Why was he impatient? They must have located *Farseer* on their sensors. Or maybe not. Sasaki had moved it to the old fighter docks because the area was shielded.

An Barik must have told them to look where Invidi ships were usually docked, on Level Two or Three. If they don't find the ship where An Barik told them, I realized too late, they'll ransack the whole station until they do. My vision of Bendarl soldiers rampaging through the rings might come horribly true. You had to be smart, didn't you? I cursed myself. Never thought the Invidi might call your bluff.

I stepped forward. "Captain."

She ignored me and tapped open her comm link, a flat area below the neck of the armor. She snapped a few words in Confederacy Standard too fast to catch. An answer in a similar dialect followed.

"We search other levels," she said, and returned to the food.

"Captain, we changed the docks," I said.

She gave no sign of having heard.

At the same time, the Invidi rolled a little way toward me. "Governor Halley tell the one where."

Stone called out, "Give yourself up, Halley. Think of the rest of us."

The captain growled at being interrupted and got up to stomp around in front of me.

"Is this true?" Her breath now smelled of garlic.

"It's in . . ." *It's in the old dock,* I was about to say, when the captain's heavy arm shot up and hit me on the side of the head.

The blow was so unexpected I spun right around and went down on top of Sasaki, who had the presence of mind to grab the other guard and anchor herself so we both didn't fall completely.

Through the roaring in my ears Lorna's voice called out something and the Achelian made a sharp, high squeal of distress.

The rough material of Sasaki's uniform scraped against my cheek. Same as Murdoch's. He . . . no, she was saying something to me.

Open your eyes. They're open, just can't focus. Legs, try legs. I grabbed handfuls of Sasaki's uniform and tried to pull myself upright. Someone held my elbows.

"Where is it?" The captain's face shimmered into unwelcome focus. She pushed Sasaki and the guard away from me effortlessly with both her arms.

I tried to answer but my head throbbed and my mouth was full of blood. I turned my head to spit and the movement sent me staggering against the table.

"Where is it?" The captain pointed her weapon at Sasaki.

"In the old fighter dock," said Sasaki. She reached out to take my arm but the captain growled, a note of warning.

"Level Eight," I mumbled. Spat, and tried again. Mouth must be cut inside, whole cheek numb. "I was about to tell you." My mouth slurred the words.

The captain cocked her head at me.

Being beaten by the Bendarl is not necessarily regarded by them as a weakness, it merely confirms their view of how the universe should work.

She slowly replaced her weapon and called her marines again. We waited while they searched, the link open. Tableau: huddle of frightened dignitaries in one corner of the room, silent Bendarl soldiers with bare weapons, the Invidi like a silver statue, Bendarl captain with her attention on the comm link. I dared not look behind at Sasaki or meet Lorna's eyes for fear the bitter bile of defeat would rise up and choke me and I'd say something we might all regret.

Finally a response crackled from the comm link. The captain wrinkled her nose in satisfaction and turned to An Barik.

"Item secure."

The Invidi shuffled toward the door where the soldiers were lined up.

"As the Council delegate, I protest this treatment." Quertianus found his voice.

"Absolutely." Stone also gained courage from the partial withdrawal of the soldiers. "I will send a full and detailed report of this outrage to your superiors and mine. Don't think you can get away with it."

The captain's eyes roved over the room and I felt sick— was she going to kill us all so we couldn't talk?

Apparently Trillith thought the same, for its color began to fade again. "I'm sure the captain has her reasons," it said. "We must not judge too hastily."

"They are in clear violation of at least five Confederacy laws and many regulations," said deVries coldly, her eyes on An Barik. "Laws that the Invidi helped draft. They have no right to break them now."

The captain ignored all this. An Barik resumed his shuffle out.

"Bring Halley," he said. And left.

Cold claws of apprehension clutched at me. I couldn't do anything from Confederacy custody. Once they had me in the system it would take months to get a ConFleet hearing.

Too fast, it's all happening too fast.

"You have no right to apprehend a citizen of the Confederacy on neutral ground. Until the Council accepts or rejects our application, this station is exactly that." DeVries stepped forward, angrier than I'd ever seen her.

"I concur with the magistrate's position," said Veatch. He wriggled his fingers nervously but he stepped forward beside deVries. The delegates and Trillith edged back, as though to make it clear they were not involved.

Florida dithered. "Ah, what the hell," he muttered, and joined Lorna. "You've got a lot of witnesses here." He spread his hands in a gesture of conciliation. "Why not just take the . . . "

"Ship," said Lorna.

"Ship, and forget about the commander?" He smiled, totally wasted on the Bendarl.

The captain looked at me. "I order you to report to *Vengeful*."

My face throbbed. I touched the cut inside my mouth with my tongue and tasted blood. "No, ma'am. I can't do that."

"Then I arrest you for mutiny."

"I hereby resign my ConFleet commission as per regulation Theta 5.3."

"You still stand trial."

DeVries came all the way to the table and leaned over it. Florida and Veatch followed more reluctantly.

"She is also the governor of this system," said Lorna, "and that position holds until the neutrality vote. You cannot arrest a senior official without due process of law, which involves . . ."

I felt strangely detached.

The captain snarled and spun around. This time I jumped back, but she wasn't interested in blows.

"Cannot, cannot. Look around you, little ones." She loomed with the promise of violence.

"Take her," she ordered the soldier closest to me.

Sasaki and the guard attempted to close in front of me but I pushed between them. "No, it's not worth it." I tried to catch Florida's eye. "Dan, tell every . . ."

Tell everyone what happened is what I wanted to say. The words were cut off as the guard pulled me away. His hand curled around my forearm like a vise. The door shut on deVries's and Florida's protests. I felt a pang of sympathy for him—he'd worked so hard to bring the delegates here and now I'd messed up his dinner.

The guard shifted his grip to my upper arm. It hurt, but so did my wrist where the captain had grabbed it and my head where she'd hit it. The pain didn't matter at the moment—it might have belonged to someone else.

The captain stalked along, growling under her breath. We followed her, two more soldiers bringing up the rear. The corridor was dark and blue, night lights only. More people, all scurrying to get out of the way when they saw the Bendarl. I kept stumbling and the guard kept jerking me upright.

An Barik's tall form filled the corridor ahead. We overtook him rapidly.

"Wait." I braced my heels as the captain leveled with the Invidi and the guard slowed down. "An Barik, please listen to me." No response.

The captain growled something over her shoulder and passed An Barik.

"Please!" I shouted at him. The guard pushed me and I bumped off the wall back almost in An Barik's path.

"At least answer a question," I panted. In the old days, An Barik was always willing to answer questions.

The guard grabbed my arm and twisted it behind me. Bright points began to blossom in front of my eyes.

"What is question?" boomed An Barik.

I sagged with relief in the guard's grip. He loosened his hold slightly and looked at the captain. She chopped her hand down irritably. "Hurry up." She continued striding on ahead.

"What is question?"

The old Barik was never impatient.

"Can the Invidi open jump points wherever you want to?" I didn't care if the guard heard. Didn't care if the whole damn Confederacy heard. "Is that why you're after Serat—because he did that?"

Immediate answer. "Serat work unstable."

Did he mean Serat himself or *Farseer?* Unstable in what way? "What's so special about that ship?"

"You answer your own question."

"What . . ." I began, but the guard cut me off by putting a coarse hand across my mouth. What did he mean? The question about Invidi opening jumps off-network—was that why *Farseer* was special? It could open jump points?

"You finish," grunted the guard.

"Yes," said Barik.

"No . . ." The guard's hot hand crushed the word against my lips and he dragged me away.

In the crawler we squished together, their armor digging into my back and hips through the thin material of the dress uniform. My arm and shoulder burned from where the guard twisted it. The pain, the heat, and the combined odors of their breath made my head spin. Don't faint, they'll probably drag you along by the heels.

More corridors. Level Three? Each time I tried to look around, another tug nearly floored me.

Then we were staring out an airlock, floating through a narrow gray tunnel, no friendly EarthFleet blue here. A standard shuttle, troops saluting. Pinned immobile in an inertia net. The three-g breakoff threatened to squeeze my eyelids shut but I forced them open, desperate for one last glimpse of the white rings of home spinning against the stars.

Twenty-eight

I did all right until they stripped me.

Kept quiet when the shuttle's rough landing threatened to scramble my insides; ignored jibes from the lieutenant in charge of escorting me to an "interview" room on the cruiser; remembered to insist I was now a civilian and to request legal counsel. They didn't listen, of course, but it made me feel better to keep repeating who I was. It helped me delude myself that this would eventually be sorted out and we could return to normal.

Resigning hadn't been an option until the words left my mouth. I felt unsettled, as an object placed in a cabin in free fall will nudge the same spot for a while before floating away around the room. I'd been in ConFleet for twenty-three years, mostly in the Engineering Corps, which contained few Bendarl and little military ceremony. If I'd been in other arms of ConFleet, maybe I wouldn't have remained for so long.

As for An Barik's words about Serat and *Farseer,* I didn't know how to interpret them. He may have meant *Farseer*'s combination of Tor and Invidi technology was inherently unstable, and I could well believe it. I didn't think active Tor technology would be content to combine peacefully with any other system. Or he might have been saying that to discourage me from trying the same thing.

As I'd almost contemplated when considering how to save information on *Farseer.*

I thought of my efforts to map *Farseer*'s system—would the Bendarl have simply removed the ship with my handcoms inside? Or would they have cleaned out all evidence of human use? More damn waste of time. I should have risked frying my brains in that direct connection in the hope of getting information more quickly.

Could *Farseer* really open jump points, perhaps the way the Tor did? It would explain the discrepancy in the coordinates when we left 2023. We hadn't entered the jump point already there because we'd made a new one. But that meant there were two jump points from 2023 to 2122, both of ninety-nine years' duration. If my theory about the radiation surge on May 16, 2023, was correct, only one of those points would survive another day. But then if *Calypso* used the remaining point in 2027, why did its correspondence shrink from ninety-nine years to ninety-five? All our experience of the jump points says they do not change length. So *Calypso* should have emerged in 2126.

I wish I'd never seen a jump drive.

When the sergeant told me to drop my clothes so they could do a full body search, I lost it completely. I yelled at him for counsel, for a medical officer, for an officer of any sort. It did me no good, and instead of one of them doing it without fuss, two of them held me down so the sergeant could get at me. Nothing personal, of course, with Bendarl. They didn't care who they hurt. Their claws scratched my skin and I cried more from the indignity and pain of their grip on my arms and legs than from the primitive medical probe they used.

After they were done, I shook with humiliation and anger in the corner of the room farthest from them, arms wrapped around myself, torso goose-bumped, knees trembling. It wasn't cold that made me shiver—Bendarl temperature controls were set several degrees hotter than humans found comfortable. It was knowing that I had been used as a tool in some Invidi game of temporal politics. Barik's involvement made that obvious.

Fear for Murdoch settled in a cold lump in my stomach. Had they arrested him as well?

Eventually the Bendarl soldiers hustled me, still naked, out into the gray corridors. The corridor lights glared too bright for human eyes. Every shadow showed black and distorted by the conduits and control points along walls and ceilings. Round, cramped doors marked corridor sections, designed to be easily defended or airlocked if necessary. We walked—rather, I stumbled. The Bendarl used the Invidi gravity field at slightly stronger than Earth normal. It dragged at my body as the situation dragged at my spirits.

The idea of trying to escape made me feel sick. Yet I wouldn't get a better chance. The ship hadn't jumped back to Central. I had worked on vessels of this class before and knew their back corridors and access networks. Only two marines accompanied me and they hadn't bothered to restrain me—probably the ease with which they'd held me down persuaded them I wasn't much of a threat. But once they put me in a proper brig cell, any chance of escape would vanish.

A shrill, insistent whoop made us all jump. Decompression alert. I hadn't heard it for years, but it sent me instantly swinging around to locate the nearest spacesuit locker and emergency shaft.

One of the marines cursed and ran to a comm panel at the end of the corridor. The other, like me, looked around for the emergency locker that should be halfway down every corridor.

Forget the alarm. The guards aren't looking at you.

I took four long strides to the closest maintenance hatch

that opened, as I knew it would, with a quick twist, push, and pull. Convenient how the Bendarl mistrust new technology.

The closest marine roared with rage and charged behind me.

A tight fit—I scraped my shoulders, hips, backs of thighs on the rough edges. Convenient, too, that the Bendarl use robots or humans for maintenance work. They'd never get through that hole themselves.

In my panic to set the hatch on auto again, I slammed the marine's stubby, clawed digits. His roar of rage turned to one of pain. I couldn't turn properly in the shaft and had to brace my legs on both sides of the hatch and bend backward.

The marine snatched his hand away, almost opening the hatch, but I kept hold and closed it. Keyed in a half-remembered, half-habitual code scramble with shaking fingers.

Get away from this area because this was where they'd start looking. The alarm still rose and fell, echoing up the shaft from a lower level. Whatever had caused a Grade One alarm, I hoped the crew was not abandoning ship while I sat here in the dim heat, a switch digging into my left buttock.

I was perched in a small, spherical space, hemmed on all sides but one by surfaces covered with snaking connections, many of them active and glowing. The open shaft stretched down with no friendly ladder like on Jocasta. I swore under my breath and wished the gravity field to hell. They must use maglev belts in these shafts, or service bots. If I wanted down I'd have to jump or climb.

A blow on the hatch at my back vibrated through the surfaces above and below me and a couple of status indicators flickered.

I stuck my feet gingerly down into the shaft, toes feeling for a hold.

The hatch exploded in my ear. I slid, and only halted the drop by bracing shoulders and knees against the sides of the shaft. Oh, hell, hell and damnation. I shut my teeth around a scream as prickles of electricity ran between my shoulders, leaving them numb and my heart racing.

In the uncertain glow I could see the hatch was still intact, despite the noise. That stupid marine must have loosed off a shot at the controls and fused them nicely. It would take them hours to get the hatch open.

A security detail would be waiting for me wherever this shaft ended. Too much to hope they'd all be too busy with the alert to have time to track one human signal on internal sensors. Unless, and I almost laughed at the thought, unless it was an outside attack and not a problem with the ship's systems, which was what I'd assumed. If someone was attacking, my place was back on the station, not stuck here in some goddamn tunnel.

I had to get out of here, find a uniform, and mix my sensor readings with the fifteen hundred or so individuals of whom, if the cruiser was an average ship, between five and fifteen percent would be human. Mostly in the service areas. Some pilots, too. Humans were small, expendable, and functioned well with interface enhancements.

A lateral shaft at last. I slid the last couple of meters down and pulled myself horizontal with a sob of relief. Don't think about how much you hurt and what you're going to do when you get out. Don't think about the alarm that still vibrates around you. Concentrate on where the shaft leads and how to crawl along it without getting burned or electrocuted.

I never realized how much difference even a single layer of cloth makes between flesh and the world of syntal, glass, and wire. Right now I'd welcome even a dress uniform.

I'd kill for a pair of boots. Like the ones a certain group of men in the out-town used to wear as a badge of solidarity. Most of them hadn't worked for months or years. But they all boasted battered, heavy boots. Vince had a pair. I'd surprised him one day in the courtyard, rubbing gravel into the toes and heels to achieve that rugged look.

I peered at the ID beside a control panel and stopped, glad of an excuse to rest. Deck Twelve, Section Fifty-two. These big warships were fifteen to twenty decks deep. Deck Twelve would be crew quarters, and as far as I could remember, Section Fifty-two contained Stores or Recreation or some such low-priority area. A good place to avoid detection, and one they would hardly expect me to visit.

I could get some clothes there, and find a way to get off the cruiser before it jumped. I'd take an escape pod at a pinch, but I'd prefer something with a bit of thruster power I could steer. And go where? I didn't know, but back to the station sounded good. Or over to the asteroid belt where I could hide for a while.

What did it matter, I just needed to get out of this tunnel.

The shaft shuddered and the jolt found every bruise and scrape in my knees, hands, shoulders. Engine hum faltered, then resumed on a higher note. They'd rerouted power through the shielded generators. We must be under attack, after all. But who were we fighting? The only threat in this sector was from organized pirates. The New Council had no ships that could seriously challenge ConFleet. Unless they'd brought the Q'Chn to fight, because all the Q'Chn needed to do was get close enough to board. But who would fight over Jocasta or the Abelar system?

At least we wouldn't be jumping out of the system anytime soon—combat mode protocols were specific to flatspace. So if I could get to a shuttle undetected, I might be able to escape and elude pursuit. Into the middle of a battle, what fun.

It didn't occur to me to doubt the outcome of the combat. Nothing in the known galaxy could stand against Con-Fleet; another reason for Confederacy stability. Bendarl were called the "wolves of space" for good reason. I'd worry about the enemy once I found a pod.

Another jolt pushed me against the shaft wall. A sharp shock fell like a lash across my shoulders and the shock constricted the cry in my throat. My heart jumped against my ribs with a will of its own.

At the same time a hissing noise drowned out all other sounds and an acrid smell drifted up behind me. Coolant leak. Now I'd need detox treatment, on top of everything else.

Holding my breath, I scrambled away from the leak. Deck Twelve was fine, anywhere except this tunnel was fine. All I wanted was to get out of that shaft, put some clothes on, and find out what was happening.

The first two hatches stuck. Or they were locked. Or the alert plus coolant leak had activated an emergency override. By the time the third hatch cover glowed beside me, the shaft seemed to be getting darker and narrower. My hand on the hatch handle seemed to twist like when you try and move something in zero-g and find yourself moving instead . . . concentrate, turn the handle.

The hatch swung outward and I followed it in a heap on the deck, unable to control my muscles enough to brace them against the fall.

Too bright. I was in a narrow room, same gray walls and low ceilings as the rest of the ship. Handholds on floor and ceiling indicated this was not always gravitized. I pulled myself up and pushed the hatch shut with an immense effort. The long wall of the room was a curious honeycomb structure. I limped over to investigate and found they'd changed the locker design. Judging by the names and size, I'd found a locker room for humans. Either that, or the morgue.

The lockers were set to open only to the owner's handprint. I leaned against them, too tired to curse, fingers too unsteady to consider trying to reset the locks. The alarm still sang, but it had settled to a slow and regular mid-tone blare. Alert and Action Stations. I had no idea how long I'd been in the shaft—it felt like hours.

An oval doorway stood around the corner from the lockers. I dabbed at its "open" pad and the door swished back. I jumped in fright, for the room beyond was filled with gaseous murk, then laughed at myself for being scared of a shower. Real water, to judge by the steam.

Nothing better. It would hurt like hell, but I'd get rid of most of the coolant traces on my skin. The internal damage would have to be dealt with later.

Four jets of warm, brackish water hit me from above, below, and two sides, a walk-through soaking. The warm, damp smell of floral scrub solution filled my nostrils. By the time I'd finished the ten paces to the end my head was spinning with pain.

"Wow, what happened to you?" A voice in my ear made me jump again.

A young human woman peered through the steam at me. Round eyes, broad nose from which rivulets dripped down to a generous mouth. A mouth pursed in an "ooh" of sympathy at the weals and burns all over me.

"I, um, got caught in a maintenance shaft." My voice drifted and I tried harder. "When the alert sounded."

My companion nodded understandingly. "I know what you mean. I got half a mission's supply of Baven eggs on top of me when we rocked around."

I shuddered at the memory of Baven eggs, a Bendarl delicacy. In their raw state they were quite caustic. The woman's plump, firm figure did give off a distinct sulfur odor. She must be in one of the Service corps.

"I haven't seen you around before." She reached out to the controls and the water changed to blasts of warm air.

Either she missed the general announcement that a prisoner had escaped, or there hadn't been one.

"I came from the station," I yelled over the whoosh of the dryers, as loud as my raw throat would permit. "I'm . . ." The wind stopped and I dropped my voice to a more comfortable level. "I'm getting maintenance experience."

She nodded again, a trusting and generous gesture.

"Trouble is," I ventured, hoping she wouldn't ask me why I'd been in the shaft, "I got lost and couldn't find the shuttle docks. And my uniform was such a mess I had to chuck it. I am in such trouble."

"I can lend you a uniform," said the woman. "We'd better get back to our posts quick." She opened the shower door. The AA alarm still pulsed from the corridor. Whatever was happening, I hoped it would continue long enough for me to get to an escape pod.

"My name's Kiri, by the way. Kiri Cook. I'm a cook's assistant, second class." She offered her hand. "You're not going to make a joke?"

"Huh?" I could easily have fainted with pain. Joke, no. I shook the hand. "Maria Valdon, Engineering tech."

Her fingers bumped the tender spots left on my wrist by the Bendarl captain's grip. I tried to ignore it but her expression clouded immediately.

"Before we find a uniform, you'd better put something on those burns."

"Kiri, I have to get to the docks. I don't want to be caught off-post in an alarm."

"Won't be a tick." Her voice rose muffled from a locker just above floor level. "Here you are, field medkit. Just what the doctor ordered."

I decided less time would be wasted by submitting than by arguing. Besides, the pain was bad.

She slapped a handful of cold goo on my back and I nearly went through the wall.

"Sorry." She peered around at my face. "Maybe you should go to sickbay."

"No, it's okay." I held on to fistfuls of air while she smoothed it in. By the time she'd finished I could flex my shoulders with only minor tightness.

"Better?"

I smiled in thanks and rummaged through the kit for detox tablets while Kiri pulled on her uniform swiftly. She seemed to realize the time she'd taken to help me. "I have to get back, too. We're under attack by someone. Or maybe that station is."

"Someone's attacking the station?" My hand shook sachets and containers onto the floor.

"Don't worry. We can handle it." She tossed me some folded clothes. "Here you are."

I pulled overalls gingerly over my back.

Kiri activated the mirror with a cursory tap. "Think you'll pass?"

The dark blue overalls would blend in anywhere on the ship, except perhaps the command deck. But my face above them, lopsided with swelling from the captain's swipe, had the anemic, smudge-eyed look typical of coolant poisoning. I swallowed two detox tabs while Kiri was putting the medkit away, then slipped the remaining tabs in my pocket and hoped they'd be enough.

"Which way's the small-craft dock? I'm supposed to report there."

"The lift will take you up two decks." She shifted from one foot to the other, impatient to be off. "Go straight along here, take a left, then a right. You can't miss it."

"Thank you."

"Take care, then."

We parted outside the locker room and she waved, cheerful to be moving, as she rounded the corner in the other direction.

A group of people were gathered around the lift doors when I reached them. Human, a couple of Achelians, one worried-looking Bendarl marine. The sight of the soldier jangled my nerves. I decided to go up the internal access shaft instead of waiting for the lift. Ten to one he'd been sent to check out an escaped prisoner.

None of them gave me more than a quick glance as I walked past. I heard a couple of snatches of conversation,

". . . between the decks."

". . . have to climb up. The AA lockout is . . ."

A human on the edge of the group caught my eye and smiled. He wore overalls and was seated resignedly on a container marked FRAGILE, which he was evidently waiting to carry up in the lift. "Nuisance, this."

"Lift out?" I slowed my stride but didn't stop. Be natural. Breathe.

"Yeah. They reckon someone's stuck in there."

I clicked my tongue in sympathy and kept going. Tough luck for the people in the lift, but anything that kept attention away from escaped prisoners was good news for me.

In the climb up to Deck Eleven I passed only one human going down and he didn't even look at me. I stopped outside the shaft well to get my breath. The pain in my back was muffled, but I had to lean against the bulkhead and put my head down before looming black blotches went away. I might as well move forward on Eleven before climbing up to Ten. Take the opportunity to get my breath back.

Kiri had said the guest docks were forward on Deck

Ten. I had the nagging feeling there was something I'd forgotten. A small emptiness.

I jogged as fast as I could to the bow end of Deck Eleven, which wasn't very fast. My body was losing the fight against fatigue, coolant poisoning, and shock. The light parts of the corridor were too light and the shadows too dark, everything in between a blur. Water. I had to find a drink of water.

Haul self slowly up connecting shaft to Deck Ten. Didn't meet anyone this time, good thing because hands kept cramping on rails and they would have noticed me hanging on and swearing.

Door, guard. He's staring at me. I try and pull my shoulders back and walk straight. As I go past, the empty feeling disappears.

Farseer's in there. Not sure how I know, but it's definitely there. An Barik or the captain must have brought it from Jocasta.

I hesitated. The throbbing in my head got in the way of thought. I might as well take *Farseer* to get away—better for me to be in a ship that can camouflage itself and maybe open the dock for me. Easier than stealing a shuttle in the middle of a battle. Especially in my present condition.

Keep walking. Don't want main door to bay. Side door, maintenance access. Small room with suits in nets and cleaning bots bolted to walls. Fine, I can be a cleantech. Anything to get out of here.

My fingers fumbled the net release, a suit tumbled onto the floor, and I wasted precious minutes sorting it out. I was glad of the suit's insulation for I was shivering. Either the ambient temperature had dropped, or mine had risen.

Water. Might stave off the fever for a bit longer. Another minute wasted before I found some in an amenities locker. I gulped down most of it with the last detox tabs from my pocket, and clipped the bottle onto the suit's utility belt.

I settled the helmet casually over one shoulder as I'd seen cleantechs do, and after hurriedly checking the dock's interior status—well done, Halley, don't waltz into a vacuum without your helmet—entered the dock area.

It was a double bay, doors shut tight as combat protocol requires, red lights around the edges. Inside the bay, three pools of light covered the area next to the main door, diagonally opposite my entry, but otherwise it was dark. Both slots were full of Invidi ship, An Barik's yacht and *Farseer.*

Farseer was closest to me. In case the guard was watching the visual pickup, I pretended to check each equipment alcove as I worked my way around the wall to *Farseer.* It loomed tall in the dark, swaying in time with the mass of conduits, magnetic lifters, and cables above. Or maybe it was me swaying. Concentrate.

I ran my hand along a ridge on the surface, shut my eyes, and visualized an entry hatch. Round, smooth-edged. Close to the deck so I could fall in.

Nothing happened.

Soft blackness threatened to overwhelm me and I leaned helplessly against the ship, cheek pressed against it, hands beside my face. *Come on, baby. Open the door for me.*

A section of the hull dissolved back into itself and the interior glowed welcome. I tumbled in and sat on the deck inside, rubbing my shoulder where the helmet had knocked.

It looked the same. Dim golden light, warm surface. The panel I'd worked on before was beside me this time and I dragged myself upright with a groan. Moved my hands over the surface, stroking the edges of triangles. Supported my weight on it and wished my head would stop pounding. Pinpricks of response needled my fingertips, then palms. The implant throbbed in time with my head, like a collar of fire. Blue lines crackled across the console in time with the collar.

Don't faint, not yet. My thoughts moved with infuriating slowness. Open *Vengeful*'s space doors without activating the alarm and without endangering containment . . . hell, I know how to do that, why can't I remember now? Leave your hand on the sensor so the ship can pick up your thoughts.

The cabin shuddered slightly. I lost my balance and slid down the side of the console, but it was all right, we were out of the cruiser and not by crashing through the space doors. The viewscreen above the console had brightened into life and showed space and stars.

I pulled myself upright against the console and ran my hands more carefully over the surface, trying to remember navigational controls. Different-sized triangles, all with slightly different surfaces, some rough, some smooth, raised at different angles. Surely there weren't this many last time I looked.

Hope it's not reconfiguring itself, like Jocasta's opsys. Making a maze to trap the unwary user.

Jocasta was centered on the viewscreen as if in a tactical holo, showing position and status. By changing the angle of the image on the viewscreen I could also see it as if through an ordinary port, a pale wheel against the dark.

There, I want to go there. Input what I think are the co-ordinates.

On the other side of Jocasta, near the jump point to Central, was a dot of light. I stared at it, wishing I could focus for more than a few seconds at a time, and the tactical part of the viewscreen enlarged it obligingly. A ship, looks like a modified freighter. Sensor details in unfamiliar script seemed to send their message directly to my brain—indeed a freighter, modified with weapons and jump drive-compliant. The smaller ships leaving it were fighters. I leaned farther to the left and was rewarded by a view of *Vengeful*, with more fighters dipping around it.

Farseer was still close enough to *Vengeful* for warnings to blip at me from the console. Radiation warnings from the bursts of weapons fire. Proximity warning, a small craft too close, skimming us—need to get away.

As I stroked my fingertips up the side of the triangle prickles of discomfort ran up the inside of my arms, twitching muscles and echoing off the pain from the implant, which was getting worse. It wasn't this bad before. Must be why it's so cold. Can't stop shivering. Could be the Tor elements . . . the Tor elements doing something. I lost the thought.

My fingers slipped off the triangle and I wasted time trying to get the viewscreen to show *Vengeful* again. Taking a while to come into focus; not sure if that's my fault or *Farseer*'s. We're farther away from *Vengeful* now. Fighters zip around it. Some of them ConFleet. Protecting the cruiser, which wouldn't be able to bring its larger weapons to bear properly on the attackers.

There was a lot of other information about automated seeker weapons and warhead content but my head hurt too much to process it. Something else I need to look at . . . Biosignals, that was it. Who was in the attacking fighters and the freighter they'd come from?

Oh, shit, it's Q'Chn. Too many Q'Chn. In the fighters. One of them stuck on to *Vengeful*'s hull and I groaned helplessly. Much as I disliked the Bendarl, they didn't deserve being massacred by the Q'Chn. And the station is vulnerable—when they finish with ConFleet they'll come after us.

Think, think, *Farseer* is a jump-capable ship. Can I get it through the jump point to Central and warn ConFleet?

I'd slid down the side of the console again, my legs as

rubbery as *Farseer*'s inner surfaces. It took a precious minute or two to drag myself upright against the console that tilted and rocked, the triangles a blurred mess. Shit, I feel sick.

. . . jump point. ConFleet. Can't do it. The freighter's in the way. And three . . . no, four fighters clustered around the point, engaging what looked like escape pods and shuttles from *Vengeful*. Did Barik get away? For a second, I thought I could see the rounded shape of an Invidi ship in the scrum, but then my vision blurred.

Farseer should be heading toward Jocasta. There, on the viewscreen. Getting larger. The station, *Vengeful*, the planet and small ship-shapes overlapped, swam in and out of focus. Murdoch's words, his deep, flat voice. *What are you going to do with it, then?* The warmth of his hand dissolves into the rhythm of Henoit's lovemaking, bears me along in a river, drowning.

Can't breathe properly. Cool, rubbery surface under my cheek. Stink of sweat, sour remnant of vomit. Am I back in the out-town?

Snap out of it. Think. You thought *Farseer* might be able to open new jump points. Could I go and warn Con-Fleet that way?

I didn't think I could find the same control sequence I'd used to jump from 2023. Not with the overwhelming ache in my head and the way the console had changed. And what had An Barik said? *Farseer* wasn't stable.

Somebody else talking. In the cabin? No, from the screen.

. . . *Invidi yacht, please respond. This is the New Council of Allied Worlds ship* Freedom. A female voice. Not human.

I fumbled upward over the console and managed to pat what I thought was the visual interface control until the outside view was replaced by a narrow figure against a fuzzy background. Humanoid. Muscled arms and torso, long plaits of hair, vertical-irised eyes staring through me. H'digh.

Henoit's voice seemed to tickle my ear. Listen.

Invidi yacht. Respond. H'digh are supposed to be patient hunters, but the female's voice rose in annoyance.

"I can hear you," I mumbled, and hoped the pickups caught my response.

You will dock that ship at the space station.

I was so slow-witted, it took me a moment to work out she meant Jocasta.

I know you're thinking: if I can stall them long enough, ConFleet will send reinforcements. But there is only one jump point in this system. Three of our small ships are waiting next to it. If ConFleet sends a ship through, the Q'Chn will be inside before they know what hit them. And soon we'll have Vengeful to use as our own.

Pause. Boom . . . boom . . . the blood in my head, the hum of *Farseer*'s engines, the sound of time dripping away.

Bring the ship back or we will let the Q'Chn loose on the station. Do it now.

Not fighting over Jocasta. Someone wants *Farseer*. I bet An Serat has renewed his ties with the New Council to get it.

Will she carry out the threat? I can call their bluff, but I don't know where I can go if I do. Jump to Central or run away in flatspace until ConFleet beat back the Q'Chn.

If ConFleet comes. Last time they didn't. They left us to the Seouras for half a year.

I leaned hopelessly on the panel and the monitor flicked back to outside view. *Vengeful* drifted dead in space. It must have decelerated just before the Q'Chn hit, because its momentum was negligible. Surrounded by a trailing cloud: wisps of atmosphere, bodies, pieces of equipment, and debris. Small ships were docked at its ventral and lateral ports, another under its nose. As I watched, a fourth clamped on to another lateral port.

And the station? I activated three vistas of empty space on the viewscreen before the white rings of Jocasta appeared. We were quite close. Despite my wavering, *Farseer* must have kept on course. The New Council freighter was maneuvering closer to one of Jocasta's docking ports. A number of smaller ships were leaving those ports, and one shaved the larger ship dangerously close in its haste to leave. As many people getting out while they could. Exactly what happened when the Seouras arrived.

This time not Bendarl marines stalking my corridors. This time the real monsters.

No. No more killing.

I wished I could see like an Invidi, but all I could do was what I thought was right at that moment. So I aimed *Farseer* at the docks in the center of Jocasta.

I must have blacked out for a few minutes, because the next thing I felt was a jolt that reawakened every ache. I slid down the tilted deck and smashed into the other wall, too dazed to do more than grab weakly at the console. My shoulder made an audible crack as it hit but I didn't feel anything. Numb all over, feeling in every limb beginning to fade. The thin pain at the top of my head from the link with *Farseer* overlay it all like a high whine on the edge of hearing.

Get up, stupid. You've docked.

I tried to repeat the words aloud through lips that didn't feel right.

The New Council is here. They're going to let Q'Chn loose on my station. Get out of this ship and go do something about it.

I rolled onto my knees and tried to put both hands on the wall for support, but one arm wouldn't answer. The hatch should be somewhere near here. Open up, please.

I tried to trace the patterns in the wall surface and visualize the hatch opening, but my fingers slipped and skated over the surface and I couldn't stay upright without leaning on it. The image of the hatch kept turning into a face, a flat circle with a toothed gash right across it and raised eyebrows that crawled up and down saying, "Assembly of the Poor."

I leaned my face on the cool wall like I did in the dock on *Vengeful*. It dug into my cheek. Etching patterns into me. Eating into me like the Tor programs eat into our systems.

"Dammit, open the door," I mumbled. Surely that New Council captain would believe I came as soon as I could. Surely she wouldn't let Q'Chn loose on Jocasta, like they're loose on *Vengeful* at this moment. What happened to An Barik? And Kiri and the corporal.

Not that on Jocasta, please no. An Serat can have *Farseer*, just let me keep the station and my friends safe . . .

The hatch slid open under my hand and I crumpled out at the base of an Invidi. He towered over me in his silver environmental suit. I let out the breath I'd gulped automatically. Atmosphere available, thoughtful of him. Or someone in the Bubble was keeping an eye on the dock.

Behind the Invidi, a small shuttle sat squeezed against the wall of the bay. *Farseer* was skewed across it. The jolt I'd felt had been from our rough landing. I'd directed *Farseer* into the open docking bay all right, but deceleration was too late. We'd slammed into the far end of the bay, padded and netted for such occasions.

One of the Invidi's tentacles reached down and tapped my shoulder. An impersonal touch, as if to confirm my position.

"It's about time," said An Serat.

Twenty-nine

The darkness smelled of Henoit. I took a long breath through my nose. It tingled in the back of my throat and streamed warmth into my gut.

Then nausea hit and I curled around it and vomited over the side of the bed. Must be flu again. Grace warned me it was going around . . .

But in the out-town I don't have a bed. I retched again and groaned, hating the taste and the way the blood pooled heavy in my nose, blocking out the H'digh scent that wasn't real. All in my head. I'll never see him again except in my head. Nor Will . . .

A voice said something I couldn't catch. Cool hands lifted my dangling head. Something soft supported it from behind. Wetness wiped my eyes and I could see.

Eleanor's face, close-up and slightly out of focus. "Lie still." It had been her voice and this time I understood the words.

Hiss of injector. The room beyond Eleanor clicked into focus. Secondary hospital block in Gamma, judging from the skylight construction. Now I could feel my whole body properly, not in patches as if through a malfunctioning atmospheric suit. Stiff joints, a throbbing ache above my left eye, and a pins and needles-like sensation in my left arm that indicated Eleanor had used some procedure involving a stasis field, which was usually to help bones knit. I must have cracked my shoulder harder than I thought.

Memory clicked into place, too.

"What happened to *Vengeful?*" My voice a hardly audible croak.

"They lost." Eleanor's voice was almost lost in the whirr of a suction cleaner as she bent over to clean the floor beside my bed. "The Q'Chn boarded them and now they're drifting."

I thought of the small ships I'd seen coming from the freighter. Small ships with Q'Chn biosignals. Bile rose in my throat again as I imagined the chaos and the carnage when they entered the cruiser.

"Some of the escape pods and shuttles got away." Eleanor dropped the cleaner with more force than necessary in its stand against the wall. "We've got a few here in the hospital. Most of them headed for the jump point. Some of them even got through." She rubbed her face tiredly. "It's a mess out there. Bits of ships and bodies floating everywhere."

"I saw An Serat in the docking bay..." I turned and sat up, but it made me retch again. The room rocked gently like a boat in a swell as I just made the side of the bed in time.

Eleanor glared at me and reached for the cleaner again. "They're here."

"Huh?" Oh, this is a disgusting feeling. "Who?"

"The New Council. Murdoch persuaded Rupert to give them docking permission."

Hard to refuse someone holding an activated weapon at your head—in this case, the threat of the Q'Chn. "Did they bring Q'Chn onstation?"

"In the docks. So I heard."

A nightmare come true. I tried to gather my thoughts but apprehension got in the way.

A human in nurse's smock put his head around the door. "They're doing another broadcast, Doctor. Thought you might want to watch."

"Thanks." Eleanor tapped one of the interface panels on the wall opposite the bed. The comm unit's visual link brightened to show two figures against one of the generic EarthFleet blue backgrounds used for official announcements. One of them was the captain of the New Council ship, Venner; the other was Stone.

Venner stood behind Stone, who sat at a table empty of everything but a Confederacy logo in the center. His hands were clasped on the edge of the circle formed by nine thirteen-pointed stars containing a diamond of four stars. Numerical symbolism had been the only kind all members would agree upon. Stone's shoulders were squared and tense, and although he didn't look directly at Venner, his eyes flicked sideways occasionally.

Venner was as calm as any other H'digh I'd seen or known. I didn't think it was a facade—Henoit never understood the sharp twist of anxiety I'd get in my stomach before an important meeting or before visiting his parents. He said the H'digh have no equivalent word for "fear," which at the time I dismissed as hyperbole to impress aliens. Later, thinking it over, I realized he'd never shown anything that could be interpreted as fear, nor did his actions ever seem to spring from that motive.

So this Venner might be the same. She wasn't physically much like Henoit, except in her flat expression. Her face was thinner, longer, the pigmentation uneven like dark freckles on the reddish skin. Her vertical-pupiled eyes were dark amber, where his had been pale yellow. She gazed steadily at the pickup—she must have had practice staring down aliens, because H'digh normally did not allow eye contact, unless with enemies or lovers.

Stone cleared his throat. "Good morning, residents of Jocasta."

Eleanor's timer showed 0800 hours.

"I have been asked by our friends, the New Council representatives, to clarify a few matters for you. First, the problem of public safety."

Venner put a long hand on his shoulder. A proprietary gesture. "We intend you should not suffer from our presence," she said. "We are *your* representatives, yes. Our work done is for your benefit." She spoke Earth Standard. Slowly, and with a nasal accent, but a great concession nonetheless.

Stone cleared his throat again. "Yes, well, I'm sure we all feel better about that now."

Eleanor snorted.

I watched Stone more carefully. His neat gray suit was the same, his light hair and face smooth. But the hands clasped on the table were whitening at the knuckles.

"What I'm going to ask you to do," he continued, "is to cooperate with Security in their work to keep the station running as normally as possible. Now, I realize some of you with business schedules to keep may have some problems. You need to refer these problems to your section administrators, who will record your particulars. We are working on compensation issues"—his eyes flicked back at Venner—"at this moment. Please be patient."

Venner's eyelids twitched in time with a muscle in her cheek.

The sheen of sweat on Stone's face began to seep into his collar. Bet he hasn't taken a pheromone inhibitor. Thinks he can cope with the effect. I'd thought the same in my first days on Rhuarl. But constant exposure without protection means you end up unable to eat or sleep. Stone would learn.

He glanced down at a handcom beside his left elbow.

"There is no access to the jump point at present. Again, please be patient about this, and we will advise you when the situation changes. If you feel you have a case for preferential access to the jump point when it does reopen, please lodge a claim with your local magistrate.

"I'm told there have been rumors of unauthorized entry of dangerous individuals . . ."

It took me a moment to realize he meant the Q'Chn.

". . . this administration assures you these rumors are groundless. Our New Council friends have promised no incursions into the residential areas will be permitted. However, you are once again asked to stay away from the center and to use the spokes as little as possible. Businesses in the spokes are urged to refrain from presenting their compensation requests until the situation clarifies."

He leaned forward. "I urge you not to listen to rumor and hearsay, but to wait quietly for further information from official sources. That's all from me for the moment. Have a pleasant day."

The image clouded back to wall surface, but not before we glimpsed Stone pushing back his chair and glaring up at Venner.

I eased my legs over the side of the bed and grimaced in disgust as I realized both legs and arms were marbled with purplish bruises from burst blood vessels. It looked awful. But at least the room didn't rock as badly this time.

"How many Q'Chn are there in the center?" I said.

"I don't know."

"Have any ships run away insystem?"

"Halley, I've had my hands full here. You'll have to ask Murdoch." She reached under the bed and placed some folded clothes beside me. Dark blue ConFleet uniform, gray regulation underwear. "You'd better go over to Security, don't call from here. Bill said the New Council can mon-

itor some of our communications. They've asked us to min-
imize calls."

I picked up the undershirt and pulled it carefully over
my head. Carefully, because even that gentle movement
pulled stabs of pain across my shoulders and neck. "Ow."

Eleanor reached for the instrument table, then withdrew
her hand with an abrupt shake of the head. "You'll be okay.
Your shoulder's back in and I don't want to give you anything until your system shows it's coping with the detox
treatment. And I'm rationing supplies. In case this goes on
for a while."

Her face was tight and pale, three worry lines etched
deep in her forehead. "Or in case something goes wrong
with the Q'Chn."

I knew she meant if the Q'Chn get loose down here.
She was scared, which shocked me a little. Even at the
worst moments of the Seouras blockade Eleanor had simply grumbled and carried on as best she could. I bit back
my complaints, slid into the trousers and off the bed. Knees
wobbly.

Eleanor watched me get my balance, pull on the jacket,
get my balance again. I had to sit down to shove my feet
into boots.

"Can't you give me something for this nausea?" I gritted my teeth against the reflux.

"Try this." She handed me a small cup with a tiny dose
of dark liquid.

"It smells revolting. It's going to make me worse."

"Drink it, or put up with feeling sick."

It tasted even worse than it smelled.

"It's based on a Garokian herb," she said, handing me
a towel to sputter into. "We've had some good results with
it so far."

I started to glare at her, but found that the nausea was
already subsiding.

She handed me a comm link. "Halley, you'll do something about this mess, won't you?'

I opened my mouth to say something sarcastic about everyone being content with Stone as head of station when things were going right, then glanced down at her fingers, clenched on my arm with sufficient force to make new bruises. Her fingernails were bitten to the quick, the skin around them red and swollen.

I fastened the comm link around my wrist.

"We'll manage," I said.

How did I sound so convincing? That gap between what we think and what we say. The potential to dissemble. It had always frustrated Henoit. Perhaps that was the biggest difference between H'digh and human—they perceived the world as a dichotomy-less whole. No life-death, black-white paradoxes. No lies. Intrigue, yes, but no falsehoods to your face.

No falsehoods, like me telling Eleanor we'd cope. Why did I say that? Memories of the Seouras blockade taunted me—over the six months of the Seouras blockade 214 ConFleet and EarthFleet personnel, 136 registered residents, and approximately 270 illegal residents died. Not counting those who tried to get away when the Seouras first arrived, and whose bodies we couldn't retrieve. At that time, Jocasta's environmental systems were stretched by double our optimum population of thirty thousand plus five to ten thousand illegals.

The hospital corridors I walked along were full of maglev gurneys and trolleys, cleaning bots, nurses and technicians. Business as usual, although people's faces were taut, their voices sharp.

The hospital door opened into the artificial sunlight of Gamma—artificial in that this level received a smaller amount of the sunlight directly reflected from the main mirrors. The throughways and residences here relied largely on secondary reflectors and luminescent panels.

I stepped into the throughway, and was immediately thrust aside as a line of people curved to avoid a pile-up between two huge trolleys, which should have been using the freight lanes at the edges of the ring. Two groups of blue-skinned Dir stood in the middle, arguing at the tops of their voices. They had all flicked their cloaks and bonnetlike headpieces inside-out to show two different guild colors, a declaration of war. The luggage from the trolleys fanned out across the throughway in a swathe of metal artwork, boxes, foodstuffs, rolls of cloth unraveling, and countless other wares.

The words "evacuate," "New Council," "spokes," and "business" could be heard amid the shouted insults and the grumbles of the people trying to get past. All the humans had faces drawn with worry. Some of them were shoving those in front with unnecessary violence.

Fear hung in the air like the red banners that clung to the upturned Dir trolley and draped the upper story of the building across from the hospital. Red banners to welcome the Q'Chn. Or deflect their anger. Legend said that red was the only color the Q'Chn saw, and the residents of Jocasta were willing to back any possibility.

A single security guard tried to direct pedestrian traffic around the accident, persuade the Dir to shut up and get rid of the mess, and reroute any automated vehicles that might try to pass. The guard shifted from one side of the throughway to the other, hands waving and alarm shrilling in short bursts. I dodged most of the people and got close to her as I could.

"Constable?" My voice was still croaky, but I could yell. "Have you sent for backup?"

She blinked at my face, then checked the rank stars. "Yes, ma'am. But I don't think there's anyone to spare."

"I'm heading up to the main office now," I said. "I'll see what I can do."

She nodded and turned back to the Dir. One of the boxes had split, and now small crablike animals were scattering from it. This disrupted the crowd's otherwise orderly detour, and I left curses and squeals behind me.

The sounds around me were different from yesterday. Yesterday the station had hummed in a way I'd never known before—busy, profitable, peaceful. In the seven years since I first came, we had experienced varying degrees of siege, terror, occupation, and uneasy cease-fires, but never peace. Today things were back to "normal." The background opsys noises formed a random pattern of cutouts, backups kicking in and small alarms as subsystems gave up the fight to stay active. Somewhere in the section a proximity alarm blared, set off probably by a faulty connection, or unauthorized access.

I felt sore, tired, and scared. This also was "normal." I didn't know whether to laugh or cry at that.

I wondered if the New Council captain, Venner, had known Henoit. I wondered why she came here with An Serat. Pretty obvious he used them to get *Farseer* back. Serat and the H'digh seemed close. Murdoch said he'd found Serat on a H'digh colony planet when he was looking for me and *Calypso II.*

Why was Venner still here? Stone seemed to be trying to keep a calm facade, but we all knew how false that was. If the New Council stayed here, ConFleet would eventually return and attack them. The station would be caught in the cross fire. Why hadn't An Serat taken *Farseer* and run, making a jump point to wherever he wanted to go? If that was indeed possible. He obviously hadn't given Venner and the New Council their own jump drive, otherwise Venner wouldn't be waiting around in a tactically suicidal situation.

I stopped at a public comm station and tried to look for Invidi and H'digh biosignals on the station-wide sensor net, but the interface informed me that I was not authorized to access that system. I groaned. Just tell me where An Serat is, will you?

Thirty

At the main Security office in Alpha the desk sergeant, Rick Banna, pointed upstairs when he saw me. A small, beak-nosed human with close-cropped gray hair and narrow eyes, Banna came with the first EarthFleet troops when Jocasta was only one and a half rings.

Now, his attention remained on the soundless complaints of a pair of Garokians gesticulating in front of him. I waited until the Garokians' hands paused and then told him about the constable in Gamma ring who needed assistance.

The briefing room upstairs was crammed with maybe thirty people. Dull green Security uniforms, light blue EarthFleet uniforms, a smattering of dark blue ConFleet uniforms like my own. I slipped in the half-open door and leaned against the back wall, invisible behind two sturdy olive-clad backs.

Lieutenant Sasaki's voice. ". . . remember, we have to stretch our resources in the best way we can. So be creative."

I squinted between the constables and saw Murdoch take Sasaki's place at the front of the room. A holographic map of the station glowed behind him, an immense tracery of differently colored threads, yellow for throughways, green for corridors, blue for vertical access including lifts and maintenance shafts. Red blips indicated the presence of Security staff. I noticed a number of them clustered at various locations within the lower levels of the spokes, but none in the center.

"Right, I'm going to recap and then we'll be off." Murdoch's slow, measured tones held the room's attention. "First, the Q'Chn."

A few voices murmured something.

"I know," continued Murdoch. "Saying it too loud makes me uncomfortable, too. But they're not legends anymore, they're real. And they're here. So let's get used to it and treat them like any other threat."

"Preferably from a long way off," said a voice, and people chuckled. The laughter skated along the edges of tension without defusing it.

"Yeah, if we can," Murdoch said. "Basically, we leave 'em alone unless they attack us. You heard what Sergeant Kwon and Constable Singh said—the Q'Chn they have up there aren't behaving like our history files tell us. They're smaller, they react different, they seem to be taking orders from the New Council." He nodded at someone in the crowd. "When I interviewed a couple of *Vengeful*'s crew in sickbay, they confirmed this—the Q'Chn are behaving less like killing machines and more like sentient beings."

"Sir, is it true they can talk?" said a voice from the middle.

Murdoch shook his head. "We don't know. The *Vengeful* reports say they can receive orders. We've only got one report of them speaking and that, with respect to Constable Pui, is impossible to substantiate. He might have just seen them gathering together. So don't go trying to invite one of them down for a cuppa to discuss its problems."

From the roar of laughter, that was a Security-wide "in" joke.

"So we're leaving them alone," Murdoch raised his voice slightly and the laughter subsided. "But we gotta be prepared for the shit to hit. We're nearly finished evacuating the spokes and when that's done, Sergeant Desai's squad is going to work with Engineering and get the spokes sealed off and the uplifts restricted. And keep it restricted, people. No letting some small-time crap-seller back in to pick up its ancient grandma's valuable heirloom."

More knowledgeable laughter. I suspected something like that might have happened last time we sealed off the spokes.

"And within the rings, I want to be able to seal off sections if we can. Which means moving luggage and people if they're in the way."

"Buildings, too?" asked a voice.

"If they're in a restricted area, yes," said Murdoch. His gaze was level and serious. "Raze the bloody things so the containment walls can activate. We need to be able to restrict access. I'm not having one of the bastards flying around like last time."

That wasn't strictly true. The single Q'Chn we'd had on Jocasta before the end of the Seouras blockade had attacked and killed three humans in Delta ring, but it hadn't flown—it had merely used its "wings" to glide from a second-story conduit ledge to the deck, slicing a couple of victims on the way.

"Sir, can't they melt their way through bulkheads?" A young voice, trying to control its quaver.

"We don't know," said Murdoch. "Someone said that's only possible in vacuum. Like when they attack a ship. It's something I'm not keen to find out. But at least we can contain them for long enough to evacuate."

I knew, he knew, the whole room knew, it wasn't enough. We couldn't evacuate the entire station in time, even if we had access to emergency transport and somewhere to go. Jocasta was too overcrowded.

"Parallel to that, normal patrols and every extra pair of

feet we have should be out in the rings, making sure all residents know their escape routes and are ready. It's important people are informed and that they *get their closest routes cleaned up themselves.*"

Murdoch paused, looked at the faces in front of him, then waved his hand back at the holo. "We can't cover all this ourselves. Don't even try. Make sure residents know if they don't confirm their escape routes themselves, nobody's going to do it for them. If they're busy clearing the corridors and access doors, they're going to be too busy to panic. I don't need to tell you we must avoid that."

"And if the Q'Chn do attack, sir?" A deeper voice.

Murdoch looked carefully around the room again. His gaze passed without seeing me.

"Depends if it's an isolated incident or not. If one of them gets down in the rings, your main priority is to get people out of the area. Ordinary plasma or radiation-based weapons are ineffective against the Q'Chn." He said the name deliberately, as though by using it he could dampen some of the menace. "The only time, and I repeat, the only time you fire anything at one of these things is to divert it from an attack on civilians."

Silence. Security was here to protect the people of the station. But they hadn't expected to have to place their lives between the residents and killer aliens.

"Sergeant Roads and myself are working on more effective diversionary measures. We'll let you know as soon as we have preparations in place. Any questions?"

Nobody said anything.

"Dismissed. Get out there and do it."

The room cleared rapidly. I waited until the last few people shuffled out the door, then joined Murdoch and Sasaki, who were looking at the holo with their backs to the rest of the room.

"What's your diversionary measure?" I said.

Murdoch spun around. His face creased into an unguarded smile. "You're okay."

His evident pleasure made me feel more than okay. I grinned back. "Pretty much."

"Nice to have you back," said Sasaki. "Again," she added with a smile.

Murdoch's eyes narrowed and he looked at me more closely. "What happened?" He touched my cheek and I tilted my head away, embarrassed in front of Sasaki in case Henoit's presence made me react to the touch, but there was nothing.

"I had coolant poisoning. Eleanor says the antidote or whatever has to start working before she can clean it up." I'd glimpsed my face in a polished door surface on the way here and it looked as bruised as the rest of me—as though I'd been under five- or six-g acceleration.

"Shit," he said, seemingly more irritated than concerned. "You really don't know when to take it easy, do you?"

"This is hardly the time for head of . . ." My voice trailed away as I realized what I'd been about to say.

"Right. You're not head of station now, so you don't have to rush out and put yourself in danger. Sit tight for a while."

"And wait for the Q'Chn to find me?" I looked at him, uncertain what his problem was. "Nobody's safe while they're here. You just said so yourself."

"You're no help if you're . . ."

Sasaki cleared her throat gently. "Ahem. Chief, do you want me to tell Roads to go ahead?"

Murdoch seemed to take a mental step back. "Yeah, you do that, Helen. I'll be down in ten."

Sasaki raised an eyebrow at me and walked out.

Murdoch and I watched each other warily.

"So what's your diversion?" I said, and tried a half smile with it.

He turned abruptly to the holo, drawing his finger through a blue column and into a white-outlined cube. "Here."

"Storage bay on Level Eight?"

"Sigma 41, to be exact."

It sounded familiar, but I couldn't remember from where. "What's it got to do with the Q'Chn?"

"That's where Veatch let Trillith store the rest of its fuel cache."

Big containers of highly flammable and explosive gases. The Sigma bays were reinforced in case we had an accident with dangerous substances, but if Murdoch intended using the fuel to make some sort of flamethrower, he'd have to modify it for use in the rings and therefore lose its power . . .

"I thought we could use the fire control system to spread flammable mist instead of retardant. Then you set a small bomb to go off among the fuel pods and boom." He said it lightly but his eyes were hard.

I winced. "You'll blow containment on that level, possibly the ones above and below. If the angle is wrong, we risk debris hitting the rings."

"We can evacuate beforehand and have bots ready to deflect any debris. As long as the hull's self-repair functions are active, should be okay. That's why we couldn't try something like this last time, remember?" He scratched his head angrily. "The only thing that'll work against the Q'Chn is something so primitive, or so advanced, that they're not ready for it."

Trillith would be furious if Security somehow used its fuel to combat the Q'Chn, even if it had come by the cargo illegally in the first place.

Then I remembered the significance of Sigma 41 and nearly laughed aloud. It was the storage bay where we found Keveth's body, after it was killed by the Q'Chn that terrorized the station at the end of the Seouras blockade. Keveth was another K'Cher, whom Trillith had betrayed and left to die. And now Murdoch would use Trillith's property to destroy more Q'Chn in the same place.

"Good spot for it."

He grinned. "Thought you'd remember."

"How many of them are here?"

He shook his head. "We're not sure. Kwon saw two of them when he escorted Stone up there for his little talk with their captain. And there was another one in Spoke Two at the same time, so that's three definite. There must be more on *Vengeful* because most of their fighters stayed there."

"So how are you going to get these three we've got on the station in the storage bay?"

"We're still working on that. But we have an edge."

"Which is?"

"We're not telling everyone, but we've been monitoring most of the communication between the New Council ship and the other Q'Chn out there. When I say communication 'between,' I mean orders going from the New Council to the Q'Chn. Seems the New Council captain has to repeat a lot of orders. The Q'Chn don't want to listen. And she lied to them about a couple of things."

"Such as?"

"Such as there being no members of the Four on Jocasta."

"You know how the Q'Chn hate the K'Cher. Venner probably doesn't want them all to head this way and leave the point unprotected. It would leave the space clear for ConFleet to get ships through."

"Mmm. Anyway, we think this monitoring works both ways—the New Council can probably pick up our comm signals as well."

"And they haven't realized we can read them?"

"Dunno. Engineering reckons not. They're being pretty free with their information if that's the case."

"We'd better not be free with ours, then."

"That's why I've put restrictions on information to be sent via comm link," he said patiently.

I thought of the Q'Chn fighters clustered around *Vengeful* and the scrum of fighters, shuttles, and escape pods around the jump point. "Bill, how many of *Vengeful*'s crew got away?"

"We monitored the jump point opening at least ten times," he said somberly.

Not many. "An Barik's ship?"

"The Bubble said they picked up an Invidi engine signature, but they don't know if it got away or was destroyed in that area."

"Bill, where's An Serat? I saw him when I landed *Farseer.*"

"I don't know and I don't care." He met my eyes. "He's in the center, as far as I know. That bloody ship is still there, too. Halley, I've got my hands full keeping people safe here. Leave the jump drive to the Invidi. At least for the moment," he amended. "We need you as an engineer."

"Why?"

"Opsys problems all over. No pattern to the disturbances, but we had major breakdowns a couple of hours ago in Gamma transport and Delta comm systems. Main Engineering reckons it's a core problem, but the New Council won't let anyone up there. Stone's supposed to be explaining to them how it could be the airlocks on their dock that fail next. Dunno if they'll listen to him, though."

"Maybe they'll listen to me."

"I reckon you should stay away from them. It was you who messed up their try at getting *Calypso* last time. You're not going to be their favorite person."

Good point. And he was also right that if the opsys problems got out of control, we were in big trouble.

"I'll contact Gamet and see what it is," I said.

His shoulders relaxed and he ran his hand over his head, as though relieved. "Thanks. I'm going to work on our diversion."

"Don't you think the New Council have too much at stake to start making enemies among the Nine and unaligned worlds like us? I mean, if they terrorize us, the rest of the galaxy's going to hear about it."

"I dunno why they're here at all. Doesn't make sense. Why risk exposing themselves at Central to make a jump here, to a system still patrolled by ConFleet?"

"An Serat must have jumped for them."

"Because he needed Q'Chn muscle to get this ship?" He frowned. "If it's that damn important . . ."

"Remember what I said about the off-network jumping?"

"You think Serat jumped the New Council here from somewhere off the network?"

"No, they came out of the Central jump point. And I don't think Serat can do it on any old ship with jump drive. He needs *Farseer*."

He frowned even worse. "That's a pretty big conclusion to jump to."

"An Barik gave me a clue."

He blew out in exasperation. "So Serat gets together with the New Council again, in order to get *Farseer* back, because for whatever reason—Invidi politics—Barik's got here first with ConFleet and beaten him to it. So why hasn't Serat got into the New Council freighter with *Farseer* and pissed off again? Why's he hanging around waiting for ConFleet to come back?"

He walked over to the wall controls and deactivated the

holomap. The complex tracery of colors disappeared, leaving the room drab and pale.

"You're right about it being a big risk for the New Council," I said. "I imagine Serat's offered them something they can't refuse."

"A jump drive?"

"What else? Or rather, a ship calibrated so that one of the Nine can use the drive."

"Maybe he's not giving it to them, and they're refusing to leave until he does?" Murdoch said.

"He could go off by himself in *Farseer.* No reason for him to wait for the New Council. More likely they're waiting for him—they won't be able to jump out of here without Serat."

"Unless they force one of the Bendarl to jump what's left of *Vengeful* for them," Murdoch said distastefully.

"If the Q'Chn left anyone alive." As the words left my mouth a sickening image of what might have happened on *Vengeful* made me turn away, so he wouldn't see the fear on my face.

I thought of An Barik's warning of *Farseer* being unstable. Or Serat being unstable. Might the knowledge of danger be keeping Serat himself from using *Farseer*?

"Bill, it's possible that using *Farseer* could destabilize jump points. An Barik seemed to be warning me not to use it."

"We used it okay." He paused in the act of putting a handcom and other small pieces of equipment on his belt.

"Yes, but only once. If using *Farseer* is dangerous, we should try and stop Serat leaving here with it."

He finished his preparations. "It's not our responsibility. The other Invidi . . ."

"Aren't here," I interrupted. "They can't stop Serat. We can."

"I was going to say, it's their technology causing the

problem. And what do you want me to do?" he said wearily. "Slap a restraining order on him? Could be difficult. Last I saw, he was with the group that's holding this station to ransom."

"Where's *Farseer*?"

"In a dock on Level Three," he said shortly.

I had a vague memory of aiming for the upper level docks when I brought *Farseer* from *Vengeful*. Also of a smaller ship buzzing me as I came in, which was probably Serat's shuttle.

"We should lock the space doors," I said. "And make sure there's a physical barrier, too. I bet An Serat can override the system locks. How about positioning one of the sweeper drones outside it?"

Sweeper drones were robotic cleanup vessels that pottered around the station keeping away larger pieces of space debris and rubbish from ships. Some of them were as large as twelve-person shuttles, most of that bulk being storage area for rubbish.

"Most of them are picking up junk from the attack on *Vengeful*. I think there's one or two left." He opened his mouth, shut it again. Then stepped forward and put his arms around me.

After a quick glance at the doorway, I relaxed into the embrace. It felt warm and comfortable, except for the handcom on his belt, which stuck into my ribs. Don't relax too much, I told myself. The last thing you want is Henoit whispering in your ear and subverting your reactions. Right now, you need to stay clearheaded.

"I'm glad you're back safe," Murdoch said into my hair. "We thought you'd been trapped on the cruiser."

Nothing from Henoit. It was so good to feel Bill without the sense of Henoit looming over me that I leaned my aching forehead on his shoulder and enjoyed the support. "I ditched a guard detail when the first alarm went off," I said. "I'm really in trouble now." The ludicrousness of this observation hit me and I chuckled—"in trouble" with Con-Fleet hardly compared with being trapped on the station with hostile Q'Chn.

He let his arms drop. "You can talk to Engineering from here. When I asked them earlier, Gamet said they were worried because they couldn't trace the cause of the problems."

"That's all we need."

He turned in the doorway. "Take care."

"You too."

Maybe I should have said something else. But what else is there to say?

Thirty-one

"**H**alley to Engineering. Put me on to Lieutenant Gamet."

Gamet here. Glad you could make it back, Commander.

"What's the status of your system problem?"

We have unauthorized access to the core. The intruder doesn't respond to comm signals and the terrorists won't let us send anyone up there.

"What's the intruder doing?"

No pattern to it. They're accessing recycling in the Smoke one minute and the Bubble command subsystem the next. Some of the systems they're not damaging, but others aren't being resumed properly so we've got malfunctions down here.

"They might be pulling material physically from a random selection."

Could be. Gamet's voice stayed controlled. But her tone rose on the next words. *We can't guess if and when they'll pull a really vital subsystem and its backups.*

Too big a coincidence if the selection was indeed random, and not deliberate sabotage. Why would the New Council sabotage the station, though? They were trying to persuade the residents that the Confederacy was the villain.

We could lose position.

Lose spin, lose gravity, lose orbit. Die.

Or atmospheric monitors.

Suffocate first.

"Lieutenant, what can I do to help?"

She paused for a moment. *We're watching vital signs down here. If you could persuade those pirates . . .*

Several voices rose in the background behind her. In spite of the proximity dampers on the pickup, I heard the words, "Confederacy," "abandon," and "these guys are the best alternative . . ."

. . . that they mustn't muck around in the core. If it's not them, we must send a team up there to take a look, she finished in a rush.

"I'll try. Keep me up-to-date."

Yes, ma'am. She cut the link quickly. Sounded like the New Council propaganda appealed to some of Gamet's people.

I tried Murdoch's link.

What is it? He was short of breath.

"The center is still having problems. Gamet thinks the New Council are interfering in the core. I'm going up to talk to them. I might be more persuasive than Stone if I can tell them exactly what could go wrong."

Right. I'll expect you to call in within thirty minutes. Otherwise I assume you're in trouble.

"Understood."

I made a short detour to take a H'digh pheromone inhibitor then approached the uplift nearest the main hospital entrance in Alpha. The New Council ship was docked at Level Three. Surely the captain would see it was in her best interests to allow us to keep the station functioning normally?

No wonder some people sympathized with the New Council. Some of them had probably been here since the early days. They had seen how the Confederacy put as little effort as possible into maintaining the station, finally abandoning it during the Seouras blockade. That neglect might be the Confederacy's undoing, for it had encouraged a huge majority of the station's residents to vote to submit the neutrality petition. If Confederacy neglect also encouraged them to support the New Council, when—if—the neutrality vote was passed, the New Council could gain a base in this sector. The main obstacle to supporting the New Council remained their terrorist activities and their association with the Q'Chn.

But some of the residents of Jocasta had also seen, close up, murders by Q'Chn. Feelings against the Confederacy must be strong indeed if these people were willing to accept the New Council. Yet I felt that their support would vanish the moment the Q'Chn threat changed to a real attack. Terror looks very different in one's own home. Venner must realize what a thin line she walked, but if she could keep the Q'Chn under control on the station, the New Council could gain support here, even if she had to leave soon after.

The throughway was crowded with evacuees from the spoke. Not all of them would stay in Alpha, but it looked like most of them were being off-loaded here, presumably so the uplifts could go back and get more. We could fit about twenty people in one uplift car. Six uplift lines in one spoke, four cars working each line. I calculated it would take at least six hours, possibly eight, to evacuate the few thousand people in each spoke, including the loading and unloading time.

Most of the people carrying boxes and bags were human. I tried to slide against the flow of their movement and my ConFleet uniform received some angry stares and muttered comments such as "useless."

The crowd thinned closer to the spoke, where a few stragglers were talking to a Security constable. Another constable tapped the comm unit next to the uplift doors, then slapped the panel with a curse.

"Has that last car gone back up?" I asked her.

She turned, and bit back a retort when she saw the uniform. Her long-boned face and expressive eyes were familiar, also the way she drew her mouth sideways in frustration.

I trawled for the memory. A break-in to the quarters I'd shared with three other women. This constable had come and taken our statements about what we'd left where.

"Caselli, isn't it?"

Her eyes widened. "Yes, ma'am."

"Problem with the lift?"

"It started to go. Now I think it's stuck."

"Stuck?" I crouched down and pulled open the controls maintenance cover.

"It won't respond to directions," she said, crouching beside me. "We're supposed to keep the lines running, or the other cars will get stuck, too."

"I know the drill," I said. Unfortunately, the problem was not with the uplift controls as such, but with one of their supporting "mother" systems. And the diagnostic function on the controls here was not enough to tell me what was wrong. I suspected it was the fault of our intruder in the core.

The other constable was now arguing into his comm link. The other uplifts were experiencing similar problems. Definitely a support malfunction, then. But I couldn't get to the core to isolate it unless the uplift was running . . .

Caselli looked at the panel above our heads and pointed. "We're on again," she said, half to me and half to her companion.

I stood up too quickly, and when the flecks of brightness stopped streaming in front of my eyes, the orange standby lights on the uplift had changed back to green. The next car on this line was approaching. "I'll be going back up on this car once it's empty. Right to the center."

She looked at the four rank stars on my collar, slid her eyes politely over the state of my face, and glanced at the cover of the maintenance controls, which I'd tapped open with a code from memory.

"Ma'am, would you mind confirming that? It's just that we were told nobody was to go back up to the spokes . . ."

Murdoch didn't answer the comm link immediately. When he did, he sounded as tense as I'd ever heard him. He simply told the constable to give me help, then when I asked him if anything was wrong, said, *We've got trouble in Section Four. Two Q'Chn have come down looking for K'Cher. Talk to you later.*

I cut the link, shocked. What could we do if the Q'Chn were down here already? Apprehension twisted a sharp-edged knot in my stomach. All right for Murdoch to talk about primitive explosions, but they couldn't use that in a residential area. For a moment I wondered if I should go back to Section Four and join him, then common sense returned. I would be no help to Murdoch there, while I could be of great use up in the core.

If only the damn uplift would come.

The gravity grabbed at my feet and stomach as the uplift stopped at Level Six. When the door swished open, a thin, scruffy human carrying a maserlike rifle was waiting. He wore oversized body armor—a vest and hip-cover—over drab civilian clothes, and a visual enhancement headpiece circled his untidy hair.

He pointed the rifle at me. "Go away," he said in heavily accented Confederacy Standard. "You not allowed here."

"Tell Captain Venner that Com . . . ex-Commander Halley wishes to speak with her," I said in the same language. Then repeated it in Earth Standard.

His face relaxed a little when he heard the message the second time, but the rifle muzzle didn't waver. He stepped back to the far side of the corridor while he activated a comm unit on his vest and muttered into it, all the while keeping me covered.

"Can I come out?" I said. "They want to use the up-lift."

He waved the rifle to one side of the door. I stepped slowly out that side. The uplift door hissed shut.

I caught the words "captain" and "uplift" from the man, this time in a guttural Mars dialect of Earth Standard.

"Wait," he said to me, and suited action to word by leaning comfortably against the door, the rifle handle firm under his arm.

"Can I see her or not?" I shifted my heels against the deck.

"Wait," he repeated.

I hadn't expected him to leave his post. I didn't expect Venner to come down here, either, and hoped she'd send someone else to take me up to the dock on Level Three.

The rebel dug something from his pocket with his free hand and popped it into his mouth, his eyes on me all the while. He chewed contentedly. I smelled the familiar, mint-like scent of *maq*. Difficult to think of this man as the enemy, when he seemed so much a part of my world. Down in the rings he would blend in easily.

"Why did you join the New Council?" I said.

His brown, watery gaze wandered over my dark blue uniform and his lip curled. Then he looked at my face and seemed to hesitate.

"Why did you join that lot?" he said.

"ConFleet?" I decided on honesty. "To get away."

"From?"

"From Earth. Family. Being trapped." It seemed so long ago. I felt a vague irritation at my fifteen-year-old self who thought that if ConFleet offered escape, it was worth selling her freedom.

He chuckled derisively. "What a luxury. Least you had a family. I joined the Council so I could get back at the Confederacy. The Confederacy didn't think my colony was worth preserving, y'see. But you ConFleet clones don't understand about that kind of thing, do you?"

"Clones?"

"Yeah. Looking and thinking just like they tell you. All the same." He glanced at me again. "Well, most of you."

I had to smile. Looking scruffy had its advantages. "What's it like sharing a ship with Slashers?" I said, genuinely curious.

"What do you think?" he said, then relaxed a little. "Makes everyone a bit nervy. Cuts down on space, too, 'cause they've got to have a whole section to themselves."

"It'd make me nervous, not knowing if you're going to wake up one morning without your head."

He snorted. "They're not completely unpredictable, you know. Not like they used to be. We've improved . . ." He stopped. "Well, anyway, you know some pirate isn't going to attack you with them around."

That was a joke—from what Henoit said, the New Council were the pirates.

Voices echoed around the bend in the corridor and two figures appeared, one walking in front of the other. The second one was a taller, sturdier version of my guard, the first was Dan Florida's lanky dark form.

"Dan." I waved.

"Commander!" He waved back, and strode a little faster.

"What happened to you?" He peered at me.

"Long story. Are the delegates all right?"

He glanced at the two New Council humans, who were discussing their respective orders. "They're okay. A couple of them wanted to get nasty with the New Council. The

only way to shut them up was to come up here and de-
liver their formal protest in person." He shook his head.
"Like a medieval messenger."

"What's she like?" I lowered my voice and poked my
chin at the guards.

"Tough. Why are you up here? Have you . . ." He
stopped.

"What?"

"Have you decided to join them?"

"You're not starting that again, are you?" I glared at
him. "I'm trying to get access to the core, that's all. We've
got opsys problems. On top of everything else."

On top of some people behaving like idiots, I nearly
added. "If you're going to start rumors about anything, you
might try talking to people about the jump network."

He cocked his head and gave me a measuring look.
"Why?"

"You might try asking people from the Bubble about
the coordinates of the jump point Murdoch and I came
back through."

The rebel who'd accompanied Florida called out to me.
"You. Over here."

"See you later, Dan." I began to walk obediently down
the corridor ahead of the man.

"Commander!" Florida called after me. "Is this your sensational tip-off?"

I turned and waved acknowledgment. "It's a start."

"Shut up, ConFleet," the rebel grunted.

Stone was in the airlock lobby on Level Three with the
New Council captain. He stood with his back to us, grasp-
ing the handrail as though he were worried the gravity field
might suddenly fail.

The H'digh female stood poised beside him, a plasma
pistol in one hand. When she had appeared with Stone in

the announcement, she'd presented herself as a diplomat, in a plain brown tunic and leggings with no obvious weapons. As if she'd been advised to tone down the popular image of H'digh, which was one of warriors always ready for battle. Now she looked more "normal." Over the tunic she'd slung a bandolier lined with an array of weapons; the dagger and the blunt kesset grip were the only ones I recognized. Probably a knife tucked into her boot as well.

Her thin, unevenly pigmented face was impassive. The iris-filled eyes focused on my shoulder. As I got closer, the pheromone effect hit me like a mild asthma attack. It wasn't too bad because of the inhibitor I'd taken.

"Here she is," said the man with the gun behind me.

Stone grunted in surprise and swung around.

Captain Venner's actual scent was nothing like Henoit's. His had been like crushed pine needles on a hot summer day. Hers was stronger, sharper, with a metallic reek to it like blood. She inclined her head with a grace that encompassed her whole body.

"Ex-Commander Halley. It is good you came. I wished to speak to you." Her Earth Standard was easier to understand in the flesh. But her voice was so similar in tone and timbre to Henoit's that I flushed, the memory of his voice inextricably bound with the dreams in which his presence invaded my body.

Stone frowned. "What are you doing here?"

I inclined my head back at Venner and smiled at him with as much friendliness as I could. More important things to do than quarrel. "First, a request for the captain. The engineers need to come up to the core to fix opsys malfunctions."

"What authority do you have to negotiate?" said Stone.

"And second?" said Venner.

If she was like other H'digh I'd known, she would not agree to anything without due consideration.

"Second, two Q'Chn are loose down in Alpha ring right now. You must get them out."

Stone faced Venner. "You didn't tell me. When did this happen?"

"Just as I came up." I tried to soothe him. "I don't have the details. Murdoch's handling it."

Stone didn't acknowledge my words and kept talking to Venner. "This is intolerable. You told me you could keep those creatures under control."

"Maybe they are under control," I said. "Killing one or more of the Four species, such as the K'Cher in Alpha, would make a useful demonstration of power without alienating potential supporters among the Nine."

Stone snorted. "It would alienate *me*."

"But not, perhaps, those unfortunates who suffered years of Confederacy misadministration here," said Venner.

"Just get them out of Alpha," I said, more sharply than I'd intended. Misadministration indeed.

"Does this indicate a willingness on the part of station administration to consider the New Council's request for permanent entry privilege? Mr. Stone has refused us," said Venner.

Stone glared at me. "This person has no authority to negotiate anything. No official position. In fact, she's in custody, waiting trial for possession of Invidi technology."

So much for friendliness.

Venner angled her shoulders toward me and her amber eyes looked me over again without meeting my own. "The Invidi ship, yes. I should like to talk to you about this ship that so interests my Invidi colleague."

I bet *he* won't tell you anything about it.

"I'd be happy to discuss anything you wish, but first get the Q'Chn out of the rings and let us make sure the station functions properly," I said. "The situation is serious and we're not sure of the cause. Have any of your crew attempted to access the opsys core in the center of this structure?"

Venner tilted her head, a H'digh negative. "No."

"Good. It's an unusual system because it was built onto existing non-Confederacy technology. If you don't know what you're doing, it can be dangerous."

"It is unacceptable for any of your people to be in this structure, even the opsys core. I cannot guarantee their safety. Both because of my Q'Chn comrades, and also because my crew becomes nervous if their identities are known."

"Please, only three engineers. I'll start repairing the comm system myself first."

"Very well," said Venner. "Three only. Unarmed."

"You can't ask them to go defenseless against the Q'Chn," protested Stone.

Nothing is a defense against the Q'Chn, I thought. And Gamet's people could conceal hand weapons in their toolkits if she wanted them to.

"Agreed," I said, and turned to go back down the corridor to the core.

"Wait." Venner's light voice snapped. "We talk."

I groaned inwardly. How much more time wasted?

"What about the Q'Chn?" said Stone. "Those sections in Alpha are important."

"What about your lower levels?" said Venner. "Are their residents not important also?" She looked directly at me, and my stomach twisted in a knot of fear.

"Of course." Stone looked from her to me, confused. His hairline was dark with sweat and he kept reaching up to rub the base of his throat.

Still hasn't taken that inhibitor, I thought.

"Maybe she can't get them out," I said to him. "Maybe the New Council is not in control of the Q'Chn at all."

We both looked at Venner but she ignored the jab. As if sick of the wordplay, she signaled to the other rebel with a single lithe movement. He had remained silent and covering us from the other side of the lobby.

"I wish to speak to Halley. Alone." She used simplified Con Standard and pointed at me with her elbow, H'dighstyle.

Stone seemed about to argue, then, to my relief, gathered his dignity about him and allowed himself to be shepherded back along the corridor. He refused to meet my eyes. Probably suspected me of conniving with the New Council. Hell, I thought bitterly, if Florida can suspect me, why not Stone?

"Why are you here?" I said.

Venner tilted her elbow in the direction Stone had gone. "He thinks it is to harass the Confederacy."

"Killing hundreds of people and taking over a warship could be described as harassment, yes."

Venner let the sarcasm slide past her, as Henoit always did. "What do you think?"

I took a deep breath while I tried to think what to do. Dissemble? Try and draw out information? But while we stood here chatting the Q'Chn might be killing people in Alpha and the opsys degenerating past repair.

"I think An Serat persuaded you to come, by offering the New Council certain technology you want badly. I think you're unable to use the jump point back or plot safe passage through Central without his help. I think you can't stay too long, or ConFleet will come back through the jump point and overwhelm you. It won't matter if Stone grants you access to Jocasta—ConFleet doesn't respect neutrality."

I paused to give her a chance to react, but she was too experienced for that.

I went on. "You don't want to run in flatspace because there's nothing out here at the edge of the Confederacy and you'll be alone here, possibly for years. Your best weapons, the Q'Chn, are developing minds of their own and to keep your tenuous grip on this station, you've had to spread your forces thin. Captain Venner, I think you should be asking me for help. You're stuck."

Her face and body were still, but something in her scent changed. Even through the fog of the inhibitor, it was enough to make the back of my neck cold.

"You forget," she said. "We have won a great victory. We have shown the Nine and unaligned worlds that Con-Fleet is not all-powerful. We have taken one of their largest ships."

"You need a Bendarl or Invidi to jump it, though. You're still stuck."

"So are you." She walked around me and stopped on the other side, so I had to turn to face her. Close up, I could see the uneven pigment on her face was indeed freckles from some kind of exposure to radiation. Her long, tight plaits were loose near the scalp, as though she'd tossed in her sleep.

"You are a traitor in ConFleet's eyes," she continued. "It will look like you stole Invidi technology and brought it to us. They'll never trust you again. Why not stay with us?"

Coming on top of Florida's comment and Stone's suspicious gaze, it nearly made me laugh. Events seemed determined to push me into the New Council's arms. Venner's arms. The idea appealed enough to make me edge backward and hope the inhibitor was not losing potency. Or that Henoit's presence was not inciting my hormones to indiscretion. He'd left me alone when I was with Bill earlier, but I could feel something now. Not much, just warmth and a feeling of physical well-being, dampened by the inhibitor.

"I did consider asking you for help once," I said. "And I might again, if it wasn't for the Q'Chn. I can't accept them as partners. Not knowing what they have done, and might do."

She was silent for a moment, her eyes lowered. It made me uncomfortable—it was such a human posture, and one I'd never seen Henoit use. I couldn't gain any idea what it might mean—was she also uncomfortable with the Q'Chn, but didn't want to admit it?

"I presume you know about my personal connection with the New Council?" I didn't want to drag Henoit into this, but if he was going to be useful . . .

"You were bonded with Henoit." She pronounced his name the H'digh way, with a guttural cough like a big cat's. "Tell me, ex-Commander Halley, have you been able to forget your H'digh husband?"

"Why do you ask?" I could see nothing in her smooth face.

"I thought you might need some guidance in our ways. I, too, have lost a spouse, and I imagine the nature of this loss could be a surprise to an outworlder."

"I can get guidance from other H'digh."

Venner stretched the muscles of her neck luxuriously. "Ah, but they won't tell you what you want to know. They will say you are bound together for eternity. His soul is waiting in that place between now and the other. They'll say when your soul leaves this life it, too, will cross into there. Then you will journey together into the other."

"The other?"

Venner tightened her forearms in a H'digh shrug. "Whatever lies beyond this world. We have dozens of interpretations. I favor the idea that one's essence is dissipated and becomes part of the universe."

"But dissipated together?"

"That's right." She watched my face closely. "He did tell you it was forever, didn't he?"

Nor death shall us part. I shook my head to clear away the echo of his voice. "Yes, but in our culture such words are no more than expressions of desire to stay together. Not . . ." Not fact.

"If you join us, I can help you make it no more than words."

"Even if I believed you, which I don't," I added hastily, "how can you break the bond? Have you done it?"

"I do not know if it is possible for an outworlder, but we can try."

I wanted to be rid of Henoit, didn't I? "What happens to the soul that's waiting?"

"I don't know," said Venner. "Some people say it wanders, unable to cross over, and eventually becomes one of the dark creatures that trouble dreams."

"And you?"

"My soul, you mean?" She laid her arm on the rail next to mine, and leaned closer.

She was trying me out. Seeing if I'm going to swoon or start agreeing with everything she said.

"My soul," said Venner slowly, "would rather spend eternity alone than with my late spouse. Do you not feel the same?"

To my dismay, I could feel Henoit's presence growing stronger, my body responding to it. Hot, itchy all over. "Henoit believed the New Council needed the Q'Chn. I think he was wrong."

She stepped back, putting an acceptable distance between us again. "The New Council needs a partner with strength. So do the Nine Worlds."

"How can you live with a partner who may turn on you at any second?"

"As the Confederacy turned on you?" said Venner. "As I recall, your spouse brought a Q'Chn here to liberate you from a blockade when the Confederacy did nothing."

"We're well aware of the Confederacy's flaws. Why do you think we applied for neutrality? Neutral or not, I told Henoit and I'm telling you, we don't deal with terrorists."

You sacrifice too much in the present for your ideal future, I was going to add. The image that entered my mind was of Will's face as he turned to follow the U.N. guide out the door of the hangar, and myself, too preoccupied with An Serat to even explain or say good-bye . . .

"If they court-martial you, you'll spend the rest of your life in a rehab colony. I have seen ConFleet-run camps." Venner's voice was quite level. H'digh don't rant. "I would kill myself rather than become an inmate."

"My future is my business," I said. "Right now I'm assisting the staff of this station and we need you to get the Q'Chn out of Alpha."

She straightened almost imperceptibly.

Here it comes, I thought. What she really wants.

"Tell me something, then. And I will recall the Q'Chn."

"What?"

"Why does the Invidi want that ship you stole from Con-Fleet?"

"Which Invidi?" I stalled.

"Ex-Commander, neither of us has time for games. I need to know why An Serat wanted to come to this station and what's keeping him here."

"Not to assist in your glorious victory?"

Her fine, hairless brows twitched with irritation. In a human it would have been a scowl. "I mean victory in the sense of a battle, not the whole war. We took *Vengeful*. Now we should retreat. But the Invidi will not come."

I spread my hands in a gesture of helplessness that I thought she'd accept as sincere. "I don't know why he stays. Why don't you just go and leave him?"

"I cannot. My superiors . . ." She broke off. "How did you steal the ship? It should not be possible."

"Its programming was incomplete at the time. I suspect Serat has since fixed it."

"A jump drive?"

"Yes." I couldn't let myself even hint that *Farseer* might be able to jump off-network. To the New Council it would offer the ultimate escape.

"You have worked with the Serat," said Venner. "If you have information about his plans, remember that it is in your interest for us to speedily leave here. The only way we can do this is with him. Our ship is set to jump for him."

"Where is he now?"

"Somewhere in this center part of the station," was the careless reply.

"But you said none of your crew had touched the core!" I stupidly banged my fist on the rail, which hurt.

"He is not my crew."

"I need to find him and see what damage he's done. You said you'd let me go in there."

She inclined her head. "If you can persuade him to leave, do so. If he gives you information, I require it."

"And the Q'Chn?"

"I shall attempt to recall them. But not while you are listening."

I walked away from the lobby. When I looked back from the corner of the corridor, she waved, an ironic lift of her hand.

Thirty-two

The comm link to Alpha was out when I tried to contact Murdoch halfway along the corridor from Venner. All I could do at the moment was hope Venner would keep her word and call off the Q'Chn. My job was fixing the opsys problems so the comm system wouldn't go down like this.

I met no Q'Chn in the center corridors or as I climbed down the tubes that were tunnels when the gravity field was off. Down to Level Eight, Section Two. The last time we had a Q'Chn on the station I did this in the dark, without gravity.

Down the ladder, past the crawler crossing, past entries to the rooms on either side. Finally my boots thudded on the uneven floor of the inner corridor, which formed the wall of the core. I counted the hatches under my feet and the doors to rooms over my head. The section names were written neatly on the light strips that ran along the wall above. Bare corridors up here, panels in various shades of gray and blue, conduits and fibers open for easy access. Transit passengers and tourists didn't come to the inner corridors, only those residents who worked here.

I tried to keep my mind on counting the sections and rehearsing what I'd have to do to the opsys, but Venner's words echoed in my ears. *You are a traitor in their eyes.* Murdoch once said I'd make a fine pirate, although he didn't mean it as a compliment. The New Council were fighting for what I'd always believed in—equal rights for all sentient beings, whether members of the Confederacy or not. I just didn't agree with their means. Yet the means we could use with a clear conscience—peaceful protest, lobbying the Confederacy Council, development of stronger links between the Four and the Nine—seemed so ineffective.

And what was it she'd said about Henoit? Could I rid myself of his strange presence? It would be good to live with Bill without Henoit peering over our shoulders, so to speak. At the moment, I didn't even know if it was Bill who turned me on or Henoit; whether it was I who turned Bill on or H'digh pheromones somehow working through me. Hell of a mix-up. But Venner's alternative sounded unpleasant for the soul, or whatever, cut loose in the afterlife. Even if I didn't believe in it, Henoit had, and maybe for his species this afterlife had substance of a kind. I didn't want to damn him for eternity any more than I wanted to spend it with him.

Nearly there, next section.

The core held much of the Tor technology we'd used when we built Jocasta, although cleansed and now inactive. Which must be why An Serat was in here now.

A quick bioscan of the center told me nobody was there at all, including the New Council crew and myself. So I gave up the scan as useless and headed for Section Two; there was an uplift access tube that ran the length of the core on that side. We used it to move maintenance equipment within the core. I suspected some of the cannier traders such as Trillith also used it to move merchandise, although this was supposed to be done via the outer freight tubes that went straight from the spokes to loading bays.

The larger hatches on the freight tube side were the only way an Invidi could get into the core. He'd never fit through the crawlways designed for maintenance bots and modified for humans. The original accessways hadn't been that large, either. Nobody but the Invidi knew what the Tor had looked like, and they weren't telling, but my guess was small, possibly smaller than humans, and maybe multi-limbed like the K'Cher and Leowin.

I reached the freight crawler safety doors, which were solid, unlike the clear uplift doors. The "open" sequence on the controls worked, and they widened slowly. The crawler shaft stretched left and right, a gray tunnel lined with a frieze of darker conduits and pipes. The entry hatch in the base of the crawler shaft yawned open. I sat down on the edge of the tunnel and slid down into the hatch. Within the entry hatch I could see the walkway that ran beside the core at right angles to the tunnel.

There was a short ramp down onto the walkway from the entry hatch. The walkway was a narrow, two-and-a-half-meter-high passage, surrounded left, right, and below by the flickering surface of Jocasta's opsys core, and bounded by a guide rail running alongside to prevent people touching the core. The space remained in half-light, like the final moments of a fine day before evening. I'd forgotten how the catwalk rattled under one's boots, how stale and metallic the air always tasted in here.

A large figure blocked the path ahead.

"An Serat," I called, not wanting to approach him suddenly from behind. "What are you doing here?"

He didn't turn, or acknowledge me, other than to say, "Go away."

I approached a few more steps. "You need to stop whatever you're doing to this system. You're causing it to malfunction and you threaten the lives of people who live here."

No answer. His tentacles wandered over a section I recognized as part of the recycling subsystem in the Smoke.

We'd attached color-coded tags to the functions Engineering accessed regularly, and this one was purple and green. Tiny traceries of energy skittered across the surface.

"What are you doing?" I said.

"I inquire further." The voicebox translated his next word as something like "Tranoradariana," but that couldn't have been right.

"I don't know that name," I interrupted. "Please explain."

"Whom you know as Tor. They are here."

"No, they're not. We overlaid it."

The Tor hardware contained the necessary directions for its use, in the same way directions for biological entities like ourselves are encoded in our DNA. When building Jocasta, the challenge was to replace—overwrite—change the Tor directions to Invidi-derived Confederacy codes. If An Serat found any areas where he could reactivate the Tor directions, the entire station was in trouble. We'd have to evacuate if we couldn't keep our opsys "clean" of Tor elements.

An Serat rocked once. "I have methods you cannot comprehend."

"Maybe. But I helped build the station and I know what we did."

"I know Tor. You and your limited stature cannot overcome them."

I thought of the gray Tor ship with its programmed trap that had snapped down on the unwary Seouras. The direct strength of that ship overwhelmed me after a few seconds' resistance. No wonder it had taken the Invidi decades to defeat them. If An Serat had spent years restricting a Tor opsys so that it would not take over his Invidi systems, he was every bit as clever as his boast.

I couldn't imagine how to use Tor elements, which was why I'd abandoned the idea of doing anything like that with *Farseer*. Tor codes were too quick to exploit weakness, too complete in their takeover of other systems.

"If you stay, ConFleet will soon fight their way past the Q'Chn at the jump point and they'll take this ship away from you again."

"I am right. They are wrong. Your arrival is evidence."

"Arrival where?"

"On your world."

It hit me what he was talking about, along with a great desire to know the answer. "You mean why I arrived before the Invidi came to Earth."

"Tor drag back *Calypso*. Tor have the power. I say this to Barik." His voicebox sounded eerily triumphant.

"Tor drag back . . ." The gray ships of the Seouras blockade were here in 2122 when *Calypso* arrived from 2027. If they somehow diverted *Calypso* when it went through the jump point and brought it to 2122, it would look like the jump had a ninety-five-year correspondence. But if the ninety-nine-year jump was also dragged back into the past the same distance, it would explain how I could emerge in 2023, not 2027 when I went back the other way in *Calypso II*.

"You mean the Tor moved the points so *Calypso* arrived in 2122?"

"I say this."

"Why?"

No answer. Maybe the Tor wanted Serat's hybrid ship as much as Barik did. But they were too early for *Farseer*. I wished I had a holo-diagram to work this out. Serat did send *Calypso* into a ninety-nine-year jump point after all. That point got skewed back four years, so that it linked 2122 and 2023 instead of 2027 and 2126. Then I went back through it to Earth in *Calypso II* and to Jocasta in *Farseer* . . . no, what about that radiation surge on 16 May? And what about the slightly different coordinates? There must be two sets of points, side by side. At least, for two days until the surge disables one set.

"Did *Farseer* open a new jump point between Earth and Jocasta?"

"You use the work." His voicebox sounded distracted.

"You must have noticed one of the points destabilized or did something that sent off a radiation surge. Does that mean one of the pairs is inactive?"

No answer.

"An Serat, please stop interacting with our opsys. What are you trying to do, anyway?"

If he could open jumps, he could set up his own jump network. One that owed nothing to the Confederacy and kept moving where he wished. If the New Council ever found out about *Farseer* and the points, this is what they would aim to use it for. Yet somehow I doubted it was An Serat's aim.

"I can go there."

"Where?"

"You use my ship. It takes you into the place of no paths and all paths."

I'd had strange dreams when I used *Farseer.* But certainly not . . . eternity. Disappointment weighed my voice low.

"I did not experience that place. At least, not so I noticed."

His tentacles twirled. "Of course. To expect that a species of your limited . . ."

"An Barik said that using *Farseer* will destabilize space-time."

"Barik is wrong."

"Why should I believe you and not him?" Some small, unworthy part of me wanted to get back at him for his being able to get so much more from *Farseer* than I did. Inferior species, right.

"Is your 'spacetime' disrupted?"

The blunt, pragmatic question took me by surprise. I said nothing.

To my further surprise, he continued, "Barik does not understand. The others do not understand. Tor power can work with Invidi. Become, as you say, greater than the two added."

"The sum of the whole being greater than the parts? But when we built the station, we had to override the Tor directives because their entire existence is based on taking over other technology when they find it. It's encoded in every matrix of every strand of every material. You either get rid of it or you succumb to it. We found no middle way."

"You are not Invidi. You do not have the ability or power."

"Then how did I use the ship?"

"Other species can use Tor ships as they will. This function is not desirable." His tentacles resumed their delicate tracing of the opsys surface and he glided farther into the core, losing interest abruptly and completely.

I followed him another twenty meters or so along the walkway. When I glanced back, the yellow light from the crawler shaft was half cut off by the curve of the core.

"An Serat, you must stop. Please stop. You are damaging our life support."

No answer.

"We'll try to find you the material somewhere else." When he still didn't answer, I edged closer and tapped on the railing next to him. "Listen to me. We've probably got some untouched Tor junk stored somewhere. Bits of jump mines, booby-trapped asteroids. Can't you use . . . ?"

I didn't feel anything. A quick flash of light that I thought came from something Serat was doing to the opsys, then I was flat on my face on the walkway.

The metal strips pushed cold and hard into my cheek-bone and my left arm was jammed under my ribs. Against it my heart beat huge and irregular and I was gasping for breath that wouldn't come.

What the hell?

Breathe in. Out.

For what seemed like hours all I could focus on was getting air and staying still to give my body a chance to catch up with what happened. Like recovering from an asthma attack. No idea what was going on. It took a while to register that the filigree of shifting twinkles to the right of my vision was in fact the opsys core, out of focus. On Jocasta. Where I'd been talking to An Serat.

The lights sharpened into focus and I lifted my head and peered along the walkway. Nothing but the eerie pale light and the metal strips curving out of sight. Had he gone? I pushed myself to a sitting position and looked back the other way, wincing at the stiffness in my neck. There he was, rolling slowly along the walkway toward the crawler shaft, sampling bits of the opsys as he went. He must have shoved me to the side to get past.

I sat sprawled on the walkway, astounded.

Attacked by an Invidi. Nobody had ever been attacked by an Invidi. Not personally. We never knew they would do that. Was it a weapon? Did Serat generate the charge naturally? An electric shock, by my heart's reaction and the way my legs and arms were twitching.

A hostile Invidi. We've never had to deal with a hostile Invidi before.

"Why did you do that?" I called out, as loud as I could.

His tentacles stilled, but he said nothing.

"I thought Invidi did not harm others," I said.

"I am not like others."

"Why not?"

"I comprehend the liberation of action. Acting frees me from the cage of knowing."

"I don't understand."

Serat rocked and the walkway vibrated under my seat bones.

"Action clouds the paths," he said. "I cannot see the web. I gain freedom."

"But you lose your future sight. How can you function?"

"As you do."

"Like an inferior species?"

He didn't answer and glided onto the ramp, out the entry hatch into the crawler shaft. I caught a glimpse of how he somehow half heaved, half rolled up the step onto the corridor wall-floor surface. I couldn't see if he was still there and my legs and arms shook uselessly when I tried to stand up.

A gentle hum overhead indicated the crawler was still functioning. Its bulk blocked out the yellow light for a moment, then zoomed on. When I finally organized my limbs enough to crawl forward, An Serat had gone.

We knew he was in conflict with the other Invidi, represented by An Barik and the Confederacy. They wanted him and *Farseer,* because he'd broken their rules, or gone too far, whether the explanation Barik gave me about damaging spacetime was the whole story or not. But so far Serat had behaved more or less like an Invidi. If what he said about acting was true, if he was unconstrained by whatever morality had kept the Invidi non-interfering until now, we were in deep trouble. Nobody had rules for dealing with hostile Invidi—we never knew we needed any.

The next forty minutes were some of the most frustrating in my entire experience. The comm system was still down and I couldn't contact Murdoch to confirm if Venner had kept her word and called off the Q'Chn. Nor could I call

Engineering for backup, or ask anyone if they'd seen where
An Serat had gone. From the state of the opsys as a whole,
it looked like he had left the core. What if he'd gone to
Farseer and left the station?

If we keep *Farseer* here we're damned because Serat
and therefore the New Council and their Q'Chn won't leave.
And we're damned if we let *Farseer* go and Serat uses it.

Shortly after An Serat disappeared, a bored-looking New
Council spacer looked down from the crawler hatch. Male,
cropped gray hair, full-face tattoos. He grunted when he
saw me and sat down to wait until I finished.

I concentrated on the closest communication subsystem
node, using a toolkit taken from the maintenance alcove in
the crawler shaft. Halfway through, the gravity switched
off and I wasted long minutes chasing tools and trying to
find the end of a lead that floated out of sight behind a
raised section of panel.

My guard amused himself by hooking his feet in the
top of the door frame and doing micro-grav exercises. His
red face appeared now and then in the half-circle of ordinary light that was the crawler shaft.

Finally I set up a comm link to the Bubble, then to Lieutenant Gamet. I explained where I was and what I'd done
so far, ignoring the New Council crew member listening
outside the tunnel.

"The New Council captain agreed to let three people up
here," I said to Gamet. "Make sure you use the maintenance shafts and bring hand-sensors because the main ones
aren't working."

I hoped they'd be all right, but what choice did we have?
The opsys must be kept running or everyone died. I dropped
my voice. "She wants you unarmed, but that's your choice.
Leave any weapons on standby, though."

Understood, said Gamet. *How does it look?*

"A lot of connections are out. But I haven't been up

here for a long time. Could be part of our usual attrition. The environmentals shouldn't be any trouble, reinitialize them from each ring."

The uplifts are running normally again. We just had a message from Alpha.

The connection wasn't good enough to pick up subtleties, but her voice held too much tension.

"What's wrong? Are the Q'Chn . . . ?"

The Q'Chn started to come down, then went back up to the center, so we thought the captain had talked them out of it. That was nearly an hour ago.

While I was talking to Venner. Murdoch had said the Q'Chn were on their way down.

Then a minute ago, the Section Two uplift went straight down again. The biosignals were pretty clear. Two of them. Looks like the New Council can't control them.

Damn Venner. So much for H'digh promises. Or she really couldn't control the Q'Chn.

Commander? I'm sending my team up now in the Section Five uplift to keep on with the work, if you want to go down.

"Thanks, Barbara. I'll get down there now."

We'll handle the core.

Thirty-three

I wanted to go and talk to Venner first, to try and persuade her to do something about the Q'Chn, but the guard
wouldn't let me into the dock lobby. Over my protests, he
ushered me to the uplift with prods from his rifle. I didn't
know whether this meant Venner was busy trying to control the Q'Chn, or didn't care what they did, or was avoiding me because of the loss of face involved in admitting
she couldn't control them.

The uplift had never been so slow. Murdoch's comm
link put me on hold. I reached Sasaki instead.

"Talk to me, Helen."

*Commander, your exit's going to open in Section Three.
Section Two is emergency sealed. We have two Q'Chn active in there. Two K'Cher and four Melot are trapped in
the Trade Hall.*

The Trade Hall was about halfway along the section.
Too far to make a quick run for the uplift and safety.

*Most of the humans are out. Looks like the Q'Chn are
only interested in the K'Cher.*

"Your people?"

*The three guards assigned to this section. They have
armor, but no special weapons. Looks like they've grabbed
some plasma rifles. Chief Murdoch's on his way with a
squad.*

"Thanks."

Four more interminable minutes. The uplifts might be working, but they weren't working as fast as they should. I tried to contact Venner and, amazingly, she accepted the link.

"What the hell's going on, Captain?" I said. "You said you could keep them out of the rings."

I promise nothing. Her voice on the link was as flat as an Invidi voicebox.

"No, you're wrong. The New Council promises much and delivers nothing," I snapped. "And I swear I'll let the whole galaxy know just how much nothing."

I cut the link, fuming. If the New Council couldn't control the Q'Chn, why had they brought them back to life?

The uplift opened, as Sasaki promised, onto Section Three. Behind me, the bulk of the spoke rose like a curved wall. In front of me lay an open section of throughway ending in the first building of the section. To my left, the gray, featureless surface of the airlock door that sealed off this section from the next one. It stretched from the spoke across to the wall of the station. I couldn't remember seeing one activated since the time of the fire during the Seouras blockade.

Sasaki and a lanky corporal stood beside the wall interface monitor in the sealer door. On my right, where the throughway led out into Section Three, a Security constable kept back a crowd of curious onlookers.

Sasaki turned as I stepped out of the uplift. "Commander Halley. You can see what's happening here."

Security's visual pickups in Alpha were the most efficient on the station, firstly because nobody vandalized them, as happened on the lower levels, and secondly because the upper building levels mostly followed the building code and left space for the pickups to be attached.

The screen split into two. One side showed the wide

throughway of Section Two residential area and the other side a magnified view of a building. I recognized the Trade Hall and the unmistakable shape of Q'Chn. Two of them, huge spindly forms, on one side of the Hall in front of a side entrance.

"Our people say the two K'Cher tried to make a run for it from the Hall to the uplift. They're trapped," said Sasaki. "The three Melot stayed inside. Mr. Veatch is with them."

"They should have waited inside the Hall," said the corporal, his voice tight. "Then our people wouldn't have to risk their lives."

On the overview of the section, three bipedal forms in green uniforms advanced slowly from cover to cover. They looked very small. I recalled Murdoch's briefing—the only time Security was to fire on Q'Chn was to divert them from attack on civilians.

"Let the Slashers get 'em," yelled a voice from the crowd behind us. Others murmured agreement. "It's not our fight," called the voice again.

"None of the Four'd save us," growled someone else.

I glanced back at the closest faces but they all avoided my eyes. Sullen, almost hostile expressions on the humans. A couple of Dir all cloaked in anonymous brown.

Commotion behind the crowd. Clatter of boots on the deck.

"Coming through," yelled a voice.

The crowd parted to let a squad of Security through. They all wore full body armor and carried squat-barreled weapons. The dark helmets covered their features completely. I recognized Murdoch's rolling walk as the leader.

"Chief." Sasaki pointed to the screen. "Caselli, Munke, and Yata. Trying a diversion."

"Follow me." Murdoch's voice crackled from his helmet speaker. He waved them forward as Sasaki opened one of the airlocks in the sealer door. We could hear the whine of weapons fire, like enraged insects. Murdoch's squad filed through and the airlock shut again.

On the screen the three small figures kept up a continuous wave of fire at the Q'Chn. Flashes from their hands left dark burn marks on the deck and the wall behind the Q'Chn. But the Q'Chn themselves showed no effect, beyond a thin halo that traced the outlines of their bodies. Natural shields. How efficient of the K'Cher, to create soldiers who need no equipment.

On the screen now, Murdoch's twelve humans spread out, their positions moving slowly along the throughway. They were running, but not fast enough.

The Q'Chn turned from the alley. The two spiky figures reared up a little as if to assess the situation. They stalked toward the Security constables, one, two, three paces. Perfectly coordinated. But not coordinated enough to split up and cover both threats at the same time.

"Get out now," said Sasaki, the tips of her fingers white with pressure as she braced herself against the edge of the screen. "That's enough."

It was more than enough. In the seconds the Q'Chn were distracted, two bulky figures shot from the alley and scurried back to the Trade Hall, the door of which opened immediately to receive them, then snapped shut. I'd never seen K'Cher move so fast, and their ungainly, bottom-heavy run would have been funny in another situation.

The Q'Chn turned, started in the direction of their prey, realized they wouldn't catch them, and stopped still for a second.

"Get back," Sasaki whispered.

Murdoch and the squad were spreading out in an uneven fan-shape, keeping as much as possible to the edges of the throughway. As soon as the K'Cher disappeared into the Trade Hall, the three constables began to retreat toward the squad.

Too late. The Q'Chn moved nothing like the K'Cher. They broke into a flat, even run that overtook the fleeing humans before we realized what was happening.

Murdoch's team put down such a barrage of fire that we could hear it through the sealer door. On the screen, a coruscating halo of flame enveloped both Q'Chn. One of Murdoch's people fired something that hit one of the Q'Chn and physically threw it off its feet. But the other one kept moving.

It reached the first constable, turned to the next one. For a second I thought it hadn't touched her. Then blood spurted, she crumpled, and something round bounced away from the headless body.

"Oh, God." Sasaki vomited beside me.

The same Q'Chn pinned the second constable against a wall. Two of Murdoch's team ran toward it, firing all the time. The Q'Chn swiveled its triangular head at them, then deliberately, slowly this time, drew its killing arm across the second constable's throat. Then it walked away as the body slid to the deck. It turned its back on the Security squad and their weapons, which sprayed enough firepower at the Q'Chn to melt the walls of the building before which the body of the guard lay, then stalked unhurriedly in the direction of the Trade Hall.

The other Q'Chn rolled over and flipped onto its four legs. Shook itself like a dog.

The remaining unarmored constable was running, accompanied by two of Murdoch's squad. They were about twenty meters away from the uplift.

Sasaki kept one eye on the screen and positioned the constable with us at the other side of the airlock, ready to make sure it opened as soon as the squad reached the door.

The rest of Murdoch's squad ran forward so that they covered the unarmored constable and his escort. I recognized Murdoch by the way he crouched to reposition his weapon. Suddenly the screen was an enemy, putting the whole drama at a distance. I shouldn't be here, I should be in there with Bill, he could get killed and I wouldn't be there . . .

I took a step in the direction of the door, realized how stupid that was, turned back to the screen. If Murdoch were killed, I . . . Quick, try to access one of the automatic defense systems. They've never worked properly, but maybe it will provide some backup.

So this is how he feels when I get into trouble. As though something inside me was being squeezed to suffocation point.

"Hurry *up*." Sasaki checked the door controls for the third time and nodded to the constable waiting on the other side of the door. He checked his weapon deliberately and settled into a ready stance.

One Q'Chn now crouched in front of the Trade Hall. The other swung its legs in a leisurely pace that caught up easily to Security's protective line. Murdoch and the others were using lasers now, because all I could see were the violet bursts as the shots hit the Q'Chn's skin and dissipated.

How the hell did they shield themselves?

The Q'Chn made two sweeps, left and right, that sent five of the guards flying sideways and backward in a crackling blue discharge of what looked like electrical energy. It hadn't used the killing arm, but its long, whiplike feelers. It seemed to flush scarlet between the violet bursts, and at first I thought Security's lasers were having some effect. Then I realized it was a skin color change like the K'Cher. The legends were wrong. Red wasn't the only color the Q'Chn could see. It was the last color their victims saw.

The remaining three guards backed up before it, firing

from the side but trying to keep between it and the unarmored constable.

I couldn't see Murdoch and a horrible, dry-mouthed panic hit me. He might be dead and I never told him anything. Never said how much his caring meant to me.

Inexorable, unstoppable, the Q'Chn reached the three running humans. They were only twenty meters from the airlock. They could have tried the uplift, I thought, then realized the Q'Chn would be too quick.

It stood on its two hindmost legs, swept the two armored guards away simultaneously with its next two legs, and killed the remaining man.

I looked away, retching. Sasaki sobbed vicious curses and thumped the airlock frame with her fist.

When I looked up a moment later, the Q'Chn had turned its back, like the other had, and was walking away. The two guards who'd been sent flying picked themselves up and staggered to the airlock. Murdoch and the others—I searched the screen anxiously, found the figures helping each other back to the airlock doors. Nobody fired at the Q'Chn.

Sasaki tapped open the airlock with shaking hands. Three medics in white oversuits rushed forward to help the two closest squad members through, then led them gently to where they'd set up a field tent on the open throughway in front of the spoke.

I hadn't noticed the medics arrive. I noticed now, too, that the crowd behind us had grown in both size and rowdiness. The constable went over to stand in front of them, his face impassive despite their shouted insults and questions.

I envied him his simple task. All I could do was keep an eye on the monitor and shiver. Inside Section Two, the Q'Chn stayed motionless in front of the Trade Hall.

Murdoch came through last. He was supporting one of

the members of his team whose arm hung at a painful angle. When the medics loaded the woman onto a stretcher, he straightened up slowly and unclicked the catches on his helmet. Each click took a long time. I stood back and let Sasaki take the helmet from him when it finally released. His face was drenched in sweat and his eyes weren't quite focused.

"What are they doing?" were his first words, spoken in a voice hoarse from shouting orders.

"They're still in front of the Trade Hall," said Sasaki. "What do you want us to do now?"

"Can we contact the Trade Hall?" He looked over at me. It was almost a plea. For what, I didn't know.

"We tried before, but nothing," said Sasaki. "I'll try again."

As she raised her comm link to her lips, mine bleeped.

Commander Halley, this is Gamet.

"I'm here, Barbara."

We picked up a signal from the center to Alpha. It must have been the New Council talking to the Q'Chn. It's in code, like when the Q'Chn started to come down and the New Council called them back.

Looks like Venner figured out we were listening to her messages.

Is there any change there?

Sasaki was signaling me frantically. On the monitor, the Q'Chn had left the Trade Hall and were ambling down the throughway toward this spoke.

"Wait on," I said to Gamet. Then to Sasaki, "In case they try to come through, run the door charge."

Sasaki nodded, and rushed to the control panel beside the spoke. She activated the electric proximity alarm and strips of bright orange warning lights began flashing over the whole surface of the door.

On the monitor, the Q'Chn got closer. Behind us, the crowd grew noisier, demanding explanations.

"They're coming this way," I said to Gamet.

Are you at the spoke?

"On the other side."

As the Q'Chn grew closer, the pickup changed to a close-up image. Two angels of death mincing their way down the blood-soaked deck. One of them had been splashed with blood, the dark patches showed clearly against its gleaming skin, now iridescent again. Its feeler rubbed fastidiously at the stains.

I wish we could see you bleed, I thought.

They were only meters from the spoke.

"Uplift's opening," said Sasaki.

"Shit," I said. "Is the alternate exit disabled?" Otherwise they could simply step in the uplift on that side, pass through the exit corridor, and step out in this section.

Sasaki nodded. "I had to reinitialize it after you got out." She checked it anyway as she spoke.

I knew the alternate exit was supposed to disable automatically, but I didn't trust all the systems after An Serat had been playing around in the core.

Got them. Gamet's voice was satisfied. *Sensors active. They're on the way up.*

"We guessed that," muttered Sasaki. The spoke quivered and the uplift standby lights blinked green.

"Why did they go?" I said, half to myself.

"Not because of anything we did," said Murdoch.

Something in the signal? said Gamet at the same time.

"Analyze it," I said to her. "I want to know what Venner told them and I want to be able to use that code and channel if I need to."

"Us?" Sasaki paused in tapping out a diagnostic of the exit program. "You want to talk to the Q'Chn?"

Murdoch shot me a look under his brows.

"The more we know about them," I said, "the easier it will be to fight them."

I'll coordinate with Lee. Gamet out.

"If I could talk to them, I know what I'd say." Murdoch's words were too precisely pronounced.

"Go and let the medics check you out," I said. "We'll handle this."

He shook his head and dragged an unsteady hand down his face. "I'm fine. I reckon we need to talk to those K'Cher. What the fuck did they think they were doing?"

I'd never seen Murdoch pale and shaking before, and I hated it. It made me feel uncertain and solicitous and I wanted to physically attack the cause of his distress or anything else handy.

"Go and see the medics," I said, more sharply than I'd intended. "I'll talk to the K'Cher."

His jaw set stubbornly. I put my hand on his arm and squeezed, then pushed gently. "Go on." I smiled. "I need to know you're all right."

He stared at me as though he'd never looked at me properly before, half smiled back mechanically, and turned away. Streaks of blood stood out against the black armor across his shoulders.

"Uplift's at the top," said Sasaki from where she stood at the control panel.

I joined her and tapped instructions, not caring that she saw my hand shake.

"We'll keep that uplift car at the center for the moment. If they try to take it down here or send for any of the other cars, we'll be warned."

We both knew the Q'Chn could use an uplift in one of the other spokes and the warning might not reach us in time. But there was little we could do.

"Do you think they'll come down again?" she said quietly.

"I don't know. Let's talk to the K'Cher while we can. They've got to stay in shelter for their own and everybody else's protection. And I want to know what they know about the Q'Chn."

The crowd were willing to disperse, after Sasaki and I pointed out to them that if the Q'Chn figured out how to override the alternative exit function they could enter this section too. News of the Q'Chn attack would spread quickly and create further bad feeling against the Four. And against the New Council. Let Venner attempt to woo the residents. If she couldn't keep the Q'Chn under control, who would believe her other promises as well?

When we entered Section Two some minutes later, halfway up the throughway the medics were lifting a covered form onto a maglev trolley.

Blood pooled in one spot on the deck near the uplift, streaks running off the pool. Near the medics, more blood had splashed in a wide arc. I couldn't look at it without seeing the Q'Chn attack before my eyes, so I kept my attention on the walls.

The walls of the buildings showed a variety of singe weals, black burn clouds, blisters, and cracks, depending on their construction. Some of it looked bad enough to have damaged the circuitry inside.

The Trade Hall was unscathed. It rose in neat, rosy-colored blocks to regulation height.

"You did say Veatch was in there?" I said.

Sasaki brought herself back from frowning contemplation of the mess on the deck. "Yes. When we talked to them before, he said he went up there to persuade the K'Cher not to try to leave in their freighters."

"I need to talk to him."

"We sent a message saying we want to talk. There he is."

Veatch hesitated in the main doorway and peered out.

He saw us and hurried over, more quickly than his usual measured walk, then he clasped his hands behind his back as he reached us.

His antennae lifted a little. "My condolences on the deaths."

Sasaki mumbled something that was either "thank you" or "fuck you."

"I want to talk to Trillith," I said. "Now."

Veatch's antennae stiffened in surprise. "Trillith? Why?"

"I need to know more about the Q'Chn," I said. "The K'Cher must know more than they let on."

"It will not come." Veatch's antennae curled apologetically. "It fears the Q'Chn will return."

"It's not that safe in the Hall," said Sasaki scornfully. "The Q'Chn only left the K'Cher alone because the New Council was calling them back. The Q'Chn can break through the building if they want to."

"Encouraging the K'Cher to panic will not help the situation," Veatch said.

"They might as well stay there," I said. "It's as safe— or unsafe—as anywhere at the moment. I'll talk to them. You go back to the Bubble," I added to Veatch. "Make sure you've got reports from all departments and divisions on their current status. Send runners to get the information if the comm links are down."

He started to protest but I glared at him and went into the Trade Hall.

Trillith waited on the second floor, in a white-walled room made tiny by its bulk. It sat still, waiting for us, a huge greeny-gray statue.

"Commander Halley." Its voicebox tone seemed subdued, its actual voice no more than a faint rustle. "You must protect us. They are here."

"I noticed," I said. "And if you want protection, you pay for it. We just paid in three lives. Now it's your turn."

Ordinarily I wouldn't use that tone to a K'Cher. They are so accomplished at rudeness, that politeness is our only weapon. Today, Trillith didn't even notice. The ridge of exoskeleton down the front of its thorax was pale and dull, as though it was in shock.

"I will contribute your required value," it said.

If I hadn't been so angry, my jaw might have dropped. Trillith, agreeing to pay me an amount I specified?

"I don't mean in goods. I mean information."

Its color deepened a little. "What are your questions?"

"Why are they chasing you?"

"They hate us. They hate the aristos most of all. The aristos created them."

The barons, of whom Trillith was a minor member, did not wield power in K'Cher society—that was left to the Few, as the aristos liked to call themselves. Even more xenophobic and paranoid than the barons, the aristos saw themselves as the brains of K'Cher pre-Change society. Below the barons, Lowers like Keveth, the first victim of the Q'Chn on Jocasta, were forced to deal directly with other "inferior" species as a result of their own inferiority. And by doing so, confirmed that they were tainted and inferior.

"The aristos emerged before the Q'Chn existed," said Trillith. "Half a human millennium ago," it added with pride. "The K'Cher at that time were genetically similar all over our colony planet network. Much greater than anything your species ever knew. Unfortunately, we could not win the war against the ancestors of Leowin. We began genetic manipulation to create the perfect warrior. The first mutations carried through the Change to breed true, and the present aristos are their descendants."

Trillith's eyes, so uncomfortably like multifaceted Q'Chn eyes, clouded briefly, then cleared again. "Then ambition overreached ability and the resulting strand could not

Change. They could not enter the next life stage. They could not breed. But the aristos chose to continue to create these creatures because they were fearsome fighters. Free of the need to allow their creations to propagate, the aristos modified further and further. When contact with the Invidi brought them the technological ability to expand their empire they did so, not hesitating to use the Q'Chn. Until the Invidi finally stopped them."

"So the Q'Chn want revenge on the aristos because they agreed to let them die off after you joined the Confederacy?" I said. "But why do they attack you? It's the aristos they should hate."

Trillith's forearm twitched and it wedged the arm under its torso, as though embarrassed. "You do not understand. The aristos commanded the Q'Chn's extinction, but the Q'Chn hate all of us because we can Change and they cannot. They cannot become more than they are now. They will never know the heights of our culture, our philosophy."

"Why are they obeying the New Council's orders?"

"I do not know. They are different to the old Q'Chn. But they kill just as efficiently."

I set my jaw in annoyance. It wasn't enough, but I didn't think Trillith knew much more. I turned to go.

"Commander?" It pushed itself to its feet with creaks and small whistles of air exhaled from carapace holes. "You will protect us?"

I thought of the blood on the deck below and felt too tired to say more than "Yes, Trillith."

Thirty-four

Lieutenant Gamet was coordinating opsys repairs in the Bubble. I stopped off there on my way to see Veatch. It had been a long time since I'd been in that round, cramped space, but my feet knew exactly how many steps to take from doorway to the edge of the upper level, and I found myself checking the readouts on each monitor, comparing them with the ideal levels in my mind. The sounds felt right—subdued voices, the hum and occasional ping of the opsys. Except for a slow, regular boop. Wonder what that is.

Three people in EarthFleet blue sat at the main consoles, and Ensign Lee was on call at the central station. She looked up as I came in, blinked in surprise, and straightened from where she'd been bent over a panel.

"Comm . . ." she began, then stopped. She must have heard I'd resigned from ConFleet, but here I was, wearing a ConFleet uniform and walking unguarded into the Bubble.

"I'm here to see the lieutenant about the core," I said, nodding at Gamet's back, which was bent over the Ops console on the lower level.

Gamet turned at the sound of my voice and raised her hand a little.

"Be my guest," said Lee.

Someone cleared their throat behind me and Lee looked over at them, then back at me.

"Er, welcome back, ma'am," she added.

She looked different, and I ran through a mental list—short dark cap of hair, same; slim figure, same; determinedly calm expression. Ah, she now wore light EarthFleet blue instead of ConFleet navy. And she wasn't an ensign anymore.

"You transferred?" I said, surprised. Lee had always been a staunch ConFleet supporter in the inevitable ConFleet-EarthFleet squabbles.

She smiled shyly. "I got comfortable here."

Someone said something about "making a love nest" and she swung around menacingly.

"Our gain is ConFleet's loss, then," I said. "And congratulations on the promotion."

"Thank you, Commander."

I stepped down to Ops, where Gamet waved her hand at the bank of readouts.

"It's not too bad. We've settled the environmentals, although Delta recycling is having problems."

If environmentals had stayed up, An Serat must have left that part of the opsys alone. "Delta recycling always has problems," I said. "What's that noise?"

Gamet listened for a moment, her head on one side. The lights from the readouts stained her nose and cheeks a sickly green. Then she grinned, understanding. "That's the subsystem monitor network. We set up access here after you left."

I became aware that the Bubble was a lot quieter than when I'd stepped inside. Everyone was carefully not listening to Gamet and myself.

"Uplifts are a bit unreliable," continued Gamet, tapping up information on each system as she spoke, spidery blue figures weaving their way down the screen. "We're monitoring them closely, especially after what happened in Alpha."

"Good. I want to . . . the administration needs to know if there's any unauthorized usage."

"There's one worrying development." On the screen to her right rotated a 3-D schematic of the core. "These energy fluctuations." She traced a series of orange patterns that passed in waves through a certain part of the core. On the periphery of the opsys, but connected to it.

"That's one of the dock systems . . ." my voice trailed away. *Farseer*'s dock. An Serat must be trying to gain information from the Tor elements of the core. Or activate them, or subvert them, or whatever he meant to do. While we'd been chasing Q'Chn, he was connecting a live Tor device to my station's core. We had to get rid of him, *Farseer*, and the Q'Chn. I wanted the lot of them off my station.

"Set up a block against Tor interference," I said to Gamet. "As close as you can to these connections with the ship. You can find examples of blocks in the database, look in the construction records for 2116, about the middle of the year."

Gamet's eyes widened and she dropped her voice, "*Tor* interference? But how can . . . I thought it was the Invidi ship."

"I could be mistaken," I said. "But those blocks are the most thorough, anyway. Set it up and see how it goes."

"Yes, ma'am."

Procedures we'd used six years ago wouldn't stop An Serat from reaching further into our opsys for long, but with any luck we wouldn't need long. If ConFleet hurried up through that jump point . . . I cursed mentally. Here we go again. Waiting for ConFleet to come and rescue us. What happens if we get neutrality? ConFleet won't come then. It's about time we learned to stand by ourselves.

"I'll need you in a meeting soon," I said to Gamet, "to coordinate with the other departments."

"I'll stand by." She didn't lift her gaze from the screen. Her fingers tapped busily, sending signals to each ring.

I left her to it and walked over to Lee. "Is Mr. Stone in there?" I nodded at the connecting door to the head of station's office. Another door beside it led to the rest of the administrative complex. Veatch's territory, a hive of corridors and offices.

Lee shook her head. "I don't think so. He hasn't checked in here, at any rate."

"What, not since the Q'Chn attack?" I said, shocked. "I saw him earlier, about ten, up in the center with the New Council captain."

"He hasn't come in here." Lee seemed half reluctant to disclose this breach of custom, but at the same time needing to tell someone. I could see a station timer on beside her monitor. It read 16:20.

"I took him the night shift's report, he signed it," she said.

"That's it?"

"He leaves tactical affairs to Lieutenant-Commander Parno and myself."

Which was, strictly speaking, the correct procedure. Head of station was supposed to be an administrative position. My ConFleet rank had been incidental.

"Where's Parno?" I said.

"He went on short leave the day before you and Mr. Murdoch got back."

"He missed the fun, then."

She smiled properly at that. "I think Mr. Stone went to see the magistrate after he finished in the center."

"Thanks."

*   *   *

I tried Veatch's office, next door to Stone's. The door opened to reveal an immaculate interior. Matte beige and cream, no EarthFleet blue for Veatch. Flat, abstract creations on two walls. A water sculpture bubbling in the corner.

Veatch stood by the enormous desk, shifting his gaze between one of the monitors on it and another monitor on the wall.

"Veatch?"

He turned. "Commander Halley."

"I did resign," I reminded him gently.

"I am aware of this. However the filework has not been completed and your record is still unchanged. I also believe that in this unusual situation morale is better served if you are seen to be an officer."

"You're very thorough."

"Of course."

"Did you get those status reports for me?"

He held out a handcom.

I took it and slipped it into my jacket pocket and stayed in the doorway. "Perhaps you could be a little more thorough in your cooperation with Security."

His antennae stiffened with shock. "My department is always cooperative with Security."

"Yes. But over in Section Three during the Q'Chn attack, the residents didn't seem as worried as they should have been. Your people should be out there with Murdoch's, making sure everyone knows what to do."

"The administration has disseminated information on all public channels." Disapproval tinged every syllable.

"Then get out there with loudspeakers or notes on handcoms, I don't care. Just give Security a hand. Get your staff off their backsides, out of their offices, and onto the throughways. The best way to avoid casualties is to have people prepared."

His face was even more expressionless than usual and his body, turned half away, also told me nothing. He's going to say who the hell are you to be giving orders.

But he dipped his antennae and turned toward the desk. "I will send a memo to all departments immediately."

"Just a memo?"

He sat down with a thud. "An *urgent* memo."

"That'll have to do. And try to get more information from Trillith about the Q'Chn." My hands were sweating. I wiped them discreetly down my trousers. "One more thing. Have you ever heard of an Invidi attacking anyone personally? One to one?"

He inclined his head in thought. "No recent information suggests it. But I remember when we discussed An Barik during the blockade, Trillith mentioned a detail from the K'Cher-Invidi war."

"What did Trillith say?" I prompted.

"It said there was such an attack, but many Changes ago and Trillith could not recall the details."

"Hmm."

"Why do you ask?" said Veatch.

"I'm trying to understand why An Serat is staying here," I said. "And how to get rid of him before we have any more casualties."

"Invidi attacking who?" said Murdoch's voice behind me.

I spun around. He looked all right. Pale, the hollows at his temples more prominent than usual.

"Me," I said.

"What? When?"

"In the center a little while ago. An Serat threw some sort of electrical charge at me." At least, that's what it had felt like. If it was an ordinary charge, though, the opsys would have reacted in the immediate area. And I observed no absorption spikes or rejection outages, which is what you'd expect.

"But I've never heard . . ."

"That's why I asked Veatch. Serat said some disturbing things."

Murdoch groaned. "Not more trouble. What?"

"He said he'd discovered the pleasures of acting in the present. To do that, he's had to give up his future-sight."

"You don't sound worried."

"I am worried," I said slowly, groping for the thought that had only just occurred to me. "But it also means he can't see what we're going to do next."

"Hah." Murdoch's chuckle held no humor. "He's not the only one. What happened with the New Council captain?"

"She's in a tough spot. Basically, she has to wait for Serat before she can leave. And I don't think she likes the Q'Chn."

He frowned, thinking. "Can we use that?"

"Possibly."

He drew his hand over his face slowly, as if he wanted to take it off. I'd seen Murdoch lose people before and it drained him in a way I was only starting to comprehend. We'd lost so many people during the Seouras blockade. I couldn't let that start again.

I squeezed his arm. He looked at me in surprise, then half smiled. And not a whisper from Henoit.

"What are you doing in here?" I said. I'd nearly asked Murdoch if he was coming to see me, then realized if he was coming to see anyone, it would be Stone.

"Passing through to Main Security."

"Wait a bit." I looked at Veatch, who was ostentatiously busy at his console. "Veatch, please notify Mr. Stone, Mr. Florida, and the chief magistrate that there'll be an emergency meeting in five minutes in the Bubble."

Veatch tapped a phrase in a handcom. "In the main briefing room?"

"Sounds good."

"What are you doing?" said Murdoch.

"We need to coordinate ourselves," I said. "If we want to get rid of the Q'Chn."

He looked at me in a way that reminded me of his early days on the station, when I'd occasionally catch his astonished gaze on me. Then he nodded.

"Let's do it, then."

We walked down the corridor together, saying nothing. His face was somber, his eyes looked inward.

The fear I'd felt for Murdoch when he faced the Q'Chn lay close to the surface of my mind, waiting to grip me again. I didn't know if I could handle this.

This was why senior officers shouldn't become involved with each other. If, in a crisis, I first thought of Murdoch, what kind of an officer would I be? You're no kind of officer, was the reply. You resigned from ConFleet. You're a political asylum applicant, a refugee on your own world. Both in this century and the last. Hah, there's irony for you.

The briefing room in the Bubble had been redecorated. It now boasted a state-of-the-art table, recliners, and chairs adaptable to all species, and a self-service multi-beverage dispenser. As we were all humanoid, we huddled down at the plain, flat end of the table and used the chairs. As this was Jocasta, the beverage dispenser would serve only tea.

Murdoch, Sasaki, Gamet, Lorna deVries, Rupert Stone, Florida, and Veatch were present. I hoped I wouldn't regret asking Florida, but we needed him to keep the delegates up to date so we didn't have to invite them.

We started the meeting with Murdoch's terse description of the Q'Chn attack in front of the Alpha Trade Hall. As he spoke, the atmosphere in the room became heavier. Stone's pale face was leeched further of any color and Lorna's normally twinkling eyes were like hard black stones.

Gamet then gave us a brief status report on the opsys—stable but fragile. The engineers had been allowed to work undisturbed in the core. "We didn't see any Q'Chn," she said. "We saw one New Council guard, but he had orders to let us through. He stood over us the whole time."

"The Q'Chn were in Alpha," grunted Murdoch. "That's why you didn't see any." He was calm in the way a star was calm before flashing nova.

"I've called this meeting because we need to get the Q'Chn off the station now," I said into the silence that followed his words. "We need to coordinate the departments."

"What authority do you have to do this?"

Stone hadn't said anything until now. I'd been thinking ahead and his interjection took me by surprise.

Lorna spoke before I could get my thoughts in order. "Security applied for her temporary release on bail. I approved." She leaned forward so she could raise her eyebrow across the table at Stone as though he were a hostile witness.

"Yes, but she has no position here. She resigned her commission," he said. Looking at each of them except Gamet, "You heard her. At the dinner."

Murdoch blew out his breath in impatience. *Finish this, will you?* his look to me said.

"I don't dispute your authority," I said. "Yes, I resigned my commission and maybe we can argue whether that resignation has been formally ratified or not. You remain head of station. Right now we need to work together, regardless of position."

"Then as head of station, surely it's *my* call what we do in the present situation," said Stone.

"Which is?" said Florida.

Murdoch rested his forehead on his hands and stared at nothing.

Stone aligned the two handcoms in front of him with the edge of the desk. "I, er, favor waiting until ConFleet breaks through the jump point. They'll overcome the enemy ships and won't have any trouble mopping up the enemy here. If the New Council stays, I think they'll run away as soon as ConFleet gets through."

"I don't agree," I said. "The New Council captain is capable of using station residents as hostages and trying to bargain her way out with ConFleet. If they come."

Stone looked up from his handcom. "Of course they'll come."

"They didn't come last time," said Sasaki. "Sir."

There was a short silence, broken by Lorna pushing her cup precisely in front of her on the table like somebody making a chess move.

"Halley's still governor," she said. "That position has to be revised by an independent review committee. Its authority overrides head of station. Hell, theoretically she can give orders to ConFleet commanders within the Abelar system."

"Didn't work with *Vengeful*'s captain," I said.

She smiled. "I did say 'theoretically.'"

"Everyone here," I said to Stone, "has tried waiting for ConFleet. We can't afford to make that mistake again. And soon we might not be part of the Confederacy. Who's going to help us then?"

"That's why neutrality is such a bad . . ." he began.

"The issue now is how to get rid of the Q'Chn." Murdoch let his hands fall on the shiny tabletop with a loud thud. "I assume you want suggestions?" he said to me.

"Yes."

"Kill them," he said expressionlessly. "Now." His hands spread flat on the table, the fingertips bloodless from the pressure.

Sasaki, Florida, and Gamet nodded. Veatch showed no sign of dissent, not even a twitch of one antenna. Lorna's face stilled as she calculated something mentally. Stone opened his mouth but Lorna beat him to it.

"You can't kill them all," she said. "There must be at least fifteen out there in *Vengeful* and the small ships. We've seen three onstation."

"They can't bring any more onstation, or they weaken their defense at the jump point," said Murdoch. "I think we can deal with the ones here ourselves and not worry about the others."

"Unless there are more on the New Council ship," said Florida, then to Stone and me, "Did you see any more up there?"

We both shook our heads. "What information do we have about them?" I asked. "Veatch, did you get anything more from Trillith?"

"Unfortunately, I did not," said Veatch. "However, based on my own observations, collated and compared with the observations of others, it appears that these are part of the first group cloned by the New Council. They seem to have a loose hierarchy, possibly based on physical strength and/or experience."

"What's the time frame here?" said Murdoch. "The history files say the Slashers live about seventy years. How long do they take to mature?"

"True," said Lorna. "It can't be that long since the New Council got hold of the genetic material. Two, three years? Earth years, I mean."

"K'Cher have a short initial maturation period," said Veatch. "Then a long stable life before they Change. I am not sure, but I believe they reach half their final body size in approximately one and a half of your years."

"If the Q'Chn are the same, then the ones we have here could still be immature," said Lorna.

"I bet they learn fast," grunted Murdoch. "They'd have to, to be any use as weapons."

"I don't know how it fits in," said Sasaki, "but over the past hour there's been a lot of communication between *Vengeful* and the New Council ship in dock here. And movement of small ships between *Vengeful* and the jump point."

"Can we tell what the Q'Chn on *Vengeful* are saying to Venner?" said Murdoch.

She shook her head. "Not yet. The Bubble team are trying to decode that message now. Or cleaning it up, something like that."

"How do you intend killing the indestructible?" said Gamet. She leaned two of her handcoms together to make a tent. "Do we have some new weapon? Biological maybe?"

Murdoch cleared his throat. "Not exactly."

Sasaki's fingers tapped on the edge of the table and she glanced from Murdoch to me.

"We're thinking of a powerful explosion," said Murdoch. "In one of the reinforced storage bays."

A chorus of dismayed murmurs greeted this. Veatch's antennae stiffened.

"A concussive explosion," said Murdoch. "The shock wave will be magnified in the enclosed space and it'll destroy their internal organs even if the exoskeletons can survive." There was no vindictiveness in his tone, merely a satisfaction with details. "We'll use the new fire extinguisher system, attach the outlet pipes to disperse atomized flammable liquid. We've already assembled a small incendiary explosive which will then detonate the mist, followed by the containers of fuel already there."

"That's relevant to what I was going to say." Stone managed to interrupt as Murdoch paused for breath. "Is the cost of this extreme action acceptable to the station as a whole? Should we not have more information about possible effects upon the residents before we embark upon such violence?"

Murdoch groaned and scratched his head.

The trouble was, Stone was partly right. "If we knew what the New Council holds over the Q'Chn, we might be able to try it ourselves," I said. "Get them to leave. There's been nothing to indicate that in the uncoded communications we monitored. There might be something in the coded messages from *Vengeful* to the New Council." And then to Sasaki, "Helen, did the Bubble team give you any idea how long it might take them to break the code for that signal?"

"Not yet, ma'am," said Sasaki. "And before we move on, I'd like to say we're having trouble getting people to cooperate in the rings," she added. "They're fed up with evacuees from the spokes and having some sections sealed off. We're using a lot of people just to keep order."

"She's right," said Gamet. "It took us twice as long as usual to get to an uplift. Not because of the detours, but because people were hanging around arguing."

"Don't they realize what will happen if a Q'Chn gets into the rings?" I said.

Sasaki shrugged one shoulder. "They know. Most of them were here last time and they're scared. But some of them are angry at having to move stuff and stay away from the spokes."

"I wonder how the New Council would handle a riot," I said slowly.

"They're the ones who caused this situation," Lorna said, her eyes unreadable.

"My initial impression of Captain Venner is that she'd let the Q'Chn loose for a while as a demonstration of power, and trust everyone to learn their lesson," I said.

"Killing and intimidating your support base is not good politics," said Veatch. "It would be extremely interesting to hear how the New Council instructs its representatives in these matters."

It all depended on Venner's foresight, or lack of same. If she valued the long-term reputation of the New Council, she'd be unlikely to initiate any massacres.

One thing for certain: as far as Venner was concerned, time was running out. Very soon ConFleet could break through the Q'Chn barrier around the jump point to Central. Very soon she would either give up on An Serat and run away in flatspace, or try to remove him forcibly in order to get through the jump point.

If it was still possible for them to go through the Central jump point, given the probable concentration of ConFleet forces on the other side. But An Serat might be able to manipulate the jump network in unexpected ways, so we couldn't dismiss the possibility of Venner escaping the way she came.

Would An Serat go with Venner? Did he still intend using the New Council, or was he content to get his tentacles on *Farseer* and let us all go to hell?

"We have the Council delegates here," said Florida. "If they take back unfavorable reports, the New Council will find its support base shrinking even further. People are very angry about the Q'Chn being resurrected anyway. If the New Council uses Q'Chn for general intimidation like this, they can say good-bye to any hope of cooperation."

And good-bye to the only organized galaxy-wide resistance to Confederacy hegemony. If only the New Council hadn't resurrected the Q'Chn.

Sasaki frowned at me. "You want us to start a riot?"

"No," I said hastily. "But you can make sure people know the New Council is responsible for all the inconvenience. Blame them for everything."

"It's going to take a lot of organizing," she said doubtfully. "Security is flat out as it is."

Murdoch and I looked at Stone. Lorna and Florida looked at Veatch.

"You, too," I said to Florida. "I want whatever the New Council does here to be shown to the whole galaxy in a . . ." I remembered the twenty-first-century phrase. "A blaze of publicity."

Florida thought for a moment. "You want me to keep feeding updates to the delegates and get a report ready to send to information agencies throughout the Confederacy."

"That's the kind of thing," I said. "Another problem is that the New Council can't leave without An Serat. Can't leave through the jump point, that is."

"Won't ConFleet be waiting for them at the other end anyway?" said Florida. "They'll be caught, regardless."

"Maybe the Invidi have tricks to get through Central," said Lorna.

Maybe Serat plans to jump them somewhere else, I thought. If he can.

"If the Invidi leaves, the New Council will leave?" said Stone. "But how could an Invidi be helping them in the first place?"

"It's a long story," said Murdoch. "He used them to get something he wanted."

"Where is he now?" said Lorna. "Shouldn't we have a guard on him?"

"I've got two people on him if he comes down in the rings," said Murdoch.

"He's up to something in the opsys," I said and then turned to Gamet. "Do we have that interference block in place?"

She grimaced. "Yes, but it's already crumbling. We can't keep up with whatever it is."

Sasaki's comm link blipped and she lifted it to her ear.

"Commander," she said excitedly. "Someone's coming along from the Bubble. They've worked out the coded transmission from *Vengeful*."

"Let's hope it's useful," said Murdoch dryly. Then to me, "You can try and negotiate with these pirates if you want to. I think our best bet is getting rid of the Q'Chn permanently."

"What do you need?" I said to him.

"A bit of time, an hour maybe, to finish reattaching the extinguisher input for that bay. And we're going to have to get all the sweeper ships down beside the rings."

The station's shields worked well against debris from space, but the areas between the rings and center had always been difficult to keep clear.

"When that storage bay goes," continued Murdoch. "It's going to spit junk out fast. We'll have to cover the ring surface completely. Last thing we want is Alpha's reflectors smashed."

"Get rid of that sweeper drone in front of the docking bay," I reminded him. The one that had formed a physical barrier in case An Serat circumvented our controls and tried to take *Farseer* out of the bay. "The way he's interfering with our opsys, the sooner he takes that ship out, the better."

"And we need to find a way to get the Q'Chn into the trap," Murdoch added.

Lorna spun a stylus thoughtfully around her finger. "We could ask one of the K'Cher to act as bait," she said.

Sasaki snorted and Veatch stacked his handcoms reproachfully.

"You could use one of us," agreed Gamet. "But it might not get all of them there at once."

Murdoch nodded. "That's the problem."

The doors swished and Lee strode in.

She glanced from me to Stone to Murdoch, before fixing on Stone. "Good news, sir. We've intercepted an important transmission. This came in only seven minutes ago."

She tapped the table beside Florida, and a bright rectangle blossomed above the table. Another tap, and the rectangle was full of Q'Chn. Everyone in the room flinched back from the many-legged figure, then glanced self-consciously at their neighbors.

We couldn't see much more than its huge, triangular head, but when it reared up it would be three meters tall, on legs that seemed spindly but were many-jointed and flexible. Kind of like a cross between a dragon and a praying mantis, covered with iridescent, overlapping armor that was actually skin. I felt my senses betrayed me—anything as dangerous as the Q'Chn should surely look evil.

A voice emerged from the table's audio processor. Scratchy and badly reconstructed, but the unmistakable flat tones of a voicebox.

. . . not to do as you say. You give us the smalleyes. You do not give us the smalleyes we attack you.

Lee froze the image and sound as voices around the table asked what "smalleyes" was. "Hang on," she said. "I'm not sure myself, but the New Council captain's answer clarifies it a bit."

She tapped the controls and the Q'Chn image changed to that of Venner, straight against a flat gray wall. An Achelian holding a huge plasma rifle stood beside her.

I will not give you one morsel of information, not one vial of material, not one embryo. It is not yours to take.

The Q'Chn again. *We attack and take it.*

Venner, her voice low and cold. *If you try, I will destroy it first. Make no mistake, I will do that.*

The Q'Chn. *You cannot get out. We want the smalleyes.*

The holoimage faded. For a moment nobody said anything. "Smalleyes" must be the genetic research with which the New Council resurrected the Q'Chn. So that was what Venner was holding over the Q'Chn.

If we could get the research information or even actual genetic material away from Venner it would help the Confederacy battle the Q'Chn. Gamet mentioned biological weapons earlier—surely knowing how the New Council made the Q'Chn would give us a chance of unmaking them.

Venner didn't have many options. Would she try and force An Serat to leave with her? Maybe leave the Q'Chn to battle ConFleet as a diversion. The Q'Chn as willing tools were useful to the New Council, but I doubted the New Council wanted argumentative allies who might turn on them at any moment.

Why did the Q'Chn want that research? According to Trillith, they hated the K'Cher for leaving them to extinction and because the K'Cher could Change and breed. Could the Q'Chn manipulate the research themselves? More likely force someone else to do it for them.

If Venner valued her crew and really wanted to keep the genetic material out of Confederacy hands, she'd have to leave now. In flatspace if necessary. Plenty of pirates and illegal salvagers found the Abelar system good hiding and good hunting. She'd survive.

I looked up to find everyone staring at me. Murdoch's eyes stayed longest on mine, but I couldn't fathom his expression.

"Uh, sorry. Did I miss something?" I hurriedly tried to recall if anyone had spoken.

"We're waiting for you," said Lorna.

"The Q'Chn onstation have communication implants," I said slowly. "That's how Venner called them out of Alpha."

"Have we seen any sign of the Q'Chn on *Vengeful* trying to contact the Q'Chn here?"

Lee shook her head, dark fringe swinging. "They sent the message only to Venner."

"Then the implants probably aren't long range. So if the Q'Chn on *Vengeful* want to contact the three Q'Chn here onstation, they have to go through Venner and get her to send a signal via the implants. Which means we might have found a way to lure our three friends into Murdoch's surprise."

Lorna beckoned to me as the meeting broke up.

"I managed to put your asylum request on record. Before you left *Vengeful*."

I dragged my thoughts back to personal problems. "I thought you needed my voiceprint."

"Yes, we can insert that now." She pinched my arm lightly. "I know it's not strictly correct. Don't look so shocked. I'm a model of rectitude normally so I can be of use in times like these."

"Thanks, Lorna."

"You need some friends in moderately high places. You know Stone's been sounding me out about challenging Murdoch's arrest?"

I stared at her stupidly. "What do you mean?"

"He wanted to know if I thought Murdoch was able to arrest you when Murdoch was on leave and anyway in the middle of a transfer. I said, makes no difference."

"Why is he wasting time on that?"

"Probably wants to get you into the brig and ready to hand over to ConFleet."

I groaned. "The station's overrun by Q'Chn and that's all he can think about? Save me from the bureaucratic mind."

She smiled and half sat on the new briefing table. "You may be glad of that bureaucratic mind soon. If Bill's plan succeeds, EarthFleet can make you pay for damages. But the bureaucratic mind remembered to allow asylum recipients to defer payment."

"Damages? Oh, hell. Lorna, there's going to be a lot of damage. Murdoch's planning a fuel-air explosion in an enclosed area."

"That's what he said."

"But if we get rid of the Q'Chn, we potentially save lives, as well as getting rid of the New Council, which will save the damage that might occur if ConFleet fights them here."

She shook her head. "All hypothetical. They can't consider something that might not have happened."

I groaned. "Is paying damages the worst likely outcome?"

"They might slap restrictions on your movements," she said, sliding off the table and patting my shoulder. "And there's the earlier charges of misuse of station property and misappropriation of funds. That won't be deferred. But don't worry, it's better than what ConFleet wants to do to you."

"Are you sure?"

"I am very sure. ConFleet wants to court-martial you, then discharge you dishonorably into the Confederacy legal system. If you're found guilty of Invidi technology possession, you'll be put in a rehab program."

"I should have stayed in the past."

Lorna cocked her head. "No, we missed you." She linked her arm in mine as we walked toward the door. "It was awfully quiet while you were away."

Thirty-five

"I'll come with you as far as the spoke." Stone's voice and footsteps sounded behind me in the corridor. Lorna's back retreated the other way, her heels echoing faintly on the deck.

"Aren't you staying here?" I said. "Security will need you to help coordinate with Admin departments."

"Maybe I don't agree with what you think I should do." His sullen tone sat strangely with his neat appearance, his gray suit as crisp as when I saw him on the broadcast this morning.

This morning seemed a long time ago and I knew I only looked a lot messier. The coarse, recycled material of my dark blue ConFleet uniform was rumpled around knees and elbows, and my face was probably paler under the coolant-poisoning blotches.

"Please yourself." I kept walking, setting out in my mind what I needed to do before talking to Venner.

My job was to keep her occupied while Murdoch and the others got ready to coordinate the attack on the Q'Chn. I hoped I'd be able to persuade Venner to leave and take the Q'Chn with her. Our attack on them might fail, and it would certainly damage the station, so persuading her to leave was a better alternative. The other worry was the

Q'Chn in *Vengeful* and the fighters. If they decided to defy Venner and mutiny, we could do nothing.

Venner could take Serat, too, and in that event I hoped he drove her as mad as he'd driven me. He must be made to disconnect *Farseer* from our core, though. Soon our outdated blocks would begin to fail—they'd been designed to defeat basic Tor systems, not a hybrid Invidi/Tor identity—and Jocasta's opsys would start to malfunction. This time there would be no easy reinitialization from the core or the ring fallbacks. I thought of the troubles we'd had setting up the station and little shivers of panic began to run around in my stomach. There had been no resident population in the early days when persistent containment failure, atmospheric leaks, and poison gas alerts, all caused by Tor mischief, plagued the station. The idea of all that happening again with the present population . . .

"I'm not happy about these decisions taken without higher authority," said Stone.

I started. He was still there, walking with me.

"If we sit around waiting for higher authority, we'll never do anything," I pointed out. "And besides, if you want to ask higher authority, you won't get one of your secret message buoys past the Q'Chn ships."

His jaw set stubbornly. It made his face look squarer and, paradoxically, more vulnerable. "I was only doing my job as I saw it. The same as you."

"My first duty was always to the station."

"Maybe if you'd thought about larger politics more, the station wouldn't be in such a mess."

"Right now we have to get rid of the Q'Chn."

But his words echoed uncomfortably in my head. I said that my first duty was to the station, but why then, had I pursued the *Calypso II* project to the extent of shutting out my friends and lying to my colleagues? Why hadn't I surrendered *Farseer* to ConFleet immediately? It would have kept An Serat, the New Council, and the Q'Chn away from Jocasta.

My problem was not that I should think more about larger politics—I needed to think less.

Stone tugged the collar of his suit straighter. "Do you really think Murdoch will be able to destroy three of the same creatures that took over a ConFleet cruiser? What if he fails and they come looking for revenge on the rest of us?"

"We'll at least have tried, won't we?"

His eyebrows rose in a horrified arc.

I rubbed my neck. "He won't attempt it unless there's a good chance of success. I know Murdoch—he won't put anyone's life in danger to prove a point. And hopefully we won't have to try his plan. Captain Venner may realize her best bet lies in leaving now."

We passed a crowd of people chatting around a snack dispenser; a series of shelves and slots in the corridor wall that provided a limited range of food and drinks. A savory smell rose tantalizingly with the steam from cups of soup. Suddenly I felt light-headed with hunger. The pale EarthFleet-blue walls were too bright and my head felt disengaged from the rest of my body.

"Lend me your ration card, would you?" I stopped and held out my hand to Stone.

"What?"

One of the people turned around. "Commander Halley? Nice to see you back."

I focused on her. Human, EarthFleet uniform open at the throat, curly hair pushed back from a high, rounded forehead.

"Ensign Zubaideh," my memory supplied.

She smiled. The other three EarthFleeters sipped and watched politely.

"Can I get you something?" said Zubaideh.

I glanced at Stone; he was rigid with disapproval. "I'd love some soup, if you don't mind."

"Any particular flavor?"

"Whatever you're having."

She tapped a combination, her long fingers moving too quickly on the input pad for me to see what. "The news said you were back. But then we heard a rumor that you'd been taken to *Vengeful*."

"Which news is that?"

She passed me the cup of hot liquid. "*The Voice*. You know, it used to be Dan Florida's service."

"Thank you."

"Are you back permanently?" said one of the others, a young man with a quiet air. He placed his empty cup in the recycle slot.

"Commander Halley is here temporarily," said Stone. He smiled insincerely at the ensigns. "She's on her way back to Earth."

"Oh," said the young man.

Zubaideh glanced from Stone to me. "I guess we're lucky you are here now. I mean, we beat the Q'Chn last time, so we can do it again. Come on, guys. Back to the consoles. Nice to see you again, Commander."

"You too, Ensign." I nodded to the others and they left, returning down the corridor we'd come along.

I swallowed a mouthful of soup too quickly and burned my tongue. But it tasted good. Not sure what it tasted of, kind of something-and-corn. With crunchy bits that probably weren't anything as mundane as croutons. The deck began to feel solid under my feet again.

"You beat one Q'Chn last time," said Stone accusingly. "Only one. And that was by luck, I read the report. You lured it into an airlock. But if it hadn't followed you, it could still have killed more people in the rings and you couldn't have done anything to stop it. Now we've got three here and dozens out there."

"You called me 'Commander,'" I said. "Not 'ex-Commander.'"

"Slip of the tongue. They wouldn't listen to me anyway. They think you're the one who's going to lead us out of this mess."

Like I expected Marlena Alvarez to be as much of a leader for people in the past as she'd been for me here. But she wasn't. And the EarthFleet ensigns didn't realize the truth about me—that I was even less of a leader than Alvarez.

"The mess you got us into," persisted Stone.

I remembered on the May Day march, saying to myself, "If Marlena was here, she'd pull them together." Maybe she would have, maybe not. But one thing was for certain, if nobody had believed in her, there wouldn't have been any EarthSouth movement and we wouldn't know about her now.

"I don't want your job, Rupert," I said. "Leaders are greatly overrated. They're just someone who goes first. It's the people who follow after who are important."

"You're not getting my job," he growled. But he seemed to relax a little.

I pushed my empty cup beside the others on the recycle shelf and wiped my mouth with the back of my hand. "I've got to go up to the center. If you've something important to say, tell me now."

He raised his eyes from where he'd watched my hand wipe itself on my trousers. His air of distaste reminded me of Henoit, which made me smile, as two more unlike individuals couldn't be imagined. "No, it's not important."

"Good, see you later."

I glanced back as I turned into another corridor. He'd gone. I didn't have the energy to wonder what he meant.

The implant was aching again and I found myself scratching, imagining what it would feel like to tear it out, like I'd often done during the blockade when the Seouras actively used the implant to communicate with me.

Maybe the Tor elements of *Farseer* regarded Serat and myself as kinds of alien technology—we are biological machines, after all. That could explain why using it had become progressively more uncomfortable for me.

So why hasn't it succeeded in taking me over? I can imagine Serat protecting himself, but a human should be easy game for a Tor ship, especially if it was aided by its Invidi elements with their biological engineering expertise. Unless . . . the Seouras implant is actually protecting me.

I chuckled aloud at this, and an overalled technician carrying a tool case stared at me as he passed.

The Seouras in the gray ship resisted the Tor for a long time, even before the ship came to blockade Jocasta. They tried desperately to get off the ship and to contact us. In the end, after the battle near the station, the gray ship steered into Abelar's sun. The official report suggested its navigational system had been damaged in the battle, but I'd always suspected that the few remaining Seouras took the only way to make sure the ship wouldn't escape.

If it is protecting me from the Tor elements of *Farseer,* my implant might be making up at last for all the discomfort it's caused.

When I reached the uplift entry, I called the New Council ship's dock directly. Standing in front of the control panel at the spoke, I remembered the last time I'd waited for the uplift—with Constable Caselli, who had died in front of the Trade Hall in Alpha. I could understand Murdoch's despair and his insistence on making sure the Q'Chn couldn't kill again.

"Halley to see Captain Venner. I'm using the Alpha uplift, then the Section One crawler. Make sure it's clear."

The captain is busy. She can't see you. The voice whispered with an Achelian lisp—probably the one who'd stood beside Venner in her message of defiance to the Q'Chn.

"She must see me. I have information she needs." I hoped my Con Standard was urgent enough.

The Achelian paused. A loud blur of voices in the background. *You may come,* it said eventually. Sourly.

The uplift rose, I drifted. Twisting to reorient my feet to what would become the floor when we reached the center, I squished my nose against the window to see if I could make out any extra activity around the lower center bays where Murdoch would now be preparing his trap. I couldn't see the bay, as it was on the other side of the center, and the only movement around the docks came from a couple of cleaning droids crawling slowly across the surface of the upper levels. The New Council freighter sat clamped motionless to her airlocks, far "ahead" or "above," depending on where you were in the uplift.

There was plenty of movement down near the rings, however. Every sweeper ship we had, every little salvage drone, took position in staggered ranks between Alpha ring and the center. The pale surface of the ring looked mottled, as though it had suddenly grown a vigorous mold culture. Several small, round robot ships patrolled up and down the spoke closest to Sigma 41. They would spread a "net" of laser beams between each other to catch small bombarding particles.

If Venner had time to look, which I doubted, she'd hopefully think this was routine maintenance. If not, surely Veatch and Stone between them could come up with a plausible excuse.

The uplift ceiling became wall, then floor. Gravity field was on. Wonder if they've kept a guard outside the lift.

The doors swished open and I was looking at a Q'Chn. It peered in the doorway, filling it completely, as I scrambled backward until my back slammed into the window, nowhere to go in this clear-walled coffin . . . I saw in my mind the lazy slice of those slashing forearms as it disemboweled people like me. Decks slippery with red.

Someone shouted behind the Q'Chn. It disappeared, and the long-limbed, furry form of an Achelian took its place. "Hurry," he said. "We do not have all night."

I let my knees give way until I was sitting on the floor of the uplift. My heart's getting too old for this sort of thing.

The Achelian rapped his nails irritably on the door. "Come on, ConFleet. You want to see the captain?"

Behind it, a scratchy, rustling sound and a faint clang, as though a blade hit metal. As though the Slasher was sharpening its blades on my station walls. But it stayed next to the uplift, hunched there like a rainbow-colored gargoyle. Or angel.

I picked myself up and wobbled after the Achelian, mind blank with relief. Then as we rounded the corner I had to quash a desire to curl up in a corner and cry. Stop it, you're alive. And a good thing you emptied your bladder after the meeting, eh?

Murdoch would have to make sure the three Q'Chn entered his trap together. I hoped he'd factored in the time they would take to move through the center levels.

At the airlock an armed guard watched me while the Achelian went to get Venner. I avoided his eyes and tried to regain some equilibrium. It was such an effort to think how I'd deal with the New Council. So many things to remember, and I was tired and shaky and the damn implant itched, worrying about what *Farseer* was doing to Jocasta's opsys was giving me a headache, or was that because last time I'd had a proper rest was a century ago and I really felt a hundred years old right now.

Venner stepped out of the airlock and waved the guard

back into the ship. I need no help with this human, said the gesture.

"Getting ready to leave?" I said.

Outwardly she was perfectly calm, but something was wrong. Instead of the usual flush of well-being from the pheromones, it felt as though I'd stood under a cold shower. The hairs stood up along my arms and the edges of my scalp.

I took an unconscious step back, away from the tension, and tried again. "Time's running out, Captain. ConFleet could be through that point at any minute."

"ConFleet are cowards," said Venner without heat. "At this moment their admirals are drawing lots to see who will die so the others can come in safely."

"Do you believe that?"

She twitched her shoulder irritably. "It is what I tell my crew. But certainly the first ConFleet crews through that point will die. And then *Vengeful* waits for those following. Unless the Confederacy decides to leave you to the wolves again," she added slyly.

I thought of Barik and his desire to keep *Farseer* away from An Serat. "Not this time. Last time they were waiting for what they wanted. This time it's here already."

"The Invidi. It is him they want, yes?"

"Why do you say that?" I pretended dismay. If Venner thought An Serat was valuable to the Confederacy, she'd try to take him with her. Although I hated the idea of *Farseer*'s technology available to the New Council.

"I went to see him," she said. "I told him we must leave within the fifth-hour."

One-fifth of a Central hour was nearly thirty of our minutes. We might still get her offstation with the Q'Chn and we wouldn't have to blow that storage bay.

"Serat knows we have a duty to take *Vengeful* to our colleagues," she said. "He knows now," she amended.

"Why don't you force the Invidi to go?" I said, not liking myself for saying it.

"He can refuse to jump," she said.

"If he does, he may be killed when ConFleet attacks you." How had the Q'Chn threat from *Vengeful* affected her? Her ship could neither out-run nor out-gun the cruiser. Perhaps she intended to continue her bluff to destroy the Q'Chn genetic material until she was close enough to the jump point for Serat to take her through.

Her nostrils flared in frustration. "I do not understand why he stays. Now his ship is connected to this station."

Connected at our core, eating into our opsys. I rubbed the implant impatiently. "Venner, will Serat disconnect his ship and go with you?"

"He was startled, as though he had forgotten us. I told him we would send a tug down to tow his ship into the hold of mine." She took a step closer to me. Too close. The deck rocked under my feet and I had to blink to retain focus on her narrow, intense face. My inhibitor was being overwhelmed by the pheromones.

"What is so important about his ship?" said Venner. "It seems to cloud his mind. He is not worried about being caught here by ConFleet."

"All I can tell you is that if you let Serat connect that ship to your freighter, it will probably take over your systems as it's trying to do to ours."

Her face was still, her eyes slid up to almost meet mine, then flicked away again.

"Henoit didn't trust any of the Four," I said. This might be my last chance to get information from her. "Why are you so friendly with An Serat?"

"When he contacted us again, An Serat said that he pretended to effect a reconciliation with the other Invidi after Henoit's death." She pronounced the name as I did this time, but awkwardly. "He said the Confederacy Council is disordered, ConFleet grows soft. He suggested a strike on our borders and offered to transport us here."

Serat had betrayed them again to get hold of *Farseer.*

"I see why Henoit did not trust the Four," she said. Her voice held no bitterness but something in her scent changed.

"Did you know Henoit well?" I had to ask.

Her eyes focused on a point close to my forehead. "There are not many H'digh in our fleet, although many work for us on Rhuarl. I knew him well."

"Did he ever speak of me?" As soon as the question was out I regretted asking it. What a sentimental . . .

"He behaved as a fully bonded adult," she said. "He accepted no lesser relations when separated from his bond mate." She paused. "I think you do not wish me to tell you how to break that bond."

"I . . ." I did want to be rid of Henoit's unpredictable presence. But what if H'digh beliefs were right and his soul would then wander in eternal loss?

"It doesn't matter now."

She waited, then when I said nothing more, raised her shoulder and turned away. "Wait here." She swung around, strode to the airlock, and disappeared inside.

I waited, wiped sweaty palms, and wondered what was happening inside the core, what was happening over in Sigma 41. Venner would be trying to contact the three Q'Chn onstation. Which she should not be able to do, if our plans were working. I had asked Lee and the communications techs in the Bubble to block Venner's signal to the Q'Chn, any way they could. I'd also asked them to use the same frequency and code that the Q'Chn on *Vengeful* used to signal Venner's ship, and make up a message telling the three Q'Chn to wait in Sigma 41 to be picked up by a shuttle from *Vengeful,* to rejoin their comrades.

One minute passed. Two. Three. I paced, chewed my fingernails, wondered if I should go now in case Lee had failed and Venner was now calling a Q'Chn to teach me a lesson. We didn't know if the conflict between Venner and the Q'Chn was a normal part of their partnership or not. If she thought the Q'Chn endangered her ship and the New Council, she might be willing to leave the Q'Chn here with us, and risk further ruining the New Council's reputation. In that case, she might tell the Q'Chn on *Vengeful* that I had taken the research material, so that they wouldn't follow or attack her. I hoped they wouldn't believe her—surely they would have realized by now that Venner had lied to them about members of the Four not being onstation. I hoped they would hold a grudge, in the way the two Q'Chn in Alpha had punished Security for allowing their K'Cher prey to escape.

The airlock door opened and Venner emerged. She held herself straight.

"We will leave, and the Invidi may come if he wishes," she said, each word slow and considered. "The jump point is too dangerous. We will hide in flatspace, as we have done before."

"What about *Vengeful*?"

"I think the Q'Chn will follow us. They need us, as we need them." Her confidence was untouched. "Can we not persuade you to join us?" Her face was expressionless, but her eyes seemed to burn a deeper amber as they almost met mine, then flickered away. "Form an alliance with us. This system's neutrality can be based in strength."

"Your kind of strength only endangers my station," I said. "Take your Q'Chn and your terrorism and go away. If you do ever want to discuss politics, come without them."

"Until then." She turned again and walked through the airlock doors.

I waited until the doors closed, then sprinted down the corridor. I didn't trust Venner. She'd told me exactly what I wanted to hear. If I were her, I'd be preparing my freighter for a run in flatspace, getting ready to take An Serat by force if necessary, and trying to contact the Q'Chn here on the station in order to do so. I would also make sure I left *Farseer* connected to our opsys, keeping us busy.

I shouldn't have mentioned *Farseer*'s meddling with our opsys.

I wanted to warn Murdoch that Venner would try to reestablish contact with the Q'Chn onstation, but it wasn't worth the risk of Venner tracing our communication and working out what the trap was. He knew she would try, he'd have people ready to prevent the New Council crew reaching the Q'Chn in Sigma 41.

Without control of the Q'Chn either on *Vengeful* or here, Venner was in a far weaker position. She couldn't terrorize us, nor force Serat to leave.

I started running for Level Three on the other side of the center. We had to persuade An Serat to disconnect *Farseer* from Jocasta. If he didn't, the opsys would begin to metamorphose into Tor matrices. Part of me wanted to let Venner take the Q'Chn and haul Serat away. I could ask Murdoch to call off the plan to kill the Q'Chn. But I couldn't trust Venner, and the Q'Chn posed too great a threat to the rest of the station.

At least, I wouldn't consider it unless I failed to persuade Serat to disconnect *Farseer*. I had less than thirty minutes before Murdoch blew Sigma 41, both to talk to Serat and to get out of the center—theoretically, only the Levels Seven and Nine directly above and below the bay might be affected, but I didn't want to test the theory personally.

On the other hand, the signal to block New Council communication to the Q'Chn might not have worked. The Q'Chn might be coming back to join Venner. And I'd be caught in the middle.

I slowed my pace a little at the thought that the Q'Chn

could be just around the next bend. Panting and wheezing, cursing the way my heart bumped in my chest, I passed the crawler entry, and slid sideways into the narrow maintenance tunnel that ran parallel with the crawler. Quicker than waiting for the crawler itself. And the Q'Chn wouldn't fit inside the tunnel. Then I half crawled, half ran along it until I reached the bright light and higher ceilings of the main corridor. I peered out. Nobody in view, either bipedal or four-legged, so I took a deep breath and walked out.

My comm link beeped at me and I jumped about half a meter into the air.

"What is it?" I hissed, flattening my back against the wall so I could see both ends of the corridor.

Commander, big problem. Gamet's voice. The background noises told me she was in the Bubble. *We're reading a big energy drain in your area. It's hard to tell because the core block is affecting sensors, but I think it's the Invidi ship. The engines are active. I don't know what he's doing, but it's affecting systems all over the station. We're compensating as quickly as we can, but more and more are going down.*

"He's probably using the energy to overcome the blocks." My mind cycled frantically through alternatives.

Do you want a Security detail up there? This was Lee.

"Yes, send a squad up. Anyone you can spare, make sure they're armored for plasma weapons." Whatever Serat had thrown at me, it wasn't a normal plasma weapon, but the armor we did have was the best protection for humans against energy weapons.

"In the meantime, I'll try and talk to him. Any movement from *Vengeful*?"

It hasn't changed position, but several of the smaller ships have left their positions and joined it. The jump point is still covered, though. And the New Council ship is initializing its engines now.

Venner was serious about leaving. The question was whether An Serat would go with her.

Security squad's on its way. Bubble out, said Lee.

Halfway down the corridor was the bay where I'd left *Farseer.* The doors vibrated gently and if I put my ear to them I could hear an uneven hum.

The outer doors opened at once. An Serat hadn't even bothered to lock them. The inner airlock doors refused to open, though, because the dock inside had begun a count-down and the airlock's recognition function could tell I wasn't wearing a suit.

Maybe he was leaving. But Gamet knew the difference between a ship preparing for departure and one merely running its engines. Must be the dock that couldn't tell the difference.

I cursed the interface's efficiency—the functions you need least are always the last to go down—and wrenched open the emergency locker in the floor. Pulled on the first suit that popped out, rammed the helmet on my head, sucked twice to make sure the air intake was clear, and tapped the inner doors open.

Farseer lay tipped on its side, ready for the dock to "kick" it out when the space doors opened. As I'd suspected, they showed no signs of doing so. All the safety lights around the edges blinked green. The growl of the engines filled the space, competing with the roar of filters as they tried to keep the atmosphere breathable.

I hardly recognized *Farseer.* The rounded curves of the Invidi ship had flattened into sharp-edged planes. Instead of a bulbous diamond shape, it was a cut diamond. In the dock's bright spotlights the color, too, had changed. It was now a flat gray, the color of the ships that held Jocasta and the Seouras prisoner for six months. Tor gray.

I swallowed uneasily and clipped my safety lead onto the airlock door in case the outer doors malfunctioned and opened unexpectedly. The blasted suit was too big and sagged around my knees when I walked. It felt like it had been made for someone Murdoch's size.

There was no sign of An Serat in the bay. Inside the ship, probably. I hoped the security detail came soon, and that they brought atmospheric suits.

Farseer's hull felt different. I put my gloved hand on it, hoping to trace the tiny paths that seemed to have opened it before. Instead of the meandering snail-trails, I felt straight ridges that intersected with each other at angles, etched deep into the hull. And the thoughts . . . I jumped back, shaking my head to clear it. The thoughts from *Farseer* had an edge. The link jarred on my mind like vibrations jarring sore teeth. I could almost hear a voice, like I'd heard from the Seouras. The implant in my neck itched and throbbed.

"Open up!" I yelled. "An Serat, we have to talk!" Then I put my hand on the ridges and thought about openings, on the principle that *Farseer* might still have the memory of how it worked last time. Serat had blamed my ease of access on the Tor elements, so hopefully I could still get in.

Farther up the hull, a small square opening appeared. I stood next to it and yelled inside for Serat. No answer. The engine noise increased a level or two. Now I couldn't hear myself shout. I stepped back and peered at the airlock indicator. No sign of Security.

Oh, what the hell. I unclipped the safety lead and climbed into *Farseer.*

Thirty-six

Farseer had changed inside, also. The same cabin features were now lit by a sharp, blue-white light that I'd seen before—on the gray ships. The consoles still integrated seamlessly with walls but now the material was smooth and hard under my boots.

An Serat stood right in the middle of the cabin, so big that he blocked my view of the other end.

I squinted in the glare and checked behind me—the square opening had shut. I also checked the atmospheric indicator on my helmet before taking it off. I didn't trust *Farseer* anymore.

"Are you leaving?" I said. Foolish hope that by saying so I could make it true.

Serat's tentacles twitched and the outside of his suit shivered. Otherwise, no response.

"Please leave," I said. "Your experiment is killing my station and endangering everybody on it. Whatever the reason, it's not worth this."

"You understand nothing." The words grated from his voicebox, as unlike his usual smooth tones as the new *Farseer* was unlike the old.

The hot rush of anger surprised me.

"I know I don't." I yelled the words at him. "And it's

not important if I don't understand. That's what *you* don't understand."

"Understanding is all." His whole body twitched and the silver-coated tentacles curled and uncurled.

"It's not all, not for us. Before that, we need to have a place to go home to every night and we need to be able to sleep there in peace. We need to be able to wake up and look forward to living the rest of the day in safety. Then we can think about knowledge."

He said nothing.

I was breathing fast and deep, as though I'd been running a marathon. "Don't threaten our safety here. Please leave, either on your own or with the New Council, or give yourself up to An Barik when he comes."

His voicebox echoed, overlaid with a metallic twang. "Barik does not understand."

"You must power down and get this ship out of the station," I said. "You're draining our energy reserves." As I spoke, I sidled over to what had been the main console. A quick glance told me the controls were in the same place, but there seemed to be more of them. I put my hand out, then withdrew it quickly. Nothing visible, but prickles ran along my fingers.

"Look at this ship now. It's more Tor than Invidi. What's it done to you?" I could take a guess—it was treating Serat as part of the ship, a biological machine to be conquered, as the gray ship had done to the Seouras. Or tried to. I put my hand over my implant, protectively this time.

"I am as always." Serat's new voice grated on my nerves, like *Farseer*'s new thoughts grated on my mind.

"Don't you see? By allowing the Tor technology to regain its power, you let it take over you as well. You're becoming what you seek to overcome."

"Not overcome. I take knowledge from all sources. All is power." His voice took on a sly tone that I'd never heard from an Invidi before. It raised the hairs on the back of my neck. As though Serat was a puppet through which another force was speaking.

"I am foremost among Invidi. You know of our K'Cher war." He didn't wait for acknowledgment. "We also know Tor in that path. How do you think," more conversational now, "we defeat the Q'Chn? They are soldiers for K'Cher then."

I stood very still. The thud of my heartbeat drowned the irregular purr of *Farseer*'s engines.

"Interested?" Serat swung his tentacles almost carelessly. "Invidi are the only ones who defeat Q'Chn. Not all Invidi. I, Serat, defeat the Q'Chn for other Invidi because I, Serat, understand Tor."

We'd always wondered how the Invidi won against the Q'Chn. If Serat was telling the truth and he used Tor technology to defeat them, *Farseer* could be a valuable weapon in our present fight against the Q'Chn. If we could control it.

"You ask me to leave," he said. "How will you defeat your enemy?"

"We'll manage." As I spoke, I reached out casually to the console. Someone's got to turn this ship off.

An Serat swished one tentacle and his entire suited form glowed. The air crackled with fluorescent flickers between us.

Shit, here it comes. I crouched in futile reaction against the console.

Serat's tentacle slapped down beside me and I twitched uncontrollably as a slight shock ran through the surface. But it was nothing like the time he attacked me in the core.

Serat stood swaying. His tentacle, which was outstretched and fixed against the console, gradually lost tension and slid off. The patina of his suit was dull, fading; something I'd never seen before. It reminded me of what had happened to some of the Seouras in the gray ships—Murdoch and I had found their bodies, life sucked out of them until they were fossilized husks.

I started forward, horrified, then stopped before my outstretched hand touched his graying suit. I couldn't leave him like this. But before I tried to "disconnect" him from *Farseer,* I'd have to power down the engines, reinitialize the dock controls. Disconnect from Jocasta's core . . .

"I'll get you out." I turned to the console. It could have as easily been me caught in the trap. Serat probably wouldn't get me out if our positions were reversed, but that didn't matter.

The controls didn't want to cooperate. Patterns of triangles shifted, formed mazes under my gloves. The simple shutdown sequence became impossibly intricate. On the edge of hearing something seemed to mock me. The same tone that Serat had used.

"Dammit," I said aloud. "*Farseer,* where are you?" Surely the original Invidi elements remained and could beat the Tor, as the Invidi beat the Tor in their long war.

An Serat didn't move. No tremor shook his suit or tentacles. He might be fighting the ship within his mind, but he couldn't help me.

I pulled off one glove slowly and hitched back the too-long sleeve. I'd have to place my hand on the console, as I did when I first entered the cabin with Murdoch in Sydney. But Murdoch wasn't here to revive me if I lost consciousness this time. It took a moment before I could breathe calmly enough to lay my hand on the controls.

The cold was so unexpected that I gasped in shock. Then again as prickles studded my fingertips and ran along my palm. Lines of pain ran up my arm and I blinked uncontrollably. Felt myself jerk away from the console. The ship had merely tasted me, licked the surface of my mind, but

I felt its need to absorb, to take over, to conquer, to turn all others into itself.

I tried to swallow but my throat stuck, dry and sore. How much would the Seouras implant help me? Or was I mistaken and would it provide an opening for the ship to do to me whatever it had done to Serat? I didn't want to end up a gray husk.

I replaced my hand and tried to reach the part of *Farseer* that I could recognize as Invidi. Remember the feeling of the first time I connected; inquisitive, interested. It wanted company.

The pain eased a little. Enough for me to cut the engines. And now I had to try to cut the connection to Jocasta's core . . .

No, said *Farseer.*

I screamed and pulled my hand off the console, sinking into a ball of shuddering horror. Oh shit oh shit, what was it? It stimulated all my fear and pain centers at once no no I can't do it . . . Not and stay sane.

I took some deep breaths, then stood up unsteadily. We'll have to strengthen the block from Jocasta's systems. Or tow the damn thing out with a shuttle and hope the opsys stays up.

You're going to give up? said a familiar voice in my mind. Henoit. He felt very close. The ache in my limbs, the trembling eased. Whenever he was close I felt so well.

You don't often give up.

I shook my head and stepped back from the console, beyond caring that I was reacting to someone who wasn't there.

"I can't. I'm not strong enough."

I am strong.

"You're dead."

That does not make me weak.

I held my head with one gloved, one ungloved hand. How can an imaginary voice help me?

Then I reached out with my bare hand to the console. Whether I received help from imaginary voices or not, I was the one who brought *Farseer* from the past and then from *Vengeful*. It was my greed for knowledge as much as An Serat's that created this whole mess. So it's my job to stop it.

Once again I reached for the Invidi part of *Farseer*. I thought of all the things the Invidi had done to help humans, how many lives their intervention on Earth had saved. I thought of the way they shared their jump drive technology, even if only among the Four. I remembered the wonder and excitement of my early conversations with An Barik when he first arrived on the station.

Stabs of pain ran up my arm and the unspeakable images that attacked me before grew clearer, but something got in the way. A warmth that covered my whole body. The memory of pleasures such as gentle sunlight on bare skin, the sound of a bird warbling, Henoit's hand on my thigh, Murdoch's breath on my cheek . . .

Farseer could not touch me while the warmth was there. But I could reach inside it, past the pain and fear, and find the connections with Jocasta. And find glimpses of a world seen through its senses. So strange that later only a few disjointed images would remain: the way a skin that was not mine stretched against vacuum, a blinding bright landscape of stars not born and those long dead, the mysterious chaotic ballet of the very small . . .

Jocasta as an immense, filigreed life form in its turn supporting other life. A tree was the closest my human experience could come to a metaphor. *Farseer* was attached to the tree with uncountable gray tendrils, and where they touched, the gray spread out into the tree, halting the flow of its sap.

So many connections. I began to pull out the tendrils. One by one. Another, then another . . .

I grew slower, lost sight of the next tendril. Where did it touch? How long had I been doing this? Blurry. Getting cold. Henoit, don't you dare leave me here alone . . .

Enough. He drew back, taking me with him. Not, I hoped vaguely, into eternity yet.

Then I was sinking down against the console, blinking in the light. Had I managed to keep *Farseer* away from the opsys or not? At least I probably bought us some time.

An Serat's massive shape loomed over me. I looked up at it and groaned. Staggered to my feet, stood behind him, and pushed experimentally. The air buzzed and sizzled around us. Too tired. I should sit down now and take a breather. Not cold anymore. Warm in here. So warm I was panting.

My heart jumped as something urged me to get up. *Move,* said Henoit's voice. Confused, I scrambled to my feet.

Then it hit me. I was getting short of breath. The ship— I couldn't call it *Farseer* anymore—was depressurizing the cabin. I fumbled the helmet, nearly dropped it, then pulled it on. A couple of deep breaths and I was lucid again.

Serat, have to get him out. I pushed him again. He moved, but in one piece, like a piece of furniture on wheels. How did he get in through that tiny hatch? I thumped on the side of the cabin with one fist, but nothing happened.

Unwillingly, I laid my palm against the cold surface again. Think of an exit, a big one. It hurt, all over, worse and worse and worse until I couldn't remember what I was doing . . . Then I got dizzy. Henoit's presence trying to over-lay the other, unpleasant voice of the ship. The cabin spun and I forgot about the pain as I concentrated all my efforts on staying upright. As I did so, a tall section of the hull gaped open, letting in a diagonal stream of light from Jocasta's docking bay so yellow it looked solid.

I snatched my hand away from the hull and shoved An Serat with every scrap of strength I had. Not fast enough, he barely moved. Henoit, if you're going to be useful, you could give me a rush of H'digh strength . . . But all I had were overstretched human muscles. Quick, before the door shuts. *Push* . . . Serat rocked forward and out. I nearly fell flat behind him on the deck of the ship but managed to scramble through after him as fast as I could.

An Serat had tipped over on the deck of the landing bay. How to get him to the airlock? I looked at his silver bulk hopelessly, when a movement caught my eye. A Security squad was running from the airlock toward us. The thud of their boots vibrated under my feet.

"Can you carry him out?" I waved at the leader and pointed to the Invidi. The leader gave me a thumbs-up and a male voice echoed acknowledgment in my suit's earpieces.

The eight of them—Murdoch must have left parts of the rings unpatrolled to get this many—slid an emergency stretcher from the airlock lockers, rolled Serat onto it, and trotted him out of the bay.

I followed more slowly, trying to get my breath. The warmth of Henoit's presence was gone, and I felt cold and shaky. Thank you, I said inwardly. Hoping, perhaps, for a response, but none came.

The ship's engine hum had ceased. I might have bought us some time, but we had to get it out now.

"We came into the bay," explained the leader of the Security squad when I joined them in the corridor. "But we couldn't get into the ship and it seemed to be powering up to leave, so I got my people back in the airlock." Sergeant Desai, a squat, powerful man with elegant dark brows, spoke slowly and precisely. His helmet sat on his shoulder, as mine did, but the others kept theirs on.

"Glad you're here." I nodded at the Invidi. "He's too heavy for me."

Desai nodded solemnly. "I've never seen one of them down. Makes you confused when you don't know if he's on his face or his back."

"We should all get down to the rings," I continued. "If the deck down in Level Eight blows . . ."

The team were busy fixing maglev lifters onto An Serat's stretcher.

I tapped my comm link. "Halley to Gamet."

Gamet here.

"The engine's off. I tried to cut it loose from the opsys, but I can't do anything more from inside. See if we can set up an automatic launch. And try to redo the block."

Understood.

"Bubble, this is Halley. Level Three Dock temporarily secure. Lee, how are the others going?"

The New Council freighter is standing off from the dock now. Although we're getting confused readings from the sensors up there.

So much for Venner sending a tug to get *Farseer*. She would, as I suspected, leave it to destroy us. "Keep a close eye on it. And *Vengeful*?"

It's moving in a bit closer, but not much. Looks like they're waiting to see what the freighter does.

The immediate problem was the Q'Chn onstation. "And Chief Murdoch?"

Last message we had from them was five minutes ago. They said the Q'Chn are being slow, but responding as hoped. Lee sounded cool as *Farseer*'s new skin. *We monitored an armed group heading from the New Council freighter down in the Section Two uplift and Security was standing by, but the uplift kept cutting out on them and in the end they went back to the center.*

I imagined the New Council crew panicking at the prospect of being left on the station. Venner had probably sent them to check if the Q'Chn had gone hunting K'Cher in Alpha.

"Good. I'm going down to the rings with Desai's squad and An Serat. We're near the Section Two spoke, so we'll use it."

Mr. Stone and Constable Guadalupi called in a little while ago. Said they were having trouble in Hill West with people wanting to use the spoke.

Hill West was the area in the lower ring on one side of the Section Two spoke.

"We'll go right down, then, and give them some backup. Halley out."

When I looked around to check on the team's progress with the stretcher, An Serat was upright. The suited Security people were standing a respectful couple of meters back from him, which put them behind and in front of him in the corridor.

His suit was still unnaturally dull and his tentacles hung lifelessly from his lower torso.

I approached cautiously. "An Serat? Are you all right?"

No response. I stepped closer until all I could see was his suit. Close up, it resembled *Farseer*'s original skin—minute indentations in the surface forming patterned trails.

"Can you hear me?" I said louder.

He might have swayed slightly. Or it could have been me.

"What's wrong?" said Desai behind me.

I stepped back to join him. "Shock, I think. Whatever it is, we need to get him moving. If I walk in front, can a couple of you give him a bit of a nudge from the other side? That way we can get to the crawler and down to the uplift entry."

But it was too slow this way, and in the end three of Desai's people grabbed more maglev carriers from the closest locker and half-ran with An Serat down the corridor to the crawler. Nine humans squished into the walls and each other to give the Invidi room, An Serat's bulk held at a 45-degree angle that made me queasy to look at. Down more corridors on Level Six, the Invidi swaying, and into the uplift at last.

Maneuvering An Serat's still-unresponsive bulk around to face the other way in the few minutes of micro-g before the ceiling became floor took so much concentration and coordination between us all that nobody had any time to look out the windows for the New Council freighter. I doubt we would have noticed unless the Q'Chn began slashing their way through the uplift casing.

In the minutes before we reached Delta the other humans quickly shed their atmospheric suits and packed them efficiently into tiny parcels. I took mine off, but ended up with a crumpled mess as I was trying to also keep one eye on Serat, and listen to Lee's update on the New Council movements at the same time.

The freighter's holding position above the center. Could be one of their shuttles is still in the bay and they're waiting to rendezvous.

I didn't like the sound of this. Why would Venner leave some of her people here?

"You haven't detected any active devices in it?" It didn't seem likely Venner would sabotage the station, but it was possible.

Nothing on sensors. We'll keep monitoring.

Venner might still be trying to contact the three Q'Chn we'd called to Level Eight. It looked like she'd given up on Serat.

I didn't want to call Murdoch, in case it disturbed their operation. Hurry up, Bill. The sooner you get rid of the Q'Chn, the sooner we can go up and get *Farseer* out of there.

Then the uplift doors opened in Hill West and it felt like we were in the middle of a riot.

Thirty-seven

Not exactly a riot. More what Security officers would call "civic unrest of an unstable and potentially property-damaging nature." That's what met us when we reached the Hill in the lower ring.

The noise was appalling, a babble that spanned several scales and contained voices, grunts, whistles, squeaks, and hoots. Moist heat rolled into the uplift as the doors opened. Wish I'd kept my atmospheric suit on.

At least three hundred people were crammed into the space in front of the uplift, a twenty-meter-wide strip supposed to be kept clear in case of fire or other emergency. The strip was normally filled with stalls, which had been pushed back to a single line beside the buildings, and a mixture of mainly bipedal species milled around.

When I stepped out with Sergeant Desai, the people closest to the lift nudged their neighbors and someone said something, of which I only caught the word "ConFleet." Following us, two of the constables pushed An Serat from behind and one guided him in front. The other three began to move through the crowd, nodding greetings at some faces and projecting an aura of calm and control.

Most of the crowd seemed to be enjoying the opportunity to get together. On my left, four humans in dirty overalls shared a plate of steaming Garokian dumplings. The aroma of the dumplings rose enticingly from a stall almost at the uplift door. A Garokian face beamed in imitation of a human smile behind the counter.

Directly in front of me I could see more humans, one of whom carried a flag on a short pole. The flag, a red and yellow design used by the dockworkers union, drooped into his eyes and he flicked it away irritably, and continued arguing with his companions. Two Achelians picked their way delicately among the crowd, fans raised to protect their noses from smells, eyes alert. I recognized them as the proprietors of a recycling center in Gamma ring.

Farther into the crowd I could hear a low, monotone chant, an appeal to one of the station's many deities. I hoped it was for protection from the Q'Chn. I could also hear a familiar human voice on my right, beyond three broad Tirenni backs.

With Desai a couple of steps behind me I eased past the Tirenni and found Rupert Stone confronting a group of ten or twelve humans, three Dir, and a tall Leowin.

"The Leowin's a troublemaker," whispered Desai at my shoulder. "Its name is Inash, and it's a professional crowd-stirrer. The Dir have probably paid it to do the dirty work because they're angry at the disruption of business. That bald human in the heavy transport overalls . . ."

The man in question listened stolidly to Stone, his arms folded.

"He was the secretary of the dockers union," continued Desai. "Got fired for taking bribes, altering files. He can't get a work permit anywhere else, so he stays here."

I nodded, then waved to Stone and called his name, giving him a big smile as well. At the sound of my voice, pitched to construction-site volume, the Leowin Inash swung around with a quick, guilty movement and Stone's eyes widened. He was drenched in sweat, his suit as limp as the anti-Q'Chn red banners that stuck to the sides of the buildings.

"Mr. Stone," I called again. "Nice to see you holding the fort." By then we were standing beside them.

"Com . . . Governor Halley." Stone shook the hand I offered him, puzzled. "I came down here to talk to the Dir trade rep, then the constable asked me to come along and give him a hand."

"Public-spirited of you," I said, wishing he'd play along and that he didn't look so nervous. Nothing to be nervous about.

"I am the head of station, you know."

"Is it a festival or something?" I looked around, smiling as I met the eyes of the closest humans.

"It iss a rally," said Inash. Its voicebox was positioned right near its mouth, which gave the impression it talked like a human when in fact its real voice came from farther down its torso. "We are protesting the lack of respect and consideration shown to uss by the administration of thiss station."

I tried to appear shocked. "Is that so? All of you?"

"Yess."

"I think some of them want to go and complain to the New Council," said Stone. "I was pointing out to them when you came that we can't allow all of them to protest in person. They can go through proper channels and we can forward the protest . . ."

"The real problem," snarled one of the Dir, "is that we've lost days of business."

"The real problem," said the bald human in faultless Con Standard, "is that the New Council think they can get away with it." His eyes, narrowed in anger, met mine. "I think we should tell them to leave."

"We've done that," I said. "They're leaving now, so you can all go home."

"What about the Invidi, then?" he said. "I thought being neutral meant we didn't have to put up with them, either?"

Rivers of sweat ran down my ribs and tickled under my shirt. I should have left An Serat in Alpha. "We don't. This one's staying to . . ." I hesitated.

"Assist us with our inquiries," put in Stone.

"And he's injured," I added. "We're looking after him."

At the back of the crowd there was a commotion. A crash and thud, as though a stall had been knocked over, followed by raised voices.

I could see Serat over the heads of the crowd. He was halfway between us and the uplift, the two green uniforms beside him.

More voices raised at the back of the crowd. An altercation about treading on someone's feet.

". . . so you see," Stone was saying, "it's no use you going up to the center anyway. The New Council isn't there."

I hoped he remembered we weren't publicizing Murdoch's proposed explosion. There'd be an announcement immediately afterward, but we didn't want people to panic or, more likely, try to get ringside seats.

There was a scuffle in the crowd behind the Tirenni. Desai cursed. Inash, the human group, and the Dir scattered, and the crowd parted. Two lines of armed soldiers confronted us. No, not soldiers. These wore scruffy fatigues and unmatched armor.

It was only when Venner strode forward that I realized they were New Council crew. They must have come down in one of the other uplifts while Security was concentrating on the Q'Chn.

"But your ship left." Stone stared at her in disbelief. He obviously hadn't got Gamet's report of the freighter waiting.

"It will." Venner took Desai's hand weapon while one

of her people covered us. The others had fanned out and were shepherding the crowd back from the spoke and uplift, brandishing a variety of weapons. Most of the weapons, I was glad to see, were laser-based and therefore station-safe.

My comm link beeped. *Commander Halley, we picked up one of the uplifts moving down to your area.*

Venner looked at me. Her kesset blade rested at the jaw of one of the constables. "Drop it," she said quietly.

I dropped the comm link without answering or deactivating the pickup. It clattered on the deck. Hopefully the Bubble would catch a little of our conversation.

"Your men are disarmed," she told the sergeant. "Don't try anything brave." She let her kesset drop and pushed the constable away, then turned and raised her voice to the crowd.

"Someone has probably had the bright idea of calling your Security forces. Please don't think we will not take hostages to protect ourselves."

The expressions in the crowd of half disbelief, half curiosity changed to fear, and many of those closest to the New Council weapons turned and tried to burrow into the safety of numbers.

"You'll start a stampede." I stepped out beside her and raised my arm. "Keep calm," I called. "Move back in an orderly way."

It didn't make much difference, although some of those fleeing turned to watch the fun again.

"Why have you risked this?" I turned to Venner. "What if the Q'Chn take your ship while you're here? You'll be marooned here when ConFleet comes."

She pointed with her elbow at An Serat. "I want the Invidi. He is too valuable an ally to leave."

The crowd were almost cleared from in front of An Serat. Reluctantly, at a nod from Desai, the Security constables also stepped back. The New Council crew now formed a little island in the space dominated by the tall silver column of An Serat.

Venner stared at Serat, her eyes narrowed. "What did you do to him?"

I snorted. "He did it to himself."

Venner nodded to the members of her crew closest to Serat, who then attempted to shove him in the direction of the uplift.

Serat's suit remained dull gray. His tentacles swayed, but his lower half seemed fixed.

"Who the hell does she . . ." began Stone.

"Enough," said Venner. H'digh didn't waste time gloating. She left the knife in her hand and called, "Get him in the lift."

"We're trying," grumbled the woman pushing Serat.

What had happened to Murdoch? If Venner had been successful in preventing our communication with the Q'Chn, she mightn't say so. But if Murdoch had blown up the Q'Chn, Lee should have told me. And we'd feel some vibration.

Venner marshaled her people with a wave of the arm. She strode over to Serat and pushed him herself, ignoring the shifting crowd. Two of her people kept their weapons trained on the Security personnel.

"We can take them." Desai tried to murmur in my ear against the racket of the alarm.

Venner's voice said something about maglevs.

"With what?" Stone had overheard. "Didn't you have enough casualties in Alpha?"

We had too many casualties, I thought. We needed Venner out of here as quickly as possible and nobody hurt. Then they'd leave and hopefully the Q'Chn on *Vengeful* would follow. Not that I wanted ConFleet to lose *Vengeful*, but it was better than having the Q'Chn threaten us.

And the sooner we got rid of the New Council, the sooner we could properly disconnect *Farseer* from Jocasta's opsys. I wanted that ship disabled and towed out to one of the orbital platforms.

We couldn't afford to have Venner hang around waiting for An Serat. What if he woke up and decided he didn't want to go with them? We'd have more delays, the Q'Chn on *Vengeful* might interfere, we'd have more casualties. No, we had to get rid of Venner quickly. She'd have to leave Serat here.

"We don't want the New Council here," I shouted. "Not when you bring Slashers to terrorize us." I waved my arm at the crowd, looking for the crowd leaders—the Leowin and the bald human.

The human stood, arms still folded, on the edge of the crowd closest to Serat and the New Council members. I couldn't see the Leowin.

Venner stopped pushing and looked over the open space between us. A calculating stare.

"There are a lot more of us than of you," I said. "Why don't you go while you can?" The crowd muttered among themselves. An ugly sound of agreement.

Venner pointed her weapon obviously at me. Then swung it to cover targets in the crowd encircling her. Shit, I thought, bad move. She'll do it.

But instead of cringing back, as she probably expected, many of them yelled curses. Maybe not a bad move.

"Have it your own way." Venner fired at a point in front of them. A circle of sparks about the width of a human fizzed as the laser ignited dust on the deck. Dirty smoke drifted upward.

She could have actually killed someone. Either she's squeamish, which is unlikely, or she thinks a death will push the crowd to attack, and she can't fight a pitched battle and get away in time. I didn't think the Hill crowd would do that—they'd melt away, as usual, more than likely. Yet I had to ask myself if she did kill someone, whose fault would it be?

"You see, ex-Commander." Venner kept her weapon pointed at the crowd. Some of them moved restlessly but nobody broke the rough line around the edge. "When it comes down to the final confrontation, nobody is prepared to go first. Because they know that whoever does, will die. This is why you need us—you need the New Council because we are not afraid to go first. Forget your squeamishness about the Q'Chn. Without us, there is no revolution."

"You're wrong. We don't need you." I stepped forward across the deck. Once I'd gone one pace, the rest was easy. Simply a matter of putting one foot in front of the other. Again and again until I stood between Venner and the crowd. Exposed in the open.

Everything went quiet.

Venner dipped her head and when she raised it, the weapon in her hand rose, too. Bluff called. Glad I'm so calm about it. Glad I told Murdoch I needed to know he was all right.

Somebody coughed loudly. Rupert Stone stepped out from beside Desai. He began to walk toward me, his pale eyes bulging with fright.

The bald man and another woman from the far edge of the crowd stepped forward, too.

One of Venner's people cursed loudly.

Out of the corner of my eye I saw Desai's hand move in a signal. I twisted around, trying to signal him not to attack. We want them to leave.

Venner snapped an order behind her.

The fire alarm went off.

The rising *whee-whee-whee* fell into the relative silence

like a bomb. Long flashes of warning lights flickered over-head.

"Oh, my God." Stone reached me, grabbed my arm.

I grabbed his, and dragged him away from the imme-diate range of Venner's weapon. We backed toward the crowd. No need to carry bravado too far.

Venner dropped into a half crouch and her eyes swiftly scanned the area. She backed toward her people, who were clumped together around Serat.

The cannier members of the crowd began to ease to-ward the sides of the throughway and back into the build-ings, remembering the last extinguisher "test." In the center, the bald man and the woman who'd stepped forward from the other side of the crowd had been joined by three, five, ten, twenty more. They all stayed put, as if reclaiming the area from the New Council.

This alarm wasn't supposed to activate. Murdoch was merely using the extinguisher system up on Level Eight to effect the explosion. We hadn't felt any vibrations—then again, we'd never blown up part of the center and I wasn't sure how much of the shock would transmit to the rings.

I managed to catch Desai's eye at last. He made a sweep-ing motion with one hand. I took it to mean stay back, or down, or something. I shook my head, meaning, don't at-tack them.

Venner wouldn't abandon Serat. The New Council crew kept pushing him toward the uplift. They hadn't found maglevs—nobody left tools lying around in the Hill.

The alarm shifted into high gear. Stone was yelling at me but I couldn't hear a thing. Then with a hearty whoosh, the fire retardant sprayed from every outlet. I managed to turn my face away in time, but a large dollop fell on my head and for a moment I was blinded. Someone bumped into me and I stumbled. Someone else bumped into me on the other side.

By the time I wiped enough of the powder-turned-slime off my eyes to see, Desai and his people had taken the opportunity to grapple with the New Council around a still-immobile Serat. The powder would have rendered the New Council's laser weapons useless, at least for the second the Security forces needed to attack. There were several fist-fights going on at once, with members of the crowd joining in, but I couldn't see Venner. I couldn't think, not with that alarm screaming at me. I pushed forward through the scrum of bodies—the rest of the crowd was eager to see the fun. Stone had disappeared. Desai was wrenching the arm of a New Council crew member and trying to keep two excited Garokians from hitting that crew member with the soaking union flag. An Serat seemed rooted to the deck.

Venner was already at the uplift, fighting a rearguard action with three of her crew. She'd finally given up trying to move Serat. She drew a concealed plasma pistol from her vest and fired at a security guard and three burly humans. One of the humans rolled away screaming and holding his arm.

The uplift doors opened. Venner met my eyes for the last time and raised her weapon in salute. The doors closed. I bumped into one of the Tirenni, who pushed me back, and I skidded toward the spoke, thudded stickily against the control panel, and recoiled away in case I hit the uplift controls. We don't want the New Council coming back down. I wanted Venner back in the center, into her shuttle, and away in that freighter.

Stone squelched over to me. His soaked head was as smooth as a seal and his suit jacket hung half off one shoulder. He yelled something at me. The alarm cut off halfway through.

". . . *stop*," he shouted, then in a normal voice. "Can we stop them?"

The controls showed the uplift was going all the way to Level One. It also showed a red warning light on Level Eight. Murdoch's explosion must have taken out the crawler access there. I should feel anxious about Murdoch but after facing Venner's laser, all I felt was astonishment that I was still here. Every action was a bonus. Even talking to Stone felt good.

"We don't want to stop them," I said. "And thank you for backing me up." Bloody good thing he did, I told myself. You were lucky.

He tried to comb retardant out of his eyelashes with fingers already sticky. "You're welcome. Don't bet on me ever doing it again, though."

Serat hadn't responded to the noise and movement around him. His silver suit was streaked with brown from the retardant slime but he just stood there.

I tried to activate sensors on the spoke panel to see what was happening in the center, but my gooey fingers slipped uselessly around the touch pad.

The uplift indicator showed Venner's car had stopped at Level One.

Commander Halley, this is the Bubble. Can you hear me? said Lee's voice in the flat monotone of someone who'd been repeating the same words for a long time. The comm unit on the spoke panel was active.

"This is Halley. How did Level Eight go? Sensors are dead down here."

Lee's voice perked up. *Chief Murdoch just called in. They had a bit of trouble before the end. Signal interference.*

Venner might have been attempting to get her Q'Chn back.

The exercise was a success, he said. They confirmed three bodies.

Stone and I looked at each other. The second victory over Q'Chn since their reincarnation.

"We can't get external sensor readings down here," I said. "What are the New Council ships and *Vengeful* doing?"

The New Council freighter is pulling out now, on a course to the other side of the system. The last shuttle from Level One just reached them.

Venner was on her way.

Vengeful is waiting for all the fighters. Looks like they're pulling back from the jump point.

And the other Q'Chn on *Vengeful* would hopefully go to follow Venner. "Did we pick up any more of their communications?" I said.

Not after the freighter left dock.

"Was there any damage to Level Eight?" Stone leaned over me into the pickup.

The chief says about what they expected. But says more peripheral damage might show up over the next few days.

Stone frowned, no doubt thinking of his repair budget. It wasn't large—I'd been pestering Earth for years to give us more resources for maintenance. And he needn't worry; if Lorna was right, I'd be paying off the repairs for the rest of my life.

"Tell him congratulations from me," I said. "I'm on my way to the Bubble. Tell Gamet we need that autolaunch for Level Three Bay 12. And keep me informed of *Vengeful*'s movements."

Yes, ma'am.

"You know." Stone tugged at my wet sleeve. "As this exercise was under your supervision, you should sign the damage reports."

"But I'm not head of station anymore."

His eyes narrowed. "You don't get out of it that easily.

You took charge because you're governor and therefore the responsibility rests with you."

"We need to sign them together, then."

"No, we don't."

A semihysterical giggle rose in my throat. We'd just averted a major crisis and he wanted to argue about signatures.

The commotion behind us, which had slackened off when the alarm ceased, started again.

"Look out!"

"He's moving!"

"Coming . . ."

A Security whistle gurgled. Both Stone and I spun around, and saw the brownish slime-colored form of An Serat rolling toward us.

"Stay back," I yelled at the constable who was about to stand in front of the Invidi. "He's armed."

The constable stared disbelievingly at me, but she did step back. A babble of voices rose in the background.

I stepped forward to meet An Serat, being careful not to get too close or directly in front of him.

"An Serat."

No response.

"An Serat, it's me, Halley."

His pace slowed.

"We need you to help us get *Farseer*—your ship—away from the station. But please don't use it. The ship has changed. It's too dangerous."

He was about two meters from me when he spoke. His voicebox sounded normal again. "I cannot stop this path . . . I cannot achieve the end without changing."

"You can't beat it. It nearly killed you. You'll just become like it. It's what the Tor do best."

He said nothing, then began moving again, past me to the uplift entry. "If I must become, I must become."

"Is it worth finding that place—what you said—if you're not yourself to know you find it?" I ran around and past him so I reached the entry first. Behind Serat, Stone spread his hands helplessly.

"You know that one of the points destabilized in the past? It could happen again if you use *Farseer*. I'm sure that's what Barik meant."

"I do not see the end." He kept moving until I could have reached out and touched his tentacle.

He stopped and we stood, nose to suit.

"Your end?" I said. "Or the end to this conflict? You said you stopped looking into the future, so of course you can't see anything. This is what being free is, you know. You have to choose. You can't see how things will turn out."

He swung his tentacle away from me. The voicebox tone was changing back to the coldness he'd had on *Farseer*. "I choose to change."

I stepped aside. "Then get off my station."

Serat slapped his tentacle onto the control panel but the lift didn't open.

I nearly laughed. Great, now we want him out of here, the station won't let him go.

The uplift doors opened with a wet swish.

An Serat was in the uplift and the doors clicked closed.

I let my knees finally give way and slid down the curved wall of the spoke. Stone and Desai were talking about what happened, or they were talking to someone on the comm link. I found it difficult to concentrate.

". . . Level Three."

"Intercept if we . . ."

Maybe I was wrong about the unstable point. The radiation could have been from another source or for another reason. Why would the jump point suddenly destabilize? Serat said the Tor had dragged the point back four years to 2122 and thus also to 2023—*Calypso* went through it once, I went through it, Murdoch went through it, and it remained stable. Yet two days after we left Earth, it seemed to have exploded or imploded or disappeared, whatever unstable jumps do. The only thing that could have changed during those two days must have been *Farseer* opening a new point to Jocasta right next to the old one. Murdoch and I had gone past the old coordinates, then jumped. Two jump points next to each other in space. Could that have created the instability? Or maybe it was the way *Farseer* opened the jump, with its Tor technology. Knowing Tor aggression, possibly *Farseer*'s point had interfered with the other in some way.

That still didn't mean it would happen the next time Serat tried to use *Farseer*. Unless he opened a new point next to an old one again.

The voices made me jump. Had I dropped off for a few minutes?

"Halley?" Stone crouched down beside me. "He's getting away."

I focused on him with difficulty. "We want him to get away. We're letting go."

He stared at me and I managed to smile at him. Serat had taken *Farseer*, I'd never get a chance to look at it again. Probably never get a chance to look at a jump drive again. But the Tor threat to Jocasta's opsys was gone, and Stone had stood with me. There were other ways to resist the Confederacy than getting the jump drive.

Ten minutes later I hurried up to the Bubble. After Venner's freighter left Jocasta, Lee had tracked it almost into the asteroid belt that extended to the next planet's orbit. Even ConFleet would find it difficult to follow in there. Closer to Jocasta, *Vengeful* finished taking the fighters on board and started to follow Venner, to everyone's relief.

But then Lee had called me to say *Vengeful* was taking

a detour—to attack *Farseer,* which was also heading away from the station in flatspace.

When I arrived, the atmosphere in the Bubble was more relaxed than earlier today. We'd disposed of the Q'Chn and the New Council threat, after all. And also the threat few of the residents knew about—*Farseer*'s attempt to draw energy from our opsys.

Stone had come up, too, and crowded me as we leaned over Lee's console.

"We thought the Invidi was heading for the Central jump point," said Lee. "But he's turning to head under our planet's orbit. That's the other way from the Central point," she added for Stone's benefit, as he was watching the wrong set of readouts.

"Why is *Vengeful* following him?" said Stone.

"Maybe the Q'Chn want revenge on the Invidi too," said Lee.

She was probably right. The Q'Chn could know nothing of *Farseer*'s special abilities, nor had they shown any inclination to capture an Invidi ship.

On the screen, *Vengeful* fired on *Farseer.* It was nearly in range, pushing *Farseer* off its chosen course.

"If that ship's unarmed," said Lee, "it won't be much of a fight. The cruiser's got more thruster power."

"They've nearly got him," Stone said excitedly.

I shook my head. "He'll jump first."

Lee ran her finger over the screen. "He can't jump, he's going the other way from the point."

"He has to jump," I said. "It's why he uses *Farseer.* He has to jump to get to the between place."

They stared at me, but I didn't mind. "And anyway, he won't go through the Central jump because his enemies are waiting on the other side."

The crew moved around, watched their stations, spoke

in low voices. The Bubble pinged, hummed, hissed, beeped, and now booped around me.

"The place you and Chief Murdoch appeared," said Lee suddenly. She began to tap through navigational records on the adjoining screen. "Dan Florida was here before the New Council came, asking for the exact coordinates."

I compared her results with *Farseer*'s present position. "Didn't think so. They're nowhere near there now."

Murdoch and I opened a new point with *Farseer* at coordinates close to the old *Calypso II* point in 2023, but the two sets of coordinates weren't close in 2122. We'd appeared in *Farseer* on the Central point side of the station, on the outer side of the planet's orbit. But *Calypso* appeared on the sun side of the planet, near a smaller asteroid belt, and I'd left from there in *Calypso II*.

And that was the direction *Vengeful* was chasing *Farseer* right now. I used Lee's adjoining screen to search for the *Calypso* point's exact coordinates. *Farseer* was heading near them, but not right for them. Even so, I felt a coldness on the back of my neck. Surely Serat knew that point would destabilize soon. He'd been on Earth on 16 May when it happened.

"*Vengeful*'s gaining," said Stone. He stood on my toe as he edged around the console to get a better view.

By now the entire Bubble was watching, breathless.

Why didn't *Farseer* retaliate, I wondered. Surely the Tor parts of it could modify existing equipment into a weapon. *Vengeful* was within range now. The Q'Chn were fools, to spend this long chasing one small prey instead of following Venner to safety.

Vengeful fired burst after burst. We could only see it on the tactical display, it was too far away for visual sensors. I looked over at the spectral display. That gave *Vengeful*'s position as a bright patch of light, glowing as each volley was fired. *Farseer* was a different color, steadily burning in a line like a comet as it kept on its course.

An Serat must be trying to get into the asteroid belt and then beyond. But he'll be too late.

Vengeful fired again and *Farseer* made the jump.

It took us all by surprise. One minute the readings were normal, the next, everything rose off the scale. Or dropped, depending on the display.

On tactical, a small whirling dot opened rapidly, *Farseer*'s signal superimposed upon it.

"Shit, that is a jump." The first time I'd heard Lee swear. "You were right."

"Look at *Vengeful*," someone said.

The cruiser veered as quickly as its lateral thrusters would allow, to avoid charging into the jump point. The Q'Chn apparently didn't chase prey that far. But the space they veered into was changing, too.

As the jump point and *Farseer* intensified in its normal burst of radiation, space nearby began to change. Every set of sensor data we had on that area showed massive disturbances. All over the Bubble lights flared and signals blipped.

"Never seen a jump do that," said someone else.

"It's not the jump," said Lee.

On the visual display, the area of space around *Vengeful* seemed to bubble. The stars and nebulae beyond stretched, distorted. A bright ring formed, seeming to enclose it, then dispersed into auroralike shimmering.

"What the . . ." Lee pored over the tactical readouts. "It's some kind of gravimetric radiation, that's all I can tell."

Vengeful's readings had disappeared, swamped in the surge of radiation. The Q'Chn would never get back to the New Council. Ninety-nine years ago this happened in space near the solar system on the other side of the jump point, now it's happening here, on our side.

"Look at the jump point," said Stone. "Is it supposed to do that?"

The tactical showed *Farseer*'s signal, motionless, in a bright spot of jump point also unmoving. For a second I thought the screen had simply frozen. Then the confused distortion of the destabilized point next to it grew larger, reached out and around the frozen whorl of the jump point, sending out amoebic arms as if to embrace it. The jump point and *Farseer* also became blurred, distorted, and started to glow red. For a moment we were looking at a twisting red cloud. It seemed like *Farseer* was trying to free itself. Then the center of the cloud glowed brighter and brighter until the protective cutoff shut down the screen.

We looked away and blinked or rubbed our eyes until the afterimages ceased to block the sight of the Bubble's wall monitors and consoles. One of the ensigns held his hand up in front of his eyes. Stone pressed on his eyelids.

Seconds later the screen came on again and we all craned to see. The red glow was shrinking far more quickly than it grew. Shrank to a dot, winked out. Only dark space remained. An eerily beautiful thing to be the end of a dream.

Epilogue

Murdoch said he'd come to see me after he got through Customs and reentry processing. He was on leave from EarthFleet after staying behind on Jocasta for a week after I'd left. Both my asylum hearing and the processing of EarthFleet charges had to be done on Earth, however much I would have liked to remain on the station.

I waited for Murdoch in Sydney by the bay where the airport used to be, although the runway where the Invidi ships landed was gone. There was a strip of sand surrounded by mangroves and shrubs, like the rest of the bay. The water still winked and glittered in the sunlight as it had on the morning Will died one hundred years ago. The seagulls still swooped, dopplering in and out of earshot.

I'd come to this place because I had something left to do here. In between the asylum hearing, which was successful, and the EarthFleet inquiry, which was not, I'd gone over to Homebush and seen where the out-towns used to be. I said my good-byes to Grace there. Not at her graveside, which was well maintained thanks to Vince's descendants, but in the tidy streets that fronted onto the green expanse of mangrove park that had regrown over the dirt and the chemicals. The best tribute to the out-towns was that they no longer existed.

Lorna was right about EarthFleet—they hadn't been

pleased at the damage we caused to Sigma 41 when Murdoch's plan worked. They refused to take into consideration our effort to save lives on the station, or the positive effect on Confederacy morale of three Q'Chn deaths. They also demanded I repay all the funds used on the *Calypso II* project.

External Affairs had to accept my application for asylum, so I was safe from ConFleet court-martial, but they included a mobility restriction clause, which meant I couldn't leave Earth for a year.

The idea of being stuck on Earth away from Jocasta appalled me, and I almost wished I'd taken my chances with ConFleet. Then when the year was over, the deferred payment for damages to Sigma 41 was waiting. Unless, Lorna said, she managed to get the charge dropped in the meantime. Or unless I joined EarthFleet or some other branch of Earth's planetary government.

A whole year. Stuck here while the station moves on. I couldn't even be there when the neutrality vote went through. After all I went through in the past to get home in time for it. But neutrality passed. Thanks in a large part to Dan Florida's boisterous publicity of the *Farseer* affair—he criticized the Confederacy for meddling in the governance of a neutral star system and the Invidi for interfering in Earth's past. No formal accusations were ever made. But when the votes were counted, Abelar and Jocasta went on record as the only neutrality petition to ever pass without direct support from one of the Four.

Sarkady had voted yes for Earth, but she lost her Council post soon after. The other yes votes were the Dir, Neron, Tell, Achel, H'digh, and, surprisingly, the Leowin. Which left the Four on the no side, plus Stegg and Chehgiru, which were distant relatives of the K'Cher and a Bendarl colony, respectively. Neutrality by one vote, but that one vote was enough.

The Invidi denied all of Florida's accusations and ignored the little evidence we had. They insisted An Serat was acting by himself and that *Calypso* had somehow gone through Central. The gravitational disturbance we witnessed when the jump point destabilized they called an unfortunate result of his experiments. Nobody else was at risk. The idea of off-network jumping was laughable, they said. A theoretical and practical impossibility.

How did Murdoch and I get to the past, then? We could have asked. But there was no proof we did go. The *Calypso II* records were well and truly gone, and Eleanor's medical records were open to interpretation. We agreed not to make a fuss, for the sake of the newly approved neutrality and for the sake of Murdoch's career—he still had one, at least.

And there was plenty to occupy us all in the present. Venner's New Council ship was still somewhere in flatspace. ConFleet hadn't found them yet, but were blaming the New Council for the loss of *Vengeful*. They were demanding stricter penalties for New Council sympathizers within the Confederacy, which were likely to come into effect, so the New Council had achieved little by helping Serat, and they'd lost a large number of Q'Chn. We all hoped they'd think twice before creating more.

I intended going back to Jocasta when my enforced stay on Earth was over, sooner if I could get the decision repealed or the time shortened. I didn't mind being a civilian or employee of the new administration, or whatever. But I wanted to be a part of the new Jocasta.

The interim administration, which was basically the arrangement of Residents Committee, old administration, and staff on loan from EarthFleet, would have to decide whether to take a defense contract with ConFleet. When I spoke with him before I left, Veatch seemed keen to do so. He thought that ConFleet's defeat by the Q'Chn and the loss of *Vengeful* would bring the price down, and they'd also be keen to prove themselves again and therefore extremely efficient.

"How about the New Council?" I said. "Do you offer them docking rights as well?"

Veatch's antennae twitched with shock, but not at the prospect of hosting terrorists. "Any application will be considered if it uses the appropriate protocols."

I thought he might have difficulty getting Rupert Stone to agree with this. To everyone's surprise, Stone had stayed on Jocasta on secondment from External Affairs, as joint acting head with Veatch of the interim administration.

"I couldn't leave things in such a mess," he told me when I asked him why.

"Veatch likes the mess," I said. "He knows exactly where everything is but nobody else does."

"We'll see," said Stone.

I spoke with another old Jocasta resident before I left. An Barik came back to the station and asked to see me. He had escaped through the jump point before the Q'Chn took over *Vengeful,* as we'd suspected. Nobody was particularly pleased to see him again—he'd run away and left us to cope with the Q'Chn. Left us to confront An Serat for him. Barik's behavior made me reflect that although An Serat had his problems, at least he did things for himself.

I said I'd talk to Barik and we met in the half-dismantled "observation lounge" in Level Three of the center. I asked Barik if Serat's research remained, and what he and the other Invidi would do with it.

"The one possesses not," he said.

"Good." I didn't like to feel pleasure at knowledge lost, but if we couldn't have it, I was glad they couldn't either.

"Some of Invidi wish Serat's work. The one does not. Your path-decision is the most open."

"I'm not really glad I helped you," I said. "Do you ever help us? Or is it all part of some self-serving plan?"

"The one is not all Invidi."

"Don't give me that crap." We were still cleaning up after the explosion and the fire extinguisher incident, and I was tired. "You must have known about Scrat's research for decades."

"The one sees only the paths of clarity."

"You mean you didn't know about it?"

He hesitated.

My feet hurt in my new boots so I righted one of the remaining chairs and sat on it. The chairs were lying at various angles all over the room where they'd fallen when the gravity field was restored after the explosion on Level Eight.

"The one moves," he said, "but Serat moves also and evades the one. He is correct in some ways and some of Invidi help him."

"Help him change human history by coming to Earth."

His voicebox sounded puzzled. "Invidi change nothing. Your history is always your history. Invidi cannot change that which is."

He's right, of course. We'll never know what might have happened if the Invidi hadn't come. The only way to change history is when it's happening.

"The one envies you. Your species," said Barik.

I blinked. Envy? The only Invidi I'd ever seen express anything like desire was Serat. As far as we knew, the rest of them were as unworldly as Buddhist saints.

"Why?"

"You possess infinite . . . what you call 'now.' "

"But your people can see further than we can. By the time we've thought of the moment, it's over. And we can't experience the next one until it's here and gone."

"Within one moment all may be."

I swore under my breath and didn't bother to hide my frustration. "I don't understand you. So how about I tell you my theory of what happened, and you can say either yes you're right, or no you're wrong."

He swayed a little. "Acceptable."

"There was one pair of jump points. One of these was at coordinates close to Earth's solar system and one was near Jocasta," I began. "This jump had a ninety-nine-year correspondence. An Serat sent *Calypso* through those points in 2027, so it should have arrived in 2126.

"It didn't, because the Tor ships that were blockading Jocasta in early 2122 dragged the jump point back four years so that *Calypso* arrived at Jocasta in early 2122 instead. There was never a pair of jump points with a ninety-five-year correspondence. It just looked that way."

I paused and contemplated Barik. He might be asleep for all I knew. "How am I doing?"

The answer came immediately, so he wasn't asleep. "Continue."

"You don't know why the Tor wanted *Calypso*, do you?"

"Tor want Invidi drive. As Serat wants Tor drive. Greed is downfall."

There must have been better ways to get hold of Invidi technology, I thought. But the gray ships were acting on the programming of long-dead Tor. Maybe they weren't thinking straight.

"Anyway, when the Tor dragged the jump point back four years at this end, the other end moved too. So it would now open four years before 2027 if anyone tried to go through it. As I did with *Calypso II,* and ended up in 2023. So did Murdoch. When we tried to go back to Jocasta in *Farseer,* though, we overshot the coordinates of that jump point. *Farseer,* using its Tor hybrid technology, opened a new set of jump points between Earth and Jocasta. Same ninety-nine-year correspondence. For a couple of days, there were two pairs of jump points."

I was ticking items off on my fingers as I went, and drawing invisible diagrams on the arm of the chair to help me get my facts straight.

"There is not old and new jump points," said Barik.

It took me a moment to work out what he meant. "You mean there's no first cause."

"Yes, no first, no second." He added with probably intentional emphasis, "No lines."

"I know. All the jump points exist simultaneously, right? But my mind works linearly so that's how I explain it." I paused, remembered where I was.

"Right. Two pairs of jump points, we went through the *Farseer* one. History files show a surge of radiation two days later in 2023 near those coordinates. This indicates one of the points in 2023 destabilized. Ninety-nine years later, the position of the other side of the jump point as it destabilizes here indicates it was the old point that destabilized, not the *Farseer* one. So there is now only one pair of jump points at those coordinates near Earth and near Jocasta. One point, which *Farseer* created, and through which Serat would send *Calypso* several years later. Then the Tor would drag it back, etcetera."

This was the strange bit. "So according to my calculations, there's still a jump point at the coordinates near Jocasta where *Farseer* brought Murdoch and me from 2023. This point will stay there for another four years until 2126, when it will disappear because the Tor have already pulled it back to last year to allow *Calypso* to arrive. Does that make sense to you?" I was asking myself as much as An Barik.

The Invidi's tentacles curled into a complex pretzel, then relaxed again. "The one thinks you will not find such a point."

He should know better than to throw me a challenge.

* * *

Murdoch and I walked along the path between the sea and the road. Vehicles ran quietly behind a thick belt of scrub. Out in the bay some white pleasure sails skidded over the water and a long ferrytrain glinted in the distance.

Murdoch shaded his eyes against the glare and sniffed the salt breeze. His face was as familiar as the sunlight and yet I felt as if I were seeing it for the first time. It had been a long week. He'd been held up at Jocasta, finishing his reports. Then he'd been held up at Central, waiting for confirmation of his extra leave, then on Titan when his transport's thruster exhaust malfunctioned. Even though he'd sent me regular messages once he arrived in the solar system, it wasn't the same as having him here.

I missed him during the lonely, boring hours of my trial and asylum hearing. I missed him when I walked the streets of an Earth I barely knew. I missed him at night as I tossed on my EarthFleet bed in my monitored quarters and tried not to relive the mistaken choices of previous months over and over again. I wondered, too, if Henoit would finally leave us alone or if I'd have to spend my time with Murdoch trying to ignore his presence. Henoit had helped me when I tried to disconnect *Farseer* from the opsys, but he hadn't interrupted on the few times I'd been in physical contact with Murdoch during the crisis.

Unfortunately, Murdoch and I hadn't had a chance to talk properly in the few days between An Serat's death and my departure with an EarthFleet escort. I didn't know where his next transfer would be. He'd said something about being sent back to Earth. Which would be good for me, as I was going to be stuck here. But maybe EarthFleet had changed its mind. Or maybe Murdoch would prefer somewhere out of the solar system, or at least on another planet.

"In 2085 they decided to restore the harbor to pretty close to its original state," said Murdoch. "I must've been about ten. Took 'em years and years." He looked away from the water to me. "You heard about the vote."

"We should congratulate ourselves."

"You don't sound very happy."

I scuffed the toe of my boot deliberately on the gravel path, sending chips skipping into the grass. "I'm delighted. I just wish I could be there to help implement it." I looked at the sea. "About here?"

"Bit farther. Might as well do it right. We've come this far."

We certainly had. A century and hundreds of light-years. A long way to find that death is final and that time always wins.

"About here," said Murdoch after another twenty meters or so. He leaned on the rail and watched me.

I held out the bunch of flowers I carried. "You want to help?"

He shook his head. "I already said good-bye."

On the other side of the rail, short grass and spindly trees clung to a stony slope, ending in yellowish rocks that stuck out into the water. The waves slapped spray over the farthest of these and swirled into near crevices.

I ducked under the rail. Stones turned under my feet and the sun beat hot on the back of my neck. The first rocks were dry and gritty with blown sand. Then I slipped on spray-wet areas until, breathing hard, I stood on the flat surface of a large rock. Up close, the waves looked rougher than they looked from the path, showing cream-veined undersides as they lifted to the wind.

The flowers emerged fresh and moist from their layer of wrapping. Small yellow and orange faces smiling at the sun. I scrunched the wrap into my pocket and untied the line that bound the stalks together.

The sun's heat on my head and hands, cool salt air against my cheek, slip-slop of waves. Only the sea and the moment forever itself and eternity. I said Will's name and threw the flowers outward. The wind laid them in a pattern on the waves where they floated with the foam.

I wiped my face, then turned around and walked back to Murdoch and the path.

He reached out to help me under the rail, then kept hold of my hands. He cleared his throat. "I couldn't stop thinking about you."

I felt my face reddening and it wasn't the sun. I gripped his hands tight, half apprehensive. If Henoit was still around, this was the moment his voice would start whispering and sending shivers of pleasure at me.

"I accepted the Earth transfer," he said.

"You want to stay on Earth?"

His hands were sweaty. "Thought I could see a bit more of Irena, too. And we could . . . I mean, shit, you made me sleep in a separate bed last time we lived together. The least we can do is try properly." He must have taken my silence for indecision. "You might enjoy it."

I wasn't silent because I didn't like the idea. I was enjoying the feeling of being alone. No voice in my ear. No, *nor death shall us part* or flush of uncomfortable passion. Henoit wasn't there. Was it because I didn't need him anymore? He might be waiting in eternity—but I suppose I'll deal with that when the time comes.

It didn't matter. He'd gone, and Murdoch was here, now.

I pulled one of Murdoch's hands around my waist and smiled. "Are you sure you want to stay with a known galactic criminal?"

He smiled back. It made the memory of mistaken choices less painful and future choices seem easier.

"I'll take the risk," he said.

"I'd love you to stay with me."

I reached up around his neck and he drew me into the kiss.

About the Author

Maxine McArthur was born in Brisbane, Australia, in 1962. Her father was an engineer and the family moved from town to town when she was a child. Perhaps in reaction to this, after leaving school she spent sixteen years in Osaka, Japan, studying and working as well as making a family. She moved back to Australia in 1996 and settled in Canberra. She has always loved reading, mainly genre fiction such as crime and SF/fantasy, and enjoyed creative writing at school, but only began writing seriously after returning to Australia. Her first published work, the science fiction novel *Time Future* (1999 Random House Australia, 2000 Warner Aspect) won Transworld Publisher's 1999 George Turner Award for best unpublished SF/fantasy manuscript by an Australian author. *Time Past* is the sequel, and features many of the same characters. Maxine has two children, a dog, and a part-time job at the Australian National University, and does far less reading than she'd like to.

WE PROUDLY PRESENT THE WINNER
OF THE WARNER ASPECT
FIRST NOVEL CONTEST . . .

WARCHILD
by
KARIN LOWACHEE

THE merchant ship MUKUDORI ENCOMPASSES THE
WHOLE OF EIGHT-YEAR-OLD JOS'S WORLD, UNTIL A
NOTORIOUS PIRATE DESTROYS THE SHIP, SLAUGHTERS
THE ADULTS, AND ENSLAVES THE CHILDREN. THUS
BEGINS A DESPERATE ODYSSEY OF TERROR AND
ESCAPE THAT TAKES JOS BEYOND KNOWN SPACE TO
THE HOMEWORLD OF THE STRITS, EARTH'S ALIEN
ENEMIES. TO SURVIVE, THE BOY MUST BECOME A
LIVING WEAPON AND A MASTER SPY. BUT NO TRAIN-
ING WILL PROTECT JOS IN A WAR WHERE EVERY HOPE
MIGHT BE A DEADLY LIE, AND EVERY FRIENDSHIP
MIGHT HIDE A LETHAL BETRAYAL. AND ALL THE
WHILE HE WILL FACE THE MOST GRUELING TRIAL OF
HIS LIFE . . . BECOMING HIS OWN MAN.

ASPECT®

AVAILABLE WHEREVER BOOKS ARE SOLD

1198

BRILLIANT, EPIC SCIENCE FICTION FROM ACCLAIMED AUTHOR

PETER F. HAMILTON

FALLEN DRAGON (0-446-52708-4)

On a rebellious impulse, Lawrence joined the military of a corporation that he now recognizes to be ruthless and exploitative. His only hope for escape is to earn enough money to buy his place in a better corporation. When his platoon is sent to a distant colony to quell a local resistance effort, Lawrence plans to rob the colony of their fabled gemstone, the Fallen Dragon, to get the money he needs. However, he soon discovers that the Fallen Dragon is not a gemstone at all . . .

DON'T MISS HAMILTON'S BESTSELLING AND BRILLIANT EPIC SCIENCE FICTION

The Night's Dawn Trilogy:

The Reality Dysfunction
Part 1: Emergence (0-446-60515-8)
Part 2: Expansion (0-446-60516-6)

The Neutronium Alchemist
Part 1: Consolidation (0-446-60517-4)
Part 2: Conflict (0-446-60546-8)

The Naked God
Part 1: Flight (0-446-60-897-1)
Part 2: Faith (0-446-60-518-2)

A Second Chance at Eden (0-446-60671-5)
short stories set in the same universe at The Night's Dawn Trilogy.

1120e

VISIT WARNER ASPECT ONLINE!

THE WARNER ASPECT HOMEPAGE
You'll find us at: www.twbookmark.com then by clicking on Science Fiction and Fantasy.

NEW AND UPCOMING TITLES
Each month we feature our new titles and reader favorites.

AUTHOR INFO
Author bios, bibliographies and links to personal websites.

CONTESTS AND OTHER FUN STUFF
Advance galley giveaways, autographed copies, and more.

THE ASPECT BUZZ
What's new, hot and upcoming from Warner Aspect: awards news, bestsellers, movie tie-in information . . .